TITANIC

A LOVE STORY

Shannon OCork

MIRA

If you purchased this book without a cover you should be aware
that this book is stolen property. It was reported as "unsold and
destroyed" to the publisher, and neither the author nor the
publisher has received any payment for this "stripped book."

ISBN 1-55166-506-9

TITANIC: A LOVE STORY
Previously published under the title ICE FALL

Copyright © 1988 by Shannon OCork.

All rights reserved. Except for use in any review, the reproduction or
utilization of this work in whole or in part in any form by any electronic,
mechanical or other means, now known or hereafter invented, including
xerography, photocopying and recording, or in any information storage or
retrieval system, is forbidden without the written permission of the publisher,
MIRA Books, 225 Duncan Mill Road, Don Mills, Ontario, Canada M3B 3K9.

All characters in this book have no existence outside the imagination of the
author and have no relation whatsoever to anyone bearing the same name
or names. They are not even distantly inspired by any individual known or
unknown to the author, and all incidents are pure invention.

Certain real people are mentioned in the book for the purposes of enhancing
and adding reality to the story, but obviously the fictionalized events involving
either fictional characters or real persons did not occur.

MIRA and the Star Colophon are trademarks used under license and registered
in Australia, New Zealand, Philippines, United States Patent and Trademark
Office and in other countries.

Printed in U.S.A.

AUTHOR ACKNOWLEDGMENT

Long before I was, there was *Titanic*. To learn of her, to use her in my story, I consulted these works. I read all with profit and appreciation—and changed some of their facts and conclusions to suit my own storytelling purposes. That is, I'm afraid, the novelist's way. Nevertheless, to all these scholars and gentlemen: thank you.

Titanic: Triumph and Tragedy, by John P. Eaton and Charles A. Haas. Norton, 1986.

Story of the Titanic: As Told by Its Survivors, edited by Jack Winocour. Dover Publications Inc., 1960.

Titanic, by Colonel Archibald Gracie. Academy Chicago, 1986.

The Titanic: End of a Dream, by Wyn Craig Wade. Penguin Books, 1986.

A Night to Remember, by Walter Lord. Bantam Books, 1955.

The Night Lives On: New Ideas on Titanic Disaster, by Walter Lord. Morrow, 1986.

And, finally, my thanks, too, to my friend Carol Powers, who told me a good *Titanic* story and said I could use it. I did.

To the memory of my mother,
Mary Magdalene Osborne,
who dreamed it all, oh, so long ago

Wednesday, April 10, 1912

1

"Come on, Smoke, come on, come on—oh, I think it's him, I think it's him—come on!"

There was such a crowd, but it was exciting. Smoke would have liked to leave Swan, her silly twin, right there, desert her in the thick of it and board the ship right away, the lovely ship, and just lean over *Titanic*'s side, and watch and watch.

If she had been a painter she would have painted this scene: this elegant scramble under an overcast prenoon sky. First she would color in the unexcited water, black and slow below the pier, breaking in a lacelike ruffle along *Titanic*'s unending ankle line. Then she would daub and shadow, low and off to the side, the neglected other ships in the Southampton dock, like the *Oceanic* she and her twin had just skipped by, hurrying, or the *New York* there; not even a watchman aboard that liner that Smoke could see. And then she'd draw where the harbor opened to the sea, beyond the channel curve there, where, for all the passengers knew, monsters waited....

Prowling sea dragons might be out there waiting, with long spiny claws. Hidden underwater, they waited to surface, invisible once the sun went down. Cloaked in misty fog, they waited for the ship to come, blind, into their white and fatal clutches.... Perhaps as a hint, she'd draw in a curl of dark green scaliness, far out, very small, unpretentious and quiet, calling no attention to itself. Only the very perceptive would notice, and even then they would not know exactly *what* it was, only that *out there* danger lurked.

And then she'd draw, with a subtle blurring of detail, the parade of passengers strutting on the wharf and up the gangway into the cavernous shining ship, its portholes aglow like stars. She'd show the passengers' bustle, the pleasure they took in themselves and in this magic ship, their *anticipation*. She'd show their never-ending stacks of trunks.... Oh, it would be a masterpiece, Smoke thought, one of many she would render—if she was going to be a painter and not the sea captain she meant, one day, to be.

She and Swan, almost sixteen, were wearing matching traveling suits of long-skirted blue velvet with dark mink trim. Their pale blond hair was tied back, each with a simple blue bow, and they wore black gloves to protect their hands from chapping in sea wind, and grown-up black shoes that laced, with one-inch heels. They were alone, unchaperoned for the moment in this foreign, exotic place. Mrs. Twigg was still at the hotel, busy packing the last of the traveling cases, busy getting the porters to carry the luggage carefully— ''Gently, gently, please, my good man. Easy does it. We don't want to crush the silks, now do we. There's a quarter in it for you, for each and every one of you...twenty-five American cents. That'll buy a good bit of meat for dinner, umm?'' —and it was just too exciting.

Though Swan was paying no attention to anything at all.

Silly Swan, intent on that English boy she'd never met. He was a rural boy, a *peasant*. He was uneducated, too. He had written, in pencil, in a broad hand, "I practiced all throo the night," trying to get himself a job on the *Titanic* as third violinist. Which he had. So he could meet Swan in person, he said, knowing—because Swan told him in one of her letters—that she and her family were coming to England after a week in Paris and then sailing home to New York on *Titanic*'s maiden voyage. He wrote to Swan, "Do you mind? I dream of you when I practice, throo it all." And once he wrote, "The potatoes spoilt and so, not telling Ma I throo out my supper."

There were other mistakes like that, which Smoke made fun of, making ugly faces while she criticized, which Swan ignored.

Because Swan liked him—so she said—and Swan kept writing.

Swan even sent him her picture at Christmastime, in a sterling silver frame, a little one.

His likeness came then, in January, old and soiled and cracked. He apologized for it. "This is the best I have, Swan, sorry to say. And I don't look like this anymore, either. It's a year old, and I've grown!" It was folded into the rough yellow-lined school paper he wrote to Swan upon. The photograph was poorly taken, unframed.

"A piece of rubbish," Smoke said. "I wouldn't touch it with a tweezer!" But Swan was pleased to have it. She slipped it into a corner of her dressing table mirror. Where it curled, she stuck it to the mirror with paper paste.

His name was Danny Bowen. Danny Terence Bowen, son of Robert, called Bob, and Anna, née Monaghan. His father was a postman—a failed opera singer. "Pa had the voice," Danny wrote, "but he never could remember all the forren words, and it hurt him inside when he belted, so he quit." His mother taught the violin and piano, at home, he'd said. His picture showed a wide-boned face, fair hair, a large mouth and a serious expression. He looked nice, Swan said; he looked like a poet. He'd be handsome, she said, if he got dressed up.

Swan was like that, generous to other people, quick to think the best of them, quick to compliment. She enjoyed being girlish and prettily dressed. Swan was romantic, and a flirt. Everywhere Swan went she captured hearts and dangled them. And when she left she took the hearts away with her and set them down in sequence, in a gold-leafed, private book.

Smoke was different, much more serious. Smoke had no time for, nor interest in, boys. Smoke didn't care what she wore—Mrs. Twigg and Swan decided the twins' sartorial needs. After all, what did it matter? Smoke was going to be a sea captain when she grew up; a sea captain like her father's father, and his grandfather, the founder of the clan, old Captain Lockholm himself—he of legend and family remorse. For everyone agreed that old Captain Lockholm had been clever but also vicious and evil....

"I am clever, too, like the old captain, our great-great-grandfather, and I do not approve of people like Danny Terence Bowen of lower London, England," Smoke told her twin one day. "I do not approve of people such as he who write to people they don't know, and then try to get to know them, twisting the tail of fate."

Swan just shrugged and let the matter drop, and kept on writing to "Master Bowen" every Wednesday night after Mrs. Twigg washed her hair, while it dried. Still—though nobody asked her—it seemed to Smoke a forced intimacy; in Mrs. Twigg's words, "an impertinence."

Smoke had written to a "pen pal," too, a boy in London whose father was at least a lord. Everyone at Mrs. Graham's had to write; it had been a school project. But Smoke only wrote the one time, asking for a reply, which she promptly got. And one letter to and from Dexter Poindexter Lloyd had been quite enough. Talk about boring! Dexter Poindexter Lloyd had sent her mathematical formulations when she wrote to him that she liked boats and hoped, one day, to be a sea captain as her grandfather had been, and his father, and old Captain Lockholm before that. Smoke suspected Dexter thought she was a boy; Smoke hated Dexter Poindexter Lloyd, and hoped to never meet him.

Most of the other girls at Mrs. Graham's felt the same about their correspondents as Smoke had, and stopped writing as soon as they were allowed to.

But not Swan Josephine Lockholm. Swan kept on writing. And Danny Bowen kept on writing. And now—at last! Swan said—they were going to meet: aboard the R.M.S. *Titanic* on its first-ever ocean crossing.

"How romantic," Swan said.

"Ghastly," said Smoke.

He had been hired as fourth musician—third violinist—for the Café Parisien. She was a privileged first-class guest, a passenger whose father, John Bayard Lockholm III, as part of the International Mercantile Marine combine of J. P. Morgan, owned the White Star Line, and therefore *Titanic* itself. "So in a way I am the boss's daughter," Swan had written Danny. "Father and mother's stateroom will be close to Mr. Ismay's, so they can get to know each other better. But Smoke and I will have cabin B-41 all to ourselves, though Mrs. Twigg, our governess and chaperon, has B-35, right next door."

Smoke hated the whole silly thing. It seemed *vicious* to Smoke.

"It's not like you're in love with him, Swanny. You're just toying with him, the way a cat does with a yellow-feathered bird. It's cruel, really—quite uncivilized. You couldn't love someone so socially beneath you, you couldn't love someone you've never met. You're just trying to swell your fan club at his expense, and I think you're vain and hateful."

"Oh, Smoke," said Swan. "It's nothing so dark, really. It's just fun, you know, to have an admirer all the way across an ocean. And——" Swan snared Smoke's arm in her quick-pouncing hands, and lowered her voice. "And it helps fill my little black book, which is awfully fun to have—to talk to the other girls about and to look through when there's nothing else to do and I'm not sleepy."

"A flirt," said Smoke. "A flirt is what you are."

"And what's so wrong with that? I'd rather have love letters to look at than those books of sailing ships *you've* got."

SMOKE, BEING TUGGED by the hand along Southampton dock by her twin, pulled back. Let Swan have her moment of first greeting with her violin boyfriend alone; Smoke didn't want to meet him. Why should she? If their mother knew about Danny Bowen's existence, she'd be furious. Which, Smoke admitted, *was* part of the fun, but still, he could never be a part of their set. Swan was just being greedy. He was a trinket for the ocean crossing, something for Swan to play with, a prize for her pride....

It was pathetic, thought Smoke. Even Dexter Poindexter Lloyd would be better than an uneducated violin-player, but try to make Swan see that.

Annoyed by Smoke's lagging, Swan dropped her sister's hand and hurried forward. Strangers moved between them. Swan ran on ahead then, not looking back, not caring if Smoke caught up. Swan ran, her blue skirt dancing, up *Titanic*'s gangway to where a boy waited on the other side. The boy was tall and solemn, his shirt collar was stiff and ill fitting. He wasn't used to starched high collars. Even from a distance Smoke could tell that.

So left behind, Smoke was alone. How nice, she thought, how good! Let Swan run to romance, the ninny; love was not to be Smoke's fortune. Hers would be to know the world, know all of it, and maybe, just maybe, to own part of it, too. Why not, if she wanted to?

Trying to see everyone and everything at once, Smoke recognized Mr. Astor, Mr. John Jacob Astor, the Colonel. He was with his new bride—Madeline, Mother called her—and he'd bought himself an Airedale pup, which he was carrying through the crowd, pressing it against the lapels of his pale blue suit.

"Hello, Mr. Astor!" Smoke called, and waved. He

tipped his hat to her, and the new Mrs. Astor, to whom Smoke had not yet been introduced, smiled from under her lace-veiled bonnet.

Mr. Astor had had a terrible divorce, and then remarried beneath himself, or so Tory VanVoorst, Smoke's mother's closest friend, had said. He married hastily a woman "young enough to be his daughter, not of his station, and not particularly beautiful," Tory had said. But Victoria VanVoorst was so beautiful herself that very few ladies satisfied her standards, so one could not always go by what Tory VanVoorst proclaimed. Nevertheless, to be honest, Smoke had heard that the Colonel—as everyone called John Jacob IV who did not call him Jack—had had to pay a thousand dollars to the minister to get him to perform the ceremony....

"Where there's smoke there's fire," Mrs. Twigg had said, which only made Smoke laugh because she took "smoke" as referring only to herself. "I'm Smoke, so who's Fire? Are you, Twiggs, are you...?"

There, you see. Smoke wanted to poke her stupid twin. There's Jack Astor, who romanced an inferior and is now judged to have married improperly. Be careful you don't end up in the soup like Jack!

But Swan, of course, had run on ahead.

John Jacob Astor's great-grandfather had been unfit for polite society, Mrs. Twigg—who knew everything and told everything except her age—had told the twins. "A disreputable man he was," Mrs. Twigg said, "but that was because he didn't know any better. He hadn't been educated up to it, as you girls have."

According to Twiggs, the fur-trading Mr. Astor

had been the lowly son of a German butcher, an immigrant, and all his life, while he made millions and millions of dollars with ease, he blew his nose without a handkerchief. "Without anything at all," said Mrs. Twigg. "Think of it. And whenever he wanted to, wherever he wanted to, in his ballroom or yours. Made no difference to Mr. A."

Such behavior was hard for Smoke Lockholm to imagine. I mean, she thought, how could you blow your nose without anything to blow it on or into? Just how in the world could you do it?

"Animals don't have handkerchiefs," Swan had said at the time, as though that explained everything, but Smoke never argued with Swan unless it really mattered, because Swan was not as intelligent as Smoke, and was never convinced by her, and so what good would it do?

But such a scandal, thought Smoke. The first Mr. Astor and now the fourth. Perhaps, as Mrs. Twigg said, sin ran in the blood....

Mother's friend, Mrs. Peerce, was scandalous, too. Dove Peerce, the marchioness of Denton's mother. She had been a widow, a brand-new widow, when her daughter, Nicola, married the English marquess and became entitled. Years ago it was, the same year Smoke's mother and father married, before the century turned. First—and shocking at the time—Mrs. Peerce had *not* postponed the wedding when her husband suddenly died. Second, she had worn much too pretty a dress for someone supposed to be in *mourning*. And third—and here was the best—Dove Peerce, less than a month a widow, like a feckless bridesmaid, reached and scattered with the rest and…*yes*…caught in a perfumed hand her daughter's bridal bouquet!

When it happened, all Newport gasped. And still, years later, they talked of it. It was a good old scandal.

Smoke did not think she would ever cause a scandal, though Swan might, on a very good day.

Smoke watched her twin's long skirt disappear into the crowd, up the broad black tongue of the ship, around a handsome older couple whom Smoke did not recognize at all. Whenever this happened in New York or Newport, and Smoke asked who they were, Mrs. Twigg or her mother would say, "I'm not sure, dear. Possibly they are Jewish…Mr. Belmont's friends…."

Mrs. Twigg had told them, too, that once Mr. Astor had wee-wee'd in a neighbor's fireplace, during a New Year's open house, in front of the lady whose fireplace it was. She'd fainted dead away when she realized—to her horror—what the old man was up to, unbuttoning his fly the way he was, while he talked unconcernedly to her about the weather and licked the crumbs of a canapé off the fingers of his other hand.

But then, maybe that hadn't been the first Mr. Astor at all. Maybe that had been someone else entirely, or maybe it never really happened…. The woman never really recovered from the shock, said Twiggs, who swore the story was true.

But Smoke didn't believe that anyone, even the wild Mr. Astor, who was always Mrs. Twigg's best example of bad manners among the new rich, was capable of such ignominy. To belch and not apologize, that Smoke could believe. She had done that herself on occasion. It made Mrs. Twigg so mad! To lust inside for another's spouse, that, too, must happen sometime. It was all her mother's friend, Tory VanVoorst, talked about—that, and clothes. But to *wee-wee in the fireplace before one's hostess?* No, no, no, no one, not even the unschooled Mr. Astor, could do that, though he had been...*a rake.*

Smoke smiled, swinging up *Titanic*'s gangway, remembering that. *A rake.* That's what she would be. Not a bad girl and never a wife, just *a rake.* It sounded like an exciting thing to be. Whereas Swan Josephine, her twin, Swan would be a shovel, see if she didn't....

The original Mr. Astor had, in his day, done something *really bad*—one evening at a debutante's ball. But no matter how Smoke pressed, Twiggs wouldn't tell her what it was. "It would ruin you to hear it," was all Twiggs would say, and she'd wave Smoke away. "Wait until you're older."

Smoke sighed, remembering. There was so much to know of life, and such fun to learn. Perhaps, if she got really *intime* with Madeline, she would tell Smoke the truth about John Jacob Astor I.

Titanic's whistle blew long and loud; the first signal they were ready to depart. It made Smoke jump. She looked up at the side of the ship, so high. People were hanging over the railings, bunched together like flowers.... Almost by instinct she found her twin. Swan was waving vigorously at her with both gloved hands. The boy beside her was waving, too. Smoke's eyes opened wider and wider as she took her first long look at Danny Terence Bowen.

Oh boy.

He was *gorgeous*, a beautiful man.

And so a fortune hunter, Smoke reasoned. He would have to be. Poor Swan, she should have known...! Or at least suspected....

Smoke could see it now. He would try to make Swan fall in love with him. He would succeed. Smoke bet he would propose to her twin before the *Titanic* hit New York harbor a week from today. And Swan, silly Swan, would say yes.... Their mother and father would have to crush it—send Swan to a convent in Lyons, France, for a year—and Swan would be scarred forevermore....

Oh boy, oh boy, oh boy, Smoke thought, Swan's really done it now. He'll serenade her in the night with his violin. He'll try to compromise her; what if he works it so they have to marry...? Oh, poor Swan!

Smoke shrugged even as she waved back energetically. You see, that's what you get, she told herself, when you play the game of love. That's exactly what an heiress must expect when she allows herself to be *pursued* by strangers not of her own class.

Well.

Father could always use him—someday—as the family chauffeur.

EDWARD JOHN SMITH, commodore of the Royal Mail Steamship *Titanic*, stood on the captain's bridge, almost a happy man.

He enjoyed, with a veteran's relish, these final, formal preparations before departure. Preparations of no consequence, really, for all had been checked and rechecked and finalized days before in Belfast. And all officers except himself had spent the night aboard *Titanic* checking and rechecking.

All was ready.

But still a captain did his duty. Captain Smith had, this morning, personally, elaborately, checked one final time the gear, the equipment, the supplies; even the boilers in *Titanic*'s hold had been caressed by his skipper's hands.

There had been a few problems, a few minor problems, but that was usual. On such an important embarkation he expected a nuisance or two, which would all be resolved—even if at the last moment—with satisfaction. Nothing wrong with that; ultimately it was a good thing. Right off the bat it got the officers and crew working together, accomplishing together. Little problems solved in port coalesced the men, made them efficient, turned them into a first-class operation, functioning as it ought to.

Seamen were superstitious, and the sooner the crew and officers accepted *Titanic* as a good ship, the better off Captain Smith and *Titanic* would be. Every time a new ship floated, the men on her had to feel her out, decide whether they "liked" her; decide whether the ship "liked" them. The old myth of the killer ship that hates its crew and passengers still thrived in seamen's minds. This crew would have to find for itself *Titanic*'s heart, proclaim her fit or foul, and no mandate from the captain and no advertising claims that even God couldn't sink the lady would affect the lads who worked in her bowels. It was up to the crew to pronounce *Titanic* seaworthy, worthy of the great waters she would sail, worthy of the good hands who would man her. So these little troubles in port were as should be. Already the crew was wooing *Titanic* and seeing how she responded.

There was, for instance, the little fire in the coal

room. The fire had been alive a week, smoldering somewhere in the middle of the coal heap since Belfast, where the coal had been loaded in—and not wet down. Because of the coal strike, just settled, Captain Smith supposed; some of the coalers not satisfied with the new wage; still bitter, not back yet to doing a proper job. But the coal fire was only a little irritation…of no consequence. Captain Smith had been assured of that by Mr. Bell, the chief engineer. The stokers were even now hosing the coal down and reshoveling the pile to get to the source of the heat. Asked by the insurance man if he, as captain, would "assume the risk," E.J., as everyone called him, said yes, he would. There was no damage to the bulkhead or hull, he had checked on that himself. No, *Titanic* was not injured, only inconvenienced. Damn nuisance, the coalers, and all other working men who blamed owners for their troubles. Class. You couldn't get away from class. Say what you would, class told, in the end. Always had, always would….

And then there was the pother about Mr. Lightoller. Mr. Ismay had seen fit, just yesterday, to take Henry Wilde from the *Olympic* and put him on as *Titanic*'s chief officer, knocking down Murdoch to first and thus, Charles Lightoller to second. And Lightoller was pouting, not taking it at all well. Well, E.J. understood. This *Titanic* tour would have been Lightoller's maiden as first, and it was just the kind of stripe on his sleeve an ambitious seaman wants, but… Nothing lost, really, everything would work out all right. Mr. Lightoller was a professional, and just to be on *Titanic*'s crew was a privilege, much less as an officer.

"Fiddlesticks whether you're first or second,

m'boy," E.J. had told him. "You're on board, aren't you? That's the ticket! Do well this time round and your career is assured. Why, you could be commanding *Titanic* before the year is out. Think of that...."

The fire drill had gone without a hitch. The certificate of readiness had been signed. The crew and staff had boarded, found their bunks, their stations. All was ready and raring to go; almost....

Almost.

E.J. nodded to himself, looking down at polished A deck from the captain's bridge. He was here at last, in command of *Titanic*, brand-new and splendid. Such a ship. Like a queen, she was, a newly crowned queen, beautiful but powerful, feminine and masculine combined. More like a goddess, truly, he thought, *a goddess of the sea*.

She would never be bettered. Lord Pirrie, her designer, had outdone himself; *Titanic* was his masterwork. And Harland & Wolff, who had built her, would never duplicate this workmanship. *Titanic* was more than a jewel, she was the body of the crown, and she would have a long reign as queen of the seas. She would right all the ills of the White Star Line, Mr. Ismay need not fear. E. J. Smith was proud to be a part of her. A significant part.... Well, he could admit it to himself, he deserved her. When you did good you got good, his father used to counsel him, and E. J. Smith had done better than good during a long career. E.J. had done perfect. Twenty-five years a captain and nary an accident, nary a single blot on his copybook....

Except, except...except for the Hawke's *collision last September....*

That was not my fault, he argued with himself. I was completely exonerated at the inquiry, held entirely blameless. It is *not* on my record, and *I will think of it no more.*

Captain Edward John Smith deserved *Titanic*, the world's greatest oceangoing vessel. And she—he could admit it to himself—had got what she deserved, the best of England's mariners to steer her o'er the waves.

Earlier he had looked over, for the hundredth time, his maps, his charts, his schedules...and his secret plan. For this, *Titanic*'s maiden run, would be his only tour as her captain, and it would be his last captaincy. This first run of *Titanic* would capstone his career: once *Titanic* returned to Southampton, E. J. Smith, commodore for the White Star Line, would retire. In glory. He would be proclaimed a hero, a master skipper; he would go down in the history books.

For he meant to set a record with this ship.

Titanic was due in New York harbor in seven days. But E. J. Smith would bring her in in six!

That was his secret plan. He would push *Titanic* through the fields of ocean, stoke her engines and throw her throttles wide. He would see what she could do and—*ha, boys!*—let her do it. *Titanic* would astonish the world.

He and her.

Titanic, first time out, would *fly* across the ocean. She would set a trans-Atlantic speed record that would live for a generation. She and he, together: they would chop *a whole day* off the established travel time.

E.J. stood on the captain's bridge and shifted. He

was eager, but stood calm and controlled, as a captain should.

There was still more crew and staff to get into place. The last-minute ones, the not-so-bright ones. The ones who were a little slower mentally and physically. The third-class staff.... There were always some of those, in all walks of life. Perfectly good people; perfectly competent. They were the salt of the earth if the truth was known. But they were not...top drawer.

And E. J. Smith did not like them. They weren't— he could admit to himself—*good enough for him*.... Not quite up to *his* standards, *his* speed....

Hurry, *hurry*, you whore's sons, he wanted to shout. But he remained as he was, silent and outwardly calm. He waited, as a war-horse waits, all the heat inside. He stood on his bridge, handsome, tall and wide shouldered, fit and polished, his white beard cropped short in the naval manner, his mustache full and white. Approaching sixty, he did not look old, he did not feel old. He felt good and he felt ready and—

Fourth Officer Boxhall, Joseph Boxhall of Liverpool, stepped up to the captain's side. Mr. Boxhall was one of Captain Smith's favorites; they had worked together before.

"Sir," said Fourth Officer Boxhall, and he handed the captain a mug of steaming tea.

E.J. nodded and took the cup.

"The first-class train has just docked in. So, barring any delay, we'll be off before the hour is out. Any further instructions, sir? Any favorite request for the band?"

E.J. had asked the Wallace Hartley band to play

in the hour before departure, to hurry the laggards aboard. Four musicians stood, now, in front of the grand staircase, playing ragtime, and champagne was being passed around on first-class A deck, on silver trays.

Captain Smith was not fond of ragtime. He preferred church hymns and military marches, either of which got a man's blood going, or soft waltzes, which made the ladies melt, every one. But if ragtime was the rage in London and ragtime was what the passengers wanted to hear, then ragtime *Titanic* would have.

Captain Smith did not answer Boxhall, but blew on his tea, an old habit. ''What do you say, Mr. Boxhall, does this do any good, any damn good at all?'' And he whistled again across the top of the liquid to demonstrate.

Fourth Officer Boxhall stood straight. ''I doubt it, sir,'' he said candidly. ''Surface area is too small to be much affected, and the force of wind is too slight.'' He did not mind that Captain Smith had not responded to his question. He was used to that. It meant E.J. was thinking, turning over in his mind each little thing.

''As I thought,'' said E. J. Smith in his own good time, referring to Mr. Boxhall's pronouncement on the effect, or lack of effect, of his blowing on his tea. ''But I like to do it all the same.''

E.J. was impatient to be under way, which, as an old sea dog, he took as a good sign. But he liked, too, and would take, this ritual look at the ladies, his first look at all the new beauties. Though he had commanded ocean liners for the White Star Line for years, one of his most-liked moments was this one, before it all began again—the dinners, the innocent flirtations, the "duty dances"—when he would see the new voyage's womenfolk for the first time, see them in the flesh, however well or modestly befrocked. They were E.J.'s new brood, the new flock, and they would be traveling with him for a week or more: in his care if not in his arms. He thought of them as his. Once they stepped into his kingdom, once they left hard ground behind, these women, *the first class women*, all were E.J.'s, no matter to whom they actually belonged. And this was the moment he appraised them, savored them as they mixed and bumped before him, like pretty baubles spilled out of a velvet sack.

E.J. handed his mug to Officer Boxhall and picked up a pair of binoculars from a stool beside him. "How about you, Mr. Boxhall," he said. "Do you notice the ladies, the first-class ladies?" And he fitted the eyecups to his eyes and filled his lungs deep with dockside air. Dockside, the air was not the same as it was upon the open sea. Dockside air was not the best, but it whispered of the wonder to come; it tempted and *lured* like a woman.... Yes, just like a woman, Captain Smith thought, scanning the crowd upon *Titanic*'s decks, and he wondered at himself. His stars must be in strange position...perhaps clustered in the realm of Venus? For usually he was not so keen as this, not so intensely, viscerally, responsive.

It must be that he knew this was the last time he would ever thus stand: ruler of a small but mighty kingdom, true adventurer, simple seaman on his last trip away from home. It gave a man pause. He had no sadness and no regrets. He had only *anticipation*.

Officer Boxhall was complimented to be taken into the commodore's confidence. He responded to E.J.'s question with a self-conscious bow toward the passengers themselves, aswish on A deck in petticoated skirts, bright with milliner's plumes in their hats, laughing with or without husbands on their arms. "The first-class princesses I leave to a man like you, sir," Boxhall said. "You've got the carriage, the looks, the authority, if I may say so, sir, to reel 'em in in schools. Me, I'll take the not-so-uppity ones."

"Go on, Mr. Boxhall," said the captain, surveying, through his binoculars, the colorful crowd. "Explain yourself."

There was a redheaded woman, statuesque, voluptuous. In midnight blue and a veil—widow's garb. She was a beauty. She caught his eye right away. But she was far too young....

"Well, sir," said Mr. Boxhall, "it's the warm, loose-fleshed ones I find are the nicest. Girls of inferior station. Girls who don't mind a fellow havin' a pint or two once the sun goes down. Girls not above givin' away a kiss or more. Your first-class 'debbies,' beggin' your pardon, sir, they're ice queens. They don't relax with a man so much as supervise upon him. Or so it's been my experience, sir."

E.J.'s binoculars had singled out a vision in lavender and gray. He thought, as he focused close, that he had never seen a better woman; the sight of her made his manhood throb and heated to scorching the palms of his hands.

She was slight, of aristocratic bearing. Her silken back was long and straight—like a shoot of lily, he thought. If I take her in my hand she will blossom as I hold her! Her back sprang from a delicate waist, a waist that defined a beautiful bosom. Her face, in three quarter profile, was shadowed by a wide-brimmed hat of Russian fox, but nothing could dim that face's radiance. Her upswept hair was powder white, as enticing as the awesome Milky Way, which all mariners knew. And her face, upturned now—ah, she had spotted him!—though she must be, as he was, of a certain age, seemed to him the face of an angel. It was perfect of feature, with a sweet overall expression. It was peach cheeked and fine boned. It was unlined. And even through the binoculars, her skin was celestial....

Captain Smith was roused.

There she was, center of A deck, beside the red-headed beauty. There she was, the kind of woman E.J. used to dream about, lust after, sob for in his bed. Used to, when he was younger...before his marriage to Eleanor. And secretly after, long after, for years. No harm, he'd excused himself, dreaming alone in his bed between continents.

Yes, he used to dream of such a woman. Maybe this very woman. *Yes, it was this very woman his hot thoughts had been conjuring, night after night for years!* In his dreams he met her, always at sea, far from the restrictions land imposed upon a man.... In his dreams she was free of other men, a woman of prodigious fortune.... In his dreams, always, they fell rapturously in love.

It had never happened, of course.

To his credit, he had not sought in life what he'd moaned for, illicitly, in dreams. He was a moral man, a good man, "true Brit" through and through. And once married to Eleanor, that had been that, more or less. His daughter was now twelve, little Helen, named for the beauty who launched a thousand Hellenic ships.... Helen adored her father; he would never do anything to shatter her heart. Still, he used to dream and had enjoyed the dreaming.... He could not remember, now, exactly when he had given up and dreamed no more. But it had been a while now, a good while....

And now, there she was, below him, accepting a goblet of champagne, smiling at the smokestacks of *Titanic* as though they were top hats being doffed to bid her welcome. There she was, *in the flesh, no husband on her arm*, aboard E. J. Smith's last voyage. This is your *chance*, his mind shouted at him, the thought so strong that his hands, around the binoculars, shook. He lowered them and closed his eyes. And still his mind roared, *You are looking now at the woman of your dreams.... What are you going to do about it?*

Aloud, he finally answered Boxhall in unexcited measure, as though his captain's heart was not leaping like a stallion's. "I see what you mean, Mr. Boxhall, but to my mind that's exactly the challenge. I like melting a woman down, like a candle's hot wax. Eh? Think about that, Joe. Well, to each his own.... But see that woman, there—she sports a white fox hat. See her? Beautiful as the devil, eh, eh?"

Officer Boxhall usually admired a vessel's steward girls or the Irish lasses in third on their way to America. Sometimes the "Brigittes" came aboard without their families, sometimes without even a friend. And almost always they were without extra pennies for extra pleasure. They were very pretty, the Irish ones, and very friendly—and in the dark, sometimes, their brcasts were wonderfully responsive. They boarded at Queenstown, last stop before the long, long ocean began.... *Titanic* was due in Queenstown tomorrow noon.

Thinking such tender matters, Joseph Boxhall noticed the older beauty who had caught the attention of his captain. "Ah," he said gallantly, "she is very fine, sir—much too fine for me. But every success to you, sir. She will make this trip very pleasant for you, indeed."

Captain Smith sighed. He liked Joe Boxhall; he was a bloody good chap.

But now First Officer Murdoch was bearing down on him, with papers in his hand.

E.J. turned from Boxhall, dismissed him with a short gesture, but thought, still, what a splendid fellow his fourth officer was. Definitely first-officer material. Perhaps as early as next year, another step up the ladder: E.J. would recommend it once he got back to Southampton.

"Yes, Mr. Murdoch, what is it?" he asked.

But in his mind the commodore was phrasing a dinner invitation to the mysterious lady who had apparently boarded alone....

What if, later in his stateroom, *much later*, after dinner, surrounded by ocean, all land lost behind, he was to take her wanton, elegant body in his naked, anxious arms, *and jack her, m'fine laddies.... Jack her till the stars paled and together they knocked at heaven's door....*

"Yes, Mr. Murdoch, what is it now?" he asked.

"We await your order, sir, to be under way."

2

Smoke Lockholm stood on the seat of a deck chair, sixty feet above Southampton dock, on A deck, watching the last of the passengers board. Her mother was one of the laggards, unusual for her, hand in hand with Smoke's father. Mrs. Twigg was just behind. They were talking to Jack Thayer and Harry Widener, two of New York's better young bachelors. Smoke did not give a fig for Jack and Harry. Though Swan might, she thought. *Might have, that is, before Danny Bowen....*

Smoke wished her twin was with her, not off with her ''poet pen pal,'' who was handsome enough from a distance, all right, but whose teeth were probably crooked, close up. Smoke made an ugly face thinking of him, but the people beside her did not see it; she was so high, shoulders above the rest at the rail, thanks to the chair.

Pushed tight against *Titanic*'s port side, she had good vantage; she could see everything from there. All around her the crowd was waving goodbye to those less fortunate than themselves, those left behind on shore, not going, not adventuring. Some of the passengers were already tipsy from the champagne freely passed on silver trays, dipped by white-jacketed stewards to this hand then that one. Others at the rail were quiet, patiently admiring the little English sea town they had come to only to leave.

But Smoke was raging to be off. She wanted to turn her face west and not look back. There the river channel curved and opened up to the ocean wild. There she would be truly water-borne, landless, the earth all gone for days and days and days....

Someday she would own a ship, a smaller ship than *Titanic*, surely, but in its own way just as fine. And when she was a captain she would not be "laced," as she was now, her frock uncomfortably tight from the too-many sweetmeats she had eaten in her first excitement on board—two, each time a salver had paused beneath her nose. And she would not tame her hair with ribbon, as Mrs. Twigg insisted the twins do during the day. When she was a captain her hair would fling free, sea-salt tangled, never quietly combed, and it would smell of the mysterious caverns of the deep. And she would not wear this heavy velvet that draped ladylike around her ankles and floated as she stepped. She would wear only what men wore, a loose shirt and easy pants, and she would stride and leap and climb a crow's nest quicker than the rest. She would pierce her left ear in a sailor's secret ritual, and a wild island native would carve her an earring made of walrus bone. She would wear it as her talisman, and sail, head back, neck bared, steadfast into a storm....

The band—without crooked-teethed Danny Bowen—was playing a dance-hall tune, and men on-shore were tossing off the lashing ropes, which a crew wound on a lower deck. The last couple was aboard—her mother's friends, Tory and Burton VanVoorst. Tory was almost eight months pregnant but ever the femme fatale. She was showing an enticing décolletage of bosom, which was quite improper before five, and it was not yet noon. The gangway was rising, well oiled and swift. The passengers were throwing flowers. Onshore, children jumped. White chrysanthemums, red roses, nosegays sailed on green-scum water. Annoyed, gulls flapped their wings and cawed and flew.

They were leaving!

In a gentle shiver Smoke felt *Titanic*'s first breath as somewhere in the great ship's belly, engines fired and turned. And then, as the band played faster and some of the couples on A deck high-step danced, the great ship moved—it moved!—glided soft, so silent, still so slow. But yes! Southampton dock was receding, and pale smoke drifted from three of *Titanic*'s four smokestacks, and a new breeze blew the gold on Smoke's forehead to disarray, stray curls.

Still, *Titanic* was not free. She was being pulled by tugs through a lowering tide to a wide place in the river, a "turning circle," someone said. And then there was a small delay as some of the crew stepped off into a tugboat called *The Vulcan*. These were "extra men," a man in the rail crowd said; crew signed on this morning in case some, previously hired, did not show up. And then...and then the bonds to the tugs were flipped away, and great *Titanic*, mighty *Titanic*, proud as a mountain, began to run. On her own. She was so quiet, even the crowds aboard and ashore were silent, straining to hear. She steamed a ship's length, then another....

Smoke closed her eyes with joy.

But something was wrong. There was shouting beside her; screams of alarm. She opened her eyes to see the river, the dull Southampton River, a moment ago sluggish and gray below them, erupting in storm. Water was roiling up from nowhere, the river parted a path, waves crashed. In their slips at the dock two ships, still tethered, strained like sister steeds at their bindings. Up and down they bucked and pitched: two ships, *Oceanic* and *New York*. Up and down, back and forth, the *New York* especially, pulled and leaped as if on springs. Unmanned, it fought against its dock lines, leaped a fathom sideways....

CRAAACK

CRAAACKCRAAACK

Broke free.

Three hawsers snapped and *New York* was unshackled, spinning in whirlpool circles. Rogue, it surged toward *Titanic*'s high port wall.

It was the suction of *Titanic*, the great pull of her draw. It had created a riptide, sudden and savage, a down draft that sucked unhaltered *New York* helplessly into *Titanic*'s path....

Smoke held to the rail post and watched with wide eyes as the unmanned ship rammed its bow heavenward, then stumbled in the head and made as though to kiss the river bottom. Another roll of waves and *New York* was head up again, swinging broadside, flying straight for *Titanic*'s left side...and Smoke.

She was going to fall.

She was dazzled by a sudden brilliant sun. Out from behind a cloud, it flashed and spangled in the river's spray; in every storm-hurled water drop it blinded her. The chair on which she stood was sliding. She was going to fall between the cliffs of the two ship sides as they smacked....

"Full astern," sounded a voice through a speaker.

"Full astern," reverberated in her mind. She was reeling, there was a cool wind on her face...and then large hands were clutching her. Under her bosom, strong hands, big-knuckled, *peasant hands* squeezed her around the waist, pulled her from behind....

The loose ship was by. Its round rump was dancing harmlessly off *Titanic*'s bow, in quieter water. It was no longer bucking; it was limping downriver, driven by a tamer tide.

Smoke fought against the hands that clasped her. They were bony hands and as strong as pincers. How dare someone pull her away from her baptism in the sea! She was the owner's daughter! She turned around to tell him to his face.

He was gawky, not filled out yet. His hair was, almost, the color of her name. He wore a uniform of dark blue, too small in the shoulders, single-breasted, black-buttoned, no stripes on the sleeves. His eyes were seaweed brown.

Her sister, Swan, was beside him. "You fool, Smoke," Swan said, "you awful, awful fool."

He was bowing. "We might have lost you, it's true," he said.

His teeth were not crooked, up close.

AUDREY LOCKHOLM—the beautiful hot-blond Mrs. John Bayard Lockholm III of New York City and Newport, the society pages called her—*the frightened Mrs. Lockholm*, paused on the open promenade of the boat deck on her way down to B deck and

luncheon. She wanted to have a solitary look at the
splendors of *Titanic* before she joined Tory and Burt
and Nicola and Dove. She was in no hurry; Bay
would not be there. Bay was in conference, dining
privately with the captain and Bruce Ismay. He had
warned her it would be like this. This trip was business for him, not pleasure. Important business.

"I'm sorry, angel." He had said it again last night
at Dentoncroft. Last night, before dinner, in Nicola's
English country house. And he had casually dropped
a present into Audrey's upturned palms as though it
were nothing, a nosegay only, loosely wrapped in
blue tissue paper cut to resemble hydrangea, Newport's favorite flower…Bay's flower.

Dearest, darling Bay….

And, as always, Audrey had been surprised,
shocked even, at the pearls, a collar of five strands
held by an ivory moon. They were, *as always*, too
costly, too rich, sinfully extravagant.

*And on the pearls was a moon, of which the gypsy
had spoken….*

She had, already, more pearls than she could wear.
Sometimes, beholding them all—she inventoried her
jewels as she moved them out of one vault and into
another, each time they changed residences for the
season—Audrey thought she had all the pearls in the
world. For she possessed the Lockholm pearls, pearls
unending, a legendary cache…which she neglected.
She who, though married into a vast wealth for seventeen years, had been born poor. She who, though
cosseted and spoiled for years as a woman of privilege, still felt that some things *were* too extravagant.

Though she had changed. No more was Mrs. John
Bayard Lockholm III an awkward, unmannered girl,

big eyed and breathless and overwhelmed by an opulence she had, before Bay, not known existed. She was now, at thirty-six, at the height of her beauty. She was now, and had been for years, at home with luxury, at ease with the socially prominent, accustomed to obsequiousness from servants and respect from tradespeople.

But seeing the moon glowing amid the pearls, she had been *terrified*....

She did not let him know. And she had learned, long ago, not to tell him he gave her too much. Smiling, she'd let him fit the pearls upon her, the moon in the hollow of her throat. She'd let him slide away her dressing gown and ease her to the bed.

They'd feigned hurry because they should have been dressing for dinner. Should have been, already by then, properly turned out, he in black mohair with amethyst studs, she in silken crepe of tomato red, banded over the bosom in satin, a shawl of thinnest red fringe over fine bare shoulders.

But Bay had made love to her.

She had not been able, at first, to relax, *because of the gypsy, because of what the gypsy'd said....*

She'd tried to shut out the memory of the hideous woman and revel only in Bay's weight burning on her body and the bliss of his breath in her mouth. But the *shining moon clasp* lay heavy on her throat, as oppressive as a stricture.

"Brandy," she'd whispered in his ear.

He brought her brandy in a porcelain cup. She drank a long draft.

And then, as he used to do before the burdens of Lockholm money had slowed his passion, Bay tasted her *there* and *there* and fired her belly, inflamed her thighs, and all fear fled.

And after, they'd descended the stairs as though nothing wondrous had transpired between them except that Audrey wore new pearls only just added to the Lockholm collection.

And so dinner at Nicola's last night had been late.

Now, peering down the tiers of *Titanic*'s decks to third-class, Audrey saw the gypsy again. There she was, *again*, an old woman staring up at Audrey with eyes like holes.

But no…it couldn't be. Madame Romany was in Manhattan, in a foul little room one rented by the day…. Trembling, Audrey thought, I must be wrong. Women such as she, unfortunate women, they all dress alike, look alike….

The woman was wearing black to match her overly black dyed hair. She was staring up from far below, beckoning to Audrey high above her…. Whatever could the woman want?

It had been Tory who told Audrey she ought to go. "She's the real thing, my pet. She predicted the Cummingses' divorce. Muriel tried to prove collusion in court, don't you remember?"

Audrey did not remember Muriel Cummings's divorce, she had never known Muriel Cummings—did not want to. But she had gone to see the gypsy…because of Bay. Bay, her husband, her great passion.

Dearest Bay, riven now with troubles….

He had tied his fortune into Morgan's IMM, Mr. J. P. Morgan's International Mercantile Marine, which was founded to capture the world's shipping industry, but was having the devil's own time—

Bay's words—simply surviving. Not the least problem was the Cunard Line, which would not crumble, would not join Mr. Morgan's combine, and was a rival to respect.

The White Star Line had "come to Morgan," but was old-fashioned and eccentric in method, not cost-conscious, not practical. "A bit of a dinosaur," Bay said.

And White Star was managed by a man Mr. Morgan did not trust, by Mr. J. Bruce Ismay, son of White Star's founder. A descendant of shipping capitalists, as Bay was. An aristocratic man, as Bay was. The man Bay had come to England to get to know. And the reason they were all here on the *Titanic*, sailing back to America.... Bay had come, secretly, to oversee Bruce Ismay while the *Titanic*, new pride of the White Star Line—and IMM—made her maiden crossing. For Bay and Mr. Morgan—and Mr. Ismay—would either succeed or be bust.

Heady stuff. Male stuff. Conquer or die. Bay in the thick of it. And, Audrey was afraid, Bay *losing*....

Worse, he would not confide in her about it. She was not to worry herself, he said, everything would be all right. But he was thin these days, and older seeming, and so much more nervous. And more tired than he should be; at fifty-three, he was in his prime....

And so she had gone, frightened even then, to the gypsy.

The woman was old, as old as once-upon-a-time, and dirty. There had been something haunting, *something familiar* about her eyes, one pale and frosted, unseeing; the other piercing, all-seeing, a faithless black. Somewhere Audrey had gazed into those eyes before. Sometime.... Perhaps it was in a dream. Or perhaps Audrey had been a child, safe in her father's hand, strolling the midway of a circus come to Newport town. Josephine, Audrey's mother, had had her fortune told. Audrey remembered the three of them, Audrey in her mother's lap, crowded around an opaque white ball.... But the gypsy she remembered not at all. She remembered only her mother laughing, and her father pleased....

"My husband," Audrey had said to Madame Romany. "He has business worries, he—"

"There will be a moon," the wretched woman said. "A cold white crescent moon. You will recognize the trouble come, m'lady, by a floating silver moon, and a woman—you know who I mean—with red, red hair. There is white all around you, maybe diamonds, dearie, or rows of stars. Perhaps a party, a midnight ball? I grieve to tell you this, m'fine lady, but your husband is telling you goodbye...."

"What do you mean, what do you mean?" It had been so hard to breathe.

"There may be a way," the grimy woman said, her mouth wrinkled and sly. She indicated Audrey's gown, Audrey's handsome coat thrown back upon the simple chair. "It is hard to see clearly." Her lips were overrouged, and there was an eagerness in her thrust-forward shoulders and a snap in her all-seeing eye. Audrey knew: the gypsy *wanted* to tell.

"Another twenty dollars, madam," whined the woman, "and we will see what we can do."

Unable to help herself, Audrey had nodded.

"Well, then, m'fine lady—" There was no hesitation now. "I'll tell you the truth. Look to your welfare. Fortunes come and fortunes go. Protect yourself, you will not have your husband long.''

Audrey flung down money and ran from the room. Last month that was.

She'd said nothing to anyone, not even to Tory, who had gone, on an earlier day, and been so pleased. ''She told me my baby will be president, Audrey, my pet, and that Burty will always adore me!''

No, Audrey had kept the gypsy's warning to herself.

And now, last night, Audrey had been presented with an ivory moon in Nicola's house, Nicola *with the red, red hair*. And she was frightened and seeing things, having no one to confide in. And Madame Romany was not down at the third-class rail looking up and beckoning with a clawlike hand for Audrey to come down, come down....

How could she be?

Dove Peerce, Nicola's mother, joined Audrey at the rail. ''I'm so glad to find you,'' Dove said. ''Let's go in together, shall we? If both of us are late to table, Nicola won't scold.''

Gratefully, Audrey turned away from the dark vision below and clasped Dove's gold-braceleted arm. ''Yes, let's go in, Dove, darling, I'm starved.''

''You are the only woman I know who has a good appetite, my dear,'' said Dove. ''You're famous for it, and I don't envy you it, although it doesn't seem to have harmed your figure, at least not yet. The trouble will come when hostesses begin to gauge the merits of their cooks against how much you eat at one table as opposed to someone else's. Then you'll be in the bucket.''

Audrey tried to sound carefree. "Then I shall follow your example, dear Dove, and stop eating entirely whenever I'm out. I will only indulge myself at my own table, in private with Bay and the twins. Then will I escape?"

"Well, if so," Dove said, and laughed, "you will have to begin right now, this meal, and I warn you, *Titanic*'s chef has been at Buckingham Palace for the king, and his grilled mutton, I've heard already, is His Majesty's noontime favorite."

Dove had been staying at her daughter's English house since August, when Nicola Lady Pomeroy returned to Dentoncroft from Kenya, a new widow. Yesterday, at tea, Audrey had seen her for the first time in a year, and yesterday Audrey had thought Dove noticeably older; still fine, but older.

And yet today she was especially delightful.

She wore, as usual, her signature color, a thin wool suit of light gray that intensified the white of her hair and the blue of her eyes. By candlelight she could have passed for thirty-five. Her hair had been white since Audrey had known her; her hair was her trademark, as white as the powdered wigs of Marie Antoinette and just as cunningly curled. Her figure was still perfect, her dresses, as ever, exquisitely designed.

Long ago, even as a debutante "coming out," Suzanna Reed Peerce, called Dove, had begun a pursuit of perfection in her physical self and in her manners; long ago she had achieved it. These days she was less obsessed with such things, she said, but the habits of a lifetime kept her up, to all appearances, to her own high mark.

But long ago she had slipped in her morals—

though other than herself and the man involved, only one other knew, and he had kept the secret; she knew why.... She had enjoyed her slipping. And now that Percy, her husband, was gone, long gone, Dove was free. I have nothing to prove and no one to lose, she, who was known for her wit, would think to herself these days whenever temptation chanced by. These days I seek only amusement. These days I am truly a dangerous woman....

But to Audrey, Dove was still an inspiration, an older woman of skilled graces, intimidating, inspiring awe. Audrey knew Dove and Nicola had never been comfortable with each other; there had always been a distance between mother and daughter, a kind of competition. A kind of...jealousy. Before Nicola had fallen in love with Rolf—and he with her—Dove used to despair, she said, of marrying Nicola off. She had been an ugly duckling, Dove said of her daughter, who was now called "the most beautiful woman on two continents." She had been a wild and willful child, her mother told on her, who was now most sought after, most sighed for, most *wanted*.

But maybe now they will be comfortable with each other, Audrey thought as she and Dove strolled, arm in arm, toward the smaller dining salon. Now Nicola was a widow, too.... Now mother and daughter would resume living together at Peerce House. They would grow close and come to love each other....

"Look," said Dove, pressing a sheet of heavy paper into Audrey's hand. "Look, but don't tell. And he sent me roses, too. White roses, a dozen, just opening, so nice."

The stationery was engraved with the insignia of *Titanic*. It bore the name of Captain Edward John

Smith. It was an invitation for Dove to join his table tonight at dinner. "Please do me the honor of sitting at my right hand," it read. "I should like nothing better."

"Why, you darling," exclaimed Audrey, knowing Dove liked nothing better than the attentions of men. "You can have a shipboard romance if you like, if you're that kind of woman."

"We are all *that* kind of woman, Audrey my sweet," said Dove. "Just some of us are better at it than others."

"Not me," said Audrey, believing it. "Not me."

Dove's laughter was light as, together, they passed down the great staircase. Men watched them descend and smiled approval.

3

Victoria VanVoorst satin her chair at the round white table in *Titanic*'s dining room as though lightning-struck. There it was, her *doom*, across the room. She had known—or feared, it was much the same thing—that someday this would happen. Someday, this very thing: she would run into her past, bang into disaster. She would be *recognized*. Her secret would be exposed, and all would be taken from her, all she was, all she had, all she loved....

She forced herself to sit tall and quiet. She knew about pretense, knew how to live a lie. So she would sit beside Burty as though she were only tired, fragile late in the seventh month of her pregnancy, seasick perhaps, although *Titanic* was so steady that for all she knew they might have been onshore. Except for a salt-tinged freshness in the air, she had no sense of being ocean-bound. As soon as she could she would excuse herself and go to their stateroom, and lie down and *think*....

She had cyanide crystals in her medicine kit. She'd had them for a long time. For years and years she'd kept the blue vial close, wherever she went, as a kind of last resort, a hara-kiri sword…if and when little Alma June Brown came back to life…and had to be *murdered* again.…

Across the room Theodore Royce marveled at her.

There are some women, he thought, no matter how long it's been, you never forget. And it must be twenty years and more since I've had the pleasure of looking at Alma June. I remember when she was no more than a big-titted pickaninny needing to sing for her supper and not always getting to, he thought. I remember when Alma June had to sell whatever they'd buy for a catfish sandwich on white bread. But always a spitfire, always a beauty. And even now, oh, she's married up has the little darlin', even now all pallid and big bellied, she's almost sinisterly beautiful, sculpted by the devil himself to beguile mankind. I'll catch up with her later, catch her alone, say hello. I'll say, hey, Alma June, remember Teddy Royce? And yes, since you ask, I still gamble. Still living by my wits. And yes, I'd appreciate it, honey, if you didn't call me Rolls.…

Tory felt so hot, sitting between Burty and Nicola Lady Pomeroy in the middle of a round table large enough for eight. They had not yet ordered. Nicola was reading a wireless just delivered, reading it to herself with a solemn expression as though its contents did not please her. And Burty sat with a gin rickey and waited for the rest of their party to join them, thumping his fingers on his bread plate amidst a great swath of new white linen and five ornate, fully dressed, empty places.

Tory saw Audrey and Dove Peerce coming. No Bay, then. He would be busy with Mr. Ismay, closeted somewhere in a private suite. And the twins and

Mrs. Twigg were probably sampling the little café outside, watching the scenery, watching the water run.

Under the table Tory took her husband's hand.

Why had she done it? Why had she got pregnant as a goose when she'd sworn to herself she never would, when she'd promised herself she'd rather die? She would be forty-two her next birthday. And years ago she'd convinced Burty she was sterile. He had been reconciled to childlessness; he expected no flowers from her womb, he said. And in another season or two she would be unable to bear children, she would cross into a safe middle age and her secret would have been...not safe, but safer. *So why...?*

For love.

Simple as that, sugar. For love of Burty, whom she'd married not to love but to enjoy. But somehow, while she wasn't thinking about it, she'd fallen in love with her husband and sensed his hurt, his disappointment, at being fatherless. And she had been so safe for so long, the terror must have died without her knowing. Her fear once constant, once ever in her mind dictating every move, every thought; the fear had slipped away in years of comfort, and she had wanted to please him, as he pleased her....

For love.

Love of Burty who had married her with all his friends against it. She was only after his fortune, they said—and it had been true. "She can have my fortune," Burty said, "I'll make another and she can have that one, too!"

He had battled his parents for her, mean-spirited Amity and henpecked Vincent. "That flame of yours comes from nowhere, dear," his parents, who had come from nowhere themselves, objected. They threatened not to come to the wedding and so, when it happened, they did not get invited; they cried then, oh yes. The father was dead now, run down by a florist's truck on Broadway, lower Manhattan, close to where his chippie lived.

Tory had come from worse than nowhere. She had come from the depths of Louisiana to the dance halls of Times Square. But Burty had married her, howling to anyone who demurred, "I don't give a DAMN where she came from! It's where she's going that matters!" He'd married her and set her up on the high ground of Bellevue Avenue in Newport, and Fifth Avenue in New York City. Strong-armed and joyously, he had lifted *torrid little Tory* out of the back street, yanked her off the stage, and set her, magnificently, upon Blueblood Boulevard.

She had, in the early days, played the marriage for all it was worth, lying all the while.

Way back in New Orleans, her first memory was of a lie she told, was of a lying silence when Sister Minni, black as sin, looked down at her in her pink dress and pink hair bows and asked so kindly, "What'cha doin' hyah, chile, in a colluhed church? You be losted? You ought'a be up de road some, in dat white church yonder. You don belong down hyah in Niggatown, now does you...?"

Alma June Brown was her name then. She had been three or four and oh, so very light—pale gold. That Sunday—it must have been a Sunday, the church and all—she rolled her green eyes at Sister Minni pitiously...

Those green eyes were her salvation. Negroes do not have green eyes. Green as greed were Alma

June's eyes in a high-boned sharp-chinned, gold-skin face; green as *go*, green as greenbacks, and lawns rolling down to an expensive azure sea—

…hoping to be carried to that other church up the road, where things were better for a girl. Even then, three or four, Alma June had known: it was better to be white than black, and she could *pass* anytime she wanted to.

That Sunday she stayed with Sister Minni. But in time she ran east, gone white.…

"What will you have, my fair one?"

Audrey and Dove had taken their places. Greetings must have been exchanged, cocktail orders taken. Tory had missed everything, lost in her secrets. She realized Burty had dropped her hand; she was twisting her hands together in her lap, and they were moist with a soft new sweat. Burty was holding the menu card for her. The sign of the White Star Line, a pennant flag with a single white star, flew gaily under her eyes.

"Consommé jardiniere," she said.

"Ah," Burty flicked the card under his own chin. "How's about cold lobster then or—this is for me— the potted shrimp. A double order, waiter, and maybe, if it's good, I'll have a third."

"It is very good, sir," said the waiter, still a boy.

Tory stroked her husband's leg. "The soup, and rice pudding, Burty. I'm not as hungry as you." She stroked his leg as though her heart were not breaking. "There's plaice fillets," she said, trying to steer him away from the fat-sauced shrimp. "You like those."

He was drinking beer, feeling better now he was going to eat. "Yes," he said, "several fillets of plaice for me, the potted shrimp and mashed potatoes. No soup, no salad. Maybe a wedge of steak and kidney pie.''

"Oh no, Burty."

"I'm on vacation, Tor." And he kissed her hand to show he didn't hold her concern for his weight against her.

Tory gave up her coaxing, but shuddered. He was too stout these days. Burty had always been robust, but now he was on the verge of becoming fat. He was not a handsome man, but not an ugly one; his eyes were bright, an alert brown, and his smile was ready and unselfconscious. He was becoming a dandy. For the voyage he'd bought himself a new topcoat—something he'd never have done a year or so ago—a cashmere topcoat with a shawl collar of Persian lamb. The pin in his lapel was ruby and platinum and matched the stick in his tie. A little too much...flash, she thought. She would have to look to it, speak to his man, Elgin....

While she, though her stomach was temporarily stretched, was taut of limb, her body curved and lissome by a lifetime of daily repetitions at the barre. Hers was an elegant neck and oil-dark hair, the face of a Madonna above the body of a courtesan. Her greatest glory was her skin, her flawless, lineless, pale gold coloring. Spanish, she explained it. "My mother was Castilian, she died when I was born...." Tawn and peach, Tory glowed. "She glows all over," Burty liked to brag. "You should see my baby in the buff!"

Some had. In the olden days....

That was how she met Burty, Burton Kingsley VanVoorst, self-made millionaire. She had been a dancer-singer who sometimes, to keep things lively, removed a stitch of clothes or two....

Thank heaven Teddy Royce was sitting far across the dining room, port side; she couldn't have borne it otherwise. He was sitting by himself, at a table for two, sipping soup. Teddy "Rolls"—for his luck with the dice—Royce, gambler, con man, collector of ladies' hearts. Handsome now—more handsome now—urbane, grown. As she was grown.... Well dressed. Ah, then. He had come up in the world, too, as she had, pulling on those old bootstraps, and polishing them, polishing them....

He smiled over at her, cocked a spoon in greeting. She ignored him.

He would be the death of her.

Audrey had said something to her, and she hadn't heard. She looked at her friend inquiringly.

"Are you all right, Tor?" Audrey repeated. "You're not sparkling the way we want you to."

Nicola was staring at her, too, with a worried expression. Nicola who, as far as Tory knew, always only worried about herself. Nicola the eagle, with her conqueror's eyes, flying alone, above them all.

Tory patted her stomach as her excuse.

Suddenly she had the urge to tell, tell Audrey and Nicola everything. Thank God, Burty was only a handbreadth away, or she might have said: One night, girls, while I was humming to myself in my marble bathroom, gray-and-white Carrara marble, darlings, from the north of Rome, Burty poked his head through the open doorway. I was in a new gown of jet and lace—I looked ravishing. I expected Burty to leer, but he yawned. He yawned and said to please forgive him but he was going straightaway to bed....

I was a long time following, sitting in my marble bathroom at my delicious best, my considerable charms ignored. I had a thin Scotch and thought of things blacker than my gown....

That, girls, is why I am pregnant now. I love him now, you see, the way he once loved me, and *I'm afraid of losing him*. That's the real reason, Audrey, my pet, I went to that fleabag gypsy on Fourth Street.... I saw myself as an aging divorcée who, no matter how well-fixed, how good-looking, how well dressed, would be remembered—it would be told and told, I know it!—as a dance-hall girl who shimmied in the all-together and got lucky. I saw you, Audrey, and you, too, Nick, and all the other women who are kind to me as Mrs. Burton Kingsley VanVoorst, with your heads close as tepee sticks, whispering over my fall from grace. I saw you all embracing Burty's new wife—my God, I wondered, who would it be! And you would all be saying how much more appropriate she was for him than I was, who had been only a hotblood...*with a trace of nigger in my veins*....

So there, girls, Tory wanted to shout, now you know. My secret is out, now I can relax.

If Burty had not been there, solid beside her, Tory might have burst out and *told it all*.

She longed to have the baby out of her, out and living on its own. I want my body slight again, she longed to tell them, lips pinched tight to keep the truth from spilling. I want to be panther-haunched again, big-breasted for my size. I want to dance under the colored lights again, I want to swivel, honey, I want to hear men sigh.

Teddy "Rolls" Royce had brought it all back to her.

She pushed back her chair. "I think I'll go lie down, if you'll excuse me," she said so correctly. "I'm a little dizzy, seasick, perhaps."

Burty dropped his napkin beside his plate, his overflowing plate. "I'll escort you, my lovely, my Madonna to be." Good-natured Burty, a *jewel* of a man.

She put her hand on his shoulder. "No, darling, please. Enjoy those shrimp, they look luscious. Maybe tomorrow I'll have shrimp myself. I think I'll just walk a bit, get some fresh air, stretch my legs. I'll take the long way round, take my time, and then I'll nap till dinner. I'll be fine—don't disturb yourself."

"Souvenirs, if you're interested, are in the barber shop," he said. "Buy yourself something, buy me something, buy something for Junior there." He was already eating again. Enjoying himself. He needed this vacation, though he had not wanted, at first, to come.

Tory took a final spoon of rice pudding. It was cold and sweet, and it reminded her of home. Not Gilt Hill in Newport, not Fifth Avenue in New York.... Real home. The Mississippi bayou and Granny Brown who walked behind her shack each day conversing with "de Lawd." Home was getting high on peach wine three weeks old, and singing the blues in a smoke-filled room to an alto sax just off the beat, sweat liming her armpits, shining on her breasts, and she twisting her thighs against the cotton of her skirt till it *split* up to her backside and the men fell over themselves, all crazy.

Home.

Tory rose, graceful, in spite of her bulk.

Across the room Teddy Royce rose, grinning wide.

The floor was floating, lazy as a Mississippi rivulet in August, but she would not faint, would not stumble. One foot in front of the other, and she was out of the dining room and climbing the grand staircase to A deck. She did not use the hand banister; she *floated up* as though it were the easiest thing in the world to do.

On A deck, the promenades, starboard and port side, were glass enclosed, so that no matter the weather, *Titanic*'s first-class passengers could enjoy the view, enjoy a walk, enjoy themselves. Tory climbed on, to boat deck, *Titanic*'s highest tier. There, in the bow, was the captain's bridge. There, amidship, was an open promenade. She reached it, a red haze in her mind, a churning in her stomach. But here it was peaceful. The wind was sharp and zestful; it sobered her mind. The sun was lowering over the approaching French coast.

She made it to the promenade rail. Gripped it…and waited.

Below, far, far below, the water churned in frosty ribbons around *Titanic*'s bow. The great ship, solid as a Newport mansion, under a calm cloud-filled sky, steamed toward Cherbourg.…

Even if *somehow* she could prevent Teddy Royce from spilling her secret, there was no way out. She had done herself in, self-destructed; she saw that now. She'd done Burty no favor getting pregnant; it had been madness. Fear she would lose him drove her to take the chance.

Stupid. Stupid.

For it would break him, wouldn't it?

And kill her...*if the baby was born black.*

"Alma June," said Teddy Royce, beside her. "It's been a long time. I've missed you, babe."

4

Happily rumpled, Swan Josephine Lockholm sat on Danny Bowen's pallet in his closet of a bedroom down on E deck, near one of the boiler rooms. With the door closed, the room was dark and very small and hot and stuffy. There was no window and only a dim electric light fixture and, being careful of the candle stub, there was barely room for one person to turn around. Certainly there was no room to dance. A second person had to sit on the little bed, or on the one above, while the first one moved around. Swan had never seen anything like it.

"This is really poverty," she said, clicking her fine black shoes together at the toes. "I wondered what real poverty would be like."

"Oh, no, this is rather good," said Danny, sitting beside her, his tunic open, a bottle of champagne in his hand. He had taken it from a tray of bottles when he was relieved upstairs from playing. "Let's celebrate," he said, and kissed her, without even thinking whether he should or not. She was so pretty, he loved her right away.

They were close to *Titanic*'s heart. Behind the wall

Swan could hear the ship's pistons thrumming. She sighed with bliss. "You were wonderful to save my twin," she said. "Smoke was so mad. Did you see?"

"She looks too much like you, it's spooky. I thought I was holding you in my arms. I didn't notice she was mad."

"Oh, she hates you," said Swan amicably. "She's jealous, that's it."

He leaned against her. "Kiss me again," he said. He put the palm of his right hand upon her breast.

She did not protest.

"I shall hide down here with you most of the voyage. Would you like that?" she said. "Though I have to go up and see things once in a while. This is only my second ocean crossing, and I don't want to miss anything. Also, I must check in with Mrs. Twigg—she's our governess and chaperon. We have to mind Mrs. Twigg in everything or she reports us to Mother. On Sunday Smoke and I will be sixteen. Sweet sixteen, which I think is heaven. Mother is giving us a party. I shall ask that you be one of the musicians. We'll be allowed two, only two. But you will be one. That way, even if we can't dance together, you will get a piece of cake."

"Take Jock and me," he said, his lips buried in her hair where it was gathered, ribbon tied, at the nape of her neck.

"Which one is Jock?"

"He's my bunk mate."

"A bunk mate! You couldn't possibly have!"

"I wish you were my bunk mate," he said.

"Oh, you mustn't say that," she said, "or even think it. I will have to run away if you do." But his hand was still closed upon her breast, and one of her hands was over his.

He kissed her velvet-clad shoulder. "All right then, I won't say it, if that's what you want. But Jock is my bunk mate. You haven't met him yet, and I have just barely. He wears glasses and he's tall like me. We'll be a matched pair of violinists at your party, like carriage horses."

"Charcoal and Peet, our blacks," said Swan. "You'd like them. We keep them at Whale's Turning, in Newport."

"You don't have an auto car?"

"Oh yes." Swan admired his hair, lightest brown, longer than it needed to be. "We have a Ford in New York. Father says this summer he will teach Mother and us to drive it. But, honestly, we only use it for special occasions. In New York, most of the time, we walk."

"Are you really rich then, Swan? Too rich for me?" The champagne bottle was empty. He whistled over the mouth of the bottle, a little tune.

She sighed. "What if I am? We can still have a shipboard romance, don't you think?"

He shrugged.

"Kiss me," she said, "while I close my eyes."

He kissed her with warm lips, kissed her eyelids and nose and chin and then her mouth. His tongue tasted of wine.

"Maybe Smoke will like Jock," she said, shifting her weight against his shoulder. Then she shook her head. "No, Smoke wouldn't. She doesn't like boys very much. She wants to be a boy herself, you see."

"Aw, come on," he said. He gave her his wine-glass, half-full.

She sipped contentedly. "I like it when the bubbles burst," she said. "She does. Smoke wants to do what boys do. She's not really a suffragette, but she wants to be a sea captain. She has a wishing book full of boats, sailing ships and yachts."

"How steady this ship is," he whispered against her cheek. "We might be in your parlor, high on a hill."

"Yes," she said, and closed her eyes again. "Yes, we might at that."

She was very lovely. He couldn't believe his luck. He had been sure the picture she'd sent was too good to be true, but she was prettier than her picture, and easy to know and fun. Best of all, she was hot. That was easy to see. He kissed her again with an open mouth, as hard as he dared.

She kissed him back ardently, her eyelids quivering.

And then her twin, Smoke, was standing in the door.

Swan struggled up to a sitting position. "What do *you* want?" she said.

Smoke looked sullen. "I knew I'd find you down here. God, it stinks."

"Doesn't. You do."

"Come away. It's time for luncheon."

"You go, Smoke. Make my apologies." Swan smoothed the nap on her velvet skirt. "Just don't you tell where I am."

"Come with me," said Smoke. Her cheeks were flaming.

Swan laughed. "If you were me, would you?"

Smoke looked at Danny Bowen, tossing back his hair, drinking off the last of a glass of champagne.

He wasn't upset that she was there. He wasn't even surprised. He was smiling at her, a slow, questioning smile. *Mr. Danger*.

"No, Smokey," said Swan, "I won't come just now." And with a polished black toe she swung the door shut in Smoke's face.

Smoke ran then, up staircase after staircase, all the way up to the boat deck. Almost everyone else was two tiers down, on B deck, eating, drinking, being *friends*. Alone, she curled into a deck chair under a blanket.

Smoke hated it when Swan was mean to her and she couldn't get even right away. Swan was supposed to be the genial one. After all, Smoke had been born first; Smoke was the leader.

Used to be.

But now there was *Mr. Danger*, and Swan had no time for her twin. After Danny had "rescued" Smoke—rescued, ha ha, she hadn't *really* been going to fall—Swan had turned on her heel and left Smoke stranded. *He* had followed her, like Mary's little lamb.

Well. If Swan didn't want to cooperate, then Smoke could always go to Mother, couldn't she. And Mother would go to Mrs. Twigg. And Swan would be confined to their stateroom for the entire ocean crossing, except maybe for their birthday party and then dinner the last night out. And then Smoke, just to make Swan mad, would sit around with Danny Bowen and maybe kiss him, too....

No.

Smoke couldn't go to their mother. Smoke never went to her mother because her mother never came to her. "Mother doesn't like me," Smoke said to the

deck chair. "And the feeling is mutual, so don't cry
for me. Mother is a cold fish where her daughters are
concerned. She cares only for Dad." Her father was
kind when she could get his attention, but he never
understood what the problem was. And she had been
told and told and *told* until she wanted to *spit* that
this trip was all business for her father, so she should
try not to be a trial—Mrs. Twigg's exact words,
every night seven days in a row before they'd left
for Paris and the spring showings.

She was missing the midday meal. But she had
stuffed herself on the departure party hors d'oeuvres;
she wasn't hungry. She had explored most of *Titanic*,
seen the men's smoking room and the gymnasium,
and booked herself a lesson with the tennis pro.
She'd got into the rowing machine and tried a few
strokes. It was harder here than in Narragansett Bay;
here it was all resistance and no water to ease the
slide. She had checked a book out of the library, a
murder-mystery, and written a postcard to her maternal grandparents, Mr. and Mrs. Lawrence Smoke
of Newport, U.S.A.

She'd been kicked out of the wireless room. She'd
gone there to see what was what, and seen a young
man not much older than herself talking into a can
faster than she could play the piano. "I am the boss's
daughter," she announced, but John Phillips, as his
name turned out to be, said White Star Line owned
Titanic and that he was busy, too many incoming
messages, and she would have to go.

"My father owns the White Star Line," she'd
said, and sat in a chair and crossed her legs as though
she meant to stay all day. But then Captain Smith
had stuck his head in the door and called her out,

and told her she was not to enter "working quarters" without permission, ever, no matter what her name was, and did she understand? Then John Phillips said that Lady Pomeroy had got another message from Captain Lord of the *Californian*, an ocean liner three days out. Smoke informed them that she knew the marchioness and would deliver the missive if the captain wanted, but he called a steward and gave the message to him, and told Smoke to stay out of the way. And so she did not know what this Captain Lord had wanted of Nicola.... But she wished she did.

And then she had set off to find her twin, whom she had found, as she suspected, in Danny Bowen's *pathetic* broom closet of a room, right next to a boiler down on E deck and as smelly as a rag. There was no window, and it was *dark in there*, and Swan was lying in the bunk with Danny Bowen, and he had her breast in his hand!

Smoke had never been so shocked.

And then Swan was telling her to go and slamming the door in her face!

He hadn't said a word. He'd just looked at her and then at Swan and then back at her, as though he were trying to figure out how to tell them apart.

It's easy once you know us, Smoke thought, sulking in the deck chair. We're not at all alike inside, and that shows through after a while, you'll see. He hadn't looked poor in his musician's uniform, he'd just looked *handsome*. She could still feel his hands around her waist. She wished he would put his arms around her, close, again.

And suddenly, as *Titanic* glided gently toward

Cherbourg, she was crying and she couldn't stop. She huddled down into the blanket to hide herself.

Tory was walking on the promenade. Come looking for us, Smoke thought, burrowing deeper. Everybody must be worried where we are, got up a search party...! No, Tory was only admiring the view, watching the sun fall.

Oh!

A handsome stranger closed upon the rail at Tory's side. Smoke saw them exchange murmurs as though they were old friends. Well, of course, Tory Van-Voorst did know almost everyone in the world, and Smoke knew hardly anyone, but still, this man did not look like Newport or New York at all. He looked like a Southern gentleman, suntanned face, white suit, dark wood walking stick. Smoke thought: If he rode a white stallion he would look like a king. He said something, something soft, and Tory turned to him and laid both her hands upon his chest.

Gee, everybody is doing it! thought Smoke. What a *swamp* is an ocean cruise. Where's Burty? she wanted to shout, but she didn't. She was obviously misinterpreting what Tory was about. After all, Mrs. VanVoorst was seven months pregnant and more; she couldn't be unfaithful if she wanted to.

THELMA IRENE TWIGG WAS on the march.

It was not that she minded dining alone in the Café Parisien. Humph, it had been a blessing. Usually the Lockholm girls were always bickering and putting her in the middle. And it was not that she thought her charges weren't on board. She had seen them both an hour before, shortly after embarking, but she had not been able to catch up to them before they disappeared. There had been such a crowd to push through. And then she had been distracted, having to arrange their trunks in their room and get herself settled in across the hall.

But they were *not* to carouse around on their own. This was a holiday, that may be, but rules got obeyed on holidays, too, and the Misses Lockholm were never, never, to go off on their own without Mrs. Twigg's permission and without her knowing exactly when they would be back.

And now here they were, coming in to dock as close they could at Cherbourg—the facility was too small for large ships; *Titanic* rode at anchor just inside the seawall and waited for tenders to bring out the passengers and take away those who had come this far only for the "channel ride"—and Smoke and Swan were nowhere to be found. Nowhere.

When she caught up to them, they'd be sorry. And she was going now, right now, to Mrs. Lockholm and complain. Oh yes, she'd get things straightened out *right now*, nothing like nipping rebellions in the bud....

Mrs. Twigg, on her way down B deck's corridor toward the Lockholm suite, paused on blue carpet before a primping mirror to reassure herself her coiffure had not been displaced in her haste. Though the wrong side of forty, she considered herself still "the right side of stout," a constant worry because she did enjoy a pastry or two at breakfast and a cup of custard when the day was done. I'm not a bad-looking woman, she thought, not for the first time, complacent at the sight of plump cheeks naturally blushed and sweet brown eyes dimmed not a whit by her lorgnette, which hung, when not needed, upon a generous bosom. This "feminine distraction," so referred, she kept well corseted and stiff by day for fear of "bouncing in her bodice and overly exciting the men." Though sometime, of an evening, she allowed her gown "the subtle provocation of dainty exposure," which never failed to lift her spirits and, she liked to think, those of the gentleman who asked her to dance. The one disappointment in her attire was in her lack of monograms. She did think scripted initials on one's handkerchief and purse—and luggage when one traveled, such as now—lent a proper air of exclusivity. But a monogram needed three initials to look right, and unfortunately for Thelma Irene Twigg, initials were impossible.

Well, one could not have everything....

She had gracious ways, as well she ought as an instructor of young women, a "walking encyclopedia" of correct behavior. And she had a fund of capsule wisdom that she used as often on herself as on her charges. "Right's right and wrong's nothing," she would tell the twins again. She had told the twins that over and over, and would probably recite it in her grave. Ah, but some does better than others, she thought, turning from the mirror and continuing on her righteous way, and those two are the worst.

Firmly, Mrs. Twigg tapped on the dark-paneled door marked B-51. Suite B-51-53-55 was one of *Titanic*'s two best. Audrey and Bay had bedroom 53, the VanVoorsts were in 55, which connected, other side of the bath, and B-51 was the sitting room. Mrs. Twigg had seen it earlier, at Audrey Lockholm's invitation, and thought it as fine as ever she'd seen.

Audrey Lockholm opened her own door. She had not brought her maid with her, nor had Tory. Mrs.

Twigg had volunteered to help as needed; it was little enough to offer since she was being given her own first-class compartment and could join in as an equal whenever she chose to—Mrs. Lockholm had said so, and Mrs. VanVoorst had emphatically agreed. Though Mrs. Peerce and Lady Pomeroy, who didn't know her so well, had not yet been overly friendly. But that was all right with Mrs. Twigg. *I wouldn't change places with none of 'em*, Mrs. Twigg thought. *I can shoot my shoes when I please, and I don't have to keep changing my clothes, nor be too proud to wield a needle. I do very well with my frocks, I've enough to suit me, and if I have a crepe suzette after dinner, there's no dressmaker there to scold me nor no man to make me feel bad, and that does just fine.*

Mrs. Lockholm was in a silk lounging robe over her petticoats. "Oh, Mrs. Twigg," she said, "what is it?"

"May I come in, madam?" And Mrs. Twigg entered, closing the door behind her.

The room was cream paneled, as large as Mrs. Twigg's bedroom in the Lockholm house on Fifth Avenue. A gray carpet covered the floor. The marble-manteled fireplace was burning a log, and double doors opened to a private promenade, from which a brisk breeze fanned the fire. This private promenade was also one of *Titanic*'s only two. Mr. Ismay, Mrs. Twigg had been told, possessed the other one, port side. Two bedrooms he had, the exact mirror of this suite, two double bedrooms, and only one of him that she'd ever seen. But rich does as rich wants, she'd noticed, and never mind the needs of other people.

Audrey Lockholm had just come from a bath. She was pale with no makeup, but her long lemon hair had never darkened, and her figure was as fine, if a little more curvaceous, than her daughters'. No bon-bons for you at the end of a day, sympathized Mrs. Twigg to herself; once a beauty the burden was always on you. Mrs. Twigg had not been a beauty, had not married, didn't miss it. Not everyone needs a man to get through this life, was how she explained it. She called herself Mrs. Twigg because it sounded more genteel than Miss at her age; she wanted no aspersions cast upon her spinsterhood, and no pussyfooting in her presence about the intentions of men, either. She knew what boudoirs were for.... Oh, gentlemen had their virtues, Mrs. Twigg would not deny it, but gentlemen *were not to be trusted*. None of them. Not at fifteen or thirty or forty-five or sixty. Men were apes when you got down to it, *apes* out of their clothes. Not their fault, perhaps. Blame it on the Lord if you want to. But the first thing you had to do with a man was check whether he had his pants on.

"Mrs. Twigg, what is it?" asked Audrey again.

Mrs. Twigg bent to her task. "Oh, madam, you know I wouldn't worry you unless I had to, but it's the twins—I can't find either one. They weren't with you in the dining room, and they weren't with me in the café. Had to have my cutlet quite alone. And they've not been in their room, and I've checked all over B deck. I thought they might be with you, or you would know where they are. Humph, if it's not one thing it's another with them. They're worse than two boys—never let a body relax."

"Oh, please, Mrs. Twigg, don't fret. I'm sure they're somewhere together. Have you tried the gymnasium?"

"Indeed," said Mrs. Twigg, her hands folded primly at her waist.

She admired the twins' mother for many things, but Audrey Lockholm was not the world's most devoted mother; Mrs. Twigg had told her that to her face.

Audrey tried again. "Perhaps they're with Nicola and Dove—B-16, Mrs. Twigg."

"We shall see. I doubt it," said Mrs. Twigg darkly. Really. Mrs. Lockholm gave her complete authority over the girls, which was as should be, but she'd think Mrs. Lockholm would sometimes be a *little* help. She took a step back to depart. "It's not good, madam, you're not knowing, I not knowing. Of course, you know that."

Audrey nodded. "I rely on you, Mrs. Twigg. And don't worry, I'm sure they're all right."

"Humph."

Mrs. Twigg turned on her heel. "They're taking liberties, Mrs. Lockholm. I saw it at M. Poiret's last week. You allowed them too many gowns and too many tea cakes. You said four frocks for the season, and they walked away having ordered seven each. I thought it a scandal—I told you seven was too much. It spoils them. And then you gave them permission for two petits fours at tea table. That was indulgence of the worst kind. Young ladies who aren't married *cannot*, I repeat, Mrs. Lockholm, *cannot* have two sweets at teatime."

"I thought just that once. Their first visit to Paris, to the famous couturier—"

"All the more reason for discipline, madam, if I may say so. And would you like to know what advantage Smoke took of your laxness? She hid sconcs in her pockets—scones as big as rocks. I found crumbs in her bed the next morning and then turned more out of her dress. She'll be too fat for her seven new outfits before they arrive.''

Audrey sighed. ''I apologize, Mrs. Twigg, I shouldn't have done it.''

''Yes. They'll take the bit in their mouths if you let them. Remember, I said that? And now you see it. Smoke first, she's a hellion, and now dear little Swan, too sweet to say no to her sister. They're running wild on this cruise ship, and we're not a day out of England. How's that?''

Audrey wished Mrs. Twigg would let her go. ''I leave them to you, Mrs. Twigg. Please find them and tell them they're to stay under your wing this whole trip.''

''Thank you,'' said Mrs. Twigg, turning to go.

Audrey opened the door for her. ''I shall not interfere again, Mrs. Twigg, without clearing it with you. You know there is a party planned for them on Sunday.''

Mrs. Twigg's bosom heaved at the thought. ''I know, it's just one thing after the other.... Shall I let you know when I find them?''

''No, thank you. Only let me know if you don't.''

''I see.''

Mrs. Twigg was out and marching again. Poor little lambs, she thought now. No one to care for them but their Twiggs. Their mother's head all full of herself and her husband, still playing the newlywed, and her daughters almost grown. Humph, she thought, congratulating herself on her good sense. I wouldn't be rich if you paid me!

She'd have them paged, that's what she'd do.

She'd go right to the purser and get them called over the speakers. And when they presented themselves, she'd lay down the law one-two-three, straight as a poker, just see if she didn't.

AUDREY SAT on the sofa for a moment, resting from Mrs. Twigg's scolding before she continued dressing. She had little defense against it. She wasn't the mother she ought to be, not the mother Josephine had been. But then the twins did not need Audrey the way Audrey had needed Josephine, needed and lost too soon.... The twins had Mrs. Twigg.

Dream children.

Everyone said so. Though born in great labor, the first not able for half a day to push through to life on its own. And the second had been turned, some-how, in the womb. For a while Dr. Lake despaired of saving the second. But then the midwife had come, Mildred Falk, and greased her long, bony arm.... Audrey closed her eyes on the memory. Long ago all that, almost forgotten. Audrey had healed, though she would bear no more children. No son for Bay.... He'd said it didn't matter.

When they were babies, Audrey used to think that Smoke, older by five hours than Swan, must be a changeling, a baby switched by the fairies while everyone sleeps, a bad one for a fair. Except of course not; that was fanciful. The twins were iden-tical. But once you knew them you never confused them, even when they were dressed to match down to the parts in their hair and the barrettes.... They were beautiful girls, Lockholm women with Bay's well-bred bones. From Audrey they had their grace of figure and golden hair. Their eyes were their own, a mixture of Bay's ocean-storm gray and Audrey's famous ones of midnight blue. The twins' eyes were vivid turquoise, the color of calm water when the sun is hot upon it. But their mouths, full lipped, belied the calm: their mouths were fine, but needy.

Audrey had never been comfortable with them.

She put away her thoughts, dressed in her simplest clothes. She was going down to third now…. Now, while the ship was quiet, before dinner. Now, before Bay finished with Mr. Ismay and came back to her.

She was going to find the gypsy.

5

Finally, the clouds had cleared. The orange sun, too shortly aflame on the horizon, dropped from sight below *Titanic*'s bow, and the profile of little Cherbourg was purpling prettily into silhouette. On the high boat deck, Nicola Lady Pomeroy, marchioness of Denton, and her mother, Dove Peerce, sat in deck chairs idly watching the new passengers boarding down below. Nicola, warm in a sable greatcoat, admired the palette of the twilight, the yellow ribbons in the sky, the swaths of parrot green, the lengthening magenta. Her mother, snuggled into silver fox, sipped from a tall rum drink and gossiped.

"Mr. Morgan, did you know, will not be traveling with us, after all," said Dove.

Nicola, who had never shared her mother's fascination in the affairs of others, feigned interest. "Why ever not?" she said.

"It seems," said Dove, in that light, innocent voice she affected when she knew she held you spellbound, "that he is regrettably trapped in Aix-les-Bains with a charming Parisienne."

"Oh, Dove," said Nicola, who had not called her

mother "Mother" since the day of her wedding, when Dove had squealed like a bridesmaid and cheated Kiki Witherspoon of Nicola's bouquet. "How in the world, sealed off as we are out here, did you discover that?"

"It was in a wireless to Bayard Lockholm," said Dove. "I ran into him and Bruce Ismay on my way up here to join you. I had to step into the smoking room for a moment to give my apologies to Colonel Gracie, who had asked for my company at dinner tonight. Bay was telling Bruce, and he told me, too. J.P. was supposed to be boarding here, with Frances, but he won't be, and she stayed entirely home.... Poor Frances," Dove murmured. "She knows J.P. is a wag. Belle Green almost *lives* in her homes with her, for heaven's sake. She never lets on, of course, but she must care, mustn't she? Still, you'd never know it to meet her, and I don't know her well enough to ask."

"I'm sure she cares terribly," said Nicola, still vulnerable to tears about Rolf. "To love a man and have him unfaithful—it must be killing."

"Or a woman," said Dove softly, wondering—with her past—how she dared.

Nicola was quiet, remembering Rolf, Lord Pomeroy. Thoughts of her lost husband engulfed her, and she was somewhere far away.... She was no longer on the great ship *Titanic* returning to America to remake her life bereft of her golden boy. She was no longer with her mother *trying to make peace....*

Her life—the one with Rolf, the one that mattered—had ended last summer in Kenya.

Last summer, and sundown, and the hunt. Rolf's long-awaited long-planned rhinoceros hunt.

It had been the third day out, all in the hunting party a little tired by then, worn-out, not used to the exertions of a safari. But not admitting to it, not giving in to it, and eager not to spoil anyone else's fun. So Nicola Lady Pomeroy did not say, lazy and bare limbed, her hair of goddess red all loose around her, "Let's stay in the tent today, Rolf, what do you say? Let's give the crew a rest, let's love the day away. Tomorrow we can hunt again, tomorrow will do as well."

No, though she'd wanted to, she did not say it, more's the pity.

There was a long trek, all day across the veld, and finally the river up ahead, bathed in African gold. A fine rhinoceros buck, huge flanked, long horned, stood sentinel on the bank, swinging his black head, lifting his nose, trying to identify what came, what *hitari* approached... *hitari* for "danger."

Rolf was excited.

He was on his knees in an instant, had the monster in his rifle sights! And then, from the bush—even their scout did not see until too late—there was a swift silent parting of gold-green grass. And, too late seen, the charging boar, thick bodied, coarse haired, one yellow tusk broken to a jagged edge, the other curved and keen....

Nicola, beside her darling, held her ground as the boar attacked; she dug in her heels and shot her rifle from the hip.

But the boar was wilder than Nicola, wilier than Rolf, and tougher than the bullet. The boar caught her golden boy, gored him, mauled him, almost tore Rolf's head from his shoulders.

And when the sun squatted just a little lower on

the far, far line of mountain, the rhinoceros buck was gone, the herd shaking the savanna with the weight of its flight. The boar was dead, eleven bullets to fell him. And Rolf Lord Pomeroy, the marquess of Denton—Nicola's golden boy—was gone. And Nicola, brave Nicola, was a widow.

Last summer, in Kenya, one day at sundown....

And now, tonight, *remembering*, she was crying again.

Her mother's hand was light on her forearm. "Darling, darling," Dove said. "Rolf told me this once—I never forgot. He said you will change the world."

Yes, Nicola thought. My mother has a way, a special way. I always admired her, she always despised me. And now, again, when I thought I was free of her spell, when I thought I was old enough, grand enough to stand on my own, she humbles me again, I feel *unworthy* of her again.... I must *conquer* that.

Nicola dried her tears.

"There was a man in Kenya," she said.

A waiter was approaching, summoned by Dove's braceleted hand.

"Two, this time, please." Dove smiled at the man. "One for my friend here, one for me."

When the waiter had gone, she said, "Do you mind, Nicola, if I don't refer to you as my daughter? Of course you are and everyone knows it, but it saddens me to think myself old enough to be your mother.... Will you forgive that?"

"Dove. There is nothing to forgive."

"Thank you, dear. You were saying...please tell me."

Nicola did not want to tell her mother, but she

needed to tell someone. She was not as close to Audrey Lockholm and Tory VanVoorst as they were to each other. Nicola and Audrey had married the same summer, Tory the one before, 1894, but then Nicola had sailed away to England, to Denton...to Dentoncroft. And though she came to New York and Newport sometimes, and saw Audrey and Tory now grown fast friends, Nicola was ever the visitor, the international traveler whose world was larger than the others'. And Nicola possessed her own fortune—that made a difference, too. Nicola was one of the richest women in the world. Percival Peerce's fortune had equaled the Astors', and he had left most of it to Nicola, his only child. His widow, Dove, had more than enough—twenty million was more than enough for anyone—and Rolf, land-poor Rolf, titled Rolf, *dear* Rolf had had nothing to speak of.... And so now Nicola was still the least comfortable of this party, but she did not mind that. She had always gone her own way and never asked for company.

Always, that is, until now, this first year of her widowhood. Now, and never again, she hoped, would she be vulnerable and needy. But now she was.

"There was a man in Kenya, Dove," she said. "He was part of our party, brought by the Cecil Windsors, I think. His name was Stanley Lord. He was not really of our set—"

The waiter interrupted, set down tall yellow drinks. Dove arched her back to see someone just arrived. "Oh, look, Nicola, there's Benny Guggenheim, being greeted by the Strauses.... Do you know them at all?"

"Not Mr. Guggenheim," said Nicola. "I met Isador and Ida once, in Rome. They're very nice, but Ida is shy with people like us, and not chic, you wouldn't like her. She lives for her husband.''

''Ah,'' said Dove. The Jewish rich didn't mix with the rest. Rather a pity, Dove thought. Difference in outlook added piquancy to a party, and some of the Jewish men were wonderfully intellectual. And they were rumored to be *stags* in the bed!

''Oh, I'm sorry, darling, I've interrupted you again. I just thought—Mr. Guggenheim is alone except for his manservant.''

''I can't tell you why, Dove,'' said Nicola with a weary sigh.

Dove Peerce wore mauve tonight, a sleek slip of mauve that bared her blue-veined bosom and her fine, taut arms. The gown flared at midcalf, fluttered above strong-heeled dancing slippers. Her hair of cloud spun around her face like a halo, and there were diamonds at her ears and five thin bands of diamonds couched in platinum on her left wrist. She shifted her weight to face her daughter, to give Nicola her undivided attention. Her fox slipped off one shoulder.

''You look very beautiful,'' said her daughter.

''It is easier at night, at my age, my dear, to be beautiful. Remember that when your time comes. After dark, in the dim, we older beauties can still fly with you others.''

Clever mother, stunning mother, perfectly turned out. Nicola's father said Dove was perfection's only four-letter word.... And then there had been little Nicola, dough thighed and freckled, sitting in a too-big chair in her mother's bedroom while Dove preened herself and shuddered at her daughter....

"It's your turn now," Dove said to that daughter. "I won't interrupt again unless the ship is going down."

Nicola Lady Pomeroy sipped at the drink she didn't want. "Oh," she said, ready to abandon telling.

"Please, Nicola, I said I was sorry."

"Yes," her daughter said, and tossed her fox-fire hair. "Yes. And I want to tell you. It's just hard, expressing it."

"A man," Dove prompted. "Lord, you said his name was...with you on safari...with you and Rolf." She said his name so gently. Nicola appreciated that.

"Yes—"

It was coming out now. She would be able to tell. "He is a boat captain, some kind of ship freighting, back and forth from England to the States. Not our set, you know, but he was there, on safari, someone's guest. And he pursued me terribly. Or tried to. I was, of course, not interested, dotty as ever over Rolf. But this man said he had fallen helplessly in love with me and couldn't help himself, couldn't behold me without passion, and that I must forgive him, it was a sickness surely, a sickness he welcomed no more than I."

"My dear, how enchanting," said Dove, who would have been enchanted in the same situation. Dove did so love to win the prize.

"No—" Lady Pomeroy had almost said *Mother*. "No, it wasn't, it was awful. Especially after," Nicola's voice dropped to a whisper, "after what happened...."

Dove was quiet, not a muscle flexed or relaxed.

She waited, but Nicola was silent and twisting in her chair.

"Go on, Nicky, get it out," said Dove. "I won't judge you."

How fine the night is turning out, Nicola thought. *Titanic* was a planet all to itself, great and black and sparkling, mast to waterline, stem to stern, with silver light.

Nicola said slowly, "Oh, no, it was nothing like that."

"Wasn't it?" said Dove, who was wicked and wise. "Well, what if it was?"

"I was shattered, Dove. You would have been, too. It was so sudden, Rolf's dying, so savage—"

"Of course, darling, of course. My God, none of us are over it yet."

"Yes." Nicola was getting excited. "So you see. This man, Lord, came to my aid immediately after the tragedy. He was gallant and patient, and he helped, Dove, he did help."

"Of course, of course. He was a good man, he did what he could."

"Oh, Mother—" There, it had slipped out. But Dove did not react, and Nicola Lady Pomeroy went on. If she stopped now it would never be told; it would return, for years, in nightmare, and she wanted to be free.

"With Rolf's poor mangled body wrapped in native cloth inside my tent." A flood of tears erupted, and there was still a ball of pain inside her.

"Oh, Nicola, oh, Nicola...."

"I—I..."

"Don't, if you don't want to, darling. I think I understand."

Dove would have taken her daughter in her arms if she'd known how. But Nicola was a bigger woman than she was, and she had not embraced her daughter since Nicola had been a toddler, given over to others to take care of and instruct. Not on Nicola's wedding day, not even when Percy died. Dove had never liked her only child, so *plain*, so headstrong, so obviously a favorite with Percy. Nicola had been almost ugly young, and Dove, beautiful Dove, had been *ashamed*. And now, indeed, her daughter was a beauty, full and lush, with hair of fire—a goddess in satin widow's weeds. But still Dove could not hold Nicola, woman-to-woman. She could not even touch, in sympathy, Nicola's tear-stained hand....

"How can you understand when you never betrayed your husband? And you loved Father less than I did Rolf, I know you did. But I let this man come to me that night, let him have his way. I gave myself to him like a whore. And it was wonderful, Mother, *wonderful*. It had never been so good with Rolf—"

There. The pain in her chest was breaking up, flowing away with each beat of her heart. There, she had got it out.

Her mother's voice was tender in the darkness. "Forgive yourself when you can, my proud girl. You were a free woman by then, a black widow, if you will. You needed comforting, and that is the way a man best comforts, and most all of them know of it. We are all of us, sometimes, Nicola, black widows, praying mantises. That's the enigma of the female. Will we act upon our natures, or will we be... respectable? We women are always, as we live, a little in danger...and a little dangerous. It's our curse, darling, and our glory. You have escaped most of the burdens of womanhood, but even you, my marchioness, even you cannot escape them all.''

"Now he wires me," said Nicola, her voice muffled in a handkerchief. ''Wires me here with proposals of marriage.'' She thrust a wadded telegram into Dove's hand.

Dove tore it in the dark of the deck; once, twice, three times. She rose from her chair and walked to the rail. The little pieces of paper, yellow confetti, drifted from her fingers, floated from *Titanic*'s port side...disappeared.

"Do you love him?''

Nicola saw her mother as a shadow in the night. "I loathe him," said Nicola Lady Pomeroy. "I've already wired his ship and told him so. He's somewhere in the Atlantic now, where we'll be tomorrow. He's out here with me on the sea. 'I've come to take you off *Titanic*,' he writes. 'I've come to take you home to England with me.'''

"There is no hope for him, no little ember for him, Nicola, in your heart? A man who crosses continents, swims oceans, to come to your side? He seems sincere in his passion, if abrupt and impatient.''

"What do I care for his passion? I wish I could undo what I did with him that night. I wish I could have left him dead in Africa for the hyenas to tear.''

"Respectability clings like a suntan, doesn't it? You can scrub yourself to the bone with lemon pulp and not get rid of it entirely.'' Dove came back to her chair, shouldered into her fox.

"I had to tell someone," said Nicola. "I'm bursting with self-hate, self-shame.''

"Oh, come, we're none of us angels, Nick. We do the best we can most of the time, and most of the time we do very well. Forget that night, it was a wildness, a nothing. You were sad and a strange man caressed you for a time. That's all it was. No great sin, darling. You take yourself too seriously. Come now, finish your drink and fix your eyes...."

With a little compact, Nicola powdered her tears away.

"Oh, look," said Dove, "there's Tory and Burt, way over there by the lifeboat pole. Tory and Burt and another man. Umm, it's dark, but he seems rather handsome.... Do you know him? See, down there...?"

Nicola stood, snuggled deep into her sable, and looked where her mother pointed.

A trio was coming toward them.

There was Tory, usually so breathtakingly beautiful, looking paler than she had at luncheon and holding her stomach as though it had suddenly got heavy; something Nicola had not noticed her do before. And there was Burton VanVoorst, easily recognizable the way his shoes slapped out sideways as he advanced, toes a little to the right, now a little to the left, smiling in his dinner jacket. Nicola noticed Burty's smile because Tory's face was drawn and serious. She looks as though she's seen a ghost, thought Nicola, though even so she must look better now than I, all chewed up in tears and self-pity....

With them was a wide-shouldered man whose dark hair lifted in the ocean breeze. He was bronze faced—even in the soft night-lights she could see the gilt of his cheeks and forehead. He wore a white suit and swung a black cane. He was smiling, too; he had seen Nicola and Dove as they had seen him. He might be a sportsman, Nicola thought, he was so muscular in the thighs. And his teeth were very white.

"Teddy Royce," he said in a deep voice, and there was mischief in his eyes. "And you, my lady, are a queen, a royal. Will you waltz with me tonight?" Bold, he took her hand between his hands and kissed it, sliding his thumbs around her emerald rings.

Nicola laughed, withdrew her hand, gave him no reply. "Shall we go down together?" she said to Tory and Burt.

"I think the baby kicked," said Tory. "It's done something, twisted itself or kicked. What shall I do?"

"Do?" boomed Burty. "Dance, Madonna. Someday you'll be the mother of the president."

"Silly." Tory held tightly to Burty's arm.

"Silly, nothing," said Burty. "I shall devote my life to it. Junior will be president, I predict."

"He means it," said Tory to Dove. "For the first time in his life, Burty is serious about something other than Wall Street."

"And you, Madonna, don't forget you," he said. "You were the best investment I ever made."

Teddy Royce offered his arm to Dove.

She took it, saying with a shade of regret, "I dine at the captain's table tonight. But perhaps you would take my place beside Lady Pomeroy. I would appreciate it if you did."

The stranger offered his other arm to Nicola. She declined it, walked behind.

He has a fire in his eyes, Nicola thought as she followed the others. A fire like mine, a fire like Rolf's. Whether or not he is truly a gentleman, he's my kind of man; eaglelike, and used to hunting alone.

In the place they left deserted, little scraps of wireless message settled beside an air vent.

And at the foot of the grand staircase, on B deck, Mr. P. W. Fletcher, ship's bugler, sounded "The Roast Beef of Old England," in a happy call to dinner.

6

In simple black so as not to call attention to herself, blond hair coiled under a close-fitting cloche, Audrey Lockholm wandered on the third-class promenade, searching for the woman who had leaned here hours earlier, leaned and looked up and clawed at Audrey to come down....

Come down....

Audrey was unsure of herself here, though the dollar she had offered a steward had opened the doors fast enough. "I am looking for an old friend," she had said, and the steward, unctuous, had taken her down in an elevator and bowed her through.

She had thought that she could still walk the streets of Newport as one of the townsfolk, at least. But she realized now, surrounded by these strange, ordinary faces, that she could not, not really. Audrey Lockholm, Mrs. John Bayard Lockholm III, was no longer Audrey Smoke, carpenter's daughter. She had not been for a long, long time. Whatever she wore, wherever she went, the years of privilege had changed her. And again, she had the unbidden thought that she had come to the end of something

and had not known it. She had crested a hill, turned
a corner and, forgetting to look behind, had not
known—till now—the way back had been long destroyed.

She shivered and drew her cape around her. It was
a simple cape, thin black satin, hand sewn, tailored
to her figure, the simplest wrap she had. But it was
a cape to be worn over one's silks in carriages and
open motorcars, a cape for the opera, the theater and
late suppers on lawns that ran down to the sea. It was
a simple thing, but fine, unlike the horse-blanket
coats worn here on D deck, heavy coats that pulled
the shoulders down; coats that were never cleaned
from season to season because with one coat it was
always time to wear it.

The dinner hour was approaching, and the deck
down here was not as crowded as Audrey had
thought it would be. Nervous, she scanned the
strange faces—the open, excited faces. The women's
were older than they need have been, and undecor-
ated. The faces of the men were quieter, more *solid*.
And there were children here, loud-mouthed children
with droopy socks and cheap new shoes.

Third class noticed Audrey, too. What was the
beautiful lady doing on D deck? What could she
want *down here*, this sleek and gleaming woman in
fine soft boots? Had she come to look, to compare?

A man stopped before her, a question in his eyes.
He was only a little taller than she was, and thick
through the chest and waist. A passenger, his shapeless hat was low on his forehead to keep it from
blowing off in gusts of wind. The hat brim threw his
face in shadow, but standing, as he did, before her,
Audrey could see him well. There were bags under

his eyes and tired lines on his cheeks, though Audrey guessed he was approximately her own age. He held a small child in each hand. Two sharp-chinned children, their faces dirty with jam.

"I am looking for an old friend," said Audrey.

"So was I," he said. "I'm from second class, and you are obviously from first. My name is Miller. I'll help you if I can."

"Thank you," said Audrey. "That's very kind. Is there a passenger list for third?"

The man shrugged. "I'm sure there must be. We can ask the purser." He looked around as though trying to spot the one he wanted.

"Hello," said the child on the man's right, a girl. On the left, the boy sucked his thumb and clung to the man's trousers. They were old loose trousers, baggy in the knees, the corduroy nap worn flat. The boy's lashes were dark and very long.

"Hello," Audrey said, smiling, but she felt a twist of fear. She did not want to snub the child or hurt her feelings, but she did not want to touch her, either, because she was not clean. Audrey did not like herself for feeling so.

"Looking down from above..." Audrey began, gesturing up the tiers of *Titanic*'s decks.

"Yes," said the man, patient, still holding the children's hands.

"I thought I recognized an old friend at the rail here," Audrey said. "In Southampton, at departure."

"Perhaps you did. Can you tell me her name? His name?" The man was still looking around for an official.

The girl child pulled out of the man's hand and stretched up her arms to Audrey, as though she wanted to be taken up. "You're so pretty," said the child. And she waited, with something shining in her eyes that frightened Audrey.

"Now, Keely," said the man.

"What's your name?" the child said. She dropped her arms and scratched at a scab on her knee.

For a moment Audrey did not know how to respond. Then she stooped and laid her hands, her black-gloved hands, on the little one's shoulders. "Audrey is my name. What's yours?"

"Cath'rine," said the child with dignity. "I'm six, and I'm going to be a veterinarian when I grow up. Do you know what a veterinarian is?" She said the word perfectly, all six syllables in a row, as though she had learned the word that morning in a grammar class and thought it excellent.

"Tell me," said Audrey.

"Takes care of animals," said the boy. He reached out and touched the sleeve of Audrey's cape. "Oooh, feel it, Keely." He pulled back his hand and hid behind the man's leg, just his head peeping out, looking at Audrey with long-lashed eyes. "Could I have a penny?" he said.

"All right, that's it," said the man. He gave the boy a swat on the behind.

Audrey had not brought a purse with her. She spread her hands and stood up. "I have no money," she said.

"That's all right," said the girl. She had two teeth missing. "Are you married?"

"Yes," said Audrey, laughing.

"Go along with you," the man said to them, giving his knees a shake to get them going.

The boy took the girl's hand, locked fingers. "C'mon," he said.

The girl took her brother's hand, but continued to stare at Audrey. "Mommy left us," she said.

And then the children ran. They both wore sturdy new shoes; the stitches showed on the soles as they flashed. They ran aimlessly, in a crooked circle toward the middle of the ship.

The man took no notice of the children.

"I know my friend as Madame Romany," said Audrey, standing tall again. She closed her cape at the throat. "But I am not sure she would be registered under that name." She saw a steward standing not far away. "Excuse me," she said and walked over to the steward, leaving the man standing with his hands in his trouser pockets.

"Yes, ma'am," said the steward. He was young and proud of his position.

As Audrey wondered whether to speak or to withdraw, she saw, out of the corner of her eye, the woman for whom she was looking. There she was, *Madame Romany*, ascending a staircase from E deck. Audrey caught her breath, whipped around. Yes, the woman was nodding at her; an old woman with one blind eye, in a shapeless black shroud. A loud-patterned cloth was wound, turbanlike, around her head.

"I've found the one I'm looking for," Audrey said and stepped away. She followed Madame Romany to the rail.

"Ah, m'lady," the gypsy greeted her. "You were wise to come so quickly."

It was dark now. Beyond, seemingly close, Cherbourg was a feast of small-hilled, scattered lights.

Amidships, the dining room of D deck spilled warm light, too, and high above, *where Audrey belonged*, strings of little glittering bulbs decorated the high lines of *Titanic*, and took the place of stars.

Audrey wanted to be away, wanted to be back *up there* with Bay. She wanted to be without care, with all her friends, at dinner with good appetite.

"What do you want of me?" Audrey said straight out. Now she had her, she would get to the bottom of Madame Romany and be gone. "Why are you here on this ship, this voyage, at all? Do I figure in your thoughts? Be quick and tell me: I won't be threatened by you. I have concerns of my own, and if I have to I will have you put away."

Audrey was afraid.

She heard the fear in the harshness of her speech. But she would confront the fear; she did not want to have to descend again to this woman. She did not want to be on D deck, or E or F—*or, next tier down, the bottomless deep....* She wanted to be back up in first class. Back where the orchestra played after dinner and the women dressed as she did, in couturier gowns. Back where the children had governesses to take charge of them and did not pathetically stretch out their arms to strangers. Back where the men were polite, did not wear dark hats to hide their faces, wore evening jackets as easily as smiles, and smoked their cigars in special rooms. *Back where she belonged.* Yes. And she wanted the gypsy gone, who did *not belong*.

"I had to come," intoned the old woman, bracing herself against the rail. "These days I see better within than from without," and she closed her blind white eye to *frighten....*

Why else…?

"I will tell you, Mrs. Bayard Lockholm," continued the gypsy. "I will tell you all I know, all I want, all there is that I can see. I have come on your account, dearie, to save you, m'lady fine, to save your husband for you, and—only last—to save my daughter."

"I do not understand," said Audrey. "If you are after money, I have very little. My husband takes care of me—I have little of my own. And if I did, I would not give it to you."

"There is no place to sit here," said the woman, gray in the twilight. "And I would not insult you with an invitation to my bunk. So come, we'll find a bench, the two of us in the night, and come to an agreement."

Audrey hesitated.

The gypsy laughed. "Come, Madam Lockholm. I will not keep you long, and you have come so far already."

Audrey followed the woman, a quick woman for one so old, so blind. And faintly familiar. Somehow, long ago, Audrey had seen this woman. Not in dreams…but somewhere…somewhen….

Down two flights, on F deck, they found a bench port side and were alone. The warm night air was sweet. Audrey removed her close-fitting hat and a light breeze played with wisps of her hair. If she had been with Bay, she would have been happy. She folded her hands over the hat, played with the brim. Far away, decks above, a lone violin played a sweet strain. Under the sweetness, this close to *Titanic*'s engines, a soft humming told of power units on, great hidden machines that fired the electric lights, the refrigerators, the elevators.... Even as Audrey settled herself, a gentle tremor glided through the spine of *Titanic* and told her they were, at last, drawing away from Cherbourg....

"Now," said the gypsy woman, shifting her old bones on the seat, pulling her drab skirts close.

"Please hurry," Audrey said. "I am wanted above."

One eye of the gypsy was white. The other was black and round and set deep in a bed of wrinkles. Cold, the eye held Audrey's. "It will be worth your while to bear with me a little, dearie. For trouble surrounds you and hems you in—a terrible trouble. You are in grave danger. I do not lie."

"How do you know," said Audrey, "what is in the mind of God? Or is it only your own mind you read? To read your mind, Madame Romany, is easy. Even I can do it. I know you wish me ill."

The gypsy's eyelids fluttered. "I have seen into the crystal, Mrs. Lockholm. Seen deep and so well that I have given up everything I am to come here to this place. This is my last stand. I have come here to perish.... The crystal says of you, my dear, that you know how to catch a man, but asks, do you know how to lose him...?"

Suddenly Audrey was not frightened. The woman was ridiculous. Who did she think Audrey was—a fear-filled girl who would write a check to anyone who vaguely threatened her...? "You talk of doom," said Audrey. "The doom of your betters. You are not to be tolerated. Explain yourself immediately. You begin to bore me."

"Remove your glove, please," said Madame

Romany. "The left glove, which covers your wedding band."

"I will not."

"Please, please," the woman whined, "be a little patient. After all, it is you who will be helped by this, you and the man you love."

"I'm sure you see an advantage to yourself, Madame Romany, if that is really your name." But Audrey removed her glove, finger by finger, smoothed it flat, and folded it inside the crown of the cloche.

"Ah."

The gypsy reached out a blunt-fingered hand, a fleshy hand, puffy at the wrist, wrinkled and black veined. The nails were long and yellow, curved like the beaks of ancient birds. Audrey stared. That hand.... That yellow, curved-nail hand.

She *remembered* such a hand!

Long, long ago it was, on the public beach in Newport. Talonlike and tense, it had arched above a newspaper...and...yes! She remembered such a hand.

The gypsy took Audrey's hand, Audrey's cool and white and perfumed, palm up, into her own. Audrey shivered at the touch. Deliberately, Madame Romany turned, three times, the wide gold ring on Audrey's third finger. Audrey resisted the impulse to pull her hand away.

The old woman closed her eyes and rocked a little on her hips. "Ah, yes, he loves you, madam, have no fear of that. And you...he fills all your life."

Audrey said nothing. Her love for Bay was obvious. And his for her—she reveled in it. She did not need the assurance of a money-gouging gypsy. Bay, full of love for her, waited even now, now day was done, waited up above to take her in his arms, to entwine his thighs with hers and melt their bodies in a seething fire where they would burn to bliss.

"You would be lost without him. You must save him if you can."

And still Audrey made no reply. Let the gypsy say what she had to. Then Audrey would be gone, and never see her more.

Madame Romany appeared hypnotized by the gleam of Audrey's ring. "Ah," she said, her chin deep upon her chest. "Ah, now it comes.... The clouds loom up—not the white, which promise joy. The dark ones rise, grow close...increase.... No, I am not wrong." She tightened her grip on Audrey's fingers, leaned into the band of gold.

"Disaster," she said at last, with satisfaction. "A white disaster, all stars and ice. An *ice fall*, madam."

And still Audrey sat calm and unafraid. What rubbish, she thought. What awful nonsense.

While the old woman talked, Audrey was *remembering*, remembering the summer of '95 when John Bayard Lockholm was only a stranger, mysterious upon a cliff top in the night. There was music around him, lovely music behind the wall of Whale's Turning, and the thought of him twisted in her heart.

"You are falling far, madam.... *He whom you love* is falling. That much I cannot prevent." Madame Romany dropped Audrey's hand, broke the spell in the ring-mirror, and lifted her face. "I cannot tell you exactly what it means, these clouds of sorrow and loss. I cannot tell you whether they are symbol or actualities. There is no left or right to a circle—one becomes the other as it flows...."

Calm, Audrey said, "I remember you now, old

woman. In the public beach house, long ago. You asked me my name then, but it had no meaning for you, and you told me yours. Why are you doing this? I was kind to you, as I remember. Why would you harm me? I only wished you well.''

The old eyelids drooped. ''Your name was not Lockholm then, dearie, and then, I had not given up hope—my daughter Daphne was still a girl. Now she is thirty, unmarried, unhappy. The Lockholms owe her…. It is not to hurt you, madam, that I crossed this ocean on an oil barge to get to this cursed ship and you…. It is to help Daphne—the crystal told me to. So oblige me. Be kind to me again as you were once…and save your husband in the bargain…. Refuse me, and I will find another way, but you will be a widow.''

Audrey leaped up, moved to the guardrail and turned her face away, into the dark. Her blood was up now, up and flying in her veins. She breathed deep, controlled her rage…. And as she did, she heard the bugler sound the call to dinner. It was dimly lighted where they were. With unseen trembling she drew on her glove again, smoothed her hair and fitted the cloche upon her head.

''Tell me now,'' she said, as blunt as board. ''Tell me what in the devil's name you want.''

Sitting, the old woman was a dull lump, clothed in shapeless heavy cotton as dark as stagnant water. Her white eye seemed to glow as night deepened, to glow and glimmer like a miniature opaque ball: *a gypsy's crystal….* The other eye stared, more and more fishlike, rarely blinking….

Audrey wanted to run, but stood her ground.

''Money,'' said the gypsy, as blunt as Audrey.

"Ten thousand dollars. It is to go to Daphne.... She knows the alchemy of beauty and wants to start a business. Cosmetics, she calls it. Give her that chance. Let her become as you, someone of consequence.... She says she will make rare unguents, almost magical. They will keep the cheeks firm and fair beyond the years of childbearing. She will mix oils to stain lips crimson, and acids to lighten a woman's hair. It is a Pandora's box you're opening, I told her. If all women are beautiful beyond resisting, the world will quick wax mad. But Daphne, she wants her chance, I won't deny her. Give her that chance, Madam Lockholm, a dying woman begs you...."

How terrible she is, thought Audrey. Why did I come down here?

"I have daughters of my own to care for," said Audrey. "It is wrong of you to insist I take care of yours."

"Ah," said the woman. "But you see, m'dear, the Lockholms *owe* Daphne. Bayard Lockholm's mother stole my husband away—you know it—and stole Daphne's father. Oh, it was long ago he left us, and the great She is dead now. But the debt remains unpaid. The debt has passed, Madam Lockholm, to you. Your husband and you. *Pay it*—and I will strike a bargain with the devil. I cannot stop disaster, cannot stop your husband's falling, but I will give my life so he can live."

From somewhere in the folds of her clothes, Madame Romany lifted a slender blade.

"Your husband lives," she said, "to cross this ocean and stand, healthy and well, in his own house, to die at a ripe old age. How's that? *I will give my life to make it so.*... Eh? And then we're quits, quits for good and all.''

Audrey would have run if her feet would have taken her. But she was transfixed by the words and the sheath of knife that jigsawed in the air in the old woman's hand. Audrey had no fear for herself. She thought Madame Romany would make—try to make—Audrey responsible for her wretched daughter by killing herself right now.

"No," was all Audrey could manage. "No, no, no...."

The tip of the knife blade touched a vein in the woman's wrist. "Ten thousand dollars," said Madame Romany. "That is only a little to one as rich as you. Ten thousand dollars for Daphne, and for one season, just one little ten-week season, m'lady fine, give Daphne your patronage when she starts up her business.... Your patronage, and that of your friends. That's it. Then the Lockholms and the Diegos are quits forever. Whatever happens after, all debts are paid. I seal it now with my blood." And Madame Romany drew her index finger down the cutting edge of the knife and showed Audrey the instant bubbles of blood.

"There," she said, "it is done."

She stood, old bones stiff already, the night still young and warm. She shook out her clothes.

"Yes," she said, "you were kind to me when you were no one special, when it was easy to be kind. All it took then was a moment's pause and a little smile at the poor old Mexican who had somehow got over to the border to take your coin in a bathhouse. Easy virtue, madam—now, it's harder. Now it will cost you ten thousand dollars and a season of patronage. Little enough, I'd think, to save your husband. Well. I'll bother you no more. Send me your answer if you like. Or don't...."

Audrey looked over the ship rail into black night pierced here and there with shore lights. She stared down to flowing black water, gray laced in pools of yellow from the porthole lights.

And mighty *Titanic*, an island unto itself, steamed on toward Queenstown in Ireland's county Cork.

"I will see what I can do," said Audrey to the woman's departing back. "Though how that will save my husband from misfortune, I don't know."

"Angels fall," said Madame Romany over her shoulder. "Angels fall every day. Why shouldn't he?"

And then she was gone. And Audrey was left alone at *Titanic*'s rail, remembering a summer long ago.... Shaded sun, white curtains gently floating in the room like angels come to escort, and a name, a strange man's name, on Bay's mother's mouth at the moment of her death. Joyously cried....

Could that man, that name—that lost love—really have been, once, the lowly gypsy's husband?

BAY WAS WAITING for her in their rooms, impatiently striding the length of the little promenade and then the width of the sitting room, back and forth, back and forth, inhaling the sweet smoke of a long cigar. He was wondering where she was, where she had been; she could read it in his eyes when, at last, hurrying, she turned the door handle and saw him there, pacing, his muscles tense in his shoulders.

She looked into his eyes, his dear storm-gray eyes, and saw his passion. She watched, her heart cavorting with happiness, as he smiled at the sight of her. His hand, unconsciously, moved to fling back the lock of hair where it fell, as always, over his forehead like a boy's, then ground to ashes the cigar, freshly started, in a dish crowded with others similarly treated.

Bay.

And then he was close and taking her *strong* into his arms, lifting her *safe* against his breast…and kissing her with a warm, wanting mouth that tasted, ever so faintly, of sweet tobacco. "At last," he whispered into her open mouth, "at last, at last," and then he kissed her throat and then her mouth again, and kissed her eyes, and her temples where her pulse reared up and flamed with his….

And then he set her down, but did not set her free. He began to unbutton her dress down her spine, starting high at the nape of her neck, his fingers hot and pressing, stroking, *stroking* the flesh now open to him…. And all the while he kissed her, sweet and slow. And now her shoulders were loose, were naked and cool in the ocean air that was as *stirred* as they were…. And then her flesh was warm under his tongue, and her dress was slipping below her hips, and Bay was kissing, kissing oh so sweetly the long white curve of her bare back.

Trembling, he lifted away her chemise and carried her as a bride, an eager, knowing bride, out to the deck to the night air. He put her down, she lush and white, and trembling, too. He bent above…and kissed, in pagan lust, in civilized control, her breasts, her loins, her stomach and the golden place between her thighs…. He kissed her limbs as he removed her stockings, caressed the windswept naked skin…until, *fired*, her thighs lifted of themselves to grip his waist, which was, somehow, now naked, too. And then he kissed the softness where her stomach was, and slid strong hands around her buttocks, and held her, naked in delight, until, *all burning*, they two ignited into one, while below, forgotten, the ocean sucked and sighed....

And then Bay slept, tired from his day touring *Titanic* with Bruce Ismay and the captain, tired of the strain he was under, *too tired these days*, Audrey thought, and she telephoned for supper in their suite, and showered and covered herself in a yellow robe that intensified the fragile lemon of her hair. She sat at the desk while he napped, found his book of bank checks, found his black pen, broad nibbed, which spread a thick black ink.

She had written few checks in her time as Bay Lockholm's wife. The accounts were joint, he had had that done in the first month of their marriage, and she was on no allowance; he denied her nothing. Bills did not come to their homes. Bills went to his lawyer, Aston Forbes, were taken care of there, and a rendering presented every season, four times a year, for Bay's perusal.

She had never questioned his system, he had never questioned her. But then she wrote such few checks, and they had always been for relatively small amounts—something to her father and Dolly from time to time, a payment for flowers spontaneously ordered and immediately delivered. And, sometimes in Manhattan, realizing she had no money in her purse and wanting a perfume or a winsome pin, something too small to have billed, she would write a check.... It was never questioned, it was always honored with a smile.

She took up her husband's pen, leaned over the checkbook. Today was the tenth of April, 1912. She wrote the date in its place. It looked so solemn on the pale face of the check, the long buff-colored check, number 17011....

Ten thousand dollars was a world of money, she thought, even to a woman as rich as I am. Ten thousand dollars must be enough to change the world.... Though she—they—spent that much each year alone on the grounds upkeep of Whale's Turning. It was a year's wardrobe for herself and her daughters, but probably only a third, or fifth, of what Tory spent on herself, or Nicola. Still, it was ten years' salary for Mrs. Twigg.... Ten thousand dollars.

It was little enough to pay, Audrey thought, for such a man as Bay. To protect him. To keep him from evil thoughts and the hate of that woman below deck and her bitter, vengeful child. It was little enough to write off the long-standing debt that woman and her daughter felt owed, justified or not. It was little enough, but it would be all.... She would pay no more.

Audrey wrote in broad black ink, wrote clear and plain, "$10,000." She wrote out the amount in words where the line was long. Then she signed her name, "Audrey Lockholm," and then, where the check asked explanation, she wrote, clean and dark, "Full and final payment." Last, she wrote out the women's names. Not Madame Romany, seer. Not Mrs. and Miss. She wrote, untitled, for all the world to see, where the line extended beyond Pay to the Bearer, "Esmeralda Diego and/or Daphne...." The names gleamed, oil slick. Where the check stub asked a reason, she wrote, quick now, "Business investment, all paid."

Bay moved in his slumber, on a chaise longue out on the open-air deck. Audrey wrote the date on the check stub and wrote the amount and her initials beside it, "A.S.L."

I would give all your fortune for you, my darling, she thought, blowing on the ink to help it dry. Why, tonight alone was worth this much, and if you do it again...

He was sitting up, fine made, smooth muscled, strong limbed. He was calling her name, because someone had knocked at the door and he was still naked.

Audrey closed the checkbook, placed it under Bay's journal, and went to open the door to supper. She was exceedingly happy.

7

Not so happy in the main dining salon, at a table for four with Mrs. Twigg and Swan and an empty chair, Smoke Lockholm ate savagely. She speared her bites of duck as though they were live and running toward the gold-medallioned plate rim; she immersed them in too much applesauce, she swallowed almost without chewing and was back for more with her mouth still full. Her fork tines clicked on the china plate; she did not pause or smile or converse.

Mrs. Twigg, of course, scolded her. Mrs. Twigg was in good form tonight, scolding. From their boat conduct to tonight's table etiquette to their attitude toward their responsibilities in general, Mrs. Twigg was eloquent, intense and long on stamina.

Smoke had been listening to an unending lecture on her lack of proprieties since she had been discovered by Twiggs on boat deck. Swan was already prisoner when Smoke was found, coupled to Mrs. Twigg by a firm handhold. Then both twins had dressed for dinner under a barrage of Mrs. Twigg's ultimatums. They had sighed, feigning regret; they had borne their rebukes in silence. Both twins, when asked for explanation, had lied. Or, rather, Smoke had lied and Swan had backed her up. They had been exploring below decks, Smoke said. Because of her interest in seamanship and ships in general, they had taken themselves down to *Titanic*'s vitals. They had been in the boiler rooms, seen the watertight compartments, which—strokes of genius—made *Titanic* the safest ship afloat. They had introduced themselves to the stokers, the so-called firemen.

Mrs. Twigg had been aghast.

But Mrs. Twigg had believed, and that was the important thing. That got Swan out of harm's way, as far as Danny Bowen was concerned. For though Twiggs knew Swan had an English pen pal, she did not know, even as she threatened in ladylike voice to lock the twins in their stateroom if they did not behave, that Swan's pen pal was employed on the *Titanic* as third violinist; that Danny Bowen, who had put his hand upon Swan's virgin breast and kissed it through her velvet bodice, was even now playing in the lounge on the deck above, even now bowing a pretty selection from the *Tales of Hoffmann*, faintly heard. That was the reason Swan sat as she did with a vapid smile on a self-satisfied face, fussing with her peas and carrots. Swan's lack of attention to Mrs. Twigg's remonstrations made Smoke even angrier, because now she, alone, was receiving the brunt of Mrs. Twigg's dressing down. Mrs. Twigg thought she had vanquished Swan Lockholm, and was pressing all the harder on the *difficult* one.

Mrs. Twigg thumped the table with plump knuckles as she ate and hectored, a familiar habit. "We'll see," she said, "what happens if I am not obeyed *to the letter*, girls. You just mind what I say. I know you have a birthday coming, and—I have discussed this with your mother, dears—*there will be no birthday party* unless I give the all right. And I promise you, Smoke Wysong and Swan Josephine Lockholm, privileged young women though you be, that if you are not *ladies* from now to Sunday, there will no celebration. No—'' thump ''—celebration—'' thump ''—at all.'' Thump, thump.

Smoke smirked in silent rebellion, but Swan would not join in. Swan was dreaming away with downcast eyes, one hand on her breast where Danny Bowen had pressed his.

Mrs. Twigg loved downcast eyes. She took them as capitulation. ''And so,'' Mrs. Twigg built to her climax, while Smoke seethed with frustration and jealousy....

Yes, she thought, I am jealous. I'm more than that....

''If you don't care about your reputations, you naughty girls, I do. It is my job to care. *I get paid for it.*'' Thump, thump. ''And you will, too. Oh, yes, you will, *when the right time comes*. You'll get handsomely paid out and then...you'll be sorry....'' This last was delivered portentously, like Nostradamus predicting the end of the world, Smoke thought. She kicked at Swan under the table, but Swan was oblivious, bent low over her plate, making the initials D.B. out of her garden peas.

''Imagine,'' Mrs. Twigg rattled on, ''the cheek of going below decks without escort, without telling anyone, without permission. Poking your nose where it doesn't belong—does not belong, I said—and you both will write that tonight, after orchestra. 'I do not belong below decks.' A hundred times each, and no sloppy penmanship or you'll do it a hundred times more for each bad line. Oh yes, my fine-feathered chicks, you've done yourselves in now...." And on and on, while Mrs. Twigg, too, dainty in ruffled blue faille and her one good string of pearls, picked her duckling clean.

But Smoke could take Mrs. Twigg; Twiggs meant what she said all right, but Twiggs could be out-foxed. Twiggs punished and punished fair, but she could be lied to and the "sentence" thereby reduced. Mrs. Twigg's flaw as a governess—and, perhaps, for all that, as a *woman*—was that a little sin sufficed.

Oh ho.

Smoke had got away with lying about being in the boiler rooms because...it sufficed. And Swan had got away with lying, too; with lying on Danny Bowen's pallet and having him put his hands upon her breasts...those long, straight fingers, the nails clean and blunt-cut across, the curve of his finger ends perfect for holding a bow and drawing it across fine steel strings. Hands made for making music and for making *love*.... Smoke squirmed at the thought, excited and uncomfortable together. Those hands had held Swan's breast this afternoon—tea had been missed because of it—and Swan had smiled. Hateful Swan, she was still smiling, nibbling her peas one by one, eliminating the initials, sensuously aroused....

And Smoke, who did not want it, Smoke was aroused, too.

Smoke could feel his hands, wide in their span, strong and tight, around her waist, pulling her back from *Titanic*'s gunwale, pulling her against him, not in panic but slowly, sweetly.... There was such pleasure in her pain.

She would have to do something, something drastic. She could not, would not, fall in love with Danny Bowen. He belonged to silly Swan....

Smoke ordered peaches in chartreuse jelly with French ice cream on the top.

"Get fat then, Smoke," said Mrs. Twigg. "You'll be less trouble then, easier to catch. A chocolate eclair for me, waiter, and black coffee and a brandy. Swan?"

"Just lemonade for me, Mrs. Twigg," said Swan, a pea between her teeth. She looked at Smoke. Tears were blurring her twin's turquoise eyes. "Oh, don't cry, Smokey," burst out Swan, "Twiggs didn't mean it. We'll have our birthday party—"

Mrs. Twigg had rarely seen Smoke cry. A kind woman at heart, she was instantly contrite, suddenly tender. "Have I been too hard on you, my dear? I'm very sorry. Of course you'll have your party, and a lovely party it will be. But you are Lockholm women, darlings, you must behave accordingly—"

Smoke reached out and touched Mrs. Twigg's hand, patted the knuckles that had gone thump, thump. "It's the music, Twiggs," she said, snuffling. "It's not you. You're wonderful, the only real mother we have.... It's the violin, Twiggs, it's so exquisitely sad."

"But they're playing a waltz, Smoke Wysong. 'Songe d'Automne.' It's lilting and gay."

"Oh no," said Swan, understanding, the way the twins always understood each other. "Oh no, Smoke, you *can't!* I won't let you."

"Can't what?" said Smoke. She thought, Can't

fall in love…? "Can't cry if I want?" she said. "I can too…! Will you excuse me?"

And she was up from her chair and gone, quick through the room, knowing her mother's friends, at a nearby table, had seen and were wondering. But her mother, of course, wasn't there; her mother was never there when she was needed. Her mother was still in love with her father, and he with her. Too much in love; it was *disgusting*…. They had no time for their children.

The twins' room was on B deck, fore of the dining room. Smoke walked quickly. Already she knew her way.

Around a turn, and she was alone. Around another, a red-carpeted corridor. Just one more, and she would be safe, closed in, hidden away. She would be able to think—

But there, before their stateroom door, there *he* stood, on his musician's break, she supposed. His eyes danced as he saw her, he played a little strain on his violin, cocking his head to hold the instrument upon his shoulder, stretching his fingers along the handle of the bow. His full lips parted in happy, conspiratorial greeting as, music done, he set violin and bow in the doorway of B-41 and held out his arms to her. He wore a dark dinner jacket. With his smoke-pale hair and thinness, he looked elegant, not like a peasant at all. Beside him, like a well-groomed hound, the dark violin leaned, close to his leg, and like a gallant's sword, the hairs of the bow were long and white. She wanted him to lay that bow on her as on his instrument, to draw that fine white thing across her nakedness. She wanted to arch and stretch under those outstretched hands. She wanted…

She paused.

She was breathing heavier than she should, and her heart was skittering below her satin blouse. Even, it seemed to her, *Titanic* lurched, or the whole world skipped, just once, for the first time. She caught herself from stumbling and walked, stately, toward him.

Oh, how would they tell Swan?

She reached him, floated silently into his arms. The jacket sleeves were rough, not mohair smooth. They were cheap serge; no matter, no matter....

His eyes, so close, were soft and dark. His hair curled at the ends above his ears. The planes of his face were beautiful—straight nose, chiseled chin, a fine natural lift to his eyebrows. His arms were strong, enfolding. She lifted her mouth, and he was kissing her, she who had never been kissed. His tongue was in her mouth, so strange, so right. His breath was hot, so nice.... She closed her eyes and melted into him. *Oh, how would they tell...*

"Swan," he breathed. "Oh, Swan."

She stiffened. She had thought to fool him longer, long enough to confuse his heart....

Oh no, she thought, it's ending.

He was withdrawing.... He held her at arm's length. "Why, you little witch," he said.

He took a step away as though he were too close, as though he wanted to stare into her face until he saw the *difference* between her and her twin so *forevermore* he would be able to tell Swan and Smoke apart....

"You did that on purpose, didn't you?" he said. "You want to spoil it for us." His cheeks, gold brown from work in his mother's little garden, flushed pink. His dark eyes snapped. His mouth, be-

fore so open, so hot, so inviting, was closed now and
turned down at the corners. "I see what you're up
to," he said. "You want Swan only for yourself.
Well, you won't fool me again. I will study her, I
will learn her well. There is a difference in you, I
can see that now."

He had the violin and bow in his arms, between
him and her like a shield. He was going, in long
quick strides.

Overcome, Smoke slumped against the wall. Her
hands over her mouth, she watched him go. Her
knees were weak, her ankles trembled. Her heart had
stopped entirely, her toes and fingers and nose were
cold. *It hurt so much.* Nothing had ever hurt so much.
Some things were not for bearing, some things destroyed a part of you.... She could feel something
inside her withering that, in his arms, had leaped so
high, just born, just risen....

She had known, of course. She had known he had
been there for Swan. She had only *pretended* it was
she he was after...because she wanted him. Let him
kiss me once, her mind had whispered, and he will
love me ever. Swan will be forgotten in my woman's
kiss....

But it hadn't worked. He'd seen through her plain
as daisies. And nothing would ever be as painful, as
abjectly humiliating, as this.

And yet...

Hadn't he known *before* they'd kissed? Hadn't she
seen—now she thought about it, now she played it
again in her mind—hadn't she seen a *recognition* in
his eyes, just before his mouth closed hot upon hers?
Hadn't Danny Bowen been experimenting, too?

Smoke's fingers played with the key in her pocket,

but she had no strength yet to move. Inside the stateroom, she would cry. Inside, she would have to think and do something final and irrevocable. But now, all she could do was lift the key and press it against her aching lips so that the cool of the iron would calm the heat in her heart.

She was standing so as Tory VanVoorst appeared at the head of the hallway. Tory was tonight in black satin, raw-gold skin gleaming as it always did like a Spanish coin. Her shoulders were bare, black bows for sleeves at the arms. Her ebony hair danced around her deep green eyes; there were emeralds and diamonds at her throat. Tonight she is so beautiful all other women must despair, thought Smoke. Surely I do, I do.

Tory's gown rustled as she came. "Forgive me for not stopping, Smoke," she said as she passed. "But I'm sick, I think. Mal de mer or the baby, please forgive…"

Smoke just stared, unable to speak. Words hadn't returned. Tonight, for the first time, she envied Tory her charm, her elegance, her perfect, no-problem life. Tory knew how to be a woman. She was loved by a man who encouraged her to whatever she wanted— a mansion, a jewel, a racing ship…. She had only to open her pretty little mouth and Burty was off to fulfill his darling's pleasure. Lucky, lucky Victoria….

While Smoke was not yet sixteen and her life was shattered. All her dreams in a moment were gone because her foolish, foolish sister had played the *harlot* and encouraged a boy she thought nothing of, *felt nothing for*, was using only for her own amusement, her own ambition….

And Smoke, stout-hearted Smoke, who sneered at

love and wanted only adventure and glory, she *had lost her heart to the boy and he could not stand her*....

It's only puppy love, she thought. It's only jealousy or boredom. But how do you stop your heart from hurting...?

Somehow, she fumbled the key into the lock, turned it, was inside an oak-paneled room with two handsome oaken beds. She was in the bathroom, rooting through her toilette bag.

There.

She picked up the scissors, faced herself in the mirror. She'd show them.... Show *herself*. Danny Bowen would never mistake Smoke Lockholm for her sister again. Eyes cold, *cold as a gypsy's crystal ball*, Smoke lifted the scissors, yawned the cutting edges wide, and began to chop away her fall of flaxen hair.

SWAN HAD PROMISED to meet Danny Bowen on boat deck after she had said her good-nights, but it would be later than they'd planned because now she had to write her stupid lines for Twiggs and had to mollify Twiggs for a little; she had to sit with her in the lounge and listen to the orchestral music.

Well, all right, she thought, my turn will come.

Her mother and father had not dined in public, so she did not have to worry about them, at least. They, as lovers so often were, were closeted away together. Well, again, Swan did not care. She would have another lemonade, listen to the orchestra, and then feign tiredness and slip away.

Danny was not playing. He was probably up on boat deck right now, waiting for her: that thought pleased. Let him wait until I am ready, she thought. Let him expect me every passing second, let him grow with longing and let him be unfulfilled. Then, finally, I will come to him, after I finish writing my lines for Mrs. Twigg. I will come to him in my thin shimmy, under my coat. I'll let him feel me in the dark. I'll drive him wild. How nice that Smoke is as jealous as a toad! Dear Smoke—she'll never be as clever as I. I'll always have more beaux than she, and she will never, never know why....

When the orchestra finished an aria from *The Barber of Seville*, Danny came in and took a place on the podium. His roommate, Jock Hume, retired. Swan scrunched down on her sofa so he would not see her. His hair was blown, his cheeks were flushed. He had been looking for her—must have been!—just as she'd hoped.

"Mrs. Twigg," said Swan languorously, around her drinking straw.

"Yes, dear," said Mrs. Twigg, soothed now by her hearty dinner and the music.

"There's a man coming toward you. I think he will ask you to dance."

Mrs. Twigg followed Swan's gaze.

Yes, there was a man; she had noticed him before. His name was Colonel Archibald Gracie. She had heard him introduce himself to Nicola Lady Pomeroy earlier in the day. He was a bachelor, or at least traveling alone. Perhaps a widower. Mrs. Twigg had watched him; she suspected he was a flirt. But he was handsome enough and obviously knew quality, for he was, indeed, coming toward her. He bowed as the orchestra struck up a waltz.

"May I have the pleasure of this dance?" he

asked. He had a long white mustache and flat, gray cheeks.

Mrs. Twigg fluttered her eyelids and wondered if she dared.

"Oh, please do, Mrs. Twigg," said Swan, seizing the opportunity. "I must write those hundred lines you asked me for, and I should see how Smoke is."

"I'll be along, then, after just one dance," said Mrs. Twigg, thinking, It's the décolletage that does it. Gets them every time. Imagine! And Mrs. Twigg swept away in Colonel Gracie's manicured hands.

Swan lost sight of Danny for all the couples dancing. Captain Smith was gliding, body to body, with Dove Peerce; their heads, white and white, like clouds together. And Nicola Lady Pomeroy was dancing, too, stiff in the arms of a Southern gentleman. Burty VanVoorst, Tory's husband, was dancing a "duty waltz" with Madeline, the new Mrs. Astor, while Jack Astor sat with a leg crossed over a knee and fondled the ears of an Airedale pup.

It was a beautiful room, *Titanic*'s first-class lounge, large and curved and high ceilinged, oak and green and gold. And beautiful people were in it.... But Swan wished she and Danny were in the room alone, swaying to a ghostly orchestra. After several turns she would recline upon a chaise while he, on his knees, undressed her and paid her beauty homage.

Ah, romance; there is nothing like romance, Swan thought and slipped, skipping, from the room. Heading for B-41 she thought how comfortable *Titanic* was, how like a hotel on Fifth Avenue in New York City. It is wonderful to be almost sixteen and having a flirtation and be crossing an ocean, she congratulated herself; truly wonderful indeed. What a pity

Smoke doesn't understand about love. Smoke is such a booby.

So thinking, she turned the handle to their room and stepped in. The light was on over Smoke's bed; it shone full on Smoke's shorn honey hair chopped short above her shoulders.

It wasn't possible, of course. Smoke couldn't be sitting in her bed, writing "I do not belong below decks" like that, as though nothing were wrong. *Scalped!* It was a joke, that space between the ends of her hair and line of her shoulders. Smoke was trying to scare her. It was a game—

"Smokey, get out of bed and turn around. Whatever have you done?"

"I don't want to look like you, Swan," said Smoke calmly. "I don't want your silly peasant boyfriend to confuse us. He kissed me in the corridor outside not an hour ago, thinking I was you, before I could stop him. We can't have that, now can we? It was awful, too. He put his tongue into my mouth."

"Oh, boy." Swan pulled Smoke out of bed, turned her around. Smoke pirouetted.

"I like it," Smoke said, as maddeningly calm as before. "I won't have to worry about my hair anymore. And we'll be individuals, not taken for each other. What do you think?"

Swan fell upon her bed, laughing. "I like it, too!" she said. "I think it's chic! It makes your figure thinner and you look, oh…regal."

"Well, you can't do it, too," said Smoke, "that would defeat the purpose."

"No, I can't. At least not till we dock. But it's fetching. You're elegant, and ever so modern. Not so cute."

Smoke stared into a gold-framed mirror. "Yes," she said. "Now you're definitely prettier, but I'm the more soigné. Twiggs will die, I bet."

"How does it feel?"

"Light. As though my head weighs nothing at all. And cool. This way, when I sail my hair won't be in my eyes."

"Oh God, you've become an instant wallflower, that's what you've done." Swan walked around her twin again. "You're like a pretty boy—what you've always wanted to be.... What will Mother say?"

"Mother probably won't even notice," said Smoke, climbing back into bed.

Swan removed her skirt. "How far have you got on your lines?"

"Seventy-two."

"What will you take to do mine? I've got a date with Danny up on boat deck." Swan was out of her blouse, out of her shoes and stockings.

"I'll do yours for nothing, Swan. Because I kissed your boyfriend. To atone."

"I forgive you that. Think of Danny as a first love—one to learn on. Once I know what's what, I'll give him to you, if there's time."

Swan was in the bath, running water in the tub. She did not see Smoke tremble at the thought. And Smoke gave her twin no reply. She lay back on her piled-up pillows and wrote, for the seventy-third time, "I do not belong below decks." And then, while Swan bathed and redressed, she wrote it again and again and again....

When Mrs. Twigg stopped in to say good-night, the twins' lights were out. Swan was in an apricot gown, cut short at the knees, pretending to be asleep.

Smoke had finished her lines and Swan's, and was lying, waiting, with a scarf around her head. She was thinking how complicated life got the older one became. Soon life would be too complicated to manage....

For hair grew again, but hearts didn't. Once hearts were broken, they only mended, and then only sometimes; only if you starved your heart until it shriveled so it could slip out, at night, between the bars of its cage. Like Hansel and Gretel.... Like Swan was going to do as soon as Twiggs said good-night. But maybe, before your heart grew dry enough, the witch decided to fire up the pot and eat you.

That's what usually happened. Usually, you just got caught.

Mrs. Twigg stood in the dim of the corridor, looking into their room. "Are you asleep, girls?" she said.

When she received no answer, she snapped on the light. "Get out of bed, the both of you," she said decisively. No fool was Thelma Irene Twigg. "Let me see what you're up to now."

"Now?" said Swan. "I'm asleep already."

"Humph," said Mrs. Twigg.

Smoke just looked. She was in for it now. She wished she could cry on demand, the way Swan could.

Swan bounced out of bed. "We're up to nothing, Twiggs," said Swan. "And we've done our lines. There, on the dresser."

Mrs. Twigg turned her attention to Smoke. "And you, young lady, out. Let's see what you're still wearing. What's that rag doing on your head?"

Smoke sat up. "All right, Twiggs, you asked for

it." She pulled off the scarf. "There," she said. "And please don't scream. I like it."

Mrs. Twigg stared, clicked her mouth shut, said nothing. She spun on her heel and left the room.

"She's gone to get Mother," said Swan.

"Yes, and maybe Father, too," said Smoke.

"Danny's waiting for me," said Swan.

"Well, he'll just have to wait," said Smoke.

"Yes. I'm going to let him kiss me and kiss me."

"You'll hate it."

"No, I won't. If you relax, nice things happen inside to you. Men want you to like it, you know. It makes them feel like wild stallions when you like it."

"I don't care what men want. I'm after what I want, a life for myself."

"Dear Smoke, I do admire you so. But you're a ninny."

I know, Smoke thought. She said, "That's what I think of you."

They giggled, sister-close.

Swan crawled onto her twin's bed. "I'll stand by you, Smokey. We'll face them together."

Smoke made room for her. On top of the coverlet, they held hands.

Audrey came, her gilt hair loose and sleep-tousled, the way the twins rarely saw it. Her face was beautifully made—like their faces would be, finally finished, in their prime. It was a fresh face, sea-air healthy from being raised in Newport. Midnight-blue-eyed, small in her thin gown and robe, she looked as young as they, and prettier. She was five foot five to the twins' five foot seven. In her flat slippers she looked more delicate than they.... And their father looked taller, more masculine, with stubble just visible on his face, and his throat and chest bare under a silken robe, the light silky hair on his chest showing where the robe wasn't closed, and an irritated gleam in his storm-gray eyes. He had a protective arm around their mother, as though he meant to protect her from them.

Both twins sighed, and held hands tighter.

"Oh, Smoke," said Audrey. She came to the bed in which the girls huddled, sat at the foot and considered what to do, what to say. "Oh, darling," she said. "Are you so terribly unhappy?" And then she reached out and took Smoke in her arms and stroked her chopped tresses and kissed her.

"Oh, Mother," said Smoke. "I had to do it." Her mother smelled of jasmine and roses.

Audrey held Smoke's face. "Why, angel?"

"Because it's time not to look like anyone but myself. We're going to be sixteen, Mother. We've got to differentiate."

Swan nodded and pushed against Audrey so she would be embraced, too. "I think it looks very well, Mother. Smoke's elegant shorn, like a fine sheep. And if she doesn't like it after all, it will grow back, Mother, don't you see?"

Bay stood with his hands in his robe pockets, wishing he had a cigar. "I don't see anything to make a fuss about," he said. "Young women experiment with their looks. Celeste was always changing her hair around. Still does, perhaps...."

Celeste was Bay Lockholm's sister, ten years younger. She lived in Paris with her third husband, Emil Hudret, who wrote novels that were not published. They lived on Celeste's inheritance; lived in a "Bohemian fashion," it was said, scandalously and well. Celeste was rumored to take "lovers" from time to time, to live fast and dangerously. Her latest husband, for instance, was younger than she, a "rare drinker and deep thinker," whom she had met on the streets of the Left Bank. A "stud," they said, "with a long club. That is all Celeste sees in him and, for her, that's enough...!" Some people said, too, of Bayard and Celeste Lockholm, that they both were burdened by "a taste for the common." Bay had married a carpenter's daughter, after all, and Celeste had married unfortunately three times—handsome men, but no-goods, of no social distinction, no moral worth. But what the truth really was no one seemed to know. Celeste had been estranged from her brother a long time; Bay and Audrey had not seen her in fifteen years. She was not often mentioned by anyone....

Mrs. Twigg said nothing. Her lips were tightly pursed. She had her own ideas how young ladies should be raised, and one of her pet peeves was permissive parents. They would be the ruination of the country. Mr. Lockholm she could forgive, he was only a man. But the Mrs.... Madam Lockholm had never outgrown her passion for her husband, that was her trouble...and Mrs. Twigg's bane.

Bay and Audrey left then, smiling in a foolish fashion, as though they did not know why they had been disturbed from their bed and were too polite to ask. They went back to each other, as they always did, even in a crowd. The twins felt the isolation, and so did Mrs. Twigg.

God keep me from wealth and idleness, the governess thought self-righteously. The rich never knew where they were. Why, this boat could sink and they'd all stand around with their hands in their pockets, saying goodbye. And what's the good in that?

She picked up the twins' written punishment. "Good night, girls," she said, determined to ignore Smoke's pathetic bid for attention. From this moment on, Smoke would care for her hair herself; Mrs. Twigg would not touch it. "We'll try and do better tomorrow, won't we?" she said.

"Yes, Twiggs," said Smoke and Swan, still together in one bed. "Sweet dreams, Twiggs."

Mrs. Twigg closed the door on the twins' stateroom and crossed the corridor to her own. There, on the threshold of B-35 lay a single long-stemmed rose. Oh! Her knees creaked as she bent to retrieve it. In the rose-tissue wrapping there was a white card. "Thank you for an exquisite waltz," it read. "Colonel Gracie," had been crossed out and replaced with a penned, "Archie."

Mrs. Twigg used the door frame to lift herself up. Bewilderment, delight, erased the stern set of her face. Colonel Gracie! He had been very nice, very nice, indeed. I must wear the yellow paisley tomorrow at breakfast, she thought. I look my youngest in the yellow paisley.

Thus distracted, thus dreaming, Mrs. Twigg did not hear the door of B-41 open immediately as she closed hers. She did not hear B-41 click shut. Nor did she pick up the tiptoed sneaking away of Swan, almost naked under her overcoat, hurrying up to boat deck…after Danny.

While he, anxious, worrying, feeling *guilty*… What if Swan refused him now that he had been

tricked by the witchy sister? What if Smoke lied to
Swan about him, told Swan that he had sought out
the wrong one *on purpose*, that he was a runaround,
after any and every pretty girl he came across?

Oh, God.

Back and forth on deserted boat deck Danny
Bowen strode, oblivious to the sweet sea air, uncon-
scious of the great ship running silently in the night,
not hearing the soft *slurr* sixty feet below where *Titanic* parted the water and foamed it white. Nor did
he see, far away to starboard, as in mirage, the dim
rise of Irish hills, growing slowly in the dark.

High above him, in the crow's nest, a lookout sat.
On the captain's bridge, behind him, two officers
manned the ship's controls. Danny Bowen saw them
not. He was aware only that he and Swan had
pledged to meet up here between nine and ten, and
that it was now after midnight, he should be sleeping,
but the darling of his heart—yes, that was what Swan
was for him—had not yet come.

He would not leave without her. He would stay
here sleepless, waiting, if he had to, till the dawn
broke and forced him down. Because he loved her.
Swan was so sweet, so pretty, so hot in his hands....
And waiting for her was the sweetest misery he had
ever known. She was the one for him, all right. Waiting for her so, he knew it, just as he knew that he
was the one for her. She had not held his lack of
high birth against him, that was proof. And she had
sighed when he played his violin for her, down in
his little room. Oh, she was some cute cookie was
Swan Lockholm, and he was mad for her, mad for
her—

If only she would come! Come as she had promised and not be angry. He would explain about her sister. Explain first off....

Someone was coming.

Yes! Flowing gold tresses under *Titanic*'s night-lights, a fast dainty step. He whirled to take her, to welcome her into his arms, then hesitated. He must wait, must make sure she was the *right one*.

"Swan," he spoke into the space between them.

"Danny."

She was walking toward him, opening her coat as she came. She was wearing something red and short, and her breasts were clearly outlined, nipples against the cloth, the breasts softly swaying, free under the shining silk.

Oh the good Lord help me, he thought, wildly happy. His baby was not hot. *Hot* was not the word for her. She was *red-hot* and in his arms....

He was under her coat, his loins against hers. She was opening her mouth, wiggling against him. He clutched her buttocks in his hands and lifted her upon him. She was light and smelled of flowers. She was golden and gorgeous, and her arms were around him, too, tight and pulling. Her breasts were hard upon his heart.... If he lifted her a little higher....

He carried her into the shadows, way back in the stern, behind an engine casing, under where the life-boats hung. He tried to tell her about her sister, but she did not give him time. She stopped him, for as she unbuttoned her chemise, all thought left. There was only flesh, taut and round and glowing, and breasts nectar sweet, and white thighs and the flat ivory of her stomach.... He was enveloped in want-ing, in *having*.

She should have, but she did not tell him no.

Swan lay, open, before him. She thought about saying he must stop. She thought about warning him never to kiss Smoke again, or anyone else, not ever, now that he belonged to her. She thought to tell him how good he felt; she thought of many things. But all thoughts drifted and swirled in silence, and she never said a word. She only let him do, coaxed him with arms that clung and legs that gave, with breasts that swung above his mouth, bright nippled. Her lips explored, her palms caressed, and she showed him, quivering, her eager secret place....

Just before he pierced her, she thought, I must stay him. But she did not. She did not want to....

Danny, then, did not know what to do. Kneeling before her, uncertain, he whispered, "Do you love me, Swan? Will you marry me?"

"Yes," she said, "yes, yes." And she lifted her womb to him.

But he drew away and closed her coat around her. "I can't do it," he said. "I must speak to your father first. He might refuse me."

Her father would refuse him, Swan knew that. Not because of Danny's station in life, but because she was only going on sixteen, and because she knew nothing of the world of men. She had not yet "come out," and she had known Danny Bowen only for a day.

Still, she loved him, she was sure of that. She loved especially, *especially* the way he made her feel. The only way she could get her father to say yes, she thought, was to do as her Aunt Celeste had done, long before....

She stretched out on the deck, modest in her overcoat. She crossed her legs at the ankles and stared up at a starry sky.

"Do you love me?" she asked, certain of his answer.

He stretched out beside her. He kissed the ends of her hair and her ears and her eyes. "I love you more than life," he said solemnly, his heart in his eyes. "I love you more than my violin, or my mother."

Swan sighed. How nice were the words of love, how exciting were the *feelings*. "If you love me, you must ravage me, Danny. Right now, under God's sky and that waning moon. Tell me how beautiful I am while you do it. Tell me how much you love me, how happy we will be."

He was infatuated, bewitched. He did not know how to refuse. Slowly, feeling manhood fall upon him like an invisible mantle, he unbuttoned her coat...and twined with her.

Thirty feet above in the crow's nest, Frederick Fleet saw the shadows coupling below, but turned his gaze away from what was not his business, and watched, instead, the easy ocean flow.

Thursday, April 11

8

Tory VanVoorst had suffered a sleepless night, alone. Burty was gambling in the smoking room; a couple of cigars and a round or two of poker with the boys, he'd said.

She sat in the dark with the bottle of cyanide pills in her lap and faced her nightmare. It had happened as she had known—though forgotten for a time—it would...one day. And that one day was now.

For after dinner Wednesday evening, Teddy Royce had stepped to her side, touched her elbow and drawn her off. "I'm embarrassed to tell you," he said bluntly, "but I'm a little short on funds. Do you think you might help me—get your husband to make me a loan—for old times' sake?"

Tory made no reply. The devil comes in many guises, she thought, and stared at him, a smile frozen on her lips.

Teddy lounged before her, shoulder against a pillar, flashing his white-toothed grin, his handsome sun-buffed face showing only charm, *all mischief hidden*, as he had learned to hide it down on the Mississippi on the gambling riverboats. "Well," he'd said, and jingled coins in his trouser pockets. "Well, *Alma June Brown*, how about it?"

And then she rallied. River rat, she thought. I've dealt with your kind before. She tossed her head to make her black curls dance. She narrowed her green eyes and lifted her chin. "Is that it, then, Rolls? Will it be blackmail, for old times' sake?"

"Ah," he'd murmured, and smoothed his own dark hair. "High living hasn't softened all your edges, has it, kid? You're still a cat, still know how to fight. Well no, in answer to you, it's not blackmail I was thinking, just a loan. I'm feeling lucky and there's a game afloat. If I win, I'll pay you right back. All I want is a stake."

"Be careful you don't get a stake through your heart. Remember, I can be dangerous."

His face changed. It firmed and hardened and brown-black eyes glinted like swords unsheathed. "I can be dangerous, too, my dear," he said softly, and leaned over her.

She did not retreat. Slight, high bellied, she stood before him, defiant, and said, "If you tell on me, Teddy, I will kill you."

"Buy your safety then, Alma June," he said softly. "Buy it now or I sell to the highest bidder."

And then, blessedly, Burty was beside her, folding money into his wallet of ostrich skin, tucking the wallet into the inner pocket of his dinner jacket. With Burty beside her, *on her side*, she was safe. With Burty as her ally, she had no reason to fear Teddy Royce.

But would Burty be on her side if he knew she had lied to him, had lied for years and years, from the beginning...? If he knew she was...what she was?

"Hello," Burty said, his face wreathed with well-being, flushed after wine and his heavy meal. Physically he was not the equal of dashing Teddy Royce—but Burty was the better man. His was an ordinary face, plump cheeked, sparse browed and snub nosed. The eyes were heavy lidded, set wide; mongrel eyes of mixed color, brown and green and gold and gray. The predominant color changed according to his mood.... In love, his eyes were star flecked, almost silver. But most arresting was their gaze. Burty VanVoorst's eyes held you, penetrated and appraised. Fearless, they peered out at the world energetic and bold, manipulative and shrewd. Sometimes those eyes showed kind, when they looked upon the things he loved. Sometimes the eyes dimmed, pretending innocence, as they measured precisely and plotted well and prepared to vanquish what stood in the way of his will.... Hypnotic eyes had Burton Kingsley VanVoorst; no fool was he. He had used his own legs to rise high, and he stood almost alone on the top of his mountain. In one thing only might he be vulnerable: it was almost laughable how much he doted on his wife.

When he stood beside her facing Teddy Royce, Tory felt, in the air around, the strength of him. With Burty, she was invincible. He was a fortress unto himself. But Tory— clever Tory, too—she knew where the battle lay between her and Teddy: not with Burty or against...but *for* him.

Teddy opened the challenge. "Are you a gambling man, Mr. VanVoorst?" he said.

"Ever know a man who wasn't?" said Burty, innocent and friendly, but behind that mask, assessing, seeing. "And you, sir, you knew my Tory as a child.

You must know New Orleans then. They gamble
there, I'm told.''

"Yes, sir," said Teddy Royce, and he jingled the
coins in his pocket. "They sure do."

"Well, it's poker in the smoking room. Are you
game, Mr. Royce?"

"They call him Rolls," said Tory, as smooth as
cream, "because he's lucky with the dice."

"Ah," said Burty, competitive instincts aroused.
"Do you mind if I try my luck then, Tor?"

She had held on to him tightly. Quick Burty, he
knew by the pressure of her hand that something was
wrong. Suave, he did not let that knowledge show.
Practiced, too, he knew how to handle a woman. He
covered Tory's hand with his, and said, oil slick, to
Teddy Royce, "Well, another night perhaps," and
he had turned to take her away.

"No—go, darling," she'd said, and released him.

Run from the likes of Teddy Royce? Not she. Let
him do his damnedest, she'd see him in his grave.
And if the truth would out—must out—let it be here,
on the high seas where pirates clashed, outlaws all.
Let it be here, before the baby came....

"Rolls has just asked me to stake him, Burtykins," she said, "for old times' sake. And I've refused. Maybe you'll be more generous. He's certain
to try you."

"I will make it worth your while, sir," said Teddy,
and his mustache lifted, wolfine, above his teeth.

Burty, who had braved the unknown before, who
had made many millions meeting the dares of other
men, bowed to Rolls. "Shall we meet in the smoker
in, say, fifteen minutes?"

"Done," said Teddy.

And he had gone and asked a waltz of Nicola. Tory was surprised to see them dancing—Nick's hair like fire against Teddy's white-jacketed shoulder, as she, pleading mal de mer, excused herself to go alone to her room.

And there she had sat in the dark—and waited. Waited for Burty to come back to her. Waited for him to burst into the room and sweep her into his arms and say, "I don't give a *damn* what color's in your veins, Victoria. I loved you once, I love you now, I'll love you ever!"

But the hours passed, and the breeze off the deck grew cooler, and all was quiet in the Lockholm bedroom next door. And the moon was a little thing, and the long blue vial of pills rattled cattily in her lap. And the baby tumbled in her belly. *Maybe frightened, too, poor thing.*

And Burty, her Burtykins, did not come. He did not come back to her last night at all.

And now it was eleven-thirty Thursday morning. The sun threw no shadows, and great *Titanic* was up St. George's Channel in Cobh Harbour, pausing now at the Daunt Light vessel to take on a "pilot" who knew the waterways, who would guide *Titanic* into Roche's Point at Queenstown.

Tory had not slept, but at nine o'clock she had done her stretching exercises, as she did every morning of her life. Curtailed only a little by the baby's heft, she had twisted and turned and pulled and held, her raw-gold skin greased with cocoa butter to keep the stretch marks down. She would swim now and then have a massage and shower. And after that she would dress in pale silk, the one with wood rosebuds for buttons, and she would go to the dining salon for luncheon as though everything was perfectly all right.... As though her husband had not found out last night she was a *nigger* and not come home to her. As though she had not been left without a word.... As though she had not lost...

The doorknob turned.

And there he was, still damp from his swim, still drunk from the night before. There Burty was, pain twisting his face in a way she'd never seen it. A rage in him bursting, trying to get out. There he was, years older in a day and *mean* in the part of him that had never been mean, that he had kept, carefully, purposefully, sweet and gentle. There was gray stubble on his face, which she could never remember seeing any way but pink and baby smooth and creamed and scented. There were bags under eyes less vivid now, red ringed and almost closed. He was in a bathing robe, white chenille, loosely sashed around his generous middle. And he wore paper slippers on his feet.

He saw his wife staring at him with a hunted, haunted face, a beautiful face, even denied sleep, and lost and pleading. Hers was a face that said, as loud as looks ever could, *love me anyway.*

No matter what I did or was or am, no matter all my faults, my lacks, my *sins*, just *love me* because I need your love, need *you.*

So love me anyway.

Burty saw those things in Tory's face, read the message straight. He threw down his ostrich-skin wallet upon the double bed, still made up from yesterday.

"Fifty thousand dollars, you cost me, princess," he said. "Chicken feed, eh, m'girl? Fifty thousand dollars, and here's the kicker—it took me all night, but I won it back.''

She looked at the bulging wallet, sat on the bed beside it. Her hair was lank with cocoa oil and sweat. She riffled the bills in the wallet, spilled them out on the bright red bedspread, looked up at her husband, started to ask because she had to, started to frame the words, ''What did he tell you—sell you—about me?'' when he lifted his foot.

Dear Burtykins lifted his slippered foot, he lifted his right leg, and *swung, kicked her in the stomach,* kicked her where their baby stirred, *maybe frightened, too....*

''Nigger,'' he said, slurring, weaving, but not drunk anymore—enraged. ''Wanna sing me a gospel tune?'' He lifted his leg to kick her again. She covered her stomach with her hands and turned, facedown, into the bed.

''Shall you get out or shall I?'' he said.

And then, when she gave no answer, he said, as though it were only conversation, ''If I didn't hate you then, why do I hate you now? Nigger cunt ain't bad, I have to tell you. I never woulda guessed it, though, never in a hundred years....''

And then he lay down on the edge of carpet that extended beyond the bed frame, and slept.

And Tory, on the bed, in the middle of the fifty thousand dollars he had paid to buy her secret then won back, Tory, at last, slept, too. She slept deep and she slept well, without dreams because she was both exhausted and relieved.... Relieved because her secret was out; Burty knew. He was angry—that she could understand—but *he was back.* He had, after all, come back to her.

And somehow they would work it out...work it out...*wouldn't they?*

NICOLA LADY POMEROY, on the other hand, opened her eyes to a beautiful morning. She and her mother shared B-16, but Dove Peerce was an early riser no matter how late she came to bed, and Dove, who had been dancing last night when Nicola retired, was up and dressed and gone when Nicola opened her eyes to find *Titanic* stopped at Queenstown.

It was too late at eleven-thirty for breakfast in the dining salon; that stopped at ten-thirty. Nicola ordered room service and, in happy solitude, enjoyed breakfast beside her port-side window. She saw there, a distance from *Titanic*'s anchor point, the long green hills of Ireland. She heard there, through her window, the voices of the tender men and the new passengers boarding. She heard their heavy boot-shod steps and soft, awed murmurs at the stately palace they stepped upon. A bagpipe, aft, wailed a melancholy air; already someone in the stern was lonely for his hills and the dry firm grip of home.

These passengers, mostly third-class, a few second-class, would be the last. Queenstown was the final stop. From here, Cobh Harbour, *Titanic*'s virgin voyage truly began. Here, sea held, the land gave up.

Out there, beyond one turning, past one final guardian, the Old Head of Kinsale lighthouse, ocean ribboned and rippled and ran. Out there, beyond one turning, was mystery untold and endless fathoms deep.... In an hour from now, or two, not more, *Titanic* would point her bow west toward the rimless, unpredictable, far-flung sea....

Nicola Lady Pomeroy had crossed oceans before:

she did not trust them. Oceans were a hindrance, an interruption of the land she loved, miles and miles of hock-deep grass and wide-mown tracks to give a horse his head and set him galloping. Or shafts of mountains that called for climbing or exploring, and ungroomed tangled forests. Fallow fields called for admiration and for planting. One could build a castle on land and string the sheep meadows with fieldstone walls to jump in pursuit of fox. On land one could walk or run and roam at will, and then return and find the land there waiting, recognizable…bearing your mark. On land there were canyons and trees with sweet-voiced birds and leaves that told the seasons. On land were deserts and savannas and the slanty shifting shores of palm-front beaches. All terra firma, solid and reliable.

But an ocean was a strange and foreign thing, belonging only to itself. An ocean was fluid, ever changing, and never as it had been before. It was vast and dangerous, a *magic carpet* that had to be traversed at risk to come, again, to beloved land…. For Nicola Lady Pomeroy the best part of any water travel was when a spine of land first showed upon a dim horizon. Ah, she would think then, soon. Soon now, I'll regain my footing and be on my way….

So she watched the land with lorn eyes as she sipped hot coffee and ate her eggs and toast. And how extraordinary, she found herself smiling; she who, since one sun-sinking eve in Kenya last August, had rarely smiled without an effort.

Could it be, as she had hoped, as she had waited, that she was healing? She did not mean to be defeated by anything, not even by the loss of Rolf, the darling of her heart. But she was finding her sorrow keener, her bereavement stronger, than she had thought any anguish could be: her sorrow was almost killing. But Nicola meant to live—and meant to love again. She liked loving. And she was young; she wanted healing....

Theodore Royce, called Teddy.

An amusing man, she thought. Attractive. Not a gentleman; a man who walked on the wild side, a man in whom charm passed for substance, a man who lived by his wits. Perhaps not altogether a good man.

Still, amusing.

She had enjoyed him last night at dinner with his tales of adventuring. Tall tales. In Madrid, for instance, he said he had been chased by a mayor's posse for a certain breach of etiquette with that high man's daughter. And in Cairo he had been ambushed and forced to build a church. A church in Cairo! And in Siam they had wanted him to stay, he told her as they waltzed, and become their sultan.... He was not to be believed, of course, but still, he was amusing.

And this morning she was feeling very much alive.

She thought she would wear the new salmon wool at luncheon. It was comfortable and showed her figure well.... To it she would add her turquoise-and-enamel necklace, a priceless piece of Roman antiquity. And after, if she was so inclined, she would invite Teddy Royce to a joust at deck quoits.... Then, when night fell, they might stroll into a shadow and she would try out that smirking mouth, try on for fit those bronze and muscular arms.

Why not?

She was unpromised....

She ran her own bath rather than ring for Mrs.

Twigg—Mrs. Prigg, Nicola called her, silently in her mind. Nicola disliked sharing a maid, but her girl had preferred to stay in Denton and not come to the States....

"Thank you, ma'am," said Agatha Leary promptly when she was asked. "Thanks kindly for the offer, but I'd rather not, really. I have me mum, y'see, I'd miss 'er bad straight off, and then there's Billy, though who knows about 'im, me boy-o from the pub...."

Nicola had not pressed. Agatha had been good enough for the English countryside, but had proved a trial in London. No, Agatha Leary belonged in Denton; Nicola had found her a place with the new Lady Casmere.

Nicola did not know what would happen once she got back to America. She knew only that she would ride again. Two English hunters had crossed the Atlantic before her to be stabled at Peerce House, the Newport "cottage," so that they would have adjusted to Yankee air and grass and be ready to run when Nicola arrived. She might make her home permanently in New York and Newport, and then she might not. She would see how she felt back home again, starting over.... Her title was hers to keep, but Dentoncroft had been attached to Rolf's title and had passed, since they had been childless and Rolf had been sole offspring, to a cousin Nicola had met once, over tea. Henry, his name was; he had been toothy and good-natured. Good luck to you, Henry, she thought, and wound her mass of auburn hair and stepped into the tub.

No sooner bathed and toweled dry, and there was

a knock at the door. She wrapped herself in a white robe and opened the door to a steward.

"Flowers for you, madam, and a marconigram." He was young, no more than twenty, with soft cheeks as though he did not yet shave. But he looked at Nicola, still misty from the tub and obviously naked under loose cotton, and his eyes fired.

She accepted the flowers and the envelope and shut the door as she thanked him. Impertinent pup, she thought, and caught herself smiling again.

Ah, good.

There were two roses, one pale peach, one white. "You and I, last night," the note read. "Teddy." And under his name he had added, "Only the white one has thorns."

So. He knew how to woo a woman, too.

There was a cloissoné vase on the writing desk. She set the roses in. They twisted in the water and climbed around each other; pretty.

And now for *the other one*.... Captain Stanley Lord. She ripped open the wireless and read.

ON SUNDAY *CALIFORNIAN* AND I WILL PASS WITHIN A SHIP'S LENGTH OF *TITANIC* STOP LET ME SEND A BOAT TO BRING YOU TO ME STOP PLEASE NICKY SAY YES STOP GIVE ME A HEARING, TRY ME ONCE MORE YOU MUST STOP HOW CAN YOU FORGET OUR NIGHT IN KENYA STOP BE FAIR, BE-LOVED, AND DO NOT BREAK THE HEART OF HE WHO LOVES YOU MORE THAN WORDS CAN EVER SAY STOP IMPATIENT STOP BURNING STOP I AWAIT YOUR ANSWER STOP

She crumpled the missive in her fist. Two suitors, and here the difference: one debonair, clever and poetic; the other dull, direct and...*dismal*.

She despised Stanley Lord. She had *sinned* with Stanley Lord. The man—as her mother might say—had no *flair*. Wanting her to come to him like a cow to the barn for milking. Writing of *fairness*—all's fair in love and war, wasn't that the saying?—as though she were a courthouse and not a woman he was *courting*....

Well, she would tell Captain Stanley Lord to go to blazes as directly as he invited her to assignation. And she would tell *Titanic*'s wireless office to accept no more marconigrams from Captain Lord. *Imagine*—mentioning that night of shame in Africa for all the world to read....

Heated, she found paper and pen. She sat at the desk, stared out the round window for inspiration. *Titanic* had lifted anchor. They were moving down St. George's Channel.

"Beast," she wrote, then crossed that out as too familiar, and began again.

SIR STOP DO NOT ATTEMPT TO CONTACT ME AGAIN STOP EVER STOP AM APPALLED BY YOUR LACK OF DELICACY STOP WILL TAKE LEGAL AC-TION IF YOU PERSIST STOP NO ANSWER TO THIS WILL BE ACCEPTED STOP SO GO HANG STOP POM-EROY MARCHIONESS OF DENTON STOP STOP STOP

There.... She laid down her pen.

She stood and pulled the pins from her orange-fire hair and watched, out the window, the last of land recede. *Titanic* was picking up speed now, steaming out to sea. Next *stop*, she thought, will be New York harbor...and home.

Happy, she whacked at her hair with a brush.

There was another knock, a softer one this time.

"Who is it?" she said. "I'm without my maid and not dressed."

The knocking became rapid, still soft.

She laughed. She saw herself in the gilt mirror, laughing. It was Teddy. It had to be Teddy, charming Rolls Royce, come to claim a kiss, perhaps, in return for the roses....

"I cannot come," she said, her lips against the door.

"Let me in, then," she heard. "I was so distracted by you last night I lost fifty thousand to VanVoorst at poker."

"You are a riverboat gambler with a mind of steel. I don't believe you."

"When I was on the Mississippi I had not met you."

Nicola sighed. Oh yes, Teddy Royce had charm. And he would know how to warm a woman, like brandy, in his hands. He would not push or urge or rip or thump...unless she wanted it, which, sometimes, she did....

What would he be like to ride, she wondered, like one of her hunting steeds? How would he feel, her buttocks upon him, her naked knees gripping his sundark chest while, as he leaped, she lifted above him, up and down, up and down, rhythmically with strong, horse-hardened thighs...?

Slowly, teasingly, she opened the door a little way.

He was handsome in a suit of tan linen. Taller than she, he leaned against the door frame with wide shoulders and a cowboy's lean hips. His dark hair waved away from his face and tousled around his ears, wild thick hair, like hers.... His eyes were dark and dark browed, unquiet eyes burning with passion not held back, yet glinted cold behind: so he could be cruel, too, cruel as well as loving. Well, she liked men who did not bend to a woman's whimsy.

"I cannot afford to lose fifty thousand dollars for nothing," he said, "so I claim you as bought and paid for."

He slipped, quick, inside the door, closed it behind him with a practiced heel. Her bathrobe covered unprotected flesh, and her hair, her flaming mane, was loose and damp and tumbling.

Teddy Royce unsashed her robe with a stroke. Without a word, where it opened, he invaded her whole body. He held her nakedness against his shirted chest, and then he kissed her, coaxing her mouth open with his tongue.... He kissed her for a long time, and she did not notice, at once, that while they kissed he nudged a trousered knee between her naked thighs, and opened them, too.

Only when she pleased did she request that he release her.

"Now you are paid," she said, her mouth below his chin. "And well paid, I say."

"Overpaid," he said with hot breath. "I shall lose to VanVoorst again tonight."

Their bodies were still together. She fumbled for her sash, lost in the folds of the robe. "Cover my nakedness," she said, "since you revealed it."

He stepped back, held the robe wide and admired her. She was tall, big bosomed, well hipped. Always athletic, she was firm of muscle, with the flat stomach of a fertile woman who has not borne children. Her legs were hard, strong and long, and her skin was as luminous as pearls.

"Oh, there are things that please a man a woman never knows," he said. "And all those things, you are.... My God, and I wanted to relax this trip." And then, ruefully, he closed the robe around her and belted her sash in a seaman's slippery hitch, which holds through a blizzard, but gives with a simple tug.

Done, he moved to a chair. He sat and crossed his legs and smiled at her, a happy man.

She let him stay.

She combed her hair before the mirror, twisted it, pinned it to make it stay. It wouldn't; it would fight its restraints and fall free the way it wanted; it always had. When I get back to the States, she thought, I will find a maid who can manage this mad painter's hair....

And with that thought the little happiness she was experiencing was gone. Teddy Royce was gone, and *Titanic*, and Nicola was back in yesterday, with him who held her heart even from the grave.

For it was Rolf Lord Pomeroy who often, as Agatha brushed her hair, used to remind her, with admiring wonder, that it was that rampant orange-red hair that drove poor Vincent van Gogh insane.

Nicola Reed Peerce had been born in 1871. In '88, at seventeen, her mother and father had taken her to Paris. There they had met Vincent van Gogh at his brother Theo's apartment. Theo was an art dealer, and that summer Dove and Percival Peerce wanted to buy Impressionist watercolors to adorn the walls of Peerce House. Vincent had instantly begged to paint the Peerce's exquisite daughter—outrageously begged, down on his knees, beating his fists upon the floor, and then his head.... Quite mad, already. He said she could not refuse him, that he must paint her or die— "Your hair is what I was born to paint," he said to her. "It has nothing to do with you. It has everything to do with me...."

He had been drinking, yes, he was utterly drunken. Still, she told him he could paint her hair, her face, her figure—nude or clothed, sitting or standing or in motion. "Whatever you please, sir," she said, "and however. Such passion as yours, Mr. van Gogh, and such talent, cannot be denied. Certainly, I will not be the one to deny it."

He had been as happy as a child. "You have given me immortality," he said.

"Come tomorrow to the Crillon," said Nicola. "You may paint me all day if you like. I'll be cooped up in suite 37 being measured by Monsieur Charles Worth...."

He had kissed her hands in gratitude.

"One day is all I need. Thank you, thank you, my Helen of Troy," he had said so sincerely that she and her father both agreed—though Dove demurred—that Vincent van Gogh, poor man, truly thought that he must put her hair on canvas or not survive. He had left then, clapping his rough hands and singing.

But the next day, Theo called to say that Vincent had complained that the sun in Paris was too faint to paint by, and he had run away that morning, "somewhere south, where the sun was closer."

"He made me promise to deliver this message to you, *cherie*," said Theo van Gogh. "Vincent will write you when he is settled, when he has found the

proper light. And then you must go to him...and fulfill his reason for being. He pleads you do not dismiss his request—his life, he swears, hangs upon
it...."

"Tell your brother I will come the instant I hear
from him," she'd said, and she had turned to her
father and asked his permission; Percival Peerce had
agreed. "Righto, Nick, we'll be honored to be summoned so. We'll be off on the instant, eh? And we'll
buy some of his work while we're there to keep him
in paints—what do you say?"

Her mother had been strangely quiet, but then
Dove Peerce had rarely waxed enthusiastic about her
daughter.

And then Vincent had not written. Or if he had,
she never received the letter. And then they heard
that he had come to grief in Arles in the Provence,
that he was hospitalized...that he had shot himself.

Years later, meeting Rolf Lord Pomeroy, Nicola
told him the story. And ever after, Rolf said of Nicola's hair that it had driven a genius insane.... Nicola chose to believe that perhaps Rolf was right.

From his chair Teddy saw that she was lost in
desolate reverie. He came to her, stood behind her
where she sat before the dressing table. "Let me arrange this glory for you," he said, and took the comb
and pins.

With a long sigh, Nicola came back to the present.
She did not tell him about Vincent van Gogh. "You,
Teddy Royce?" she said, making the effort again to
be gay. "You're such a masculine man, and you
would brush a lady's hair?"

"Only the strong can be gentle, Lady Pomeroy.
Only the good can be wicked."

His hands were deft. He was skilled. An interesting man, Teddy "Rolls" Royce…. Still, she wanted to weep for what she had lost. She forced herself to stay in the present, with *this* man, *this* moment.

"Your hair was made for diamonds," he said. "Do you have diamonds, Lady Pomeroy?"

"Everyone has diamonds," she said lightly, instantly alert. For while one's possessions may be displayed for others to admire, they were not to be talked of—nor tallied up—with strangers.

He set another curl into place. "And emeralds and pearls?"

She did not answer this time. She watched, in the mirror's reflection, his eyes darken down to a satin glow. It is not only I who interest him, she thought. He is lured by money, too, and status. Well. Perhaps Rolls Royce and I will play more than a game of deck quoits….

She raised her hands to her head and took his hands away. "You must leave me now," she said. "My maid will dress me."

"Join me at luncheon," he said.

"I regret," she said, and touched perfume to her wrists.

He was a smart man. He knew he had erred.

It was amazing, she thought, as he left without another word, without a backward glance, what a rose or two could get from a woman. Forgiveness…. Always that. A kiss. A smile, an invitation….

But not, she thought, opening a velvet box to lift out the turquoise-and-enamel necklace, not a bank draft for fifty thousand dollars.

9

Captain E. J. Smith was annoyed.

A large crowd was watching as they steamed away from Queenstown. And everyone, it seemed, had box cameras and was taking pictures of *Titanic* departing. All well and good, thought Captain Smith. But one of the boiler room stokers had climbed up the fourth funnel, the nonfunctioning one called the dummy. The man had shimmied up the inside ladder and was poking his head through the top hole, was looking a fool, grinning and waving at the townsfolk back on-shore.

Captain Smith did not want *Titanic* to sail off to America undignified.

"Damn the man," he said to Officer Boxhall, who was at his side. "Get that man down immediately."

"Aye, aye, Captain."

Probably the fireman only wanted a view of his homeland, thought E.J., or was after a stolen breath of smoke-free air. Maybe the gentle-playing bagpipe of that newly boarded passenger in third, Mr. Eugene Daly, had lured the man from his boiler the way, it was said, sea sirens do who sing a sailor into jumping to his death in a storm-racked sea.

Why ever, the fireman was dirty from his furnace work, and therefore black of face. And even less than indignity, Captain Smith wanted no "dark surprises"; no ill omens to mark this, *Titanic*'s final touch with land until destination.

Some of the crew would take it for the joke it was, but not all.... Not near all. And so that stoker would be hard disciplined. For those who lived their lives with only a bit of board between themselves and the soft coffin lid of the deep took anything and everything as signposts portending good or ill.... And all were especially sensitive the first time out.

Damn the man.

For this stunt he would work extra shifts, the hardest shifts. It was the only way to teach such as he. You had to bear down on the rambunctious rabble; only way to keep them disciplined was to lay on the whip....

Another stoker had just deserted. One John Coffey. He hid, Mr. Boxhall thought, with the mailbags sent ashore by tender. And just now, now they were under way, he had been discovered missing.

Well, damn John Coffey, too.

Such things as these happened all too often these days. The world is changing, thought Captain Smith, changing for the bad. There was a time when a man's acceptance by White Star Line set him permanently into his life's work. A man was proud to be taken on by such a company. So it had been for E.J., so should it be for all.... But now a lad signed on to work, then "jumped" when he got where he was headed, and never mind the ship's crew was thrown short because of his desertion. Trash, thought Captain Smith, and good riddance. He would see this laggard's name recorded in the black book, and if he had used his true name to be hired on, John Coffey would never work for White Star Line again!

The stoker atop the fourth funnel had been called down, Boxhall informed the captain. "Called down and dressed down, and back at work, sir. Seems he has a girl in Queenstown."

"We all have girls in Queenstown," said Captain Smith, and thought, always a woman behind mischief—or a woman blamed. And he remembered himself, last night, with the delectable Madam Peerce. He had acted the fool, too, but he, as a proper one should, had kept it private—trying to impress the exquisite lady. Lusting to please her…to win her heart…. Ah, we're all alike at bottom, he thought, we men. Every man jack one of us ends walking a plank of our own devising, trying to climb inside some woman's skirts….

With a snort he brought his thoughts back to *Titanic*, where they belonged.

He stood at his captain's place on the bridge surrounded by the guarantee staff of Harland & Wolff, builders. These were the men who knew *Titanic*'s intimate workings, all her engineering, her systems and mechanical abilities. *Titanic* was forty-six thousand tons of ship, nine hundred feet of ship; from top to bottom she rose the height of an eleven-story building; she exposed a cliff of more than sixty feet above the water line. She was capable, said the guarantee men, of sustaining a speed of twenty-three knots in a steady sea, and maybe more….

And maybe more again, thought E. J. Smith. Beginning tomorrow, I'll give her a chance to show it!

The guarantee men knew all *Titanic*'s secrets, knew where every screw and lever was, how her winches functioned and her powering motors, what each wire lead to, and every pipe and tube. They knew the electrical system, the refrigeration, the four elevators, the fifty-telephone switchboard and the new five-kilowatt Marconi station. Most important, they knew *Titanic*'s physical blueprint: they knew her steam boilers and coal furnaces, her triple-screw turbine engines, double-bottomed hull and three propellers—they knew *Titanic*'s heart.... They knew everything.

The guarantee staff had been sent along on this first voyage to explain, wherever needed, how something should be done, to fix anything faulty or loose or stubborn, however insignificant. They were there to show, to solve, to soothe *Titanic*'s first crew, these men who knew her best. And they were to file reports when *Titanic* finished this first run, and grade their prize on her performance.

With Captain Smith and the builders' staff were those ship's officers not currently on duty, and the two owners' representatives, Messrs. Bruce Ismay of White Star and Bayard Lockholm of IMM. The captain was conducting an inspection tour, and giving the two owners, E.J. hoped, reason to rejoice in their new liner.

Captain Smith demonstrated, from the bridge, how the fail-safe emergency system worked: alarm bells for ten seconds and then, automatically, the safety doors, fifty in all, descended between sections of *Titanic*'s bowels and sealed off each of the sixteen boiler rooms. These doors, called bulkheads, made each boiler room separate and watertight from the others. So no matter the destruction from collision and subsequent flooding to any powering part or sections, the other boiler rooms would be safe, and *Titanic*, after any injury—however unlikely any calamity was—would have fifteen-sixteenths of her power, or seven-eighths, or some such significant fraction. Built to be thus self-sufficient, *Titanic*, if she had to, could steam around the world on only a half, even *a third* of her available power.

"Or the doors can be worked manually, individually, you see, sirs," explained one of the builders' men, "by any member of the crew as needs to. Or if occasion arises and no man sets them off, they'll work by themselves, automatically."

"How's that?" asked Bay Lockholm, wanting to understand exactly.

"Water on the floor, sir, of any compartment will cause a float to rise that connects to the setting-off device. When the water gets high enough—boom!— the door slams down." The man was proud of *Titanic*'s "waterproofing"; his smile showed that, and the way he rocked his shoulders.

"So you see," said Captain Smith, proud himself, though not displaying it, "it would be impossible for this ship to be sunk by any collision whatsoever. A great feat of engineering, gentlemen," he said to the builders' men. And to a man, they nodded, self-satisfied.

"She is a jewel who will never be bettered," said the swaggering one. "Never in a hundred years."

Bayard Lockholm, of a long line of shipping men, questioned the bulkheads amidships. While at bow end and stern the doors rose five decks from the double-bottomed hull—another safety protection—between boiler rooms six and five and four, the watertight walls extended only four decks high and did not reach all the way to the ceiling.

"Aye, yes," said the one from Harland & Wolff who was acting as spokesperson. "But they reach, sirs, as high as need be. Far above the water line, and very high indeed. Higher than she'd ever need and more. We guarantee it."

The others from Harland & Wolff nodded agreement. "Nothing can sink this ship, Mr. Lockholm," said a younger member of the guarantee men. "Not even God Himself could sink *Titanic*."

"Oh, don't say that," said Bay, repressing a tremor. "That's really tempting the Fates."

"Throwing down a challenge?" said the spokesman, and he smiled and flexed his shoulders, complacent.

"Something close to that," said Bay, and wondered why, again, a shiver ghosted up his spine.

"Laughing in the face of God you are," said Bruce Ismay primly, his first words since the group had begun its inspection.

"Don't fear, gentlemen," said the guarantee man. "*Titanic* will outlive us all. She's perfectly made."

"Wonderful she is," Bay agreed, but he was not as confident as the builders' men about those bulkhead doors....

However, his job was to get to know Bruce Ismay, to find out what manner of man he was. So far Bay had found Ismay formal, perfectly courteous and aloof. "Will you join my wife and me for a drink and luncheon?" he invited the manager of White Star

Line. "Audrey hasn't properly met you yet, and she's been looking forward to it."

Bruce Ismay had all the aristocratic bearing of his class and little of its charm. His eyes were hooded with suspicion and constant appraisal; his personality was stiff and humorless. He bowed in acknowledgment of Bayard Lockholm's invitation. "Thank you, sir, I accept," he said, and ran a finger over his thin mustache. "Mrs. Lockholm is a very beautiful woman. I am honored."

"Captain Smith, will you join us?" said Bay, and sensed, as he did, Bruce Ismay stiffen as though in silent disapproval. But surely, Bay thought, a captain on a ship at sea is of the highest ranking. Surely the captain is *good enough* for Mr. Ismay's company.

"Excellent, that's just the thing," said Captain Smith easily, "for I've already invited your wife, Mr. Lockholm, to join her friend, Mrs. Peerce, at my table. So what say I join you in about fifteen minutes?" Captain Smith gestured to the entourage around him. "I've a bit more inspecting yet to do— do the whole ship every day, that's the way to avoid problems—and then I'll be along. You're welcome, of course, to tramp along with us, go around below decks, inspect those bulkheads for yourself, Mr. Lockholm."

Bay looked at Ismay, since he had just invited the man for a drink. "Would you be interested, sir?"

Bruce Ismay nodded. "I should be most pleased," he said, and passed his hands over his thinning light brown hair to keep all strands in place.

So Bay followed in the wake of Captain Smith and Bruce Ismay, and thrust his thoughts of White Star's manager to the back of his mind.

The elevator going down to the bowels stopped on D deck, opened its door to two stewards waiting there. When they saw that the cab was occupied by their superiors, the young men stepped back, happy to wave it on. But in the pause, looking out, Bay saw his wife.... She stood there on D deck, where she did not belong, talking to a dreary woman with bent back and loose, dark dress.

Bay lifted a hand; he was going to cry out, but he was hemmed in behind Captain Smith and the talkative man from Harland & Wolff. Audrey was facing the elevator, Bay saw her clearly, though her face was bleak and slack as he had never seen it in all their time together.

Gilt-haired, slight-figured, unconsciously elegant in a morning gown of soft dull red, his ever bride was clasping her hands together tightly at her waist. The other woman, of swarthy skin and, Bay thought, a certain menacing demeanor, was holding a long white envelope, was sliding the envelope into the folds of her own dark bodice. And Audrey, his Audrey, was staring intently and talking sharply, and was, oh, so deathly pale....

What in the world? he thought.

As the elevator door began to slide shut, the old woman abruptly turned in his direction as though she had felt, in the air, his startled eyes upon her.

He did not know her. She was an ugly woman, a hag with one white, useless eye and one that was cold and black and farseeing. Long-reaching, that one eye caught Bay just as the elevator door closed him off. But the eye saw and *recognized* and *pierced*, and in that instant Bay Lockholm saw, too, and was afraid.

IT WAS NOON when Swan opened her eyes to her first day as a woman.

She stretched, lithe in her bed, and thought about the soreness between her legs and wondered if her face was changed. If so, she would only be more beautiful, as her mother was increasingly more beautiful, loved by a man, and as Tory VanVoorst was, and Nicola Lady Pomeroy. Though Nicola, Swan thought, was possibly less lovely of late, now she was a widow. Swan wasn't sure; she did not know Lady Pomeroy so well.

The sensation of love had not been celestial, as she had hoped. It had been exciting, oh yes, but...uncomfortable. Danny had liked it. He had been overcome by his passion; he had sworn he would love her forever. She hoped so. That was pleasing....

Making love must be like anything else, she thought. It was like learning how to dance or how to sail; it got easier and better the more practiced one became. Muscles got used to the stretching, and the mind knew, in time, what to expect. The body relaxed, the senses fired...one began to enjoy.... That must be the way it was, for love, *true love*, was always built on passion, and not the other way around. And then families were made, children were born, and fortunes passed along, all in the name of love.

Some men ruined themselves forever, in thrall to a bad woman. Bad, because she would know the arts of love too well to be resisted. Bad, because she would give her body in the act of love, but not her heart. A woman who knew many men intimately was bad, and it was wrong, too, to profit from love outside of marriage.

I would rather be bad, thought Swan, than to be unfortunate, to be a woman like some who, in the name of love, let men beat them, abuse them, ignore them. After all, Napoléon made his harlot, Josephine, an empress, and Henry VIII, several times, *murdered* a good woman he no longer loved so he could wed a bad one he did....

I would rather be Josephine than a woman like Mrs. Twigg, Swan thought. I would rather be Josephine than be like my mother who, happy as she is, has known only Father's love, and is content.

Swan was glad she was finished with inexperience, which only got in the way. She wanted to know what she was doing—and what she had to do—to catch any man who tempted her and to hold any she wanted to keep. That was the way to happiness. Like a man, you sampled...and then you chose.

Swan stretched again, suddenly smug. She was finding the art of the femme fatale easy to master. I'm talented, she thought, and Smoke isn't. It's as simple as that. Smoke wants to be a man—I'm more clever. I want to love like one. I shall have it both ways then, a woman's pleasures and advantages in life, and a man's experiences. That's the best....

Stupid ol' Smoke, cutting off her hair. Where was she, anyway? Swan wanted to tell all about last night, wanted to tell about *doing it*, and what Danny said after, and the night breeze and the shadows.... Really make Smoke jealous! Where was the *virgin*...? She was probably running around bothering the ship's staff, getting herself chased off instead of being chased.

And Swan swung out of bed, flung off her nightie, and skipped, carefree, into the stateroom shower.

The twin she sought was up on boat deck in a lounge chair, immersed in a novel of adventure. Smoke was wearing a white day dress trimmed in navy blue like a sailor's uniform, and she looked boyish, with her hair curling now above her shoulders instead of falling, almost waist long, down her back.

Mrs. Twigg was beside her, talking to Lady Lucile Duff-Gordon, called Lady Lucy, whose sister, Eleanor Glyn, had written a scandalous and disreputable novel, *Three Weeks*. Lady Lucy, for all her title, was not, in Mrs. Twigg's opinion, quite respectable, either, but she was a good gossip, and in lieu of "better" company, Mrs. Twigg was happy to sit with Lady Lucy and chat. Mrs. Twigg had asked Smoke to stay close to her today and to try to stay out of trouble, and Smoke had shrugged and said all right, as submissive as Mary's little lamb. Heartbroken, probably, thought Mrs. Twigg, now she realizes what she's done to herself, *shorn* like that.

And there they were, happily ensconced on boat deck, with only the ocean to see in every direction, while little Swan, thought Mrs. Twigg, slept sweetly in her cabin. This was the way the whole voyage should be, she thought, ordered and lazy and quiet, with good food at table and a little entertainment at night to tickle—but not overexcite—the senses. And then a wee nightcap and a good night's sleep, and another day much like the one before, with only a different frock to mark the passage of the days.

"It was I, you know, who coined the word *chic* for a fashionable woman," Lady Lucy was saying, "and it has taken root wonderfully well. Cosmo, that's my dear husband, heard before we set sail that the French Academy is officially adding my term to the language. And that's such an honor, don't you think, Mrs. Twigg?''

Lady Lucy was middle-aged and looked it, but she dieted strenuously and corseted herself tightly and wore beautiful clothes. Young, she had been a beauty, and beauty clung to her still, though her nervousness and aggressive mannerisms were what one noticed first. Were, at least, what Mrs. Twigg had noticed first. But to have a word accepted by the French Academy—

''That is high honor, indeed, Lady Lucy,'' said Mrs. Twigg. ''I'm quite overwhelmed.''

''So was I,'' said the lady, ''though in all modesty I must say I deserve it. I also have my own clothes design business, did you know that? I've just split the skirt.''

''I did not,'' said Mrs. Twigg. ''I congratulate you. But to *split* a skirt, madam, surely there's no need for that—''

''Ah, Thelma, if I may call you that, you are of the old school, I see. Well, let me assure you, even as we cross the ocean on this marvelous new vessel, the world is readying itself for revolution.''

''Revolution?'' said Mrs. Twigg. ''You shock me.'' And she glanced over at Smoke to see if the girl was listening, but Smoke was immersed in her adventure story, a novel of sea catastrophe by a Morgan Robertson, called *Futility*.

''Revolution,'' said Lady Lucile, ''is not too strong a word. We women will soon have the vote, you know, in America at least, as they do now in Finland—pathetically *only* in Finland. In England all royalty and the parliament stands against it, to their shame. But once we females are released from the bondage of disenfranchisement, everyone will be wearing my split skirts. Even you, Thelma Twigg.''

"Oh, I hardly think so. Forgive me for saying so, but it sounds...rather indecent.'' And Mrs. Twigg smoothed her long skirts over both knees to emphasize her point.

"Pother,'' said Lady Lucy. "It's just an aid for walking. Paul Poiret will not keep women forever in the hobble skirt, mark my words. And if my designs for the modern woman happen also to please men, well—'' and Lady Lucy winked and patted Mrs. Twigg's covered knees. "Well, as I say...revolution.''

Smoke stood and set down her book. "It's gone one o'clock, Twiggs. I'm going to get Swan out of bed. Shall we meet in the café to eat? I didn't have breakfast.''

Mrs. Twigg was torn. She wanted to ask Lucile Duff-Gordon about Hollywood, but had not, for fear of overinteresting Smoke. And she meant to keep the discipline on the Lockholm twins, now she had it. "Promise you won't be long, dear,'' she said. "Fifteen minutes at latest.''

Smoke scratched at her elbow. "This book is extraordinary, Twiggs,'' she said. "It was written years ago, ten years ago at least, and it's about us, about the *Titanic*. Only it's called *The Titan*. It predicts disaster for us, Twiggs. According to Mr. Robertson we're about to hit an iceberg.''

"Stuff and nonsense,'' said Mrs. Twigg. "We're as safe as houses. Really, the novelists of today—'' But then she remembered about Lady Lucile's sister, and did not finish her uncomplimentary thought.

"Well, it's awfully exciting," said Smoke. "I can't put it down." And she tucked the thick book under her arm and strolled away.

"Now there's a chic girl," said Lady Lucy. "How daring—and how fetching—chopping her hair that way."

Mrs. Twigg reclined her head on the lounge rest and closed her eyes. "You can't mean it, Lady Lucy," she said. "The poor child has ruined her looks for two years, the two most important years of her life. They're twins, you see, and so pretty, and now one will be a wallflower and the other will be a belle, and they will both be injured, Swan feeling guilty for her popularity, Smoke resenting Swan's beaux—they'll be debbies next year, or, at least, are supposed to 'come out' then. I was so looking forward to it, but now I just want to cry."

"Darling," said Lady Lucy, "that girl is a stunner. She'll dance every dance. Why, I saw her yesterday and liked her, but thought her too comme il faut to be interesting. But now...why, she'll be a sensation. She's got character now, and mystery.... There'll be dancing tonight. Turn her loose if you don't believe me, and just sit back and watch."

"You continue to amaze me," said Mrs. Twigg, truly overcome at the thought of anyone finding Smoke Lockholm attractive with her hair like that.

"Live and learn," said Lady Lucy breezily, used to shocking conventional women like Mrs. Twigg. "Oh look, there's Cosmo. Catch you later, dear." And Lucile Duff-Gordon rose to intercept a tall, gangly gentleman in immaculate morning dress who, nevertheless, staggered as he came and reeked of whiskey as he passed.

Travel *is* broadening, as they say, thought Mrs. Twigg, watching the famous couple depart. So many different ideas one hears, so many different *kinds* of people.... Lady Lucy was obviously no lady at all. She was an adventuress and one of those "liberationists," who fight for the rights of women. Still, under it all, like most of us born common who get "up," under it all, Lady Lucy is a snob.... A little grilled sole would do me well right now, I think, and duchess potatoes, very hot. A little more of the duchess potatoes, please waiter, she rehearsed her line, to settle my dyspepsia....

SMOKE AND SWAN SAT in a far corner of the reading room on A deck, their heads close. For the first time, without being mad at her twin, Swan had chosen a different frock than Smoke had. Swan wore pale amethyst with milk-white collar and hem and cuffs, and Smoke sat still in her sailor's dress. Still, sitting together as they were, their hands folded one upon the other, the one whispering, the other listening big-eyed and intent, still they looked each other's reflection. Even with one whose hair was plaited in a single braid straight behind while the other's was short and crooked and a crown of curls, even so, at this moment, they were identical. There was the same tender line of cheek, the same lilt to the chin, and the same trembly fine needy mouth. There were the same dropped eyelids and the same soft lashes shadowing vivid blue-green eyes. To choose either would have been to choose the same, at least outwardly.

But when the one finished talking and the two young women stood, even though they joined hands to exit the room and walk together, there was a difference in them. A new and permanent difference. It showed in the way they held themselves, it showed in their eyes. It was a difference that would always mark them now, would never reconcile, so long as they both should live....

No one would ever mistake Smoke Wysong Lockholm for Swan Josephine, or vice versa, ever again.

DURING LUNCHEON, Captain Smith and Dove Peerce were almost lost to the others, rapt in each other's company.

The captain's table, instead of being isolated and grand, sat in the midst of others just like it, to the fore of the main dining salon just beyond the grand entrance. It held only eight, an informality E.J. had begun long ago in his young skipper days. But for E.J., today, his table held only himself and the beautiful American who, last night, had smelled of English heather when he held her close in the dance, and who had leaned her fine head upon his sturdy dark blue shoulder and whispered, with breath that warmed and teased, an intimate invitation.

Ah, women; he did admire them, their delicate bodies, their pretty, pretty ways. And this woman he could love, if she would let him. Last night she had let him think he *might*....

So Captain Smith sat oblivious to the tensions at his table. His own troubles were light. The ship was perfection, running as smooth as a train. And everyone, even Archie Butt, adviser and closest friend of America's president, Mr. Taft, had remarked on *Titanic*'s firmness and lack of vibration. The weather was fine, the sea was easy under steady winds.... And the woman of his dreams had materialized at his side, as smitten as he was, for she had accepted his after-luncheon invitation to view his captain's quarters.

Champagne was waiting there, icing in a bucket. His man, Mr. Layton, had laid on fresh sheets. The captain wouldn't be missed for an hour or so…and if an emergency should warrant his attention, perhaps the lady would wait for him, a naked angel in his bed.

E.J. ate robustly and dreamed his pirate's dream.

Others at the midday meal were less sublimely satisfied. Bruce Ismay talked interminably about *Titanic*'s operating expenses. There was too much waste of space, he said; the walking areas were too generous on *Titanic*'s decks and the staterooms were excessively large. "We could have added a third more rooms, Mr. Lockholm," he remarked, "if we had cut down a fifth of the public space. I tried to get that done in blueprint, but was not listened to. Still, it could be done yet, in renovation. What do you say?"

And then, not waiting for an answer, he went on to criticize the kitchen. "We offer too many fragile foodstuffs, sir, in my opinion," he said. "The refrigeration we need to keep the fish and creams unspoiled pulls so much electricity it would make your hair stand on end to know how much. And the freezing compartments are as heavy as whales. Why, think, man, what it costs to pull that extra weight across an ocean."

"I hadn't thought," said Bay, genially. "I tend to think first safety, then comfort and pleasure, and mark it up enough to make fair profit.… Do you have the cost figures, Mr. Ismay?"

"I'll get them for you," the Englishman said.

"We can save on things that don't show, you see—the things no one worries about. Like the lifeboats. Sixteen is too many. I doubt we need six. The builders—think of it!—had wanted twice that amount. But of course the law says we do not have to carry emergency seating for every soul on board, God forbid, so they were not listened to on that. One life jacket per person is adequate protection on such a ship as this.... What do you say, Mrs. Lockholm?"

Ismay turned to his right where Audrey sat tremulously beside him, sat tremulously because *Bay had seen her with Madame Romany*, and was waiting for an explanation.

The old woman had seen Bay with the captain, recognized him in the elevator when it paused and opened its door on D deck. She had said to Audrey, "Now you're done. You and 'im, dearie—he's seen us sure. He'll be wantin' to know why you handed over ten thousand dollars to a peasant in third, won't he now? And what'll you say? Will you lie, pretty lady, or will you tell the truth...and damn 'im to Davy Jones?"

Audrey had paled, but answered back. "You can see into the future, Madame Romany, so you tell me."

But Audrey's mind had raced to black conclusions. Bay wouldn't give her the money if he knew. He would wire his bank and stop the check. He would laugh at her, dismiss the gypsy's doomsaying, and take Audrey in his arms. "You leave the future and the money to me, my love," Bay would say, his mouth against her mouth. "We have put the curse of Phineas Brown behind us, long ago. We'll speak of this no more."

And Audrey would not be able to make him see—

Sly, the old woman watched Audrey's face and read the fear.... "Do not tell him," the gypsy said. "You'll lose 'im if you do. I'll let him *ice fall, ice fall* to a bottomless, watery grave...." And her one long-seeing eye held Audrey's like a predatory bird's.

"Know this," Audrey had responded to the threat, her eyes snapping, her mouth pulled tight. "If my husband dies, *Esmeralda Diego*, I will kill you myself, with my own hands. I swear it. I will find you and I will drown you, and I will laugh as you sink."

"Pretty words from a pretty lady," Madame Romany had murmured. But she had retreated a step, and her stare broke, and she blinked.

"I expect to die out here," she said, "but not by your hand, gentle lady. So do not tell, t'will do no good, and let happen what will. Let your husband live to step whole on yonder shore, and let my daughter Daphne have her chance at life. Ten thousand dollars is little to you, but I have sold my soul for it."

"You have your money, take it and go," said Audrey, "and never see me more. Whatever happens, contact me never, or I will have you jailed."

Madame Romany extended her hand. "We will shake on it, and it is done."

Audrey had clasped the old hand with her own, felt its heat and the strength of its grip. "Goodbye," said Audrey.

"Good luck," said the prophetess. "I will pray for you."

Audrey had swept away, and not looked back. She had run away, to Bay....

But in their suite, she and Bay had had no time to talk. He asked her to meet him back in their rooms after luncheon. His book of checks lay on the bureau, open to the place where the check she had written had been torn out.

What would she say when Bay asked her *why*?

And now the English ship owner had asked her opinion of *something*, and she must not embarrass Bay—

"Please, sir, ask me again," she said to Mr. Ismay.

"Safety, Mrs. Lockholm," repeated Bruce Ismay, flicking his fingernail against the stem of his wineglass. "Do you think it should be required that an ocean liner as superb as this carry *lifeboats* at considerable expense to its owners? Or do you think a life jacket a person would be enough?"

As he waited for her answer, he cut himself another piece of fish.

Audrey glanced at Bay, but he was only smiling at her, she could read nothing in his eyes. And the others who shared the table were looking at her, too, smiling expectantly as though they hoped she shared their view in such matters.

"I am braver than most on water, Mr. Ismay," she said, "as I am a good swimmer and fisherman, and I know how to sail. And all my life I have loved the ocean, having been born and raised in Newport, Rhode Island, which is—or was—an international harbor and port. But to know the sea is to know she is capricious and mighty.... I would always choose safety over cost, and I urge you—and my dear husband—to do the same."

"Well said, Mrs. Lockholm," said Bruce Ismay, and he lifted his glass to her. The men of the guarantee staff followed suit. "Well said...and yet, as a businessman I am not persuaded."

"It is his pocketbook, you see," said one of the shipbuilders' men.

"But my skin," said Audrey.

Everyone laughed, even Bruce Ismay, and the meal concluded. Captain Smith excused himself and Dove, the men of Harland & Wolff bowed themselves away. Mr. Ismay mumbled that he always napped after luncheon and asked Audrey to save him a dance, if she would, in the lounge after dinner when the orchestra played.

And Bay took her hand and guided her toward their stateroom.

"All right, I will tell you," she said, even before he asked, even as he led her. "You must indulge me in this, Bay, it means so much to me, you see...."

But as they turned the corner of the corridor to their rooms, they were stopped by Burty lurching out of his room.

Burty was dressed, inappropriately, in evening cutaway; from the rumpled look of him, he was still in last night's clothes. His shirttails were out of his trousers and his collar was gone. His suspenders swung from his waist. He was shoeless, in black silk socks, and unshaven. His hair was disheveled, his eyes were bloodshot. He was loaded down with two valises, one in each hand, and he was pushing a third with his knees.

Bay, walking ahead, hastened to their friend's side.

"Something's unsatisfactory with the suite," said Bay, and he lifted the third suitcase. "I'll carry this for you till we get a steward."

"Goddamn stewards, goddamn wives, goddamn

every goddamn thing—except you, Bay, you're all right." Burty was sober, but he staggered as though overloaded, or perhaps worn out from a sleepless night.

Audrey did not understand what was happening, but she thought, *It's starting. Whatever it was Madame Romany saw, it's starting and I can't stop it—* "Oh, Burty," she said, "what's the matter, please tell me."

And so desperate and terrified was her voice that both men paused and looked at her.

"It doesn't concern you, Audrey," said Burty, and he gestured to his and Tory's door. "Ask *her* if you want to know.... Thanks, Bay, this way." And he hoisted his suitcases and squeezed past Audrey and bumped along the corridor.

Bay lifted the third valise. "Wait for me, Aud," he said, and blew her a kiss as he followed his friend.

Audrey let herself into their room, crossed the sitting room the two bedrooms were meant to share. She knocked on the door of Tory and Burty's bedroom. "Tor? Are you in there...? Can I come in?"

There was no response.

Audrey thought, as Burty had indicated, that Tory was inside. But if her friend did not choose, right now, to respond, Audrey understood. Sometimes a person wanted to be alone, wanted to sleep or think...or simply wanted to cry and have no audience.

She went out onto the little deck, sat in a chaise longue there, astonished and frightened.... And waited.

10

The room was a mess. Burty had thrown open the drawers, thrown his things and hers around, packing in a dreadful silence. There had been no tender words from him, no attempt at understanding, no regret expressed. There had not been, even, disbelief. Told— *sold*—by Teddy Royce, he had accepted it as *truth*; he had not come to her for explanation. No, there had been only snarls of hate and hurt from Burton Kingsley VanVoorst...and then, at the end, the pitiful end, there had been only his indifference.

She could not bear it. She would not bear it.... The pills bounced, joyful, in her hand. She'd show him. She'd make him sorry yet....

Would they bury her at sea, wrapped in black to match her blood? Would the orchestra play Louisiana blues?

From the bed she watched him pack, her knees drawn close to her swollen stomach, her raven hair loose and swinging formlessly around her face.... Raw gold, she used to call her complexion. Unconsciously she rubbed at her arms, her legs, trying to get the color out, while Burty said with a flat voice that he was leaving now, moving to another room. He would see his lawyers in New York; she could see hers.... He would provide for her, provide for the child; she didn't have to worry where her next meal was coming from, he said.

And then he'd gone, just gone, half packed, ill packed, undressed. He'd gone with no goodbye, no "go to hell," no one last kiss for old times' sake.... With nothing. He'd just gone, rolling his eyes, avoiding her with his eyes, and shuddering.

Oh God in heaven. The heart breaks but goes on beating. How can it go on beating?

There was the door, closed between them: she inside, dying; he, somewhere out there, suffering but going on. Scarred, she hoped.

Please let him be scarred a little.

But he would live, go on, find *another*.... She wouldn't. How could she? He was all her life, always had been since they met. Silly of her not to realize that till now. Silly to have thought, as she used to think, that she could live very well without him, that she did not love him, plain, plump Burty who worshipped at her feet....

Used to.

Ah, but she had known she loved him. She'd known, but had wanted him not to. For that way lay dependence and vulnerability...her happiness in his hands. No, she had preferred him to think that she was the centerpiece of his existence, not the other way around.

Ah, she thought. Even beautiful women lose. All of us, *the womenfolk*, we lose in the end.

She should be happy she'd had what she'd had, as long as it lasted. Lucky her. She'd had no right to him in the first place, had pickaninny Alma June; no right to bright white Burton VanVoorst. She had dared, though, and got him, little raw-gold girl who thought she was so fine.... Little gutter girl; she'd climbed high. Oh, it had taken deceit and guile— love always did, don't kid yourself—and it had taken thinking herself smart enough and *brave* enough; it had taken thinking that if she ran far enough and pretended *hard enough*, she could make the lie come true.

Yes, she had lied. Who didn't who'd come from where she had? Name one.

And yes, truth to tell, back when she met Burty, she would have married any man—any white man— who had had a bit of money and who would have loved her for a lifetime. It just happened to be Burty, and he just happened to have a whole lot more than most. The little nigger from the bayou had got lucky, got much more than she deserved, got much more than she'd hoped.... Who she'd got had been Prince Charming, and he had made her life a dream.

But—to be fair to herself—she had tried in her turn, *oh, how she'd tried*, to be his dream girl, to be his Snow White. And she'd succeeded. Burty was a happy man until—

Damn Rolls Royce.

Though...she was the evil one in this, not Rolls, not Burty. She was the fraud. She had married her prince under false pretenses and tried to keep them up. Had kept them up for a long, long time: so good for her. She had paid large sums of *his* money to keep her secret, to have birth records changed, her name changed, and support for a fictitious past created. But she had never tried, in the best of times, to come clean and tell him true.

Perhaps if she had...

Perhaps if she had lain upon his chest one night after she had pleased him, after he was sated and drowsy and still damp from love; perhaps if she had begun to weep, then, under his arm and told him she had something shameful to reveal...

Perhaps he would have said, as he so often had said, "Whatever it is you've done, dear Tor, I forgive you. You just get it off your chest, tell Daddy, and then we'll forget all about it. All right now...."

If she had let him coax it out of her then, while he comforted her, while he kissed her and petted her and promised her yet another gemstone bracelet and made them both another drink... Perhaps he would have—yes—been mad...yes, been *aggrieved*...but his heart would have been open and his love would have been flowing....

He *might* have forgiven her then.

And then he would have helped her shield her secret from the world. He would have understood—she would have *told* him everything: why she'd lied about not being able to have a child; why she'd had to lie about the little twist of chocolate blood that didn't show. He would have understood why she worked so hard to keep herself physically perfect—afraid of being *rejected*, Burtykins, don't you see?—afraid she was not good enough, not *white*.... He would have understood, and he would have forgiven *everything*....

Why, he might even have said the words she'd always dreamed him saying.... "As you are, whatever you are, and as you will be, Tory June, you're

mine, all mine, and I'm yours and I love you, forever
and ever and around again…. Now blow your nose,
sweetest, and give dear ol' Burty a kiss. There, that's
better. That's my baby.''

Oh, he might have said those precious words she
had rehearsed for years in her heart. He might have,
if she had owned up.

But she had not been brave enough. She had been
too afraid; she'd had too much to lose. For what if
he *hadn't* forgiven? What if he'd acted the way he
was acting now? There would have been so much to
account for, so much to explain…. She had been
right to lie. Hard as it was to pretend, it was easier…and so much safer.

Except, of course, it wasn't safer. Wasn't better.
It was fatal. Of course, she knew now.

Now he'd found out from someone else. He would
never forgive and forget and love her again. Now he
had *bought* her secret for fifty thousand dollars and
then won the money back at cards, and so had found
her out *free*….

It broke her heart—*crack*—in two….

He had called her "nigger cunt." He who used to
call her "Madonna" and "heaven-sent" and "Victoria the Great." She put her palms upon her private
place and closed her eyes. Nigger cunt, who used to
be a queen.

How could long-ago forebearers count for so
much? Why don't my white ancestors mean as much
or more? So what if I have a little *black blood*?
We're all red where we bleed. And what makes your
white blood, white skin, Burty, better than mine, *pale
gold*?

And what makes me worth less today than yesterday? Just yesterday I set the stars in the heavens as far as you were concerned.

Ah, ah....

Tory pushed back the shutter to the little deck and stepped out to see the world one last time. It was a beautiful afternoon. The sea was blue glass, the sun spangled the surface, and lace-edged waves rolled undisturbed for miles. Solid as a planet fixed in its course and as imperturbable, *Titanic* steered through the lovely, silent blue. Around and high behind, a parade of gulls, white, wide winged, followed *Titanic* like escorts sent by the god of the sea. Rough-voiced, they called and glided and dipped and soared.

Why is it, Tory wondered, that birds of the sea have no pretty songs to sing, no sweet-tongued voice? Not a one can match the music of the simplest sparrow.

She uncapped the thin bottle, spilled fat, round pills into her hand. Pale yellow they were, as she was. *No good*, as she was.

Poison, as she was.

Fatal, if taken to heart.

Tory raised the first of six pills to her lips...and saw, not far, Audrey Lockholm staring at her, speechless, petrified.

Audrey stood, watching, her eyes huge with fear and indecision. She was holding both hands over her mouth, and tears, *tears for Tory*, were streaming down her cheeks.

Tory paused, surprised, not understanding how Audrey could be there before her, suddenly materialized. And in the pausing, Audrey cried and leaped. As in a daze, Tory lifted the pill to her mouth. Audrey ran at Tory, knocked her to the floor, stuck fingers into Tory's mouth, pulled out the pill. She tossed *whatever it was* over the deck side and began shaking Tory's shoulders. Audrey screamed and screamed. And Tory, shocked back to reason as something deep, deep down loosed and broke...Tory was screaming, too.

And then they were laughing and crying together, and Tory, not thinking, dropped the other five into a pocket of her gown, along with the pale thin bottle. The two women rolled together in a flurry of petticoats and silk. They rolled like children, laughing while tears spattered their bodices and ruined the luster of their complexions.

Finally, breathless, out of tears, Audrey held Tory's hands and said, "I don't care what you've done, you silly, *I* forgive you!"

"I haven't done anything," Tory said, and they collapsed against each other again in hysterical laughter.

"Oh!" said Audrey when she could, holding a stitch in her side. "Well, all right then, what's the fuss?"

And they laughed some more, triumphant in friendship.

Tory snuffled, found a handkerchief and blew her nose. "He found out, Aud. He found out about me, what I really am."

Audrey sat on the floor of the deck in her dress of soft dull red, and leaned on her hands. "What you really are is wonderful," she said, and tossed her lemon hair.

"What I really am is a mixed breed, Audrey. I'm not really Spanish, I'm...I'm..."

But Tory couldn't get it out. She'd never voiced

it, never spoken the word *Negro* regarding herself. She wiped her eyes and dried her cheeks with her hands. "I'm...I'm..."

"Shh," said Audrey, and lifted Tory's hair and twisted it into a giant curl at the nape of Tory's neck. "I don't care if you're Creole, if that's what you're trying to say. I don't give a fig if you're Eskimo or Mongolian or anything, and neither does Burty. Nobody cares, not really, don't you see? Remember when I was just beginning with Bay and didn't know what to do, and you helped me? I'd love to help you now, if you'll let me. I'd love to be able to prove that none of us, darling, cares. Not one."

Tory sighed a long sigh. She thought her sigh would never end. She hoped it wouldn't, because with the sigh so much was leaving—years and years of fear and pain and suspicion. She was getting pounds lighter just sitting on the floor of the little deck and sighing, and feeling...feeling the weight of a lifetime lift. Gull-like, the weight glided up, cawed harshly and flew away, taken by the wind....

"Creole," Tory said, and squeezed Audrey's hand. "What a pretty way to put it."

"What do you say we have a drink?" said Audrey. "Champagne, just us two, right now, in the middle of the afternoon. We'll have a snootful. We'll celebrate ourselves."

Tory reddened. Her eyes swam, anew, in tears. Her mouth was cotton and she couldn't speak. But she nodded and swiped at her runny nose.

"Done," said Audrey.

She got off the floor and shook out her dress and went to the telephone in Tory's room. She ordered a magnum of champagne, very cold, and two glasses.

She saw where Burty had ransacked the drawers. She saw he'd left his hairbrushes and a leather-framed picture of Tory's face. He'd left a pair of black shoes and his new lamb-collared overcoat. He's left his heart behind, too, thought Audrey, even if he doesn't know it. Men are strange creatures. Like women they run on emotion. Unlike women, they deny it.

When Bay came back to the suite, he found his wife and Tory out on the deck, sitting on the floor. They were drinking champagne, and Audrey was combing her friend's dark hair.

"I can't come to you now, Bay," said Audrey. "Tory needs me now, you see."

"Yes," said Bay Lockholm. "Burty told me about it. He's moved in with Bruce Ismay. He's very upset."

"Silly Burty," said Audrey.

"Yes," said Bay. "I told him that."

He left the women together and went up, by himself, to *Titanic*'s highest deck and watched the sun sink into endless ocean.

THE TROUBLE with getting quietly drunk, Burty thought, was that the drunker one got, the less quiet one wanted to be. It had been all right, chasing Bruce Ismay out of the sitting room after the man had offered the bedroom in his suite to him and Burty had accepted. That had been just fine. Bruce Ismay was a prude, and like most prudes, was much too interested in the sins of other people.

Burty understood men like Ismay. They were cautious men, frightened men who tried to preserve, not expand. They hoped *not to lose*, they did not *try to win*. They were yesterday's men; men who clung to traditions, to "the conventions," as common men clung to their guns, for protection. Bruce Ismay and his ilk needed *protection* from men such as Burton Kingsley VanVoorst, who were *better* men, men who could make it on their own, men who did not need to be shored up by family money and family connections. Ismay was afraid of Burty, *as well he ought to be,* Burty thought. I can buy you and sell you, Ismay, if you were worth buying, which you ain't.

Men like Ismay kept men like Burty out of their clubs for a while, marshaled "combines" against them, tried, by ignoring them, to make them go away. But the VanVoorst kind of man did not go away; he ate you up and ground you down and spit you out. And men like Ismay either joined what they could not beat, like *good little boys*, or got out of the way: they stepped back, or they got rolled over.

So Burty VanVoorst didn't give a damn for Ismay's hospitality. Ismay would shine his boots, too, if he was asked. Ismay's honored to share his suite with me, thought Burty. He wants in, he wants to be friends.

Ha.

"I knew a chap this happened to," said Ismay to Burty, after the purser, smiling, thankfully, had deposited the bedraggled and slightly pugnacious Burton VanVoorst in bedroom B-56 of Bruce Ismay's suite. "He went all to pieces for a bit. But he met a lovely woman and straightened right up. They've been married now for years—grown children. He forgot all about the other one."

Burty found a cigar in his jacket pocket. "Do you mind?" he asked, rolling the shaft of tobacco in his hand to loosen it.

Bruce Ismay was wearing a fawn-skin smoking jacket over eggshell-light trousers and a red ascot. A smoking jacket, thought Burty, though he didn't smoke.

"Go ahead," he said to Burty. "You need it."

Sure don't need you, thought Burty. Aloud, he said, "What did you say happened to this chap?" Chap, Lord Almighty.

"Met another woman within a month, a proper woman, and turned out right as rain." Ismay's feet were sockless, clad in velvet slippers with fox heads on the toes. Ismay was sitting in a damask armchair, legs crossed, swinging one foot.... A fox head with red-glass eyes. Probably garnet, thought Burty. First it's garnets on your feet, then it's diamonds in your ears.

"Chap's first wife wasn't proper?"

Burty was going to punch Bruce Ismay in the nose, then beat him with his fox-head slippers. Pansy's what he is, Burty thought, for all his wife and children....

"Oh, my dear sir," said Mr. Ismay, "I didn't mean to imply..." He left his sentence unfinished, but Burty waited in belligerent silence for the rest of it. "I say, I am sorry," Mr. Ismay said.

"Nigger," said Burty. "My wife has colored blood. Did you hear? Becomes her, though, don't it?" His glass was full of whiskey, his mouth was full of smoke. He exhaled a cloud of fumes and warmed his lungs with Bailey's Best.

Ismay was uncomfortable. Burty liked that. He liked to watch worms squirm. He'll run soon, Burty thought. Another minute or two and he'll run like a hare.

"In your country," said Bruce Ismay finally, "race has the same social problems that class has in mine. We don't mind color so much in England, but an improper background..." He shrugged—trying to be buddy-buddy, thought Burty—and did not complete his sentence again.

"You'd marry a nigger in England?" persisted Burty, enjoying this. He licked the rim of his glass with a fat tongue then drank off the top.

Ismay pulled at his smoking jacket sleeves and leaned toward Burty in the appearance of intimacy, confidentiality. "It's been done, sir, done and got away with. Of course, the children suffer."

"You friggin' British fart," said Burty.

"I beg your pardon?" said Bruce Ismay, his voice ascending with each word. Then he rose. "You're not yourself, sir. I'll leave you for a bit."

"Bet your booties," said Burty. "On your way."

"Please make yourself at home here," said Mr. Ismay as he retreated toward his bedroom. "Please, treat this suite as though it were your own." He closed the door between them, gently, and Burty heard the lock turn solidly into place.

So he'd scotched the Englishman right enough, Burty thought. The ol' bunghole. *Of course, it's the children who suffer.* Friggin' prig. I bet he calls his cock a Richard and only pulls it out on special occasions.

In his suitcase he had two fifths—no, one and one-third fifths now—of Bailey's. That'd keep him going till dinner. Then he'd run down the riverboat gambler and take some more of his money. Take the rest of it. Nobody likes a snoop and tattletale, Burty thought, not even the one who gets let in on the dirty little secrets. And Burty did not like Rolls Royce. He was a con man, oh yeah, but Burty could respect that; B.K.V.V. had a bit of the con in himself; you had to have, to succeed by pulling on your own bootstraps. But Rolls was all con, and that made him a rascal. Probably got all the women he wanted though, and more; he was a handsome rascal. Kind of man who had to fight the ladies off with brickbats.... He hadn't got Tory, though. Burty knew that. She had come to him virgin, and never let him olly-olly-ox-in-free, neither, until he'd married her, beringed her, and driven her in style to Niagara Falls.

He drank off the rest of his glass, filled it again, Bailey's neat. Carefully he tapped the ash off his cigar. He let his head fall back against the chair cushion, scratched his unshaved jaw and tasted the stale breath in his mouth.

Ah, it was good to be a bachelor again, and not give a... What a night, his wedding night. *Their* wedding night. He'd been tired, and so anxious. Scared, even, that he wouldn't please her. Ah, Tory had been too good to be true. *Always was too good to be true, that kid.* Loving and funny and the sexiest, prettiest thing any man ever saw, anywhere, anytime.

He'd trembled when he undressed her: that had been her idea. *Good idea*; he'd been so *ready*. But first they had to shower together, she'd said, and that was a good idea, too. Her body dazzled him—*still* dazzled him. He'd never seen another, before or since, so perfect. And then, damp, like Adam and Eve, she'd said, they'd stretched out and—*bang!*— he was on her and in her and off. He'd pulled out all bloody: her hymen, she said. "You've torn away my virginity, Burtykins, now I'm yours...." But she hadn't been his, not yet. He, who knew, knew better.... She'd waited quiet, on her back, taut thighs spread wide while he cleaned the blood away. And her golden breasts, so big on a slender body, *so wonderfully big*, so *naked*, waited for his hands, and the dark rose nipples shivered for his mouth.

She'd waited, patient. And when he was ready, it was her turn. He loved her, then, all through their first night. Four hours, she told him after, he made unflagging love: stroking, tasting, warming, *teasing*. Four hours of bliss it was for him, and it ended in triumph for her. For just as a cold dawn streaked the white Canadian sky, "torrid Tory June" truly became his bride. His baby climaxed. She really hit the roof and took that magic carpet ride...first time down on the blanket....

He'd been so *fucking* proud. They'd been so *fucking* much in love.

Goddamn.

He drank half the glass's whiskey in two swallows. It burned all the way down.

It's the things you get that break your heart, he thought. The things you *don't* get stay always as they were, stay perfect because they're far away. But once you got your paws on heaven, it dulled and shriveled like a used balloon. Once you got a thing, you got to *know* it, and maybe only the unknown seems perfection. Aww...he was getting sentimental. The whiskey was softening his brain.

Burty drank again, a sip or two this time, and tried to conjure thoughts of other women, new, exciting, *unknown* women. But he couldn't visualize them sharply. They floated, breasts and hips and lips and arse, disembodied, jigsawed. And they all looked like

Tory, imitation Tories, not so slim of waist, not so lithely limbed and roundly curved. Not so *raw gold, more beautiful than peaches and cream.*...

There was a divorcée on board. She was blond and buxom, not half-bad. Helen Churchill Candee, that was her name. She had Archibald Gracie all crazy, and several other guys. He could give "Candy" a try, after dinner tonight....

"Would you care for a stroll on boat deck, Mrs. Candee, to look at the moon? Or better, to give the moon, a lesser light, a look at you?"

And on the strength of that, Burton Shakespeare, would she come to your bed?

He doubted it. She was looking for a husband— all women without were—but she was a respectable woman with a reputation to maintain. She wasn't going to tumble into bed midocean with Burton VanVoorst while his pregnant wife cried abandoned in her cabin. No, even if she wanted to, she wouldn't. It wouldn't do....

Maybe he could ask one of the cleaning staff Umm? Umm?

Or he could invade second. Seconds didn't worry so much about their reputations.... No, he would be noticed and reported on; second was too close....

But third now...ah, there he might have luck. Lots of young Irish minxes down in third, coming to America looking for work, their pockets turned out empty. Why, if the dolly played her cards right, he could move her right into Godsend as housemaid.... Well, maybe not. His nigger wife would get the Newport cottage in the settlement. Given her choice, Tory would take Godsend, just because he liked it best, damn her....

His glass was empty again.

Aww, Tory was all right. He'd always liked Tory…loved Tory…. High yellow, they called what Tory was. Well, she was a high yellow to end them all; fooled him for almost twenty years…. Hell of a can on that woman, though, hell of a can. Made to order for a man…. And could she twist it….

The cigar was a cold stub. Burty fingered for it, knocked it out of its ash plate. He bent to look for it and was filled with nausea. The stub lay two feet from his dangling hand. It was dark and dry and wrinkled…. Oh my God, Burty thought, the baby. I forgot all about Burton Kingsley VanVoorst number two. Hell of a thing.

He sat back, forgetting the cigar. The nigger brat. She'd saddle him with that, too. Child support, college, corn pone bills for eighteen years. Hah, he had to laugh. Women. Just when you thought they were doing something for you, they were doing it *to* you; stickin' it to you right up the butt….

But now wait a minute. Just wait a goddamn minute.

How had Tory been going to explain that baby? I'll just bet, he thought, it was an accident. All that stuff she told me about how she couldn't conceive— bitch liar—*because she didn't want me to find out she was a jiggaboo*. I'll just bet she didn't know she was pregnant until it was too late to stop it. And she's been going through hell's own torture, worrying how that baby's gonna look, white, black or pokey dot. Ha! He'd call her up and ask her.

With drunken care he asked the operator to connect him with their room, her room now.

"Hello," she said. Her voice was calm. She didn't sound as though she'd been crying.

"Tor?"

"Yes, Burt."

"Have you been worried what your baby's gonna look like, you bein' a nigger and all?" He could hear the mean in what he asked, so to cover it he raised his voice to gruffness. "You tell me the truth now."

"Yes," she said. "I worried all the time. I pray—still pray—the baby will be white. It should. You're the father, and there's just an ounce of colored in me."

"Tor."

"Yes, Burt."

"How come you never told me yourself? How come you let it happen this way, huh?"

He could almost *see* her at the other end of the line. His beautiful darling, full bellied now and pale, but oh, so beautiful....

She was saying, "Sometimes you keep on going because there's no place to get off. You know, Burty-kins? You ever have that feeling?"

"There's always a place to get off, kid," he said, tired now. "You just have to know how and when and where. Like me now, I just got off the boat, but you're the one who's high and dry."

"Goodbye, Burty. Please don't call me like this again."

"No," he said.

The telephone was dead in his hands. The mouthpiece he was holding was black—like his wife—and wet.

That's how he realized he was crying.

11

He awoke to black night, almost midnight, to a dim, cloud-cast sky and the dull reflection in thick, strange water of *Titanic*'s high-strung lights. The air around felt close and damp and still.

However the day passed for others, for Burton VanVoorst that Thursday was spent in bedroom B-56 in drunken slumber. He did not hear Mr. P. W. Fletcher's bugle call to dinner. He heard no sweet and playful orchestral dance tunes, he saw no brilliant blue Atlantic tumble into cold gray green as R.M.S. *Titanic* steamed into its northern sea-lane and headed toward the forty-second latitude and a few degrees west....

He awoke to black night, almost midnight, to a dim, cloud-cast sky and the dull reflection in thick, strange water of *Titanic*'s high-strung lights. The air around felt close and damp and still.

Burty stood out on Ismay's suite's deck, port side of the ship. His head was as dull and heavy and bleak as the ocean looked. His mouth was dry, his tongue was foul. He was still in last night's evening clothes, now rumpled to the point of comedy, and his face was scratchy with a full day's growth of beard.

Vacations.... He had not wanted this leisured respite from his work. He had been lured to it by...Tory.

Damn Tory, he thought.

He stretched out his hands and clasped the deck rail. His hands were steady, the ship was steady. He could feel no vibration of turbine, no jerk of piston; he could hear no throb of engines beating. There were only ice-white ripples, long and fine at the water line to mark *Titanic* moved, that and the clammy breeze: she was a good ship.

And he was a good man who had been misused.

He turned away from the night and the ocean— the blasted ocean. All he really wanted was his office and his telephones and a club where he could get a hot meal and be *undisturbed*. Land, solid old land, that's what he liked, and work, exciting work. Forget all this folderol window dressing of fancy rooms and fancy meals and fancy places. He didn't give a rap for exotic places—he got enough foreigners down on Wall Street, thanks—and he had better rooms than *Titanic* in all his houses, and better meals, too, if he wanted.

Work. That's what he liked.

Home? He still wanted to go home, get to someplace he owned where he could drop his hat and unbutton his collar and pour his own whiskey into his own damn glass.

But vacations? You could have them. *She* could have them. She could spend the rest of her life on water for all he cared.

He dropped off yesterday's clothes and rang for a steward. Naked, he handed over his trousers and jacket and shirt and socks— ''Here's the whole caboodle,'' he said. ''Get it all fixed up right for me, eh? That's right'' —and asked for a pot of black coffee in his room. In the shower he stood under the hot spray—less forceful than his own showers back home—a good long time until his headache went away. He shaved himself, he who was usually shaved by others but, what the hell, before he made his first million there were years and years—thousands of days—when he'd scraped his own face with a self-honed straightedge and done a good job, and combed his own hair, too. Tomorrow he would be shaved in the barber shop and have a manicure and a haircut. He got into his second set of evening clothes—first things he'd packed, leaving *her*—and congratulated himself on not bringing Elgin along on the trip. His valet had wanted to go....

"Oh, Paris in the spring, sir, and England in the country and the maiden voyage of the *Titanic*? Oh, heaven, sir...!"

"Please," Burty had responded. "My wife's not taking Anna, so I can't take you, I'm sorry. But I'll bring you something from Bond Street, Elgin.... What would you like?"

His valet had clapped his hands. "Gloves, sir. Would gloves be too much? Two pairs of white gloves made to measure to my fingers...?"

Burty had the gloves in his suitcase, along with the paper patterns of Elgin's right and left hands. Burty had bought his man a dozen pairs and a set of silver valet brushes engraved with the initial E—Mrs. Twigg's idea—in a doeskin case of chocolate brown.

But, much as Burty thought Elgin a splendid example of his profession, servants were certain spreaders of gossip—they spread scandal better than they handled soft butter on bread—and Burton VanVoorst did not want it all over Fifth Avenue and Newport's Gilt Hill that he had been gulled into marriage by a

"Jemima." He needed another drink just thinking what a field day his mother would have. She would lift her thin, thin brows and stretch her eyes in their surgically tightened sockets until they almost popped. She would pretend sympathy.... "Oh, poor little Burt," she would say, "you see? Didn't I tell you so...? Yes, and your poor dead father, too. We told you, dear, but you wouldn't listen.... How much is she taking you for...?"

Women. Get you every time, they will. Even *mothers*.... There was no escaping the claws of women.

When the pot of coffee came, he ordered a bottle of gin and a bucket of ice. Hair of the dog, he thought; sometimes it was the only thing kept a man going.

He was dressed when the steward returned. The steward—Hunter, said the man's name tag—helped him with his collar and studs. And if he looked a little less than his best—not as starched and pressed and perfect as Elgin would have had him—well, Burton VanVoorst's best was not so fine he had to worry; he left the sartorial splendor to Tory...had left, he corrected himself. And Burton VanVoorst did not depend upon how he was turned out for social success. His pocketbook was his ticket into any drawing room in any house he wanted to enter: he could look like a bear and be granted an audience with the king of England; he could look like an elephant if he chose and marry a queen.

With money like mine, he thought, still trying to set his satin bow tie just right, I could strut naked on Main Street and call my bare ass new clothes, and any town in the world would give me a parade.

So there.

He gave up on the bow tie and finished two fingers of gin with one draft, and left the room, ready. Ready for Freddy, ready for Rolls, ready to play a little poker with the boys in the smoking lounge. That was how he'd get through the rest of the voyage. He'd stay up all night, every night to come, and sleep all day until time for cocktails. Then he'd up and play bachelor with the boys and avoid the *niggah*.

Try to avoid...

How could she have lied to him all these years...? How could *he* have been so dumb...? *How* had she gotten away with it...?

In a little more than an hour he had lost back more than thirty thousand dollars to Rolls Royce, so he knew his luck was running bad, would get worse before it got better if he kept on, so he quit. Smaaart. Even up against it, I'm smaaart, he thought, standing away from the table. Rolls and the two Archies—Archibald Gracie called Colonel A., and Archie Butt, famous as the confidant of President Taft, called Major A.—thanked him for the pleasure of his company and promised him a chance to get even tomorrow night. No one mentioned his wife or his changing his room or his constant knocking back of gins on ice.

Which only went to show that it was men, after all, who knew how to handle delicate social situations, and not the spoiled little darlings. Split-tails, he used to call them derisively when he was a boy. Nothing between their legs—or in their heads—but air.

Burty thought he'd stroll on down the back staircases to third and find himself a little split-tail: nothing like a new woman to make you forget…when you wanted to forget…the old.…

For a while, anyway.

He paid five dollars, putting a finger to his lips, to the steward on duty at the door of lower deck D. The steward caught the idea straightaway, good man.…

It was the dead of night. Probably there wouldn't be anyone around, no one interested in making an easy twenty…maybe thirty, if she pleased. After all, he was a generous man.

Several times in his married life—a few times—*rarely* he thought, he had comforted himself in a strange woman's body. Never with the same one twice, never with a woman he'd known, never with a woman he'd especially sought. Just a woman, a *bad* woman, a professional *floozy*, once in a while when he was lonely in Manhattan and Tory was at Godsend, far away in Newport. It was no trouble; he picked them up around the midtown hotels. They were easy to spot. They were always alone and in bright dresses that showed all the law allowed of their bosoms, and they lifted their skirts up to the calves when they sat and crossed their knees.

Easy pickings, easy lickings.…

But he had never done what he was doing now— in the company of friends, with his wife on board— slinking down to a netherworld to snatch at buried treasure.…

"Hello." He had bumped against her in the dark. She was a child, maybe seven, maybe eight; small. She was hunched down on her heels under the deck rail with a towel around her shoulders to break the wind. A small boy was tucked in beside her. He could not have been more than five.

"Oh, dear me, sorry," said Burt. He tried to pass on, but the girl held on to his trouser leg.

"Do you have a quarter, sir?"

She was not a particularly pretty child, and she was dirty. Her face was smudged and her palm, which she extended, was black. The boy was pretty. He had a sweet face with long dark eyelashes.

Burt fished in his pocket for two. He would give them both one, he thought. Rotten little buggers.

"Do you have a name?" He drew out a handful of change.

"Yes, sir," said the girl and then the boy and then they giggled and the boy stretched out his hand, too, palm up. His hand was as grubby as the girl's.

"Well, what is it? Cat took your tongue?"

He laid a quarter in each soiled little hand. Fingers closed around the money like flowers folding or butterfly wings becoming still.

"My name is Keely, which is short for Cath'rine."

"My name is Keef," said the boy.

"Keith, not Keef," the girl corrected.

"Keef," said the boy, and put his thumb and the quarter into his mouth.

"Look at you," said Keely to her brother. He spit the quarter out into his hand and smiled. "Thibault is our real last name, but Daddy's using Millor now. It's an alias, Daddy says. We have to do it.... Do you know what an alias is?"

"Yeth," said the boy. "We've been kidnapped. Daddy did it."

"He had to," said the girl.

"My, my," said Burt, thinking he'd just forget it. "Isn't it time you were in bed?"

"Yeth," said the boy.

The girl took her brother's hand and edged away. The boy pulled at his short pants, drooping at the waist. Without another word they faded beyond the pool of night-light, and Burty was alone, hearing only their soft steps retreating.

He thought a moment about his own child ripening in Tory's belly, a "soiled" child, too. Would his offspring, someday, wander neglected, unwanted, wondering where his father was...? He did not want to dwell on *that*....

Someone else was there, in the shadows of the stern.

Burty approached the figure, a stout figure garbed in black, a mature figure. A man, then, restless, as he was.... No, a woman. A short wide woman with shoeblack hair, wrapped in dark folds like bat wings.

He stopped, repelled. The figure turned to face him, and as it did he heard, far away, a bell toll.

The woman was old, with one blind white eye. The other snapped with life. Nothing else in the gypsy's face moved.

Burty heard again, faint, on the edge of hearing, a bell toll one note, which quivered in the sea-shushed silence.... And then again the bell clapped. The woman moved, folded her arms in a cross upon her chest, and rolled the eye that could see up into her head so that it showed white like the other.... And then she stood there, stolid in the shadows, still as a noose hanging from a spar....

Burty had never been so terrified.

He heard the bell—a buoy bell it must be, a marker in the sea being made to sound by a swell of waves rolling through. But where? They were miles from land, *hundreds* of miles from land now, surely.

Titanic was where no markers were, where man did not mark but only passed through, a temporary shadow....

The bell rang harder now, quicker, and the woman moved. Without a greeting, head bowed, she started toward him. Burty was dumb, immobile. The witch *crossed his path*, her arms still in an X upon her chest. And then she was gone, lost in the dark amidships.

And Burty heard the buoy bell no more.

He was shaking. His knees were weak and he was panting slightly. Suddenly cold sober, he walked back to the stairs that would take him up again, and away. He avoided the elevators; the elevators were too public. He wanted the dark and the time that climbing the stairs would take.

That bell, that knell of doom...and the air, now, as soft and damp as ghost fingers. His hair was prickling at the back of his neck. I have looked into tomorrow, he thought. I must make my peace with this world....

He would not, could not, now, think of Tory. Thinking of her would only break his heart.

But Ismay, for instance. He had been rude to Bruce Ismay, who had only been generous to him and helped him out when he was in need of a bed, a room, companionship. Burty had been callous in return. He must fix that.

I am not a bad man, Burty thought. Imperfect, certainly. But an ethical man who played fair and gave good value and who had done right in this world, by and large.... I am going to die, he thought, and in his mind there played again the *bong* of the bell—

mysterious, out of nowhere, gone now, but foretelling.

There was a light under Ismay's door. Burty realized that he had climbed two flights of stairs and encountered not a soul. He had traversed the middle portion of B deck and seen no one. He had passed the starboard flank of *Titanic*, passed the corridor that led to Tory's room, his former room, without a thought.... Horses remember the way back to the barn forever, he thought. I've forgotten how to get home in twelve hours....

Tory.... He loved Tory....

He knocked gently on Ismay's door.

"Come in," he heard. The voice did not sound surprised or annoyed or sleepy. It sounded almost as if he were expected. But how could that be, after the way he had acted this afternoon...?

Ismay was in bed, reading, in royal-blue silk pajamas. There was a snifter of brandy at his bedside table.

As Burty entered, Ismay set the book on the table and gestured to a wicker armchair. "Come in, Mr. VanVoorst. I've been wondering where you were."

"Where I was?" said Burty, and he smoothed his hair from his face, distracted, not knowing what to say. He had not expected brotherly affection, that was sure.

"Well, you know, old chap, you need looking after right now. Your bed's been made up, fresh linen and all that. Your wife hasn't seen you—I checked with her. And the boys in the smoker said you'd given it up an hour ago."

Burty sank into the chair. He was tired now, but

he felt better just being in a warm dry room, cozy with fire logs smoldering, cozy with electric light.

"I was just wandering," he said. "A man can get lost in this palace, it's quite a production. Your builders did you proud."

Ismay swung out of bed, slipped his thin feet into the fox-head slippers, and padded to a burled-cherry bureau that served as a bar. "Snort of brandy go well now? You're pale, if you don't know."

"Thanks, I will.... I came to apologize for my behavior this afternoon."

Ismay waved the etched-crystal stopper of his decanter. "My good man, I understand—understood at the time. You've suffered a great crisis."

"Ah." Burty took the snifter Ismay offered, swirled the liquor, watched it, thick, coat a curving circle on the inside of the bowl. "I love her, you see."

"Of course you do, and why not? She's an admirable piece of work." Ismay went back to his bed, stretched out on top of it. "Here's to Mrs. Van-Voorst...and to reconciliation."

Burty smiled at the thought, and drank, was warmed and uplifted. Great invention, alcohol, he thought. Wonder how they did it? "Ismay..." He was going to ask if the owner of White Star Line had charts for this part of the ocean, maps; if there was, somewhere, not far, a jut of land with a lighthouse on, perhaps with warning bells....

But Ismay interrupted him. "Please, call me Bruce," he said, "and I'll call you Burty, how's that?"

Burty nodded and drank. Languor enveloped him.

He relaxed and stretched out his legs. "Ah, that's good. Here's to you, Bruce," and he sipped again.

The decanter of brandy was at his elbow. Ismay must have brought it over with the glass. Burty poured himself another hit. The scent of the brandy was sweeter than a woman's perfume.

"God, I'm tired," he said.

"Come to bed," said Bruce Ismay, and he patted the pillow beside him.

"Eh?"

"Come to bed," Ismay repeated easily, and patted again the pillow beside him.

Burty was surprised—astonished. What a day this had been. Still was....

"I've just been looking for a woman," he said, and drained his glass.

"Exactly," said Bruce Ismay, drinking off the rest of his. "And not finding one."

"Yes," said Burty. He was almost asleep, and yet his mind was alert, on the edge of keenness, watching Ismay. The soft yellow light, the rich oil-rubbed furniture. It was very cozy, very comforting, very much like home. "Yes, no luck in that department."

Ismay turned off his table lamp and tucked himself under the sheet and blanket. "Don't be shy," he said. "You can close your eyes if you like and imagine I'm a woman, a hot-hipped, big-titted Bessie."

"Belinda," said Burty, passing a hand over his face. "Belinda is better."

"Belinda, then."

Why not? Burty thought. He was so tired, so tired.... And he had been so frightened, so lost. Now he was found. Rescued...by a bloomin' *poof*.

He stood up to undress, hauled off his dinner

jacket. "Why me?" he said, and yawned. "I'm not a glamour puss. Don't guys like you like 'em sweet?"

Ismay folded his hands on top of the coverlet. "You've heard of the expression, a girl in every port?"

"You mean," said Burty, as he dropped his trousers and sat down to strip off his shoes and socks, "you mean any port in a storm, I think."

Ismay smiled. "Yes, that's the one," he said.

Burty came toward the bed, his side. Hoisted himself in. It was a wide bed, the mattress firm and soft with goose down. "Ah, that's good," he said.

"You have beautiful pectorals," said Bruce Ismay.

"It's not my pectorals I want rubbed, bub," said Burty. Despite his flying thoughts, his eyes closed. He sank into a cocoon of comfort. Beyond his eyelids the fire, embers now, glowed red and yellow and black. Nice.... Very nice....

"You Americans are quaintly primitive in your sexual attitudes," purred Ismay, hovering over Burty's exhausted body. "I find you very exciting."

But Burty never heard the compliment nor felt a thing. He slept, like one of the dead.

Friday, April 12

12

On the bridge Friday morning, enjoying a croissant and coffee, Captain Edward John Smith was enjoying, too, the most pleasurable feeling of his life: he was in love. Truly, ecstatically, in love.

What a strange emotion, he thought, celebrating it in his mind. Love made a man distracted, made all the things he had spent a lifetime thinking the most important seem as superficial *obstructions* to the real meaning of his existence.

Love.

It was more than passion and more pervasive than lust. It was a roiling storm over the quiet currents of friendship and admiration. There was a song in his chest, a roar in his vitals, and attending to the morning's chart positions and location measurements, each day's first priority, was suddenly, just now, for the first time, only a dull task upon which his mind would not stay focused.

Ah, Dove.

He had found, at the end of his career, the love of his life. It was terrible and wonderful all at once; it was inevitable and impossible together. Worst—or

maybe best, who knew?—it would be short-lived....
It would be brief—much, much too brief, and there
was heartbreak at the other end; but it was, oh yes,
yes, yes...it was sublime.

"Sir." It was Second Officer Charles Lightoller,
the correct and careful Chuck Lightoller, whom E.J.
respected but did not like. E.J. especially resented the
interruption while his thoughts were with his beloved. For again, today, they would secretly meet in
his cabin after luncheon. They would tumble and
tango in love's sweet dance— He checked his wrist-
watch: hours yet to go.

"Sir."

"Yes, Chuck, what is it?" Nothing in the captain's
voice reflected his displeasure.

"We have wireless communication from *Empress
of Britain*. She congratulates our first sail, wishes us
long life, and warns of ice ahead, between forty-one
and forty-two degrees latitude, forty-nine and fifty
west. Field ice, she says—rather heavy, some growlers and some bergs." Lightoller handed over a typed
marconigram.

"Ah, yes," said E.J., taking the paper and sliding
it into his logbook. "See a duplicate is posted for
the men in quarters. But ice is not unusual out here
in April, is it, my good man?"

"No, sir, quite the norm." Lightoller had not yet
got over being moved down from first officer to second by Mr. Ismay at the last minute in Southampton.
Everyone had been bumped down, but Lightoller had
taken it the hardest. Hit in the heart, E.J. thought,
and sympathized, being ambitious himself. But E.J.
could not condone pouting. His guiding principle

was, stay a soldier, a good soldier, no matter the turns of fortune, and do your duty like a man.

E.J. laid a gentle hand upon Mr. Lightoller's striped cuff and said, "So how are you faring, sir? Getting along with Mr. Wilde, are you?"

Mr. Lightoller was appreciative of the attention. "Yes, sir, thank you, sir. He's a good sailor and I am learning from him."

"That's the way," said Captain Smith. "Well, then, is there anything else?" He would be making his full ship's inspection soon, and he did not want to be late. He wanted all his chores wiped up, slicked off and finished by the time of the midday meal...so as to be *free* after.

Free for her.

"There are other messages, sir, off the wireless," said Lightoller, laying a stack of marconigrams on E.J.'s podium. "All much the same. Congratulations to you and *Titanic*, and information of ice sighted."

"Well, post the news. If anything new develops, let me know at once. But you don't expect undue trouble?"

"Oh no, Captain. We're fine. Position checked, all clear ahead."

E.J. consulted his log. "Only covered 386 miles on Thursday, I see. That's a bit slow, I think."

"We'll get her speeded up, sir. I'll see to it right away."

"Good man," said E.J., dismissing him.

His captain's thoughts rolled on to the distance still to be covered. *Titanic* was steaming at barely half speed, he could tell that by the ease with which she moved and by the amount of coal she burned to do it. Ismay insisted speed was not the first consideration of a White Star Line ship—comfort was. "A little slower gives the passengers another meal," Ismay said, "another happy night at sea. A reputation is built on luxury and dependability, and luxury is what sells tickets.... Leave the 'hurry' to Cunard Line—let them gamble with the risks of speed...."

And as a result, Cunard was killing White Star in the passenger wars, Captain Smith thought. The world is speeding up, Ismay; that's why you sold to IMM. White Star was failing under your command.... Bayard Lockholm, now, he seemed of a more open mind. He agreed with Captain Smith that "fast" was a selling point, though he thought it best not to emphasize speed unduly. "If it comes as a result of our efficiency, Captain, that would please me very much, yes, and Mr. J. P. Morgan, too. But we must move carefully in these matters and not seem to be sacrificing either safety or comfort for a record ocean crossing. If, however, such should prove the case—if, not seeking to, our superior vessels traverse an ocean quicker than the rest, well, that is not to be despised, is it, Captain Smith?"

That was Lockholm's oblique directive, and E.J. accepted it as unspecified permission for him to try, on the quiet, to bring *Titanic* in to dock in New York's North River sometime on Tuesday, 16 April. *Anytime* on Tuesday would be a record....

Captain Smith circled Thursday's run of 386 miles with a thick pencil point. They'd better run five hundred miles today or he would know the reason why....

He gathered the stack of marconigrams Lightoller had passed on to him and put them, unread, between the pages of his log. All very nice of the fellows to acknowledge the maiden trip, he thought. Damn thoughtful. And then he remembered she who inflamed his heart and blazed his bed.

Soon, he thought.

Soon Captain E. J. Smith would ascend to paradise...again and again and again....

SMOKE LOCKHOLM WAS wretched.

She sat in the Café Parisien at a table for two, by herself, listlessly finishing a bowl of cut fruit. Her twin was down in the bowels of the ship, not back on B deck yet from her secret all-night with Danny. And Mrs. Twigg was breakfasting with "new friends," Sir Cosmo and Lady Duff-Gordon, who had, for some inexplicable reason, taken Twiggs under their wing. Colonel Archibald Gracie was at the Gordon table, too, flirting openly with the governess, to Twiggs's utter satisfaction.

Puke, thought Smoke, unladylike. Simple peagreen puke.

Smoke felt halved, cleaved from her twin, who was so immersed in sin and deception that she had become, *through carnal knowledge*, Smoke thought, a different person entirely. A "round-heels," like Aunt Celeste who lived in Paris and of whom the twins were not supposed to speak, she led so disreputable a private life. Well, the truth is, Smoke thought, spinning a purple grape in syrup, Swanny and I are twins no more. We do not look alike or act alike or think alike, or even dress alike, and we are never together anymore.... Swan had *severed* them forever, in a night.

Smoke could not even hate Swan for what she had done. Hate might come later; Smoke hoped so. But now all was pain. The twins had been so close, *a part of each other*, like heart and soul, and mind and body. Distinct, but integral....

Smoke, who never felt sorry for herself, was feeling very sorry for herself. Everyone else on board was plunged into activity or crisis or emotion—*something important*. And Smoke was being ignored...completely left out.

Forgotten.

Everyone, for instance, pretended not to notice her cropped-to-the-shoulder hair. Even Mrs. Twigg. Twiggs was in a dither, anyway, acting the fool over the attentions of the courtly Colonel Gracie who—if Twiggs only knew—was paying court to every unattached woman in first class with the exception, *sure*, of Smoke Wysong Lockholm. All right, Colonel Gracie was an old man, much too old to smile on Smoke, but still...it was abysmal to be neglected.

And her mother and father—they were impossible, and Smoke hated them. Her father wasn't interested in her problems; that's what Mrs. Twigg was for, Smoke supposed. Twiggs was hired in the first place to keep the children out of their dear parents' hair....

When Smoke went to him yesterday and asked him to play deck quoits, he said he couldn't just then. But he could have; he wasn't doing anything important, just waiting for Mother to come back to him from Tory's room. He said he would buy her an ice, if she liked, or a souvenir, but she did not want either, and she couldn't just burst out and tell her father that Swanny was sleeping with a fortune-hunting violinist down on E deck in a dark closet of a room and *screwing* like a rabbit with nothing better to do.

She'd wanted to. She'd tried to, but she just couldn't....

And her mother? Ha. Mother was incommunicado behind closed doors all day with Tory VanVoorst, who was heartsick in her bed—and might lose the baby—over her breakup with Burty.

Which I never would have imagined, Smoke thought, and swallowed the grape whole. It slithered down her throat and into her stomach, cold and round; she could feel it.

Burty used to kiss Tory's feet almost, he adored his wife so much. Smoke looked for another interesting piece of fruit, settled on a small wedge of pineapple. She speared it with her fork, lifted it boldly to her mouth, and began to lick the syrup off: an egregious breach of table etiquette, which, if Twiggs was paying attention, would have made her as mad as Mildred's cow. But Mrs. Twigg wasn't paying attention—she was smiling at some *drivel* Colonel Gracie was explaining to their table, all hand gestures and winks. No one was paying any attention to Smoke at all....

Burty must be a snob, Smoke thought—though before yesterday she would have bet against it. Because Burty had been on a drunken tear since he found out *Tory's secret*—it was all over the boat, everyone knew, and Nicola was mad at Mr. Royce, who, according to Twiggs, had "spilled the beans." That was exciting, all right, Nicola dancing with the scoundrel, too, even after she knew what he had done....

Burty had moved in with Mr. Ismay, and who knew, now, what would happen? Twiggs said the VanVoorsts would have a terrible divorce. It would be in the newspapers—about the worst thing that could happen in a divorce—and Tory would be *lost to society forever*; Twiggs's prediction. And then Burty would, again according to Mrs. Twigg, probably make a *big mistake* like John Jacob Astor IV and marry in a hurry *a wrong woman*. This was because men needed sex, Twiggs said, and marriage was the only respectable way to get it. Well, Twiggs had a fixation about the Astors; they were her favorite American family. Whatever happened today, the Astors, one of them, some time or another, had done it before, done it better or done it worse....

"Follies and triumphs, climb and fall, it's all there in one genealogy, Smoke, dear. Attend, and learn...."

Smoke found it tiresome.

She hoped Mrs. Twigg went to work for an Astor someday—for Madeline, Mrs. John Jacob Astor IV, the "wrong" one, who seemed to Smoke one of the nicer women on board. The new Mrs. Astor told Smoke her hair was wonderfully cut—"French modern," Madeline called it—and she'd let Smoke play with the Astor puppy, an Airedale named Kitty, which made no sense, but still, Madeline had been friendly and kind. Working for Madeline would fix Twiggs, all right, and that would make Smoke happy.

Ignominy for Twiggs: that's what Smoke wanted. The old bag deserved it. Dumb old thing, never had made love to a man in her life, and still she sprinkled her bosom with rice powder to keep it "cool" on the dance floor...silly ol' Twiggs. She'd never *climaxed*—that's what they called it. She never would, but she giggled like the twins over the single rose Archibald Gracie had sent her.

Phooey.

Smoke ground the pineapple wedge between her teeth.

And the novel she had spent all day yesterday reading had depressed her, too. *Futility*, such a sad title. It was an old book, written way back before the century turned, but it seemed to Smoke like a diary, almost, of their *Titanic* voyage. Except that, of course, nothing happened in the novel that was happening now *except*, as in the novel, they were crossing the Atlantic in April and *ice had been reported just ahead*.... In the novel, the ocean liner struck an iceberg and all lives were lost. Silly, oh yes, nothing like that would *really* happen, but still, the book depressed Smoke and made her angry.

Angry at being left by herself.

Angry at being left out....

Angry at being *unloved*....

Well, Smoke Lockholm was not going to sit with her chin in her hand and mope. No, no. She pushed the dish of fruit away. She was going to run away: jump ship. Create a scandal of her own. She had it all planned....

"Idleness is the devil's workshop" was what Twiggs said whenever she wanted the twins to do something they weren't doing. Smoke thought that, maybe this time, Twiggs was right.... Because Smoke—idle, ignored little Smoke *with nothing better to do*, had gone snooping yesterday afternoon...and discovered *gold*. She'd gone to the wireless room for the demonstration she'd been promised by Captain Smith, and John Phillips had shown her how to work the Marconi apparatus's levers and dials. Harold Bride, the other Marconi operator, had loaned her a book on international code that included the alphabet of dots and dashes.

And then she'd been ignored *again*, in the telegraph room this time, while Harold and Jack—they said to call them by their first names—worked on the incoming messages from Cape Race, a relay station far away. Smoke sat at the "sender's" desk and looked through old messages jotted down as they had come in over the wire. Translated from code to English, they were typed up and sent to whomever they were intended; the originals were collected on a spindle, ultimately to go into *Titanic*'s files.

And there the gold. Leafing through, Smoke found the last wire of Captain Stanley Lord of the *Californian* begging Nicola to come to him. He would send a boat, he said; they would be reunited. Nicola refused him in the next wire, emphatically refused him; Smoke found that one, too.

But a girl could change her mind, couldn't she?

So all last night while Swanny—foolish Swanny—was baring her body to the peasant Danny Bowen, *throo it all*, Smoke was writing up a marconigram in code to send to Captain Lord…. Smoke, pretending to be Nicola, wrote that she would be pleased to accept his invitation *after all* and for him to send a boat for her *at Saturday midnight*.

"A quiet little boat," Smoke wrote. "Two oarsmen only, trusted men."

Upon which boat Smoke Wysong Lockholm would step, disguised as Captain Lord's beloved. For the "trusted men" would not know Nicola by sight. How could they…? And Smoke would be secretly borne away, not missed, perhaps, for *days*…. And if, when Captain Lord discovered he had been deceived, he demanded the pleasure of Smoke's body in recompense, well, she would give it to him, proudly, disdainfully, even if he was fat as a friar and had a hook for an arm and was filthy dirty. For she would refuse to return to *Titanic*, and she was prepared to pay her way, ask what he would....

She would go to London then and start a new life. She would become a ship's officer in the British navy. She would excel. And then she would be captain of the greatest, fastest ocean liner afloat. *Titanic*, herself, perhaps, in a few years' time.

She knew how to send the marconigram; Mr. Phillips had shown her. While he was busy with something else, she would send it off, and no one would ever know.

No one would even care.

Smoke stood away from the little table, her breakfast done. I shall go and send it off right now, she said to herself, lest, on thinking it over, I waver....

But Jack Phillips, working in the telegraph office, would not let her in. "I'm sorry, miss, I'm much too busy for you now. Bride is sleeping, and I'm all alone. Come back when I'm caught up a little, say around teatime, there's a good lass." And he hunched over his gadgets and his papers and went on translating incoming information.

To be obstinate she delayed going. She stood with her arms folded and read, for a while, over his shoulder, message after message, all saying much the same thing: greetings to *Titanic*, new ship, and beware the heavy ice ahead.

Just like in the novel she'd read....

Finally, Smoke wandered away. She took a tennis lesson, but did not do well, unpracticed as she was and unable to concentrate. She swam then, and went back to her room to change into an afternoon dress. No one talked to her. She did not see her sister or her parents or any of their party. Even Mrs. Twigg had disappeared—Mrs. Twigg whose job it was to keep the twins company, had found something better to do than spend the day with Smoke.

Hurray.

Dressed in off-white linen trimmed with brown braid and buttons, her short pale hair brushed back from her forehead and behind her ears, Smoke drifted to her parents' suite, just on the starboard corner to the corridor of first-class cabins. Instead of knocking, she leaned her head against the door, heard nothing. She moved down to Tory's door, but it gave away no secrets, either. All was quiet and private...and closed away. Smoke was not included in *anything*.

She wanted to cry, but did not. She lifted her chin. They'll be sorry soon, she thought. When she was gone, they would be very sorry. Perhaps they'd think she'd drowned. Well, if she did, it would be their fault. Like kittens were drowned when they weren't wanted. You put them in a sack before their eyes opened, so they wouldn't know what it was all about.

Ocean crossings were supposed to be fun. The trip from New York to Paris had been fun—Swanny had been a real sister then, and Twiggs had been excited, too, full of scandalous stories about the rich. Smoke's mother had told her she would have an exciting time aboard *Titanic*. Mrs. Twigg had said the voyage would be "much more than only educational and recreational. It will be historical, my dears."

Well, all right then. Smoke would make history on her own. She had the wireless message written out, in proper dots and dashes, in her pocket. All she had to do was get rid of Jack Phillips for a while, and that would be that....

Burton VanVoorst was coming along the corridor. "Hello, my dear," he said. He was perfectly sober now, and properly dressed in a suit of narrow pinstripe.

"Shame on you, Burty," Smoke said, not smiling, straightening her shoulders and leaning backward to let him pass. "Your wife is a great credit to you, and I think you're monstrous to care about what some riverboat gambler said about her. He was only doing it for money."

She was impertinent, yes, but she knew him well, and she wanted to like him yet. But if he mistreated Tory, she would hate him till she died.

He made a funny mouth and nodded and passed her by. He paused at Tory's door, glanced back at Smoke staring back at him, and raised a fist to the door to rap upon it with his knuckles. There was no response from within; Smoke waited to see. So Burty reached into a jacket pocket and pulled out a letter in an envelope and slipped it under Tory's door.

"Go along with you, Smoke, if you please," he said to her. "This is not your business."

She whirled away. Of course it was not her business. She *had* no business. She'd only been trying to help.

She trudged, as though to her own hanging, up to boat deck and the wireless room. Inside, she found it empty. What luck. Wherever Jack Phillips was he wouldn't be gone long. He had told her before that an operator must always be in the wireless room in case of emergency. And the fact that there were only two operators made for twelve-hour turns. "There should be three of us," Phillips had said. Smoke had offered to be the third, but of course they had not taken her seriously. They seemed to regard her as a nuisance, "the owner's daughter," to be treated gingerly and warily with the hope that she would soon go away.

Well, she would be away soon. Far, far away, forever and ever.

She sat down at the sender's position and prepared to send out. No one bothered her. Officers passed behind, guests invited into the officers' area and up on bridge deck strolled unconcernedly behind her open door. Smoke thought she saw Dove Peerce, Nicola's mother, glide by under a parasol, but she didn't swing all the way around to make sure.

She was sending! By golly, she was sending! It was working...! Dit, dit, dit....

Suddenly the incoming board flashed and aborted her message. Oh fox, she thought, what should I do now? But even as she wondered, she took down, slowly, the incoming signals.

It was from *La Touraine*, of the French Line. Bound for, it said, Le Havre, out of New York.

"Ice," the message ran. "Heavy ice around the forty-first parallel...." Something like that. Ice, and greetings, the same message as others earlier. Nothing new....

But she wrote it down, carefully, and set it beside Mr. Phillips's transmitter. Then she turned again to her own business: dit, dotdotdot, dit...

"You wicked girl," she heard behind her.

Her fingers fell away from the apparatus. She

turned to see Harold Bride looking as though he wanted to strangle her.

"Oh, Harold," she said, "you gave me a scare. But it's all right. Earlier when I looked in, Phillips said I could come back at teatime, when things are slower. I've taken in a message—there was no one else here to do it. It's right there, for Captain Smith.... And how are you?" She smiled at him and tossed her hair.

Harold Bride was young, in his early twenties. Jack Phillips, the senior operator, was not much older. Smoke thought of them as servants and was not intimidated; indeed, it should be the other way around. Still, she did not want to alert Bride's suspicions...her message was just going. And the way to divert Harold Bride's attention from the telegraph station was to act like Swan...and flirt a little.

"I'm waiting for my next lesson," Smoke said. "I'm getting rather good, I think."

Bride unbuttoned his uniform at the neck. He was still angry, she could tell. "I'm surprised you are so interested in marine communication, Miss Lockholm. Young ladies such as yourself usually are not so tuned to the nautical arts."

Smoke dropped her eyelids. "I would like you to show me how to send again, Harold," she said. "Just to make sure I've got it."

"I've just come on duty, miss. I've things to do. Perhaps after dinner, if you'd like to come up with your father, I'd squeeze in some time to—"

So that was how it was going to be.

"Oh, all right, Harold. If I must disturb my father before you will accommodate me."

"Please, miss. This wireless station is important

business. We are on an ocean liner and we are on our first voyage. There is more work already than the two of us can do. I'm sorry, but we'd need a captain's order if you're going to settle down with us. We can't get our proper work done with you around, miss, that's the truth of it.''

"Indeed," said Smoke. She swung back and forth in the swivel chair. Soon she would huff and go, but not quite yet. To give up too soon would be suspect....

The Marconi apparatus began to flash. Excited, he waved her out of the chair. "Please, Miss Lockholm, you don't realize how hard you're making it. Please let me be about my duties."

Smoke rose languidly, taking her time, smoothing her skirts as she did, hoping to annoy him.

"Oh, have at it then, Harold. You're beginning to wear on me, too, I'm afraid. Father will be disappointed to know."

He cast her a miserable eye. He did not want trouble. But he said nothing. He began translating the incoming message, and Smoke read, over his shoulder. It was to Nicola Lady Pomeroy, on board *Titanic*, from Captain Lord of the *Californian*.

MY PRECIOUS DARLING YOUR MESSAGE RECEIVED STOP EXPECT THE TRANSFER BOAT LATE SATURDAY STOP I AM A HAPPY MAN STOPSTOPSTOP

Fudge, thought Smoke. Now Nicola will get the message and tell him to go rot and ruin the plan. "I'm off to join Lady Pomeroy and my mother, Harold. Shall I take this message with me now? Or should I stay on here and bother you?''

He did not want to hand over the message to her, she saw that. But he wanted rid of her, she saw that, too. Finally he ripped off the typed marconigram. "Do take it along, Miss Lockholm, and thank you. I'm sorry, I can't do more. Perhaps the next time you travel, the Marconi men will have more leisure.''

She folded the paper between her hands. "Thank you for your courtesies, Harold, and good evening.'' And she gave him her back.

He loosened his tunic another notch and settled down to take yet another message.... Already, she thought, she had been forgotten.

Well, she had got her way.

She marched out the door, then meandered amidships around the open promenade. No one who interested her was taking the air. That was good, very, very good. Her foray on the bridge had not been noticed.

Back toward the stern, under a great pole where lifeboats hung, hoisted high, she ripped Captain Lord's reply to her missive into little pieces, little yellow pieces. She let them fly from her fingers over the rail into the Atlantic. They lifted in the wind and spun like tiny butterflies.

While in the wireless room Harold Bride, just to cover himself, copied out again *Californian*'s message to the marchioness. He gave it to a steward to take, personally, to her. He wrote upon it, "duplicate copy,'' when he sent it off, so she would not be confused. Better two than none, he thought.

He did not trust Smoke Lockholm, and he did not

like her. Needs a spanking, he thought. Needs to grow up.... Prettiest girl I've ever seen, but not worth salt; just another spoiled rich brat, born to make men miserable.

13

Mrs. Twigg would not stop bellowing. She would not stop pacing the rug in front of Audrey's bed and bellowing.

It is strange, thought Audrey, white lipped, her sleep-needing eyes, long famous for their deep blue color, dull now in her face. It is strange how, no matter how good we try to be, our little sins keep tripping us and finally pull us down.

All night she had stayed up with Tory. Her friend had alternately wept and laughed, and had told stories of her youth. Hour after hour, sitting side by side in deck chairs, under blankets, as the North Atlantic blew icy cold, Tory told Audrey the deep dark secrets of her secret-twisted life....

But it had been a wonderful night. They drank champagne and picked at cheese and grapes together, and told their secrets to each other, friend to friend.

Audrey told about Madame Romany down below, the gypsy who was really Esmeralda Diego of Newport's public beach, wronged by Bay's late mother and come, now, to take revenge. Audrey told Tory before Bay—who was waiting to know—about the check for ten thousand dollars she had written without Bay's consent. Audrey told of her fear for Bay, driven now by business pressures, the Lockholm fortune slipping.... Audrey said she would do anything to save her husband...*anything*—it was a flaw and she would pay for it—and she told of her decision to bribe the gods through the check to Madame Romany.

Tory told of the pills still in her pocket. Deadly cyanide, hoarded for a lifetime. Laughing like naughty children, they threw the tablets overboard, one by one, and then the pale blue vial itself.

Burty called, and Tory was all dignity. He will get drunk now, Tory prophesied, and seek out another woman.... They had laughed until their sides ached, suggesting who the woman might be. Mrs. Churchill Candee...? Mrs. Twigg, perhaps...? Or the gypsy, Madame Romany, herself, who would tell him his fortune while he ground away upon her belly, reeking of gin?

"For Burty does pound from time to time, Aud, and he grinds, too.... Does Bay?"

And then, amid hushed laughter and covered mouths, Audrey, who had never uttered one word about her husband's "bedroom manner," told Tory how Bay warmed before he heated and how he liked, sometimes, to tear away her nightclothes bit by bit, and that she liked it, too.

"Ripping, is it?" Tory said, and they had fallen off their deck chairs laughing.

And so in tragedy, new pleasure. In sadness, new depth of friendship. In loss, some gain....

But then, as faintest pink tickled the gauze at the horizon, Tory excused herself to go to her lavatory and was gone too long a time. Hesitantly, fearfully, Audrey went after her, and found her standing before the mirror, gripping the washbasin with hands stiffened into claws, her mouth open and slack, and one last yellow pill dissolving on her tongue....

"Oh, Tory!"

Audrey had taken the pill away and flushed it down the toilet, and washed out Tory's mouth with peppermint water. But Tory was as pale as linen, and her eyes rolled, and she lurched, holding her high stomach as though to protect the baby from herself.

Audrey helped her to the bed and lifted the telephone receiver to call the ship's doctor, but Tory held Audrey's arm as in a vise and shook her head. "Get the gypsy, Aud," she whispered. "She'll know what to do, and I—I would be ashamed to have the doctor—he will tell. I—I think the baby's coming, or I'm dying...."

And Audrey, who was unused to anything stronger than a single glass of champagne but who had, by then, consumed an entire bottle on her own, Audrey obeyed, without a word. She wrapped herself in a velvet cloak of ruby red that hung in Tory's closet and, avoiding Bay sleeping—or perhaps not asleep but waiting for her in the bed next door—she let herself out into the corridor of B deck. And then she ran in soft slippers to the back staircases, unlighted after midnight, but with all *Titanic*'s length and height glowing with small lights, she could see dimly, well enough....

She pattered down the flights of decks...to D deck, and the gypsy.

Down there she hovered in the shadows, and was startled to see *Burty* there, stopped by the children who had earlier surrounded her. Motherless, those children; motherless and lost. She almost called to him, but something held her back. If Tory died, if the baby died, it was better Burty not be involved. He might reproach himself too much then, he who was already grieved....

Burty found Madame Romany for her, not knowing that he did. The gypsy seemed to come like a spirit, materializing out of air; Burty seemed to summon her out of night-shade. The old woman passed him by, though, shuddering. Audrey saw that...and shuddered, too. Burty was dazed and very drunken. Audrey had never seen him so. He left D deck as she hesitated, uncertain what to do. He stalked, slow, back up the stairway. He did not notice Audrey pulled aside into the dim, trembling. When his footfalls finally slapped upon the staircase landing and faded around a turning, Audrey stepped out of hiding and called to the retreating gypsy's back, "Esmeralda."

Madame Romany turned, looking, somehow, older by years than the day before. But she was still shrewd, still alert. She paused, her face shrouded by hood, and held out her hands. She said, out of the dark of the ship, "Who calls me now? I'm tired, my tasks are done, leave me be."

But Audrey called out to her, "I paid you and now I need you, Esmeralda."

The old woman came. Nick, nick, nick, her heels moved on the deck wood firm and quick. She came to Audrey and waited, wrinkled and somber, one blind eye staring.

"Do you remember my friend, a dark-haired woman, very pretty?" Audrey said. "Her name is

Victoria VanVoorst. She is having her baby early and does not want the ship's doctor to help her—she wants you.''

Madame Romany passed a hand over her mouth. "I remember," she said. Audrey waited, but there was no more.

"Then follow me," Audrey said, and the woman did.

Afraid of the elevator, not wanting to wake a steward and call attention to themselves, Audrey and the gypsy tramped up the two flights to B deck.

When they arrived at B-51, Tory was sleeping or in a trance. Her breathing was shallow and each breath came slower than the one before. She was curled on her side and her arms were wrapped vine tight around her stomach.

"Leave us," said the gypsy.

Audrey obeyed without protest. She went to her own room by way of the private deck. Dawn had conquered the night by then, but not yet won into day, and Audrey was tired, so very tired, though her mind raced....

And she was no longer afraid of the future, though danger surrounded her like sharks.... She would do what she could, and what she could not she would leave....

Bay was in their bedroom, half asleep, half awake, but waiting for her, waiting to enfold her in strong arms. Dearest Bay, loving even in anger.

"You must tell me now," he said, and kissed her forehead. "Even if you're tired you must tell me about that woman below deck and the check you gave to her."

She told him instead about Tory, all about Tory:

about how she was only an eighth colored, but had lived, all her life, a lie. She told how Tory's maiden name was not June but Brown, of the line of Phineas Brown.... Audrey told how Tory had—and had not—tried to kill herself and how, now, the pill poisoning and her body fighting back, the baby was coming...a month too soon, coming furtively and secretly and ashamedly.... Audrey told that, too, how Tory did not want *Titanic*'s doctor, and thus the world, to know what was happening, and so she had sent Audrey for the gypsy, Madame Romany or Esmeralda Diego, take your pick.

And Audrey told him, while he held her and day took the sky and made it beautiful, she told him about Esmeralda Diego and her daughter Daphne, and about his own mother, Edmunda Lockholm and her profane love of Jeoffry Eckkles.

Bay listened, holding her, stroking her hair. He did not interrupt with question or exclamation. When she was finished, he kissed her closed eyes, kissed her dry mouth. ''Ah, my brave darling,'' he said, softly, into her ear. ''I know you are tired, but I need still to know more. I need to know why, without telling me, you wrote that desperate woman, Mexican or gypsy or whatever she is...so large a charity in my name?''

She was so tired. She was warm under goose down and snuggled along his length, and a sweet paralysis flowed in her limbs. She said, and it took all her effort, ''There are some things, dear Bay, a woman cannot tell. Some things men cannot know....'' And then she broke and began to weep.

He said no more then. He held her, and she slept. And now, only several hours later, she needed more rest, much more. But now Mrs. Twigg had burst into her room and would not stop bellowing....

Audrey wanted to know how Tory was and where Bay was, and she did not want to understand what she understood only too well: that because she had been an improper mother one of her children had just been caught by Mrs. Twigg herself in the outrageous heinous sin of copulation, fornication, *whoredom*, with a ship's musician.

"The lowest of them," Mrs. Twigg said distinctly between moans of anguish and announcements of resignation. "The *substitute* violinist...." Swan had been caught in the act—"run to ground," Mrs. Twigg called it—by the governess herself and, Mrs. Twigg *bellowed*, she had never been so shocked and shaken...so abused...in all her days....

It was all Audrey's fault, Mrs. Twigg cried on and on, for Audrey had not been a good mother, always too busy *futzing* in the bed with her twenty-year-older husband to pay any attention to her children, who, of course, needed a mother as well as a governess!

And if the fact that her beautiful, once-virgin daughter was irrevocably now *ugly and ruined* was not enough to stir her mother's heart, then Mrs. Twigg was happy to tell Mrs. Lockholm that her other daughter—the one who had mutilated her hair in a desperate bid for attention—had sent a duplicitous message to a suitor of Lady Pomeroy by marconigram. In it she asked to be taken off *Titanic* on midnight Saturday, the eve, *in case Mrs. Lockholm had forgotten*, of the twins' sixteenth birthday, the most important birthday to a girl, and the third most important day in a woman's life, after her "coming out'' ball, which was second, and her sacred wedding day.

Mrs. Twigg's world had come to an end, she said. Lady Pomeroy was *furious*.... Lady Pomeroy was, at this very moment, sending a *vicious* telegraph off to Captain Lord of *Californian*, telling him she had not sent him an invitation to abduct her, an ''impostor'' had. Lady Pomeroy had informed Captain Smith himself that no messages from Captain Lord addressed to herself were to be taken by his wireless operators, and Mr. Ismay and Mrs. Lockholm's very own husband were with the marchioness now, agreeing to her demand.... As for Smoke and Swan, they had been locked in their room.... It remained for Mrs. Lockholm herself to handle the situation because Mrs. Twigg was *resigning* on the spot, she had never been so mistreated, so shamelessly ''brought down'' by a family who was supposed to be ''the upper end of the upper orders....''

It is so strange, thought Audrey, dull in her bed. I hear all Mrs. Twigg is saying, and I plead guilty. And yet my heart is turned to Tory.... It's Tory I must go to first, Tory I must see about, not my daughters. They can wait.... It's Tory needs me most....

''Have you news of Mrs. VanVoorst, Mrs. Twigg?'' Audrey eased herself slowly from her bed.

''I have not,'' said Mrs. Twigg, snapping off each word with a click of her jaws. She sat herself down in an armchair without an invitation and said, ''That comment is just about what I would have expected of you, though.''

''Forgive me, Mrs. Twigg,'' said Audrey, ''but I'm worried for my friend. She's not well, you see. And these other things, hard as they are, can wait.

You have the twins now firmly under your control.
You have hounded out their sins, broadcast their
wrongs. Thank you. Thank you very much. I'm sorry
you are leaving us, but that will have to wait, too,
until we're off this ship, I think. So until then, I hold
you to your contract—"

Mrs. Twigg sat where she had planted herself and
bellowed.

"Now YOU'VE done it," said Swan to her five-hour-
older twin. "If your hair was longer I'd give it a
yank."

"*Me?*" said Smoke, surprised at the venom in
Swan's voice. "*Me?* What about you?"

It was almost teatime, and they were both sitting
on their respective beds, their shoes kicked off, their
toes in thin cotton socks gently soiled on the bottoms
from all their jumping up and running to the starboard window to see—one if Danny was coming to
her rescue, the other if the *Californian* was anywhere
nearby. Neither held out much hope, but in the cir-
cumstances, neither knew where else to look. And
out the window there was only ocean, a brilliant
ocean of spangled blue, and a cloudless sky and brisk
cold wind. *Titanic* ran through the deep as though
the water itself were going her way, flowing before
her to clear all obstacles, flowing behind, lending
propulsion.

But the twins did not care, at the moment, for the
glories of *Titanic* or the day. Locked in their room,
they were both, for the first time, uncomfortable with
each other, both, suddenly, not knowing how it happened that they were enemies.

"So stupid," said Swan, plucking at a velvetappliquéd rosebud on her skirt of a darker red. "Lady Pomeroy's beau. *Really*, Smoke."

Smoke said nothing. She was restlessly, distractedly, turning the pages of her scrapbook, looking at pictures of merchant ships, long curved schooners with flying, wind-filled sails—not seeing them, but looking, idly, because she did not want to look at Swan. Her cheeks were warm with emotion and her heart was chilled.

"If you want to run away, sister dear," said Swan, going on with it, being mean and arch and condescending, "an ocean liner is not the place to do it. Anyone could have told you that. *Really*. You've been reading fairy tales again."

"Oh, stop," said Smoke. "It was just a game, that's all. I was bored, with nothing better to do."

"Well, your *childish* game has ruined my wedding plans. Almost ruined them, that is, not quite."

Smoke stopped turning pages, but she did not look up. Whatever did Swan mean, wedding plans? Carefully, she said, "I don't know anything about that. Tell me more. I burn to know."

"Danny and I are getting married as soon as we get back home. He won't be going back to England. He'll stay with us until he's settled. He'll probably go to work in a nightclub band or for a theater troupe. *I* will sponsor him and perhaps invest in theatricals. Father will help me."

Now Smoke did look at her sister. Smoke's face was flaming; she knew it, didn't try to hide it any longer. "Marry that peasant, Swan? Just because he seduced you? Don't be ridiculous. You may be a harlot, but you are not mad, I hope."

Swan was lounging back on her bed pillows,

knocking her toes together the way she did when she was especially proud of herself. She did not protest at Smoke's insult. She smiled like a cat that was up to its whiskers in cream. "I am not a harlot. I may be a slut, but I am not a harlot. Sluts give it away to those they fancy, harlots charge."

"Oh, I'll bet you charge," said Smoke. "I bet you charge plenty. Maybe not money, maybe only a wedding ring, but you didn't do it for nothing. No, no, not you."

"Maybe you're right," said Swan, as though she did not care one way or the other.

"I don't know you anymore, Swanny. You're different."

"Some grow," said Swan, off her bed and looking out the window. "Some stay stunted."

Smoke closed her scrapbook gently. She put it aside, on the rug, just under her bed. She did not want to hurt her dream book if she got into a fight.... "You're being insulting, dear sister, as well as mysterious. I don't see why."

"Danny hates you," said Swan. "He says you are jealous of me. Of him and me. And I agree. You are."

"But I am not!" Smoke said. "You know me better than he does, who doesn't know me at all. Why would you let that *nobody* speak against me that way? I can dislike a person and not be green-eyed jealous, can't I?" Outraged, she stared at her twin.

That was all it had taken, she thought: a boy.... One full-lipped boy and her twin had turned against her. She had never been so unhappy, so miserable!

"I *don't* think you should sleep with him, that's right," Smoke said. "And I *don't* think he's worthy of you, that's right, too. Nobody would. He's socially beneath you, financially beneath you, educationally beneath you—will you grant that? And I *don't* think you're in love with him—how could you be?—you've not met anyone else to compare him to. He's just your wretched, precious *pen pal* come to life like a toy, and you're enchanted. You certainly haven't matured enough to know what you want. You couldn't have. And Mother and Father will never let you marry him. Danny Bowen is a nothing—he can't even spell—and you're an heiress. So who's stupid now? And since you have been a perfect dunce *throoo it all* and been deflowered by a cheap jazz-hall musician, you'll just have to get over it and get over him."

"My, my," purred Swan, "and is the lecture over, Miss Green-eyes?"

Smoke sat up, too stirred to remain quiet on the bed. "And if you're pregnant, Swan," she said, falsely sweet, "you'll be ruined for life. You'll have to stay at home and care for the dim little bastard, who'll live in the attic, and you'll be a spinster till the end of your days—"

"You!" Swan hurled her hairbrush at her sister. It struck Smoke's chest, dropped, silver, into her lap.

"Oh," said Smoke. She picked up the brush and began pulling her sister's long golden strands from the boar bristles. "Oh, Swan...."

There was a silence then, both overcome by the violence between them. Both hung their heads, re-gretting.

"I'm sorry, Smokey," said Swan. "I didn't mean it."

She wriggled off her bed and came to her twin's. "Please forgive me?"

Silently, Smoke moved over, and Swan climbed in beside her. They laid their heads back together and held hands, fingers interlocked. Finally Swan sighed elaborately and said, "It's just that it's so good, you see, Smoke. I must be like Aunt Celeste. I liked it almost right away.... I went looking for it."

"Making love, you mean?" Smoke closed her eyes with shame. How could you, Swanny...?

"Yes. I knew I'd love it, and I didn't want to wait. I couldn't share that with you before because you weren't interested—you don't understand. So it became my *secret*. I wanted to tell you, oh, way back. But when I tried, you always pooh-poohed. So then I stopped and told only my diary."

"It makes me squeamish to think of it," said Smoke sadly. "Getting naked in front of a boy and him getting naked, too, and then letting him put his— *apparatus*—" she shivered "—into you...."

"Oh, it's wonderful," said Swan. She clicked her heels together. "I made Danny do it. He wouldn't have, on his own."

"I thought men couldn't control themselves."

Swan squeezed her sister's hand and released it. "Maybe after a certain point they can't, but Danny wouldn't let himself reach that point, you see, unless I urged him on."

"And you did, Swan? Why? Why ever why?"

"Ah, because I get this funny soft feeling inside sometimes, when I see a handsome boy. And I get daydreams that he's touching me, and my skin just *itches* for him to do it.... I don't *try* for it to happen, it just does." Swan thought a moment, thinking how to explain. "There're two kinds of women, I think, dear sister. There're hot ones and cold ones—parrots and penguins, let's say. And I'm a parrot and you're a penguin, Smokey. I'm a heat wave, you're a snow-storm. So even though we're twins outside, inside we're absolutely different—I got all the hot stuff. See?" Swan kissed her sister's cheek. "See, Smokey...? Please see."

Now it was Smoke's turn to sigh, because what Swan was saying wasn't true: Smoke got hot. *Danny Bowen, for instance. He made Smoke hot, too....* But that, she did not tell.

She said, instead, "But to marry the first boy you like? You haven't even come out. Don't you want to be a debbie? There'll be so many pretty dresses to wear, and parties to go to and fun. You could marry after your deb season, marry anyone you want, but don't you want a flock of beaux to choose from?"

Swan considered.

"Yes," she said after a while, "yes, I do. But—" she shrugged "—one can't have everything. And I want Danny, Smoke. He's darling and dear. And he's not a fortune hunter. All he wants out of life is to play his violin and teach it when he's old—that's not the ambition of a gold digger. And..." Swan snug-gled down and laid her head on her sister's breast. "And I *like* him. He makes me feel so good...that way, you know. I'm the one who proposed. 'You'll have to marry me now,' I said. 'I hope you don't mind.'"

Smoke scrunched down next to her sister. "And what did he say then?"

Swan giggled. "He said he would love to, but he

didn't think it would happen. He wasn't good enough for me. My parents wouldn't allow it.''

''Well, that's true, that's all true,'' said Smoke.

''So,'' said Swan, and she pinched, just a little, the skin at her sister's elbow. ''So I figured out how to fix it.''

''What do you mean?''

''Listen. I wrote an anonymous letter to Twiggs. I put it in an envelope and licked it closed and wrote 'PERSONAL' on the outside in capitals, and then I had one of the stewards deliver it to her right after luncheon.''

''What did the letter say, for heaven's sake?'' Smoke felt a gnawing near her heart: Swan's game was going to be better than hers had been: she could *feel* it coming....

''It said,'' said Swan, smug in victory, ''that one of her charges was, *at that very moment*, stupping with one of *Titanic*'s staff. On E deck, in room 224, not far from the boiler rooms.''

''No!''

''Yes. And as soon as I sent it off to be delivered, I jumped into the kip with Danny.''

''Oh Swan, I just don't understand.'' But she did understand, a little.

''It's very simple,'' said Swan. ''I had to force a crisis, but it couldn't seem to come from me. So there came Twiggs, of course, on fire, thundering down.'' Swan laughed. ''She brought one of the ship's officers with her, a Mr. Boxhall. They were ready to batter down the door. But I'd left it unlocked, and so...''

''And so you let yourself be *discovered* like that?

In the altogether?'' Smoke was horrified at the thought.

"Unveiled, in the buff. That's right. Danny almost died of fright. But other than that, so far it's worked like a charm—"

"Swan! Didn't he know what you were up to?"

"Of course not, silly. He'd never have agreed to it."

"You astonish me," said Smoke. "Twiggs has gone to Mother about both of us. We've been *locked in*. I fail to see the charm in that." She slithered off the bed and went to the door and turned the knob. The door did not open. "Father will probably come and beat us."

"And Mother will disown us and forget we ever existed."

"And Lady Pomeroy will have me put in jail for false impersonation, and you'll find out you're pregnant and grow fat as a whale."

Swan clicked her heels, contented. "That's as may be," she said, "but I'm getting married. To Daniel Terence Bowen. And that's the important thing."

AUDREY HAD ESCAPED AT LAST from Mrs. Twigg. The governess had finally slowed and said, "I will carry on if I must, Mrs. Lockholm, but only until we dock, and I demand my reference now." Audrey had written her a good one, and Mrs. Twigg had tucked it into her bosom and fled. And Audrey tiptoed into Tory's room.

It was late afternoon, the sun was setting early as it did in the north in April, and the darkening day made the hour seem, to Audrey, later than it was. The lights of *Titanic* sparkled beyond Tory's bedroom window like magic just out of reach, for Tory's room was dim, illumed only by the window's light. And Tory, slight in the bed for all the lift of her stomach, Tory struggled as she slept, fitfully, in her sheets.

Madame Romany was with her, flabby arms bared, long black sleeves folded back and pinned. The gypsy sat in a graceful wicker chair, an ungraceful woman. She was tired, too. Both eyes, the good and the bad, were red rimmed with fatigue.

Audrey stood by Tory's bed, took her hand and held it. The hand was hot and tense, the muscles flexed against the pain. Tory's face was dull, the radiance gone. Yellow blighted her cheeks and a purplish tinge sullied her lips, and her hair, just yesterday glossy jet, spread upon the pillows as rough as rope. Her mouth was slack; she seemed not to breathe....

Behind Audrey, the gypsy said, "She vomited for hours. Whatever poison she swallowed was a good one. She is lucky to survive that."

"It was on her tongue only," said Audrey. "A small fat yellow pill, not yet dissolved. Cyanide of potassium, she said it was. I took it away."

The gypsy shifted in her chair, heavy, slow. "She is little and tight," Madame Romany said. "She has torn something inside fighting the poison, and the baby is trying to come too early as a result. She will suffer long...."

"Is she conscious?" Audrey asked. "Does she know?"

"She comes out of the deep sleep for long stretches and labors in silence. She asks for nothing. Once in a while she moans. And sometimes she tries to get out of bed. When I stop her she reaches out to me and says, 'Don't tell, no matter what. Don't let them tell the doctor or Burt....' I have promised her, m'lady, no one will tell.''

"No one will tell," said Audrey. "If you are ready to go back, I will watch her now."

"How long can you stay?"

"As long as it takes," said Audrey.

Madame Romany snorted softly. "You would not last a day, lady fine. I will rest now, a few hours. I need that. Then I will come back."

Audrey turned to face the woman. In the faded day Madame Romany was exposed as very old and very tired. Over her sightless eye, the eyelid drooped and twitched. Her many-wrinkled face quivered in the bones beneath the folds of flesh.... She was witch-like—perhaps that was why she shrouded herself, Audrey thought—though once she must have been one of the prettiest girls in San Francisco.... Jeoffry Eckkles had loved her. He had killed a man for her, married her. He had come back to her after his time with Bay's mother, Edmunda. He had provided for her before he left for good. Audrey had seen Esmeralda's daughter: Daphne Diego was a rare beauty. The Mediterranean women, Audrey thought, bloom early, gorgeous and exotic. But if not cared for they grow frowsy, *overblown*, as they say of the rose when it is past its prime. Whereas women like me, New England stock, we grow dry and brittle and bloodless if we are not loved.

"Sleep in my bed, Esmeralda," said Audrey. "I'll stay here until you come back to her. And...thank you."

Madame Romany creaked up out of the graceful

chair and lumbered from the room without a word. Within moments Audrey could hear her, next door, snoring like a pirate overcome by wine.

Audrey settled herself in the wicker chair still warm from Madame Romany. She folded her hands in her lap to watch over her friend. I hope she dreams of heaven, Audrey thought, while she endures her living hell.

CAPTAIN STANLEY LORD of *Californian* stood over his wireless operator, reading the incoming message from *Titanic*. It asked him not to use the Marconi apparatus to contact Lady Pomeroy, *Titanic* passenger, ever again for any reason. It said his doing so would be considered "breach of conduct," by his employer, Leyland Line, which was owned by IMM, and as such would be marked against him. Lady Pomeroy was aboard *Titanic* in the party of one of the directors of IMM, the communication ran, and she did not want, indeed she was suffering from, his attentions. As a result, the director of IMM was personally demanding Captain Lord "to desist from ignobility and resume, forthwith, his proper duties...."

Captain Lord was livid.

As soon as he had the missive in his hand, he crumpled it in his fist. *How dare she....* Not only had the lady refused him, then changed her mind and led him on, she had broadcast his affection—*the bitch!*—and toyed with his infatuation. Tired of the game, she had then *reported him to his superiors, perhaps ruined his career....* He had enjoyed command of *Californian* less than a year; he was still on trial, for God's sake. What was the stupid woman thinking of...?

She was a pig; there you had it. She was a beast!
Didn't she realize *lives* were at stake…? *His* life,
at least—worth ten of hers!

No, love could not survive such abuse; passion
would not survive such humiliation.

Captain Lord turned and marched, stony faced, to
his private quarters. Well, she did not know the man
she had spurned. She did not know his measure: he'd
get her back for this if it took a *lifetime.*

Wanton bitch of a whore. Slept with him in sight
of her husband's corpse, and it not yet cold. *Piece of
garbage.…* In his room he locked the door against
interference, poured out rum three fingers deep.

Let her rot, I say, at the bottom of the sea.

He raised his glass and drank to it.

"Ho, ho, ho, Davy Jones," sang his caged green
bird. And it flashed its wings and shivered, and
stretched out its claws for a cracker.

BURTON VANVOORST STOOD before the bar in *Titanic's* Palm Court, eyes vacant, wondering what
next to drink. He'd been bolting stingers all day, and
they were beginning to pall.

He'd missed dinner, but what the hell. Popped a
few peanuts though, and a couple of those hot prunes
wrapped in bacon. What was the name of the damn
things anyway—devil's raincoats? Something like
that. He liked devil's raincoats, he decided. He
needed such a raincoat for himself, devil that he
was.… Have to order one from Hoskins, his tailor,
first thing he got back on terra firma.…

Okay, so he'd been wrong. Okay, so he'd been an
insensitive bastard. He'd make it up to her, beg her
forgiveness. Tell her the truth: he didn't care if she

was Eurasian, Hindu or Hottentot polka dot. He loved her, was abysmally miserable without her.

He wanted her back.

"Listen," he said to the bartender, and waved a pruneless toothpick in the air.

The bartender was a Negro, a deep, shining black. He was an elegant man of middle years, about Burty's age, in a white coat and black tie, with hair of grizzled gray. "Sir," the bartender said.

"Listen," said Burty. "What's your name?"

"Wisdoms, sir." The bartender wiped the mahogany bar with a rag.

"Well, listen, Wisdoms," said Burty. "What I want to say is that nobody's perfect."

The bartender smiled.

Just like a white man, thought Burty. He didn't grin like a jiggaboo. He smiled just like a white man!

The bartender's teeth were fine and very white, and one of the upper molars showed a little diamond chip close to the gum. "Thasso, capt'n," the bartender said. "The Lord, he say even the righteous man sin seven times a day. Thinkathat, capt'n, seven times a day, even the best of us."

"Listen," said Burty, "I'd like a pink lady. Do you know what that is? Can you make one of those?"

The bartender snapped his rag. "Sure can, capt'n. Comin' right up."

"Good man," said Burty.

"Thank you, sir," said the bartender. He broke an egg deftly, separated yellow from white with the halves of the shell.

"I'll bet you don't make many of these for gentlemen, Wisdoms," said Burty, watching the bartender add cream and grenadine to the egg white, and gin and ice before shaking it all.

"Not too many, capt'n, but it's a popular drink with the ladies. They like to sip it slow, you know, through a little colored straw."

"My wife is a pink lady, Wisdoms. Very beautiful, very nice."

"Thasso, sir?" The bartender poured the cocktail into a long-stemmed glass. He put a napkin with the White Star Line pennant on its face in front of Burty and set the glass upon it. "There, now, capt'n, how's that?"

Burty nodded and took a sip. The drink was sweet, like the meringue on lemon pie. Burty pursed his lips, rolled his lips over the glass rim. "This is an awful ladylike drink," he said.

The bartender laughed and the diamond chip flashed. "Well, you can throw it away if you want," he said.

"Oh no, no, this is just what I want." Burty sipped again. "Reminds me of my better half. Tory, Wisdoms. That's her name. Victoria VanVoorst, three *V*s in a row."

"Victoria VanVoorst," said Wisdoms. "That's a name for a queen, sir."

Burty looked at the man. "That's what she is," he said. "That's just what she is, Wisdoms, and she's going to have a baby. Our first."

"Thasso? Congratulations, you must be a happy man. 'Propagate if you would be great,' so saith the Lord. What will you name him, sir?"

"It just came to me," said Burty. "I'm going to name him after you." Burty took half the drink in his mouth and swallowed. It was a god-awful drink.

"Me, sir?" The diamond chip winked.

"You," said Burty. "You're a gentleman."

The bartender bowed.

Burty thought he'd have another god-awful drink his next go-round, a double grasshopper in lots of shaved ice. "Wisdoms Kingsley VanVoorst," he said, finishing the egg-white confection. "How's that sound?"

"That sounds right fine, cap."

There was a line of foam on Burty's upper lip. He dabbed it off with the napkin. "Would you give a man with a name like that your vote for president?"

The bartender cocked his head and shrugged. "I'm Jamaican-born, sir. Never voted in my life."

"Well—" Burty waved his hand "—if you were American, what then?"

Wisdoms shook his head. "I wouldn't want to commit myself on that one ahead o' time, sir. No, no."

"You'd want to look him over first," said Burty. "Is that it? See if he was...a righteous man."

"Thassit, yes, sir."

Burty nodded. He put a crisp new dollar bill on the bar. "Good night, Wisdoms, and thank you. That was a very fine drink."

"Good night, Mr. VanVoorst, been a pleasure...."

In the bar of the smoking room Burty ordered a double grasshopper on the rocks. He leaned against a pillar and idly watched the tables of gambling men. He was waiting for Teddy "Rolls" Royce to show. When Rolls walked into the room, Burty was going to intercept that raincoatless devil and bash him in the face for the trouble he had caused.

He'd beat the son of a bitch to a pulp is what he'd do, and then beat the mutt out of all his money, too.

Saturday, April 13

14

For three hours John Phillips and Harold Bride, wireless operators for *Titanic*, had been toiling together trying to get the machinery to operate. Inexplicably, at 11:00 p.m. the box had sent up a short hiss and died. Phillips, senior officer, was on duty. After working for some minutes to repair the device on his own, he called Harold Bride from his bed to help. Patiently, young Bride read from the manual; carefully John Phillips traced through the workings and wires trying to find the cause for failure.

A little after two, Joseph Boxhall joined them. Everything else on board was working perfectly. Even the night was sweet aired and calm, the visibility clear for miles, and the ocean as gentle as a bay.

"How's it progressing, Phillips?" Boxhall inquired. He brought the two men mugs of hot coffee.

"No better," said Phillips. "Thanks for this."

"We're still working on it," said Harold Bride. "It'll be something simple when we do find it, like a wire gone loose. What do you say, Phillips?"

The senior operator just shook his head and

yawned, and went on gliding his fingertips over a thin cap wire.

"E.J.'s got a woman in his bed," said Boxhall conversationally. "A rich American. He noticed her on departure—pointed her out to me."

John Phillips was young and going to be married. He was not envious. "Is she a looker, Mr. Boxhall? Would she be the beautiful redheaded widow or that blonde—what's her name—Candee?"

"Now that would be telling, wouldn't it?" said Boxhall. "But she's a looker, I'll give you that."

"If I had to choose, I'd take the redhead," said Harold Bride. "She's the best on the boat, my vote."

"She's more woman than you could handle, pup," said Boxhall. "You stick to the young lassies. Lady Pomeroy would eat you up in no time."

Harold Bride considered. "That's probably true," he said. "But how I'd try to please her—oh, how I'd try." He watched Phillips's hand move to another wire.

"What about you, Joe?" said John Phillips, running his fingers blindly over invisible lines, trying to feel where he could not see, under the wire cap.

"Well, I like the young ones. Those blond twins are nice."

Both wireless men groaned. "Don't mix with the short-haired one, sir," said Harold Bride as he unscrewed a dial. "She's a pain in the hindquarters, she is."

Boxhall lounged in the doorway so he could talk and still see the watch on the bridge. "I saw her in here earlier, just sitting around. She must like you, Bride—your name probably appeals."

Bride vigorously shook his head. "Lord help me,

no. She's a terror. Got all high-handed with me she did, when I wouldn't let her send. She's one of the brass's daughters, you know. Lockholm, of IMM. Best leave that one alone. She'd have you out of a job in no time.''

"Aye. I leave them all alone in first class. I know my place.''

"So E.J. used to,'' said Phillips. "Maybe it gets to us all, in time. The cat's away, the lady is willing, no one's looking and no one'll tell. So the rat begins to gnaw the cheese....'' He kissed his fingertips to ease the hurt of finger-testing the screws.

Boxhall folded his arms on his chest. "I'll tell you this,'' he said. "The captain's in love, told me so himself. 'First time in my life,' he said to me tonight. 'May it happen one day to you, Joe....' Well—'' he shook his head disapprovingly "—I don't like it.... Let me know when you've found the trouble, will you?''

"As soon as we're sending, we'll report,'' said Phillips. "Thanks again for the Java. It helps.''

Boxhall nodded and ambled away. He had seen what he'd come to see: the stack of ice warnings on the spindle had grown an inch high. It was unusual, so many, with the wind and water temperature still comparatively warm, and there was no storm nor rumor of one—just ice, always ice, straight ahead and lots of it. Well, the lads would fix the wireless and everything would be all right. If E.J. isn't worried, thought Fourth Officer Boxhall, why should I be?

Loud voices on A deck rose to the deck above. Boxhall bolted for the stairs. The whole bloody boat would wake up. Part of his job tonight was to preserve the peace. The peace and safety of *Titanic* and her passengers, that was his charge.

Whole bloody hell, he thought, shouts were coming from the smoking room. That meant the gambling men were at each other's throats, one accusing another of cheating, or someone, in his cups, turning surly at a downturn of luck. Boxhall was glad he was not a gambling man: it made for grave instability of character, he thought, even among the privileged.

NICOLA HAD ADMIRED in her late husband—among many other things—his lighthearted integrity. Rolf Lord Pomeroy had worn his virtues gracefully, and one of the most endearing was—for all his enduring love of sport—his insistence never to wager on happenstance or competitive outcome. Other men could gamble and be great, other men could lose or conquer fortune: Rolf Lord Pomeroy would congratulate or condole easily and sincerely, and feel no temptation heat his heart.

"Oh, that's ripping, Nick—see how fine." Or, "Worse luck, Nick, Will's horse ran dead last." Good-hearted, well-wishing, attentive and appreciative: those were the attitudes Rolf Lord Pomeroy brought to sport. He left, with no regret, the blood-stopping excitement of the bet to those who, he said, used their money as a measure of their fate.

And Nicola, though she did not share the passion of men who spun the wheel of fortune while they leaned their souls, their minds, their bank accounts upon it, Nicola liked to watch what happened in men's eyes when they won...or lost, small amounts and great. Nicola, who was a different woman, who was as much a conqueror as any man; who was—

who always had been—exactly what she wanted to be, Nicola liked to see what men wanted to be…and were not. Such intimate glimpses often showed when men gathered together for sport and gambling; often in the crisis, there would be…a revelatory moment.

So Nicola Lady Pomeroy, restless with boredom, sauntered, late, to the smoking lounge. She came with her small glass of Cointreau to idly sit awhile. She would watch Teddy Royce at risk, she thought; he who was too interested in her jewels to be a gentleman, he who was too tempted by her estate to feign indifference. She would watch him stake his manhood upon the caprices of a deck of playing cards, and mark him how he fared.

Burty VanVoorst was there, against a pillar, red nosed from drink but correct of bearing. He waved to her and she crossed to him. She wore thin-threaded silk of hunter green. Mandarin collared, it shimmered upon her breasts and hips, highlighted by her turquoise-and-enamel necklace, and set her hair to burning.

"Dear Burt," she said as she reached him. "Your Tory is ill. Have you been to her?"

Burty had a drink in his hand, a fresh drink, the glass was nearly full. His eyes were red-shot with tiny veins. But by conscious effort he held himself erect, though something he could not control pulsed angrily in his throat. Still, he smiled upon her and spread his legs a little to steady himself, and said with a dignity Nicola found touching, "However she is, Nicky, I love her still."

And then he was silent. He drank, a long draft.

She put her hand, white gloved, long gloved, upon his arm. "You must go to her, Burt. Go now. She needs you. More, she wants you. You are a fortunate man.''

He rolled a bit as she touched him, then straightened and smiled affably again, a tender smile for so alcohol-soaked a face. ''You're a beautiful woman, Nick,'' he said. ''You stand proud, independent, like a statue. I'd love to love you, but—'' he shrugged like a boy ''—Tory has taken all my heart.''

''Dear Burty,'' she said, and thought, So it will be all right, anyway, about Tory. How right, how good.

''My dear,'' he said, pulling pathetically on the points of his vest to correct the results of his two-day binge, ''would you give me a little kiss? I know I'm all liquored up—if I weren't, I wouldn't ask— but I do want a beautiful woman to kiss me now. Just once. Just a little.'' His eyes swam and blurred, then cleared because he willed them to.

Nicola leaned forward and kissed him on the lips. It was a light, chaste kiss; it lasted only the briefest moment. But he seemed very pleased. He raised his chin and threw his shoulders back and expelled all the breath in his chest. She smiled at him. ''You're one of the lovely men, Burt, one of the goodies. Now, will you escort me to a table? I've come to watch the gambling for a while. Will you play?''

He offered his arm. She touched gloved fingertips upon it. He brought her to a table, drew back a chair. She sat, crossed her knees, and sipped at her drink. He drained his and set the empty glass on the ivory-inlaid tabletop.

''I cannot leave you here unaccompanied,'' he said.

''Oh, yes, you can,'' she said. ''I wish to be alone. I can't sleep yet, but soon, I hope. So good night, dear Burt, and don't worry, no monster will get me unless I wish it.''

"Ah, Nick," he said. His head hurt terribly, but his heart was suddenly happy. "Rolf was worthy of you, he was a splendid fellow. But where will you find another?''

"Ah, Burt…" she said. "Good night.''

She liked him enormously. She was glad it was going to be all right between him and Tory. She thought that for the baby's christening she would give it a pure white pony. By the time the tot was two, it would be riding astride, already a soldier….

"Good night, dear lady.''

He left her because he had to. He was waiting to start a fight, and Nicola could not be any part of that. He was waiting for Rolls Royce, the bastard who had started this whole sorry business with his *nigger tattletales*—

There the rat was now.

There he was, already in and seated while Burty's back had been turned to the beauteous Nicola. *There the son of a bitch was, already playing a hand.*

He would have to wait then, just a moment….

Teddy Royce looked with cocked eyebrow at Nicola, stunning and alone, but kept his thumbs over the slightest fan of five cards couched deep into his palms.

Burty studied Rolls's handsome face, sea tanned and chiseled, mustached and dark-haired over an ivory linen jacket. Rolls was handsome as Burty would never be, had never been. But so what? thought Burty. He believed that looks were never the measure of a man. That bird will never make a million on his own, thought Burty, filled with contempt. He'll have to have it handed to him...or marry it....

And then Burty glanced at Nicola. She was looking at Rolls with that detached-and-amused air she had, as though however wonderful something might be to anyone else, to Nicola Lady Pomeroy it just missed going over the top. It might be very nice indeed, but it would not be...*marvelous*. Burty admired that. He wished he had been higher-born only so he would appreciate more thoroughly all the joys life offered.... Thought was making him sober. He had, he realized, in his life, not given over enough time to...*appreciation*. He hadn't had the time. He had been too busy gathering, amassing, *scrambling*.

He, like Theodore "Rolls" Royce, Burty realized with the greatest clarity, was not quite yet a gentleman.

Well.... His *son* would be a gentleman then! Gentler than himself, more cultured. But less of a go-getter. He would pile; his son would spend. In three generations, unless Burty looked to that, too, the name of VanVoorst would cease to disconcert. He would look to it as soon as he got home....

Burty turned his mind back to the handsome worm who sat so at ease at the round felt-topped table. Nicola Lady Pomeroy could never love a rotter like that. She would never think Rolls Royce *marvelous*...though she might, Burty conceded, find him *nice enough* for a couple of North Atlantic sea-bound nights.

The hand at Royce's table was over and Rolls had won it. Burty watched the blackguard rake in the chips. The man's wrists were thick; the muscles in his back and shoulders rippled under the linen jacket.

Big as he is, hard as he is, he'll never take me, Burty thought. Anger weights my fists like iron rings....

And then, ready, he was standing at his enemy's back. He tapped Teddy Royce on the vertebrae at the nape of his neck. "Sir," Burty said. "I demand you step away from this table for a moment. You and I have private business that must be attended to."

Teddy Royce had seen Burty come, seen the set purpose in his jaw and seen the plump cheeks lock with purpose. Rolls knew he was in for it, for what could he do but let the jester play the hero? Lady Pomeroy, *interested, the darling*, sat three tables away, intently watching. Teddy would play to the lady's *maternal instincts* and let himself be bested....

He bowed to his company. "Excuse me, please," he said. He pushed back his chair, started to rise out of it.

Burty, furious at Royce's self-possession, lost his. Burty swung from his heels, where he stood, an overhand right. His fist connected from behind with Teddy Royce's underjaw and kept on going.

Rolls had not seen the haymaker coming, had not expected it. A gentleman in a drawing room or in a first-class smoker, however offended with another, did not swing from behind before one was ready; that was rude, that was blindsiding, that was street brawling. It wasn't done.

Rolls staggered under the blow. His chair skidded behind, he lost his balance and crashed to the floor. There was pain in his chin but it was dull, as though the jaw were numb. And it felt good on the floor, rather comfortable, he thought, though he would have to struggle up and make a proper show of it....

He was on his knees when Burty pounded him again, on the temple this time, and then rained blows upon him, battering and furious, drumming his ears, his eyes; the man was drunk-loony and a maniac besides....

Men were pulling the nigger-lover off him. Through puffed eyes he saw VanVoorst canting backward, arms pinioned by a dozen concerned citizens. The bugger was fighting them, too, taking on the whole room....

Teddy Royce rolled over to see where Lady Pomeroy was. She was out of her chair and shimmering, ocean green. She was gliding toward him, angel quiet. She did not look alarmed, only curious.

Fascinated, he watched her come. He smiled, and all his face protested. Still he smiled, for she was exceedingly beautiful. She crouched beside him and her breasts moved within the silk of hunter green. He thought he loved her truly.

A shadow fell over him—not hers, his enemy's. He looked, swollen-eyed, at VanVoorst, free of the men who had pulled him away. "I apologize to you, VanVoorst," said Rolls. He extended his hand. "I should not have sold, you should not have bought. I regret it."

Burty did not take his hand. Burty looked at Nicola, who was silently studying Rolls Royce's face, and said, "Forgive me, Lady Pomeroy, making you a witness to this, but it had to be."

Nicola felt pity for them both and love for them both, too. Stooped beside Teddy Royce, she looked up at Burty and nodded, and smiled slow and sad. She said nothing, though her lips parted.

Burty turned away then and walked from the

smoking room. Other men watched him go, glad the fury was over and no great harm done.

"Cabin fever," said one to his companion. "Even on such a ship as this, it gets to some."

"There was some trouble about VanVoorst's wife," said the other. "She used to know this Royce chap before she married, I believe."

"I see," said the first, and smoothed his whiskers with a finger, and thought of Mrs. VanVoorst, a luscious woman. "I see, yes, well..."

In Burty's heart now there was only a great wound, a chasm only Tory could fill. He was going to her now, coming home to her now.... He knew he had brought on her labor early, and she had been battling alone and long....

His fault.

They might lose the baby.

He promised in his mind: He would never leave her again, until death did them part—

"Tory!" He shouted out her name, began to run. "Tory! Tory...!"

She heard him calling as he neared. Worn-out, she pulled herself higher on the pillows to greet him....

Nicola continued to stare at Teddy Royce, lolling on the floor before her.

"Do you often get yourself into such scrapes as this?" she said, and lifted back a lock of his hair that had become displaced.

"There are those," he said, and it hurt him to talk but he ignored that, "who depend upon amusement to define their lives. You might as well know, I'm one of them."

"So this is amusing," she said as evenly as she might ask the temperature.

He nodded and began to laugh. He thought his face would burst from the pain the laughing caused, but he couldn't stop. He *liked* the pain. It validated the evening, validated his life. And the pain had brought Lady Pomeroy to his side, dressed in a conqueror's hunter green.

"Get up now," said Nicola, and she waited, offering no assistance.

Still laughing, still hurting, he stood. He took her arm and tucked it around his own. They headed out, then, he chuckling and patting her hand, she as gracious as a queen bestowing knighthood.

AND AUDREY COULD NOT find Bay.

Most of Friday she sat with Tory, while Tory alternatively strained and slept. Audrey watched the day pass, out the window, watched the Atlantic Ocean tumble, serene and beautiful. As the sun fell the ocean's color faded from brilliant blue to deepest ice-flecked gray.

At six, Madame Romany relieved her, and Audrey asked a steward to find her husband, but the steward returned and said Bayard Lockholm could not be found. She ate in the dining room at the captain's table with Dove and Nicola and the Astors and Bruce Ismay, but Bay did not appear. Mrs. Twigg, also, was not heard from or seen, and the twins were locked in their room until Bay and Audrey would go to them.

She would have to confront her daughters before Sunday. Sunday was their birthday. And she wanted to consult with Bay before she did, because what were they to do about Swan, *soiled so easily* by that boy…? She blamed herself. She had not truly been a mother, always there, always guiding, the way Josephine had been for her. She had chosen Bay over the twins, chosen love over motherhood. She thought she had *attended* to her daughters by giving away their care to others, but Mrs. Twigg was right after all: Audrey had neglected her children. She had failed to love Smoke and Swan as they needed her to, and now the girls were paying her back. Paying *them* back, Bay and her.... Dearest Bay. Her life, her love.

And now she couldn't find him, and she wanted him desperately. Now she sat in their room, alone, in mink over her nightgown because the air was cold, waiting for her husband, afraid of her children, loath to face them, and terrified what tomorrow would bring because tonight at dinner the table places had been graced by *paper moons....*

Moons, as the gypsy had foretold.

She would sell the pearls with the clasp of ivory moon that Bay had given her as a bon voyage gift. She could not bear to look at the piece; it was beautiful but deadly. It lay now in its box, unworn after that one night, unfondled. She'd slipped it deep into her jewelry case, down to the bottom.... If she had been wiser, she would have given the necklace to Madame Romany instead of that check; the necklace was worth more. She would sell the pearls in New York as soon as they got back. She would restore the money to Bay's account....

Where was he?

Maybe the gypsy knew....

Half gypsy, half Mexican, fraudulent or true, Madame Romany or Esmeralda Diego, the old woman next door at Tory's bedside had proved her worth in this: she had insinuated herself into all their lives and was having her effect.

Oh, where was Bay, and what was he doing that he had so abandoned her?

Echoing through the corridor she heard Burty's calling, waking everyone.

"Tory, Tory!"

He was trumpeting like an elephant.

Miserable as she was, Audrey smiled to hear him. She closed her eyes and tucked the mink coat higher under her chin. Burty's hurrying footsteps passed her door: one of their husbands, at least, was safely home.

BAYARD LOCKHOLM, MORE RESPONSIVE to Mrs. Twigg's complaints than was his wife, had listened while she told him—though she, reciting the catastrophe a second time, had been calmer, too—of Swan's indelicate fall from grace.

He had been shocked, and she had been sorry for him. He had grayed before her eyes as she told, and she grew gentler, ever gentler, in the telling. When she was at the end, she told him, apologetically, that she had locked both girls in their stateroom, and gave him the key. She had resigned her position in anger, she said, to Mrs. Lockholm, which action she now regretted. She asked to continue on in her place; the twins needed her, she said. And she was as much at fault, if not more, than he or Mrs. Lockholm, for it had been her task and duty this voyage to look after the young women, to see to their safety of person and reputation, and she had failed utterly.

Bay had just sat there on A deck listening, as ashen as death, and then he had thanked her for all the good work she had done. "Of course you must continue on with the twins," he said, and told her she was not to blame herself, life was full of such tricks, and all of us, at bottom, must rely on something inside ourselves to see us through. Then he asked her to escort him, if she would, down to Danny Bowen's bunk room. He wanted to meet the lad, he said, have a talk with him.

Humbly, she had. Yes, Bayard Lockholm compared better in this affair than his wife. Uncharacteristically, she wished she had broken the news to Mrs. Lockholm differently; perhaps that would have somehow helped.

All day Bay Lockholm had stayed down on E deck, closeted in with Daniel Terence Bowen. In the evening, when Danny left to play in the Palm Court, Bay Lockholm sat on. Mrs. Twigg sat outside and waited. She had his dinner brought, and hers. They ate together, in silence, in that dark little closet of a room with no window and a harsh overhead bulb. Then she went outside and sat again, though her derriere—as she referred to it—was numb and her knees were stiff.

Late, Danny returned and went into the room and closed the door, and still Mrs. Twigg waited. She slept fitfully. She dreamed of silly things, bits of her childhood, her first kiss.... Splendidly begun, that one infatuation, but later too much heartbreak. She'd never tried love on again, had never before brought him to mind, not even in dreams.... Awake, she remembered her decision to go into service as nursery maid and governess—the decision that changed her life irrevocably.

Finally, finally, Mr. Lockholm came out of Danny

Bowen's room. He took her arm, *took her arm as though she were a lady,* and squired her up to B deck on the elevators.

Arrived, he walked her to her room and thanked her for her loyalty and steadfastness. "I'll not forget it, Mrs. Twigg," he said. "Thank you very much for all your help. Good night."

And then she heard a rowdy commotion coming from the public rooms—the men's smoker. It was after midnight, nigh onto one, and the noise was stirring up the entire deck. Quickly she whisked herself inside B-35 and locked her door against it.

She had given Bayard Lockholm the key to his daughters' room, directly across the hall. She heard, rather than saw, him fit the key into its chamber and throw free the bolt. And then some arrogant fool— oh, it was Mr. VanVoorst; it must be!—began hollering "Tory! Tory!" Mrs. Twigg thumped herself down on the side of her bed—something she would not allow the twins to do because it sagged the springs—and stripped off her stockings.

Somehow, she thought, yawning wide and not covering her mouth as there was no one to see, on board this ship I have become, for better or worse, part of this family....

And then she was snoring, still dressed and sideways, all matters set aside until the morrow.

SMOKE AND SWAN WERE ASLEEP, curved close to each other in Smoke's bed, when the key turning in the lock woke them.

They opened turquoise-colored eyes to see their father, their tall, elegant, reserved father, now coldly stern of face, contemplating them where they lay.

Neither girl moved. They waited, and Smoke's heart quickened as she struggled up to a sitting position and thought, Twiggs has told. Oh, what will Father say? Swan was wrong to do it, he is very angry—

Outside there was shouting, some stir, but Smoke paid no attention. For her the excitement was here, right here.

Swan was unafraid; she was eager for the confrontation. Under the bed cover she nervously tapped the sides of her feet against each other and patted her twin's hand to reassure her. Swan did not try to sit up when her father entered, but remained as she was under her father's eye, stretched out, at her ease.

"My dears," their father said, and crossed to the bed and sat himself at the foot, on Smoke's side where there was room.

Still, neither twin said a word.

"I've met the young man, this Daniel Bowen, Swan. He says he is in love and wants to marry you. He knows he is unworthy, knows you both are young, knows he cannot support a wife on his own. He has, he told me, a poor family and a mother to help financially, as he can. He is willing not to marry you now—"

"No," said Swan, interrupting, and now she did sit up and let the bright blanket fall away from her blue-ribboned nightdress. "No, Father, we must marry immediately, I insist on it, you see. I've already taken him as my husband, Father, don't you understand that?"

"I do understand, Swan Josephine, and I am grieved by it," said Bay. "Deeply grieved. You have lost, for no reason, what I—and the world—value more than beauty in a woman.''

"Well, then, restore my virtue, Father," said Swan. And composed, she began to plait her long gilt hair. "A married woman keeps her reputation."

Smoke thought of their father's sister, Celeste, but held her tongue. Mentioning Celeste would *really* get Father going.

"'Well, then' yourself, my little yellow daisy...." said Bay. He did not smile at her or pat the blanket encouragingly, as was his wont. He was rigidly composed, and that was frightening to Smoke. She saw what Swan did not, that their father was raging in his heart. He said, "You are in no position, missy, to tell me or the world what you will do. I will tell you, and I tell you this—you will not marry the lad this year or next—"

Swan screamed, "I will, I will, or I will die!"

"Nonsense," said Bayard Lockholm. "You will not see this boy—"

"He's not a boy, he's a man, and I will have him, you won't stop me—"

Swan flung herself from the bed and was running, barefoot, toward the unlocked door, but her father was there before her. He slapped her full across the face, once, very hard. The sound, unknown before in Lockholm homes, resounded, carried over the water out the window, rippled away.

Shocked into immobility, tears sprang into Swan's eyes, and the bright red mark of her father's hand stood out like stain upon her cheek. She swung around, retreated to her bed, marched to it, unrepentant. She climbed in, sat straight backed and stubborn against the pillow, and crossed her arms upon her breast. "I will marry him, Father. I will I will I will."

"No," said Bayard Lockholm. "You will grow up first. I am sorry I brought you along now on this trip—you are not ready for travel. When we are back, you will go to a convent-school, Swan Josephine. Switzerland, perhaps. Smoke will stay with us. You will be separated not only from this 'man,' but from your twin, from your parents, from your homes. I hope you will learn away what you could not learn from us—"

"Do you mean violence, Father?" said Swan. Her eyes had dried and were flashing, vivid blue.

"I mean," said her father calmly, "the attitudes of a lady, proper esteem for yourself and those about you."

"And if I don't, will you whip me like a slave? Hang me by my heels and lash me?"

He did not rise to her taunting. "If, when you have come of age, when you have passed your twenty-first birthday, you choose to lead a life of dissolution, my dear, I will not stop you. But it will be on your own funds and without my blessing. The choice is yours. That is all I have to say to you now. Tomorrow, perhaps, your mother will come to you.... Smoke—"

"Will we be locked up the rest of the voyage?" Swan interrupted again.

Bay shook his head. "No. Mrs. Twigg has decided to stay in charge of you. She asked to be relieved of that duty after what happened, but she thought again and took her position back."

"Hurray for Twiggs," said Swan, and she kicked out, under safety of the blanket. "She's a silly old maid, and if you want to know, I get around her nicely.''

"However foolish she is, she is a lady and I like and respect her," said Bay. He turned to his other daughter, stiff with surprise. "And now for you, Smoke."

Smoke was marveling at her sister. Swan had never performed like this in her life; Swan had been the dutiful, the exemplary one.... "Yes, Father," she said around the lump in her throat.

"Tomorrow Swan moves into Mrs. Twigg's room. You will remain here. That is not to say you cannot be with your twin. I hope you will be, and continue to be her friend."

Oh, he had never been like this before, either, so dark and final and punishing.... Swan was a triple fool. Hadn't she told Swan that a hundred times...?

"Yes, Father."

Bay rose. "The young man in question has agreed to stay away from you the rest of the crossing as a show of good faith. Don't ruin his chances as you have ruined yours, young lady."

He left them then, turning off the light and closing the door quietly, not locking it, behind him.

Both lay back in silence, wrapped in their own thoughts.

After a while they heard the light strains of a violin beyond their window: "Songe d'Automne," played for the one, though both sighed to hear it. Neither moved nor spoke. They lay together, listening to the music. At last both slept and dreamed of Danny Bowen—both the knowing one and the virgin.

JUST AS THE DAWN blushed palest pink onto monotonous swaths of gray, John Phillips found the burned-out ''secretary'' and fixed it. With that simple replacement, the Marconi apparatus flashed to life. The first incoming message was from the steamer *Montcalm*. ''Ice alert,'' it said. ''Heavy ice, all along the lane, between 41° and 42°N, 49° and 50°W. Field ice, pack ice, growlers and bergs....''

The other messages waiting to get through read much the same.

The two engineers sent the watchman to inform the officer of the day that the Marconi was repaired. They handed over all up-to-date warnings of ice. Then, feeling they had done their duty for a time, they turned off the device and, too exhausted to crawl back to their beds, lay down their heads on the sending table.

15

Captain E. J. Smith was the happiest of men. The night was clear with a thin cold moon, the waters of the North Atlantic were as placid as he had ever seen them. *Titanic* had more than doubled her miles on Friday, and he had increased the push for more of the same today. *Titanic* was responding, showing no strain; she was knifing through the water like a train on tracks. Engineer Bell had informed him at the end of this morning's inspection that the coal fire, four days smoldering in engine room six, was finally only dry ash; the chef and the sous-chef were talking to each other again—all little problems seemed solved....

And best of all, the lady loved him. *Best of all*, beautiful Dove Peerce, his dream come to life, *loved him*. Just now she had told him, sinuous and lace tumbled and thoroughly *poked*, she had confessed she loved him as madly as he loved her.

Ah, why hadn't he found her sooner? Life would have been so different then....

"I can't let you go now, E.J., ever," she said. "We'll have to marry as soon as we can. You couldn't go back to Eleanor and be happy, nor I to Newport alone. I'd waste away longing for you, and you'd die of boredom with her.''

She was very lovely, her cloud-white hair, her dawnlike cheeks, her elegant, lissome figure. Whatever age, her breasts were round and as white as rice, with peony-pink nipples that lifted firm and tasted sweet when he held them in his mouth. Where Eleanor—never a beauty—had spread in the natural way of women, with slackened breasts and a stomach that rippled when he laid her flat, this heaven creature's belly lay smooth upon its bones, and her legs curled around his buttocks when he took her for his own. Oh, this mistress of his heart was all a man could want.

''But I cannot marry you, my angel,'' he said. ''I have a family in Southampton—a wife that needs me and a child.''

''Oh, yes, you can,'' she said, languorous and gay, and she let him stroke her where he pleased, and sighed beneath his hands.

He considered it for a moment: divorce was an ugly thing, unbecoming to a man of decency and principle, ignominious to a man of achievement such as he. No, he would never leave Eleanor; after all, he loved Eleanor, *too*. She had been his childhood sweetheart; they were comfortable together; he read the funnies to her from the papers on Sunday mornings while she fixed his favorite breakfast, chipped beef on day-old toast. She always knew where his slippers were, and sewed his service stripes on just so, just right. She kept his bicycle oiled for when he came home, and the air in the tires up...and she was the mother of his child. No, he could not, *would not* leave Eleanor even for this swan of the sea, this miracle of grace and sin.

"You do not want an old sea walrus like me, my dear," he said, his mouth upon Dove's navel. "You'll tire of me by the time we dock in Hudson Harbor."

She smoothed his hair with a perfumed hand, hair thick and full, though not so white as hers. "Oh, yes, I do, dear Edward," she said. "You'll love Newport in the summers. From my bedroom in Peerce House you can see the ocean as far as where the sound breaks around Gilt Hill. We'll keep a little boat at the foot of our lawn, and you will be my brave captain. We'll entertain on the lawns in summer, and in the fall we'll do the New York season from my house on Fifth. You'll love my friends, you'll love America, you'll be the happiest of men, you'll see."

The happiest of men.... Hadn't he just thought that of himself a moment ago? And already that moment was fading and now he was uncomfortable because he loved her madly and he did not know how to tell her that he would not love her soon.... Off *Titanic* he would not love her; their liaison belonged here, belonged to now, his *fantasy*. He did not want to live with this American society woman the rest of his life. He was Brit through and through, solidly middle-class; he had no airs. He was a seaman and a good one—forget that bit of bad business with the *Hawke*. He was no drawing room gentleman stiff all day in starched shirtfronts and nothing to do but read the papers—and not even Eleanor to hear them—while his wife went shopping or visiting or was measured for yet another gown. No, dammit, she would become, in her own milieu, a Medusa, and he would be strangled by her, mangled by her, turned to stone....

"Would you turn over, my angel?" he said. "I long to kiss the bottom of your spine. Your back should have been painted by Ingres, your buttocks have driven me mad."

Dove said, soft, as she obliged him, "You've just never been unfaithful to your wife before, my love. The idea is new to you. But I understand these things, and you and Eleanor are done. Even if we part, you'll never love her again. You'd spend the rest of your life comparing, remembering, resenting her and wanting me."

E.J. lifted himself, joyously, upon her. She was right, he found her irresistible. He would stuff her now in the *belugas*, roll his sausage up her *roodle-doodledoo*. Eleanor never let him do this; Eleanor thought this kind of lovemaking dirty.... He parted Dove's beautiful backside and kissed where he wanted to go. Ah, he would explain it all to her later...much later. For now—

The telephone at the bedside rang.

To hell with it, he thought.

He was hoisting himself into position. Lust was roaring in him, such a joy.

The telephone rang again.

Ah....

E.J. rolled off his paradise and answered the call. It was nothing; a small correction of reckoning Lightoller wanted him to approve.

Naked, he hung up the receiver and looked down upon his lady. She was waiting for him, thighs spread, buttocks quivering, long arms delicate in bracelets of purest gold. Her head was thrown back, her throat curved, she was drinking champagne from a crystal goblet. The sight of her was so intoxicating, so rousing.

"Yes, I will marry you," he lied to make her happy—he wanted her to be happy, too—and then he threw himself upon her; again, for one long moment, the happiest of men.

Beneath him, Dove relaxed. She knew the battle was not yet won, but she knew, too, that she was winning....

And she did so love to take the prize.

MADAME ROMANY DISAPPEARED as soon as Burty opened the door to Tory's bedroom—now his and Tory's bedroom again. She'd been startled to see him; frightened. One dark black eye fired once, then dimmed. The blind one leaped in its socket, wanting to see, then died, hooded by a wrinkled lid. She uttered not a word to him. She shrank away and closed the door behind her, as though she had never been. He thought he understood: he must seem threatening, storming like a bull, full of drink and sudden decision, come to reclaim his wife.

But Tory slept, deep in some potion that eased pain and took all consciousness.

Burty was glad. He was weary from his debauchery, too tired now to be eloquent asking forgiveness. He would wait until she woke and found him beside her. Then would come the time of reconciliation. He wished he had a jewel to please her. When they got home he'd take her to Cartier's; Tory liked Cartier's.

He undressed in the dark, dropping his clothes on a chair, used to his man, Elgin, tidying up for him. Before he crawled into his wife's bed he stood, in his undershorts, out on the private deck. The night air was chill, the breeze from *Titanic*'s forward speed almost icy. The mast-high lights, strung carnival-style along the ship's great length, beamed down on the ocean below like captured stars. They threw jagged circles upon the whispering sea; exposed it eerie green. Like eyes, the little lights penetrated the moving blackness, but not far, not nearly far enough: they did not pierce the *mystery*....

Burty breathed deep; the air was icicle sharp, cleansing. Funny, he thought, I never in all my life ever thought about the colored, or what it means to be a woman. I'm just lucky, I guess, goddamn lucky to have been born a white man....

And then he went back to Tory, curled around her and covered her drum-tight stomach with a protective arm. He hoped, before sleep took him, she wouldn't be too hard on him when he awoke.

Tory shook him a little after four. Her water had broken and soaked the bed. She had rung for a steward. "Burty, you've got to get up," she said.

"Baby, say you forgive me," he said. "I was angry, I didn't know what I was doing or what I said. Say you forgive your Burtykins, please, purty-please?"

She was sick, weak from struggling. She was unmade-up, undressed. Her hair was wild, unpomaded, uncombed...and she was gorgeous, even with those dark circles under her sea-green eyes, even with that tiny thread between her brows that told of worry. She was the most beautiful woman he had ever seen.

"Burty, the baby is coming. The bed's got to be changed."

He didn't budge. "Tell me you forgive me, Tor, then I'll move."

"Oh—" She hopped to the bathroom, and he heard her vomit in the sink.

The door was slightly open. He stood on the other side of it and said, "Tell me you forgive me. I'm sorry. I was a fool. It was such a surprise, that's all. You should have told me."

The steward came then, with a young woman from housekeeping. They changed the bed without expression while Burty stood before the bathroom door in a double-silk bathrobe embroidered in dragons against a white ground, and Tory remained behind the door, quiet; all Burty heard was water lightly running.

When the ship's staff was gone, Burty went back to his job. "Tor? Tor, can you hear me?"

She came out. She was in a new dressing gown of ruby red. Her hair was combed, there was what seemed a natural blush upon her cheeks. Her lips were pink, and she smelled of exotic flowers.

"I forgive you," she said. "Let's never talk of it again."

"I'll kiss you after I shower," he said, "and we will talk of it. We'll talk it out. I've so much to tell you. I punched out your friend, for one thing, in the smoker. How's that for a start?"

She laughed, the old Tory. But then, "I'm in such pain, Burty," she said. "I think I'm going to die."

"I'll get the doctor," he said, turning toward the telephone.

"No." She held his arm. "Please, no. I don't want the ship to talk if baby isn't…isn't right. Please bring back the woman, the gypsy. She'll help."

He wanted to argue. Sense told him a doctor was warranted. But Tory was still ashamed, and he was going to play it Tory's way. "I'll get Audrey, if I can," he said. "Is that all right?"

Tory nodded, doubled up. Blood was running between her legs. She threw off the red dressing gown, stumbled back to the bath.

Burty crossed the outside deck to Audrey and Bay's room and knocked. But all was dark through the curtained pane, and no one came.

He went back and called to have Audrey paged, and then he sat down in an armchair to await the birth of his child. It won't be too long, he thought, and then her purgatory will be over....

But the time lengthened; Audrey came and went to seek the gypsy and returned, hours later, empty-handed, and Tory lay on the green-and-white tiles of *Titanic*'s most luxurious bathroom, on towels that Burty replaced when they became too soiled, and suffered.

And still the baby would not come.

Sunday, April 14

16

So much had happened since Audrey first readied herself to lie to Bay—for lie she had decided she would, about the money. She would not say she was bribing whatever gods-that-be to preserve his life. She would not tell him that she *believed* Madame Romany saw with a special sight, and that Madame Romany had glimpsed *something dark* ahead for him, though the gypsy always described it as filled with light.... Bay would not understand that, and he would not want to be protected....

Audrey would tell him all the truth she could. She would tell him how Esmeralda felt *owed* because Bay's mother, Edmunda Lockholm, had taken Jeoffry to her bed for a decade, and Esmeralda had not told Bay's father.... Audrey would tell him all the past as she knew it; she would only omit—because he would not believe—*the future*....

She had been ready so long, but he had not yet asked. And she had to face her daughters, too.

And now, this Sunday morning before service, Bay was dressed—she almost was—and he asked her to wear the pearls for him; the pearls he had presented to her at Nicola's country house in Denton.

Nicola of the red, red hair....

"You will recognize the trouble come, m'lady, by a floating silver moon, and a woman—you know who I mean—with red, red hair...."

And Audrey, who had been so long ready to tell Bay *some* of the reasons she had written a check for ten thousand dollars to a gypsy woman, Audrey did not know how to say, "I am afraid to wear those pearls, dear Bay, afraid even to look upon them. I am afraid they spell your doom."

"Oh, Bay," she said. And then she told him everything.

He did not laugh as she had thought he would. He was not impatient. They missed service she talked so long, and he listened, sitting beside her on the sofa, his arm along its back, around her shoulders. When she was done, confession complete down to hating and fearing the pearl necklace he had only, a few days ago, given her, he held her face between his hands and kissed her. He said, "That being the case, golden girl, when we get home I shall return it, and you shall choose what pleases you, instead. How's that?"

She did not say she wanted no more jewelry, that she had more than she appreciated. "Yes," she said, "yes, yes." She would choose tourmaline from now on, she thought, tourmaline and platinum, as in the Lockholm crest. Tourmaline was semiprecious, not so costly as gems, and it was the deep dark blue of her eyes. Yes, she would have a necklace made like the Lockholm crest, a platinum sailing ship over three waves in chips of tourmaline.

And suddenly she was very homesick and nostalgic for long ago, when there was no *Titanic*, no business worries for Bay, only him and her, and Bay not older seeming and too often called away, and their daughters as small and pretty as dolls who had not, one of them, given herself **away**—*like Celeste*—to a hot-mouthed boy.

"We must go to the girls," she said. "Today they're sixteen, the party's planned, and they've had a bad crossing so far. What do you say?"

A shadow crossed his face. But he stood and slapped his hands together as though the prospect pleased him. "I've presents for them," he said. "Not pearls. Silver pins. That's all right, isn't it?"

"Oh, yes. They don't deserve them—" She stopped herself. "I mean, they deserve silver pins and more. I've neglected the twins, I think, Bay. I must make it up to them. I've presents, too, awfully extravagant—mink sweaters. Mrs. Twigg will think I'm spoiling them again and be very mad."

He shrugged, and his hair fell over his forehead, boyishly. She laughed. "I know how to fix Mrs. Twigg," she said. "We'll give her a raise."

Bay touched his chest to make sure his cigars were still there. "If we raise it high enough, will she let me smoke during the party?"

"Oh, no, I don't think so," she said. "Mrs. Twigg thinks smoke discolors ladies' dresses, don't you remember?"

And they went out together, hand in hand, to face their children.

IT WAS A BEAUTIFUL DAY, the North Atlantic and the sky intensely blue, and the clouds stretched long and white, and swirled in spirals high above. But it was bitterly cold, that invisible, frigid corridor through which *Titanic* passed.... Audrey was glad for her greatcoat and glad for the sweaters she was giving to the twins.

But she was nervous about seeing them again.

They were sixteen today, children no longer, though not because of a date on a calendar. No; they had, the both of them, forsaken childhood on their own, each in her own way. One had jumped, too soon, unprepared, into womanhood, taking that strange boy into her body. And the other had privately mutilated herself, cut herself in protest against something that Audrey, her mother, did not understand: Smoke had only severed her hair this time, but could it not as easily have been a wrist, a throat...?

I must attend to my daughters or lose them, she thought, and the same with Bay. And if I have to choose, I know, and they know, that he comes first. Maybe that's their problem—maybe I'm their problem, and I do not want to be.

Audrey knocked at the twins' door because Bay carried the presents. She hesitated before she entered. She felt, in the chill of the air, a foreboding. She was afraid.

Oh, how silly—

Of what should she be afraid?

The twins were seated on a settee of buttercup-flowered chintz and wicker. Bright yellow, it set off their hair, just a shade less golden than Audrey's, and showed their turquoise eyes to advantage. But there the resemblance between them ended. Audrey was startled: they sat as strangers, to each other, and to her.... The twins had always looked alike, all their lives been dressed identically. They moved alike and laughed alike, and were, in essence, so alike.... Audrey had thought of them as one soul broken perfectly into two, one flower branching into double blossom.

Their birthday dresses were different. Smoke wore wool of sophisticated gray, plain, high necked, close fitting over the hips, with an ornate gold belt to define her waist. Swan was in tiers of bright red, loose sleeved, soft cuffed, wide skirted, its round necklace skimming the swell of corseted breasts.... Smoke's sheared blond hair curled at her shoulders; she'd combed it straight back behind her ears. Swan's tresses fell straight to the middle of her back; she'd pulled the sides up and secured them at the crown of her head with a wide red bow.

And they sat differently, Smoke stiff with her knees together, feet planted side by side like Mrs. Twigg. Swan's legs were crossed at the thigh, and the delicate foot not touching the carpet swung saucily, its slipper loose. But mostly the difference between them was in their faces: each was veiled now in the mask of the adult—a woman, each, with something to hide. They sat, cleaved from each other, separate in the world, each behind her secrets as though behind a shield: two shields, meant to disguise, and flashing. Two shields blinding to the viewer.

"Darlings, happy birthday," Audrey said, and controlled a need to cry.

Swan cocked her head. "Thank you, Mother," she said, but made no move. And Smoke only smiled and looked along her lap where her knees curved the fabric of her dress. Different even in their masks.

"Will you open your presents?"

Audrey wanted to kiss them, but her two daughters sat so cold—as cold as the day was, they sat, backs stiff against the chintz cushions of the settee—she did not know how.

Smoke wet her lips. "If Swan is to go to Switzerland this fall," she said, "I should like to go to school in London. Swan would like a hunting horse, as companion and exercise when she isn't skiing, and I would like a two-sail boat. I'd keep it on the River Thames. I would take proper instruction from the merchant marine, and be very careful and most appreciative."

"And we will both write to you once a week," said Swan, "unless that is too often, in which case, once a fortnight."

"Also," said Smoke, "we are both agreed we are too old, now, to have a governess, and we have decided to accept Twiggs's resignation and not have her with us anymore. We understand—"

"That is just about enough," said their father.

"We'll decide your futures another time, darlings," said Audrey. "Let's have fun today. Here, open your presents," and she took the silver-papered boxes from Bay and thrust them forward.

Dutifully, each twin extended a hand and took her gift, sat back and unwrapped it. Smoke was first to have the box undone. She opened the lid, admired the thing inside, waited for Swan to see hers, too. Swan smiled with pleasure, having looked into Smoke's box, and lifted the lid of her own. "From Father?" she said, and lifted out the pin and held it high.

Then Smoke handed hers to Bay and said, "Oh, it's lovely, Father. Will you put it on me?"

And Audrey saw and felt the blood stop and back up in her veins.

No pearls, he had said, no pearls.

But moon pins, crescent moon pins.... In the curve of the crescent, the moons held, each, a diamond star, flickering, winking at Audrey like the cold white eye of the gypsy.

It was come, as Madame Romany had prophesied: the cold, the moon, the little stars....

Audrey sat on the edge of her chair, her breath gone, unable to say a word. She sat, certain that catastrophe was upon him whom she loved. But Bay was just as always. He accepted his daughters' kisses and fastened on their pins. He strode around the cabin smoking a cigar while the girls, frost gone from their faces but not their new reserve, tore away Audrey's pink-and-white striped bows and wrapping paper, and exclaimed with delight at their cardigan minks.

Her daughters kissed and thanked her, and Audrey, befogged, *frozen around her heart*, patted them and laughed with them, and stood with them to go to their party in the Palm Court.

And Bay was just as always, just as always....

Nicola came to the party; she brought the handsome man, Teddy Royce. And Dove came, and Captain Smith, the two of them obviously enamored. Bruce Ismay came alone, and Mrs. Twigg brought Colonel Gracie, a charming man with a sense of fun for all his erudition.

So there were eleven at table, and two musicians played, Danny Bowen and Jock Hume, violinists. The musicians stood along a wall, beside two palms, before a window. And behind them, splendid, the sun blazed in a blue, blue sky. The food was good: vichyssoise and a crab soufflé and asparagus under cream.

Audrey tried to concentrate, but there was a film over the afternoon for her, a film of fear, as real as sweat. It blurred her perceptions. On the watch for everything, *anything*, she saw little; nothing registered in her mind. She sat in her place and dimly smiled and...waited.

She was not sure which boy, the taller one with the poet's face or the one with the wholesome, athletic look, was the youth who had spoiled her Swan. She knew his name was Danny and that he played the violin, and that Bay had allowed him to play today in return for his oath to stay away from their daughter for two years. Danny had given his word of honor. They could correspond—that, only, was allowed. And then they would see, Bay had said. Then, if the fire still burned in both their hearts, after Swan had compared this boy to others, then...

But not even her curiosity about her daughter's *lover* lifted Audrey's dread. She ate. She drank pink champagne. She oohed at the cake, a pretty thing in the shape of two hearts, covered with icing roses of pink and yellow and white, and the twins' names written on it in green under the "Happy Birthday." She clapped when the girls blew out, together, their candles. She ordered ice cream with the rest. But all was vague because what she was really doing was waiting...waiting for the blow to fall.

So that when, toward the end of the fete, she heard shouts from below deck and felt a tremor in *Titanic*'s bowels as the great vessel slowed, she set her napkin down and rose. She was ready. Whatever, she was ready....

Then there were many shouts, and the sounds of running feet. The ship swung in a half circle port side. Something had happened—*something had happened!*

"What is it?" she said to the air around.

She heard a splash, a great splash as though something had been hurled overboard.

Frantic, she looked for Bay. But there he was, enjoying himself, stepping with Smoke in a dance. She looked for Nicola...and there she was, queenlike in almond taffeta, surrounded by Teddy Royce and Colonel Gracie. The three of them were laughing at a joke.

But somewhere people were running; Audrey could hear hasty footfalls on stairs.

"Oh, what is it?" she said, and ran, without excusing herself, to see.

The Palm Court was on A deck where the promenade was glassed against bad weather. Audrey ran down the stairs to B deck. Several stewards were running down, too.

"What is it?" she demanded of one, taking his arm so he would answer.

"Woman overboard, madam. Third-class, I'm told," he said, and ran on ahead of her.

NO!

No, it wouldn't be Tory; it wouldn't be. Tory was all right now, wasn't she, yes? Burt had come back; they had made it up. Tory was sick, but the poison was passing. And the baby was saved, she hadn't aborted.... No, it couldn't be Tory.

No.

A crowd was gathered around the rail, aft toward the stern. Audrey ran to where they were, couldn't see, pushed through. "Oh, let me see, let me see—"

There. A man gave her his place. He was taller; he could still see behind her—

There.

Black skirts floated in a blue-orange sea. Black skirts like a great sea anemone spread and lifted, filled with air here; sank, water heavy, there. The whole bobbed and turned, slowly, black on blue, black on red, now black on silver orange, as the sea shifted under the body and changed colors in the sinking sun. But the black, *the shroud*, stayed ever as it was.

Two life belts had been thrown out, and a donut-shaped life preserver, bright yellow and as jaunty as a children's toy. But the body was facedown and turning, gently floating on the swells.

No. Could it be…could it be Esmeralda…?

Yes.

And such a chill took Audrey's heart and squeezed it. I am a murderer, she thought. I've bought that woman's life in trade for Bay's….

Oh, God will punish me.

Audrey turned away. She was shivering with cold and fear. Yes. Yes.

Fear for Bay….

But she retraced her steps slowly, emotionally drained, body exhausted: she was carrying such a weight.

Bruce Ismay was striding ahead of her. She caught up to him, with effort. "Mr. Ismay," she said, "what has happened? Do you know?"

"Mrs. Lockholm, come away," he said. He

handed her a piece of paper distractedly as he looked over her head as though searching for someone else.

It was a marconigram. "Greek steamer *Athenai* reports passing icebergs and large quantities of field ice today: latitude 41° 51'N, longitude 49° 52'W...." Audrey handed it back. "I mean, Mr. Ismay, there is a woman overboard...."

He patted her shoulder. "I'll look into it, right away," he said. "It was a stowaway, I'm told, someone caught down in third, trying to get away. Don't worry yourself, Mrs. Lockholm, it is not important. Excuse me." And then he was gone, the paper she'd returned to him pushed into his pocket.

Not important...? A life gone, and it was *not important?*

Audrey climbed the grand staircase back to A deck, so tired. But she hurried, wanting Bay.

She found him in the Palm Court, the party over, tipping the waiters who had served. Everyone else was gone, the tables were nearly cleaned away. She came up and embraced him; she did not care who saw. "Bay," she said, "the woman I told you of—"

"I know," he said, "let's go now. Let's see how Tory is."

Tory....

Audrey had forgotten her in her consuming fear for Bay. Who would attend Tory now the gypsy was gone?

"I must summon the doctor," she said. "He'll have to know now."

Bay guided her toward their suite. "Let's check in, first, shall we? I've brought pieces of birthday cake for her and Burt."

Birthday cake. She had forgotten the twins, then, too.

She followed him where he led. He was safe; he was all right. The nightmare was over. She could relax now, couldn't she. She could be happy now....

Inside the suite they could hear, from the Van-Voorst's bedroom door, Tory moaning. Audrey went to the door, knocked and called, "Burty, may I come in?" She tried the knob but it was rigid, locked the other side. "Burty, it's Audrey, please let me in."

Burty's voice was just beyond, "I've promised her no one, Audrey, go away. The baby's coming, I'll help her. She's telling me what to do...."

"Oh Burty, you must have assistance. You must have the doctor—"

"No," came his voice. "We're doing this together, she and I. Don't interfere, it is not your business."

And then she heard him step away. She whirled to Bay, but he was beside her at the door. He said, through it, "Burt, old man, we've birthday cake here. Come out and have some and let Audrey in, she's better than you at—"

"Leave us alone!"

And then there was no more, only Tory moaning, writhing unassisted in childbirth....

"I'm going for the doctor myself," said Bay, speaking to the door. "I promise you his discretion in this. Audrey will be here, Burt, ready to help—"

"NO!" It was a scream.

And then Bay left the room and Audrey heard Burty pushing something heavy against one door, and then the other.

Audrey drew a stool close, and sat and began to

talk. She spoke of meeting Tory, long ago, when she was a bride, and how Tory had helped her learn the ways of Gilt Hill, and how they had grown fast friends. She rambled, whatever came into her mind, anything to calm Burty and reassure Tory, if she could hear. Behind the door Audrey heard movement sometimes, water running, short curses, and always, like a tide, the bed protesting and Tory struggling.

The ship's doctor came, but Burty would not let him in. "Go away, go away, let us alone, we're all right," was all Burty would respond. And then, after a time, he said nothing, and Audrey sat on her stool, silent, too, only listening. The ship's doctor left when Bay refused to allow him to use force to open the doors, and Bay ordered coffee in, and waited, too, smoking another cigar and walking down the private deck and back again in bitter cold.

In the grand salon there was a hymn sing going on. While Tory birthed and Bay and Audrey waited, the sound of many voices lifted in lilting prayer and filled the cavernous ship. Audrey did not know if the singing had been called for the drowned woman's sake, or if it was the custom, on high seas, to spend a Sunday evening so. Going over to Paris they had arrived Sunday morning....

Paris...and Dentoncroft: the pearls and Nicola of the red, red hair.... How long ago it seemed already. And home, Newport, her father and Dolly, and Whale's Turning on Gilt Hill. And the house on Fifth where she could walk to extravagant stores. And the operas and stage plays, and the sumptuous dinners.... She in a fine new gown, surrounded by friends in new gowns equally beautiful, everyone chatting and dancing, being gay. Tory often there with her, close for whispers, ready for a laugh; exquisite Tory, proud Burty at her side....

A sound. A new sound. Audrey glanced up at the door, looked to see if Bay had heard it, too. Yes, he was coming in from the private deck, shutting the French doors behind him. He had thrown away his cigar and his breath was visible, great gray clouds around his face.

There! Again.... A cry, faint and tiny, like a mew.

Bay pulled a second footstool close, and together they leaned on their laps toward the bedroom door beyond.

Now all was silence. The bed no longer protested, Tory no longer moaned. Burty was not stomping around....

Soft, they heard water splashing and then—oh yes, a lusty cry!

Bay took her hand. She was crying. Quiet little tears, but so many, they ran down her face and splashed upon her hands; tears of sorrow for the gypsy, tears of guilt, tears of relief for Bay and Tory, tears of joy for a new VanVoorst.

"Oh, Bay," she said, and took the handkerchief he offered.

"Congratulations!" he shouted at the door. "Congratulations, Dad, come out and have a drink!"

But though the babe cried again, there was no answer from Burty, only footfalls back and forth, back and forth.... And nothing, nothing at all, from Tory.

"Oh, Bay...."

He ordered supper in their room, enough for four. When Burty came out, he would be hungry, and maybe Tory would be, too.

Audrey got off the stool and sat on a sofa. Bay

rolled the dinner table away and smoked another cigar. The food cooled as they waited; they were not ready, yet, to eat. The rooms were chilly; Audrey did not remember Newport even in winter being as cold as this. She put on her heaviest wool dress and stockings, her sturdy walking shoes, and then one of Bay's sweater-vests and her long pale mink. He had two sweaters on under a knickerbocker suit-jacket of gray flannel, and two pairs of long socks. And over all that he wrapped himself in his silk bathrobe, navy blue and white.

"You look rather nautical, after all," she teased, "even in your knickers."

He sat beside her. "And you look as though you know just what to wear on an ocean cruise."

Finally, she picked at a breast of pheasant. He ate the dinner rolls and the fruit sauce.

And they waited.

17

Captain Smith was jubilant. He was going to do it! Five hundred forty-six miles they'd run from noon to noon, and they would go faster yet, *Titanic* was only *strolling*.... He would bring her in sometime on Tuesday, perhaps even before sundown; the trans-Atlantic crossing record would be his. Oh, it was a fitting finale to his captaincy. He deserved it; it would erase entirely that bad business with the *Hawke*.... He would be remembered only for *Titanic* and for speed.... He would go down in the record books!

Arriving unexpectedly, there would be no fanfare waiting. Well, all right. Let the band and congratulatory press come Wednesday, after *Titanic* had cooled in the harbor overnight, been cleaned and shined *shipshape*.... The passengers could depart on docking if they chose, or stay aboard, sleep over and enjoy the Wednesday celebration: however they wanted it. Captain Edward John Smith would have his record, that was the important thing.

And his woman....

Would he have her, too?

He was in his quarters, and Dove was in his bed,

under blankets because she was naked. He had bedded her after the Lockholm party, a hot and lovely romp, and the wanton was waiting for him to come to her for another tumble; she was as hot as embers, this one, despite the cold....

But he could not enjoy her again just now. He had much to do and so many messages: they must each one be read and logged. They annoyed him, all very much the same. "Ice here, ice ahead," as though he didn't know. Hadn't they been sighting field ice on their own, loose ice, for hours now? And didn't he know what it meant, this sudden plummet of temperature...?

He had the water temperature measured, too: drop a bucket down the side, an old mariner's trick, and then hoist and test.... The water at 4:00 p.m. was very cold, thirty-two, thirty-three degrees, right on the freeze point, but, of course, running far too fast for that. So he knew what he was about; he did not need Lord of *Californian* sending another such warning, trying to "buddy up" after being scolded the way he had. But here he was again, wiring about three bergs he'd sighted.... E.J. gazed out his window: visibility was good, and the sea was as calm as a bath. Let there be a hundred bergs, E.J. thought, we'll come through....

"Tell me you'll divorce her," said Dove from his bed.

E.J. turned, surprised. He had forgotten her for a moment, lost in dreams of his ambition. He crumpled the remainder of the wireless messages and pushed them into a side pocket to be read later, at his leisure, from the bridge. "Oh, my angel," he said, and told her the truth. "I cannot, I will not. She needs me more, you see."

"No," said Dove, "I do."

E.J. sighed and went to her, sat down on the bed and took her luminous-skinned hand into his rougher one. He might as well face up to it, confront her, *end it now*. She was demanding more love than he could give, more loyalty than she was entitled to...more time than he had to spare. It would be painful, for he was facing up to an old dream, *rejecting* the fantasy of youth for the *achievement* of maturity. He had enjoyed her, oh, how he had enjoyed her, but his life was in Southampton in a cottage on Winn Road with a modest view of the harbor and the ships.... And after this, after *Titanic*, he wanted to go home. His heart, if not his passion, was with Eleanor and little Helen.... For all her glory, for all her charm and beauty, Dove Peerce was, after all, only a distraction....

"I shall always be grateful for you, my dear," he began, and he saw her eyes harden. She was wise, this worldly woman; she knew from his tone, from the way he began, that he had been thinking how to tell her he wanted to be free, that this was no spontaneous decision, leaped to in heat. She could tell: he meant to leave her and would not be swayed.

Well, all the better....

"You have misled me," she said, "and stolen my heart. Will you now break it in its time of greatest happiness?"

E.J. sighed again. "I love you more than heaven, dearest, I've told you that. But I'm not cut out to share a life of...constant waltzes. I'm a simple sort of fellow, who thinks of himself in terms of his work.

I like—I want—a simple life that matches my tastes…a beer-and-sausage life, dear Dove, that's the one for me. And one of my own devising, surrounded by my own dear and familiar things and dear, familiar faces. I'm Brit, and want to be. America is not for me. And I'm from the working class…. I love you as a man loves his erotic dreams—you're a perfect mistress. But you're outside the normal way of things, you know. You are an angel, too special for the likes of me. You're a once-in-a-lifetime-woman, darling, you're not for…every day…. I have thought it over, and I—I do adore you, but I would hate to live your life.''

There. That was frank enough.

She did not scowl or weep or rant or plead. She merely gazed at him with pure blue eyes and sweetest face, and said, as though that settled it, "Then I'll live yours, E.J., with you. I'll be a Brit, as you say. I'll lead the rustic life—"

"Oh, my dear."

He did not know what to say. His mind rushed from yes to no, possible, impossible…. Eleanor's face rose accusingly into his mind, flashed vibrant; sweet Eleanor, who did not deserve to lose her husband in her old age because an idle American woman, too rich for her own good, too beautiful for *his*, wanted a new plaything. And in his mind he heard Eleanor say quietly, as she watched out their chintz-curtained kitchen window, for his returning, "She will tire of you, Edward, after a season. Her kind of woman does not love forever, as my kind does…."

E.J. stood up from his bed. Suddenly he had to distance himself from this woman. *She irritated him.*

"Will you get dressed, my lovely?" he said. "The Widener party has already started, and I must look in. I promised.... Will you accompany me, as though we really were a union, for one last time?"

She did not argue. She slipped from the bed, and dressed, unselfconsciously before him. He marveled at her beauty, her grace in every action. He was excited by her clothing, so beautifully made. He was roused seeing her sweep up her angel hair with an ivory comb, the way she lifted her slight arms. He watched her touch her lips and cheeks with rouge and wanted to lick it all away. Oh, she was a devil, his angel; she was a destroyer of men. He would never forget; he would always be grateful. And yet, as of this moment, *he wanted only to escape....*

As soon as he could, he left her with the Wideners, promising to see her later.

He went, a little before nine, to the bridge; Second Officer Lightoller was there. The air was stark cold, it revived him. A mug of tea was brought. E.J. sipped the tea and felt better, felt almost himself.

Here was where he belonged, he thought. He had been foolish to chase a dream, a boy's dream. Why, he had almost been snagged—hadn't he?—like a flounder, by a man-hungry adventuress.

"There is not much wind," he said.

"No," said Lightoller, "it's all flat calm. I wish there was more. We'd cut through the ice much faster then."

"Are you worried about it?" said the captain, taking up a long-glass and sighting through.

"Well, sir," said Lightoller, "ice at night.... I like to have a bit of wind to stir up the water along the base of a piece. Helps to define and differentiate the shape.''

''Aye,'' said E.J. ''I see nothing very big out there just now.'' He collapsed the telescope and handed it to Lightoller. ''Tell me what you see.''

Lightoller looked through. It was a splendid night, midnight blue, both sea and sky—blue-black satin, like a lady's gown. And over all, above for real, below reflected, a million pinpoint stars glittered like shards of diamond, each distinct and sharp, cutting sharp, different from the softer glow of *Titanic*'s electric lights, strung high on lines the length and breadth of her, and mirrored, miragelike, at her feet.

''I think I've never seen a sharper night, sir,'' said Lightoller. ''The black so bright, the lights... There's nothing out there now to bother us, but I'll worry a bit about a monster with a blue side toward us, till we're through.''

Captain Smith nodded, understanding. New ice: the big slabs moved down the cold current, hit a warmer tide and forced the warmer water up. That caused the mass to calf, they called it—break up into twin pieces, and then calf, or break, again. Freshly shorn, the ice not crystallized yet by air, it was dark, mirror clear. The sailors called it black ice then, or blue. Sometimes it took hours for the air to frost a new side of calved ice, and that was the time of danger. That was when the outline of a berg was hardest to see, blending as it did with the dark reflecting water and the dark invisible sky....

''Who's lookout tonight?'' the captain asked.

''Fleet, sir,'' said Lightoller, ''a good man. Keen eyes. Too keen for his own good, I tell him. He depends on them too much, forgets sometimes to take binoculars up with him.''

''Don't we keep binocs in the crow's nest at all times?'' said E.J. ''We should—I want them there. Let's see to it.''

''Yes, sir.''

''Well, then, good night, Chuck. I'll be inside if you need me.''

Lightoller hesitated. He knew how the captain had been spending his nights. Finally he said only, ''You'll be in your quarters, sir?''

E.J. laughed and slapped him on the back. ''Aye, I'm spending tonight, all of tonight, with you.''

''Thank you, sir,'' said Lightoller, and blushed, unseen.

''Don't hesitate to call, now, Chuck. The smallest thing.''

''Yes, sir. Good night then, sir.''

In seven steps E.J. was in his cabin. He shut the door and smiled to see it. He was home again...alone again. He looked around for evidence of *her*. There was lipstick smudged upon the rim of a drinking glass. He took it into his bath, scrubbed away the stain, washed the glass, dried it, set it in its proper place.

There was still a hint of her perfume in the air. He opened his window wide; he would weather the frigid blast. There was a strand of cloud-white hair— no, two, three...on his night table where she had combed her hair. He picked up the hairs and twisted them together and turned them into a curl. He would put them into his diary, he thought, as a memento of what a boy could dream and despair of having, and a man have and despair of getting rid.

ALL DAY THE ICE had worried Captain Stanley Lord of *Californian*. He had never seen so much loose ice nor such massive solid pieces. Like white beasts newly arisen from their watery grave, huge hulks of ice slouched down his ocean lane, silently threatening, hulking...hovering too close to his ship.

Three great bergs had drifted by to starboard at twilight, with not a hundred yards between them and him, like three moving mountains. He was glad they were behind him now. *Californian*'s bow had been nosing through a sea of slush ice for three hours, and now there was a glow ahead in the darkness, a wide belt of brightness as though the sun, turned to ice, was frosting the rim of the world. There must be a continent of ice sliding down the sea, he thought; the better course would be to pull around and wait out the night, stopped, surrounded. Let pass what would. Tomorrow would be time enough to find a way through. Tomorrow in daylight, tomorrow in a melting sun....

About to leave the bridge, now his decision had been made and executed, he saw, east, a light.

"Groves," he said to the officer on bridge watch, "there's another vessel struggling with this stuff."

Third Officer Groves looked where his superior pointed and considered. "There shouldn't be, sir. According to the charts, no one should be that close to our position. It must be a star, sir. They're piercing tonight. I've never seen them more brilliant."

Captain Lord went over in his mind the ships he knew in the vicinity. *Antillian* only, and *Titanic*.... He had wired both the present situation. He'd had to do that, even though asked not to communicate with *Titanic*, he'd had to alert all nearby ships of the ice danger or he, as a neighbor on the sea, would be derelict in his duty. *Antillian*'s captain had wired acceptance and thanks; there had been no such courtesy from Captain Smith.... Ah, to hell with *Titanic*, thought Stanley Lord, with all its personnel and all its passengers. And especially to hell with Lady Pomeroy.... Resolutely, he pushed *Titanic* from his mind.

Still, he thought, watching from his rail, that was a vessel, not a star, off the starboard stern. It was a steamer, too, by God, and approaching faster than it should through an ice-infested sea.

Cold, even in his long coat, he went down to the saloon and had a whiskey and called for Mr. Mahan, his engineer. He wanted *Californian*'s steam kept up through the night, he said, even though they were stopped, in case they needed to shift position quickly due to ice crowding in.

"We don't wannit growin' too thick round our feet, Cap, that's right," said Mr. Mahan, and he helped himself to a grog. "Thissen here's morn ice I've ever seen, and I'm talkin' fifty years. Cold as a witch's tit, too—ain it?—but damn purty. It's because o' nights like this, sir, that I first put out to sea. Always found th' ocean purtier than any gal I ever knew." He had thick lips and a walrus mustache. He smacked his lips over his hot cup, a big man with a gentle smile.

"Pretty is as pretty does," said Captain Lord, thinking of Nicola Lady Pomeroy. A man like Mahan wouldn't meet a "gal" like the beauteous Nicola. She rivaled the beauty of the sea, she did, *the bloody tart*....

"Ah, we'll come through, Cap, don'cha worry,"

said the engineer. "Ice ain nothin' next to a gale in the tropics. Then you got yourself a bit o' trouble, aye." And he slurped his rum and rubbed the steam from his eyes.

"I know I'm in good hands," said Lord, laying his hand on Mahan's shoulder. And then he left him, and saw again, closer, the unidentified ship steaming up, *almost flying*, off to starboard.

He went in to his wireless man. "Evans," he said, "are there any ships around we haven't notified of ice? I see a steamer maybe ten miles broadside, southeast, running like the dickens."

"That would be *Titanic*, sir," said Evans, and yawned. He was the only wireless operator *Californian* had, and he was tired, exceedingly tired. He had been at his station since early morning, sending, receiving.... He'd missed his dinner; no time to stop.

No, thought Captain Lord. It is not *Titanic*, it's too small. But he felt, in good conscience, that he must try to signal her.... Up to the bridge again, and Groves. "Try to contact that unidentified steamer by Morse lamp," he ordered.

Groves, shrugging, did as he was told. He stood on the deck, and click, click, clicked away in the icy cold. But the vessel sent back no response, so after a while Captain Lord said to give it up, and went to his quarters.

"It is not *Titanic*," the captain told his parrot, "and even if it is, I've wired her, my duty is done."

"Ho, ho, ho," croaked the parrot. "Davy Jones, ho, ho, Davy Jones...."

Captain Lord pulled off his boots and poured himself another whiskey. Where was *Titanic*, if not there, broadside ten miles...? Where was Nicola of the burning copper hair and long, strong thighs? Who was she kissing...opening her belly to?

"Davy Jones," he echoed his parrot, and sat in the dark of his room, and drank.

18

Funny, Tory thought, how your world can be crashing down but you get so tired it doesn't matter. And funny how you think you know what love is, and that you've done it—loved hard, up to the hilt—for years and years, until you see the one you love loving you while you struggle and suffer in pain, and then you know you haven't even begun to love him as you ought.... And funny how it doesn't matter what you've gone through once it's over, and funny how good it feels just to lie back, content, and see Burty at your side, Burty all exhaustion and concern for *you*.... Burty's heart all broken, given up at last, and put, in little pieces, in your hands, for you to take and fit together, stronger than before....

"Oh, Burtykins," she said, and squeezed his hand. "We did it, didn't we?"

"Don't talk, Tor, just rest. It's over now." He was happy, too, she saw that clearer than anything. He loved her. He didn't care about the color of her blood: he really didn't care!

"Oh, Burty," she said, "I love you miles and miles."

"And I love you, pet.... Will you marry me?" He was slumped in his chair beside her bed, his head back. She knew: he would never leave her. It was so good to know that.

The babe was at her breast, making little kisses as it sucked, toothless, kneading tiniest fingers into her flesh. Her bosom was *paler* than the baby's skin. She was raw gold against the infant's mocha cream....

"We can give her away," she said, "set up a trust and have her adopted."

He lifted his face, and she saw that he was crying. She had never seen Burty's tears before. She lifted a hand, caught a tear upon a finger. "I'm sorry, darling. I only wanted to make you proud, to give you—"

"Hush," he said, and wiped his tears himself.

"She's pretty," Tory said. "She has your eyes, I think."

He nodded. He did not want to explain, to think....

"You wanted a boy. I know," she said.

Funny how, now it was over, now the baby was obviously mulatto, so her past was irrevocably exposed—funny how it just didn't matter...because Burty *loved* her, *really loved her*....

The baby coughed up a little spit. Warm and bubbly, it dribbled on Tory's breast.

"Has she had enough?" he asked.

"I don't know," she said. "I don't know anything about babies."

"Neither do I," he said, "neither do I."

He looked at the strange little creature. The top of its head was soft and fuzzy with red-gold strands. Her eyes were closed now as she nursed. The face was delicate, cool and smooth, not red and squeezed the way he'd thought it would be. It did not look like Tory nor like him…but it might grow up to be beautiful, *it might*…. The body was long and slight boned and all a fawn color. He stared at the bare little body…. It's a beautiful color she is, he thought, and in that instant loved her. He filled with love; he swelled with love.

"Wisdoms," he said, sitting up, no longer tired, excited now. "That's to be her name. Wisdoms Victoria VanVoorst, and she *will* be president, if she wants to be."

Tory's mind had been drifting. She had not seen his eyes explode with love for their daughter. She knew only that Burty loved her, Tory. "What name?" she murmured, slipping into sleep. My stomach will be flat again, she was thinking…. I can wear my Poiret gowns again, she was thinking. Maybe tomorrow, or Wednesday when we dock….

"Wisdoms," Burty said. He knew that Tory slept, but he wanted to say it again, out loud. He reached out and took the babe from the nipple. It didn't cry; it bubbled and opened silky eyes and stretched out tiniest tawny arms. Burty held his daughter against his heart. He had delivered her all by himself: engendered her and delivered her. He lifted the little thing high. Just-born legs tried to unbend, pushed against the air. He wrapped it in a towel emblazoned with a red pennant holding a single white star. He tucked it beside its mother. The baby smiled at him— he thought it smiled at him—and pursed its lips…and slept.

He would go out for an hour, tell the bartender in the Palm Court he had a namesake who would be president; he would buy Wisdoms a drink. Hell, two drinks...maybe three.

"Welcome to the world, Wis," he said. He was a father. For the first time in his life he was feeling...fatherly. He must find Bay and Audrey, too, tell them, show them...

He pulled away the armchair he had, before, pushed against the bedroom door. He went out into the living room of the suite. And there were Bay and Audrey, huddling side by side on stools, dark rings under their eyes. They had been waiting, too, worrying, too.... But their eyes smiled to see him.

"It's a girl," he said, and shut the door behind him. "She's sleeping now and so is Tory. She's beautiful, the color of coffee and cream, and her name is Wisdoms Victoria VanVoorst."

Bay handed Burty a cigar. "And will she be president, Mr. VanVoorst?"

"Without question," said Burty, and kissed Bay on the mouth.

"Perhaps she will only marry into it," said Audrey. "That would be easier."

Burty lifted Audrey from her stool and kissed her on the mouth, too. "Not a chance," he said. "She gets the whole castle, the whole fairy tale. I shall devote my life to it. So come now, we must find her namesake—he's a wise man—and we'll all have a drink."

"It's polar out," said Audrey. "You'll need a coat."

"Not I," said Burty, "not tonight. There could be a blizzard and I'd not need a coat tonight. I'm going to have too much liquor in me."

"All right then," said Audrey. She did not ask of

Tory, though she wanted to. She took Bay's hand and straightened her shoulders.

And they went.

"WELL, THAT'S IT," said Danny Bowen to his bunk mate Jock Hume. "I've been let go. From now on I'm an official nonperson. I can eat and sleep all right, and wander free, but I won't be relieving you boys no more. I'm out of the band for good and off the list of White Star Line musicians forever, I guess."

"Rotten luck," said Jock. "She's a pretty lass, but she's costing you a lot."

"Well." Danny turned the cloth, polishing his violin. "I'll put it away shined good, at any rate. Take care of your tools, my dad says, and they'll take care of you."

"Aw, it's too bad, Danny boy. These ocean liners are good gigs. What if you gave Swan up? Could you get hired back on, then?"

"I dunno, Jock, but I wouldn't do that," Danny said. "I love her, you see, and she loves me. I can't see her no more, not to speak to, that is, but we can write. So I'll write her tonight, the way I used to when I was home and she was in America. We'll just get through it, you know, somehow. I think of it as a test."

"Sounds like a hard knock to me," said Jock. "Not what I'd want."

"Hey," said Danny, "let's forget it, shall we?"

"All right. Want to go up top then and see what we can see?"

"Maybe I'll see her from afar," said Danny, locking his violin case.

"Yeah, dancing with another bloke," said Jock.

"Without music? I don't think so. C'mon, let's go...."

Each in his coat and muffler against the cold, they climbed up the back stairs until they came to the top deck, where the promenade was open to the air. There were almost no passengers. It was close to midnight, and the cold had long since driven people in. But there was staff on the bridge, more than usual, Danny thought. Well, maybe they're restless, too, like me....

He leaned over the starboard rail and filled his lungs with air so cold it hurt. His father, who had had a voice and worried about his lungs, used to tell him to be careful not to breathe too deep in winter air. "A man can freeze his lungs that way, my boy," his father'd said. "Permanently injure your wind...." Danny thought that was "singer's superstition"; he'd not believed it. But he might change his mind, he thought, if he was forced, night after night, into such an air as this. It was strange air: barely a wind, the water wrinkled only, not even rippled, much less waved. And yet, a *cutting cold....*

And all so beautiful. The night was like a church, the sky burnished black into a cathedral ceiling, and the stars like distant chandeliers. And *Titanic*, a magnificent floating *pew*, filled with rich people, poor people, and all people in between....

Danny leaned as far as he could over the rail. *Titanic* was steaming smartly along; no slowdown for her because of all the ice.... Straight ahead, it was so dark. He tried to see. Something huge was out there, something huge and cloaked. Like a ghostly galleon, unlighted and silent. It was creeping through—

Three sharp bells. Three clangs of the clapper, up in the crow's nest.

Danny looked around. Jock was gone. Up on the bridge the officer on watch was picking up a telephone. Danny leaned back out, over *Titanic*'s side.

He could see it now. It was a mountain of ice, higher than top deck; it reared above Danny's head. It had two peaks, the closer higher than the second, and it was *blank* on the side that faced him. The whole side was clear...*invisible*. It shone, and it was black, a gigantic mirror....

A moment ago it had been a steep black curtain—

Now it showed itself as two *huge fangs framed in crystal edges*, and so *close*, so *high*.

My God, it's going to ram us! he thought, and then he heard, like his heart, the engines deep in *Titanic*'s bowels stop and reverse, and he let his breath out in a swoosh of gray mist, relieved.

"We'll miss 'er now," he said.

But then the ice cliff seemed to lift, to ascend like some monster yawning out of the sea.... Silent, it *leaped*, it *attacked*.... It was upon them! The ice was alive and shimmering and towering over—he would be *smothered*. He fell back from the rail, and the great white thing clawed along *Titanic*'s side...*shuffling, scuffing, crunching*...as soft as a wolf scratching snow. A spray of ice engulfed the deck, pounds and pounds of tiny sharp-edged slivers cascaded with a whisper, and skittered and gleamed.

And then the beast was past, as a scrap of paper in his face might pass, whipped by wind, or the silent wide-spread wing of a swooping gull. Blank faced, it sighed and hissed and then was gone, gray already off the stern...now dim...now black...now gone as though it had never been.

He was wet from the ice fall, his face scratched a little and burning, but he was all right. No bones broken; he'd not been swept over the side.

He brushed ice from his coat with his hands and looked toward the bridge. Gee! That had been exciting, thrilling even, and thank God we're all right.... For *Titanic* was steaming on, engines turning, and the officer on the watch was standing only, talking into the telephone.

Unsinkable, they called her, Danny thought, marveling. And unsinkable she must be. But what a ramming there could have been! And now, where was Jock? He'd just missed all the fun....

CAPTAIN SMITH ANSWERED the telephone in Dove's stateroom on the second ring. Even as he put down the receiver, he was reaching for his trousers and cursing himself. Why had he gone back to her? Why had he not stayed where he belonged, in his own room, next to the bridge...?

Because she had given in, that's why, given up. Because she had called him, knowing he had left her, and said, "All right, E.J., my darling, go back to her if you must, but be with me *now*.... Nicola, at my request, is sleeping in Bruce Ismay's spare bedroom."

And the boy in his heart had whooped for joy.

He had *rushed* back to her, hastily dressed, more quickly undressed, and, yes, he had *reveled* in her scented, profligate arms....

And now, slow in finding him, Hitchens at the

helm had followed First Officer Murdoch's command: he had bumped the engines into reverse, and *Titanic*'s forward motion, so abruptly stopped, had swung the ship a length or two to starboard—into collision.

E.J. was running for the bridge.

Arrived, he was glad to see Boxhall there. "What have we struck?" he asked Murdoch.

"An iceberg, sir. I have closed the watertight doors."

"And rung the warning bells?"

"Yes, sir."

"Stay at your post, then, Murdoch. Boxhall, you come with me."

Captain Smith looked carefully, starboard side from the bridge, for damage. But other than an ice-scattered deck, there was nothing...nothing visibly out of place, nothing wrong.... He sent Boxhall to inspect below and called for Engineer Bell. He ordered *Titanic*'s engines pushed to half ahead, and then, grinding his teeth in anger held in check, still buttoning his Norfolk, he waited for word of the disaster.

How bad would it be? he wondered. Please, not as bad as *Hawke* was, he prayed....

STOKER FRED BARRETT ALREADY knew how bad it was.

While E.J. was still licking the fulsome breasts of his beloved as Dove stretched excitingly beneath him, down in boiler room six Fred Barrett was fighting for his life.

In the act of shutting down his dampers as ordered, he heard a solemn, sudden boooom.

And then there came a soft *shredding* sound, like cloth tearing.... Only six inches of double hull suspended him above the sea, and that six inches had been *cracked, split, sundered* where he stood.

Suddenly, immediately swamped by an onrushing flood of ocean, Fred Barrett ran for safety, but the watertight door was descending. Someone had ordered all doors down, with him within, imprisoned! He sloshed through ocean up to his loins, his waist.... His trousers were waterlogged; they dragged at his legs. His feet were heavy in water-shackled boots. Waves of water, like fiendish tentacles, broke upon his back and tried to suck him down....

Ah, the door was banged closed—locked....

Barrett lunged for a rung of the escape ladder. Slippery with ocean, it rolled in his hands, but he held...and pulled. He held, and pulled again, another rung up.... Mad, the water rose with him, surged over him faster than he could climb. He clambered, he scurried, he *scuttled* up the ladder, flung himself over the top of the door, *which did not reach to the ceiling,* and scrambled, half falling. He slithered down to the floor of engine room five, where the ocean was only ankle-deep for now *but rising*...and then ran on, gasping, *not safe yet,* for higher, drier ground....

CAPTAIN SMITH KNEW now.

Titanic's engines were all shut down. Only the electric generators that kept the lights on and the elevators running still functioned in *Titanic*'s belly. But instead of silence, the backed-up steam from the boilers was roaring out of the funnels, as loud as trains. Joseph Boxhall had computed their final position: E.J. delivered it himself to the wireless room.

"Call for emergency assistance, Phillips," he said, and laid on the table Boxhall's figures: 41°46'N, 50°14'W.

Without a word Phillips went to work. "CQD, *Titanic*," he tapped. "CQD.... Require assistance, come at once.... CQD: Position..."

"Good man," said Captain Smith. "And you, too, Bride. Carry on." And he left them to it.

It had not been fifteen minutes since he was summoned from Dove's bed, and already the water in *Titanic*'s lower decks had risen fourteen feet above the keel.

"How long have we?" he asked Harland & Wolff's head man, who had joined him on the bridge.

The man considered. "An hour and a half, possibly two. Not much longer."

"We'll have to lower the lifeboats, Boxhall," said E.J. "Summon all passengers topside immediately."

AUDREY AND BAY and Burty were having a fine time, virtually all to themselves in the Palm Court, with Wisdoms, the bartender. Burty was standing all rounds; they were singing "Alexander's Ragtime Band" for the fifth time through, trying to teach it to Wisdoms, who was a strong baritone.

A steward at the door interrupted them. "Please," he said. "All passengers are to come to boat deck immediately with their life belts on. This is an emergency. All passengers are to please come at once...." And then the steward passed on.

"Who's that?" said Burty, and finished his Pimm's Cup. "Paul Revere...? Now where were we?"

But Audrey did not make fun. It had come as Esmeralda predicted, Audrey thought, and was almost content. So long, it seemed, she had been waiting. It had been a great strain. Only hours ago the gypsy's body had floated on the face of the deep in *Titanic*'s wake.... Audrey had known then—believed then— that the terror had begun, only yet unseen, unfelt. She had had to wait, pretending calm, while whatever Esmeralda had seen in a crystal ball *loomed* and *humped* in the shadows....

"What is it?" she asked, but there was no one to tell her. No matter.

Now, at least, she could *do* something. Now she could face the trouble and do whatever she had to...to save Bay. For this she was resolved: she would not leave him here, far-flung between two continents. *No matter what it took*, should she have to hold his dead body in her arms for three days, she would bring him home—somehow—to Whale's Turning on Gilt Hill.

Burty ordered another round, but Audrey put her hand on his arm and said, "We must see to Tory. We must see to ourselves. Will you go up on deck, Wisdoms?"

"Yes, ma'am, I'm on my way, soon's I lock up this liquor."

"The ship has stopped," Bay said. "Come on, Burty, something's happened."

"All right, all right, put this bottle on my bill, Wis," said Burty, and he helped himself to a fifth of peach schnapps.

"Blessings on your new chile, sir," said Wisdoms, and the diamond chip winked in his fine white teeth.

"Wisdoms for president," said Burty, but he allowed them to lead him away.

They passed others drifting up to boat deck. Some were dressed appropriately for the icy cold, but others had shuffled into topcoats over pajamas or gowns, and had slippers only on naked feet. Many of the women wore hats to hide hair let down or pinned up, and many of them were pale, having washed the color from their faces.

Audrey saw Mrs. Straus, who had been a companion at dinner the other night. "What has happened, Ida, do you know?"

"They say we've struck an iceberg, my dear, and are stopped, that's all I know."

"I see, but where is your life belt?"

"Isador has it, don't you, dear?"

Her husband was beside her. He lifted the bright contraption. "I'll get her into it, never fear, Mrs. Lockholm. She says she doesn't want to be made uncomfortable if there's no need."

"I hope there is none," said Audrey, "but there may well be. Please let your husband help you, Ida." And then Audrey passed on, pulled by Bay's hand and at Burty VanVoorst's heels.

At the purser's desk, people had queued up to retrieve their jewels and money.

19

The mattress, dancing, woke her.

Now what was that? she wondered. Burty? No. She looked around, remembering. The room was dark and empty and cooler than she liked. The mattress shivered again and then was still.

Could it be the baby bouncing?

Where was the baby...?

It slept against the small of her back. She might have rolled over and smothered it in its first slumber.... Tory pulled herself up upon the pillows and lifted the baby up. She did not know what time it was, but it must be late, because the ship was so still and the room so dark.... And where was Burty, dear, dear Burtykins? Had he gone to grieve...or to celebrate?

She unfolded the towel and held the babe up so that the lights of *Titanic* shining in from the private promenade shone upon it, illuminated it.... It was obviously of mixed blood. She shook it and the little thing opened its eyes—funny, lashless eyes, not yet focusing. "You won't be able to pass the way I can,

Miss VanVoorst. People will know you, right away, for what you are.''

The baby moved its mouth…trying to smile or trying to find a nipple; it didn't cry. It was silent, a thin little body hanging helpless and naked from its mother's hands. Tory searched the new face. No bones stood out yet; there was no *definition* to it. The eyes were dark, no green Tory eyes for this one, though the hair was light. The hair was brown, darker than the skin, yes, but the light shining in haloed it like an aura into highlights of auburn and gold.

A red nigger, Tory thought, that's what you'll be. Red niggers are rare….

The nose was just a snub, but you couldn't tell about noses, you had to let them grow and wait and see. The mouth was wide, well formed, pink lipped; no teeth. The body was pitifully slight. She will be delicate then, Tory thought; she won't want to exercise at the barre like her mother and grow supple and sculpted as though by a madman inspired….

She will be sickly and spoiled if she lives….

Oh.

Tory wrapped the baby in a blanket and put her to her breast, but it slept instead, pushing tiny fingers into its mother's flesh and forgetting to close its mouth.

If she lives.

Would Burty care?

Or would he be relieved?

She heard movement out in the corridor, people up and passing. There must have been a party, she thought, and I missed it. "You made me miss a party," she said to the babe, but she didn't really care. She didn't want to go to a party. She felt wonderful: Burty knew, knew the worst of her at last, and he didn't give a damn. And the baby had come; her stomach was almost flat again. Tomorrow, first thing tomorrow, she could exercise again....

Everything was *almost* perfect.

"If only you were out of the way," she said, and unconsciously she stroked the baby as it slept. "Then everything could be just as before."

The knob of the door was turning. Burty was back.

"Hello, Mother," he boomed, and Tory was glad to see that he had been drinking and was in a good mood.

"Burty," she said. "Where have you been?"

"Celebrating, my beauty. Drinking with Aud and Bay and Wisdoms."

"Who?"

"With Wisdoms, our daughter's namesake. Wisdoms is his name, and so it will be hers. Wisdoms Victoria VanVoorst, one *W*, three *V*s. It will look like ducks flying in initials, very grand."

"Burty, no." *Such a colored name....*

"We must get you up, princess, we've gone and popped into an iceberg, worse luck, and now we have to put on life belts and go out on deck. It's cold, you'd best wear the sable and wrap little Wisdoms there in the chinchilla."

"I've never heard anything so silly."

"Nor I, but those are the captain's orders." He huffed down to his knees and looked under the bed for the life belts.

"No," said Tory. "I mean you can't name a baby Wisdoms."

"Why ever not?" He was at the closet, looking

on the shelf. "Ah, here we are. Two adult life belts, but none for little Wisdoms. What shall we do?"

"Oh, Burty."

"There, there, my dearest, what's the matter, eh? Would you like a wheelchair to hold our offspring in your arms, is that it?"

"Oh, Burty, whatever are you saying?"

He sat, with a thump, on the bed and twiddled the baby's ear. "The water, forward, is already pulling the bow down, Tor. Do you know what this means?"

"No," she said. The baby squirmed and squeezed shut its eyes and sighed.

"How are you feeling?" he said. He was looking at the newborn, fascinated.

"What does it mean, Burtykins?"

He got off the bed and ran a hand over his chin, feeling the stubble. "It means we're sinking, Tor, and we have to get up and put on our coats and then these life preserver things and then go up on top deck and hope we get rescued."

"Oh, silly, *Titanic* can't sink, you said so yourself."

"Hurry, Tor."

"Burty, would you have minded if…if the baby'd been born dead?" She closed her eyes so she wouldn't try to read into his face what wasn't there.

"Never thought about it. Now come on, Tor."

"All right, all right, I'll come."

She swung her legs over the bed, found her partridge-feather slippers with her feet. "I'll wear my yellow wool suit, that's the warmest," she said, weak.

"Yes," he said. "Wear the yellow and every fur you own."

"Silly. I've only got the chinchilla, the rest are in the trunks."

"Give my new topcoat to Wis then," he said. "It has a lamb collar. I'll wear the old mohair—don't think I packed it away." He rummaged again in the closet. "Hey, here it is…. Hurry, Tor."

Someone knocked on the inner door that led into the suite.

"Yes," Burt called, "we're coming."

Bay stuck his head in. "Hello, Tory," he said. "Congratulations."

She smiled but did not hold the infant up for him to see.

"I've been talking to Bruce Ismay," Bay said to Burty. "The water has covered the squash court now, G deck, up to the ceiling."

"Dear God," said Burty. "Tory, do you hear? You must hurry…. Thanks, Bay, we'll see you topside."

Bay was gone.

"Go with Bay, Burt," said Tory. "I'll be along. I have private things to do I can't let you see—woman things. I'll only be a minute." I'll throw her out into the water, she thought. Burty won't care….

"I don't want to leave you," he said.

"Please, Burtykins. I'll be right along, I promise."

"Shall I take Wis with me?"

As though in answer to her name, the baby began to cry. Instinctively Tory's hands closed around it. "No…no…. She'll be fine—"

"Are you sure?"

"Oh, please, *go*, Burty, please—"

He backed out, leaving her life belt behind. "You

get this on over your coat if you can," he said. "I'll buckle it for you later."

"I'll meet you by the first pillar where the promenade begins on A deck," she said, up and carrying the baby toward the bathroom. "I'll only be a second."

He stopped to look at his wife and new child. "I love you, kid," he said. He started forward to kiss her but bit his lip and backed away, closed the door and left her, as she'd asked.

Now, she thought as the door closed and he was gone. *Now, now, now—*

The floor was tilting just a little. She had to hold on to furniture with one hand, the babe in the other, to get out to the little deck. She stood there for a moment, alone in the dark, looking down...not so far down now, to placid water shining in *Titanic*'s lights, yellow-green and green-black. Above, there was a roaring, like radiators bursting their seams, but no other sounds, not even the water lapping velvet-tongued up the great ship's side. She saw that the bow was definitely down, a steep list to port.

Why, we're sinking, she thought. We're really sinking. And then the baby was crying. Tory held it close.

"It's a perfect opportunity," she said to the person in her arms. "I stumbled, you fell." She kissed its nose, the first time she'd kissed it. It smelled like fuzz and warm milk. "I didn't mean to," she said. "I was rushing, and the ship lurched, and suddenly, you were gone."

The baby's face was red with rage. It cried, lusty and long.

"Or I could wait until the water creeps in beneath

the door, and rises, just enough. Then I'll lay you down to sleep, Wis, which is a ridiculous name for a girl child. It's painless, drowning, I'm told. You won't mind it. You won't even know what's happening...."

The babe had found where Tory's breast should be, but the nipple was covered by Tory's bed jacket. The baby burrowed its pink-brown face against quilted satin, and tried to suck and whimpered.

"All right, here you go—" Tory pulled the baby away and held it out over the rail. Its head fell on its right shoulder, and it blinked. Hands, wanting the warmth of its mother, clenched, unclenched in the frigid air.

"Goodbye, Wis," said Tory, "and good riddance—" She swung her arms wide....

There was a hiss of light, arcing upward.... Tory recoiled, *held the baby tight*. And then the sky ignited in a soft explosion and a rain of silver sparks. Tory watched little tears of fire drop.... And then another rocket hissed high and burst.

And Tory clutched Wis to her heart.

Who was she fooling...? Who, if not herself, was she trying to hurt...?

She held the little head, too weak to hold itself. She swayed with it in the rhythm of motherhood. "Mama's sorry, Mama's sorry," she whispered. "I didn't mean it, Wis...."

I didn't mean it. I've just been so scared of being colored for so long.

The babe tsk-tsked its tongue, wanting to suckle.

"We've got to hurry," Tory said. "Got to change your name, too—" She was laughing and crying together. "Got to find the jewel bag, got to run."

She laid Wisdoms on the bed and pulled out, from underneath it, a small doctor's satchel with her initials cut into the leather in gold: V.V.V. Her jewel case. She was lost in reverie, imagining W.V.V.V. cut into crystal wedding goblets, when the water nudged open her bedroom door....

Monday, April 15

20

Second Offiger Herbert Stone had been on watch duty on *Californian* for less than an hour when he saw, from the steamer they had all been watching, a rocket leap into the sky and fire. Or at least he thought it was a rocket. If that ship was *Titanic*, as he supposed, it was probably just a party celebration. *Titanic* was a floating party, after all, wasn't it, a great big floating party palace...?

Still, he picked up the speaking tube. "Captain, sir, I see rockets from that unidentified ship to starboard, dead abeam."

Captain Lord's voice sounded furry through the tube, as though he had been asleep. "Rockets, Stone? Not firecrackers...not shooting stars?"

"I think they're rockets, sir," said Stone. "They're all white."

"Keep trying to make contact, then, with signal lamp, and keep me advised."

"Yes, sir. Will do, sir."

Stone set down the speaking tube and picked up the lamp. He began to flash it, beaming it toward the other ship's bow.

True, he thought, it would be a bit tricky maneuvering through the pack ice to get over the ten miles to that liner. But if he was captain, they would have been there an hour ago. They weren't going anywhere tonight; Captain Lord was just turning in a circle till daybreak. We should shovel on through, Stone thought, nose over, nice and easy, and see what's going on for ourselves. Gee, *Californian* was used to heavy ice, this was her regular crossing lane, after all, and she was a tough old tub.... Bloody hell, everybody knows rockets mean distress.... I don't get it, he thought, and he flashed the signal lamp on and on....

Captain Lord was drunk now, solidly drunk. His booted feet were on his bunk, his chair was tipped on its hind legs, its back held up by a wall. From his vantage point he could see right through a porthole south-southeast, starboard. With a long-glass he could see the steamer plain. She was stopped, all right, and spangling rockets in the air.

"Perhaps," he said to his parrot, "it is *Titanic* out there. So what? We've done all we need to, according to law. I've tried to telegraph, we're sending signals by hand, and they refuse to answer. They could be all down, I suppose, and still refuse to acknowledge me because that daft bitch told them to write me off. Would you go to help a man who slapped you in public, Zeke? Would you stoop to give a hand to a woman who had publicly humiliated you?"

"Wock," said the parrot, and shuffled on its perch. The captain's quarters were dark, and the bird was sleeping, its belly full of beer-soaked seed.

Captain Lord banged out of his chair and strode, almost soberly, to his window. He steadied the telescope upon it and tried to see a little better, a little clearer.

"I'm not going to threaten the life of my crew trying to cut through this ice tonight," he said. "I'm captain, and I say there's no need. Let another skipper play hero, damage his own tug, get an accident on his record—not me...." He shivered in the cold, but he liked the cold. It braced him and made him meaner. "And if that is *Titanic*," he said to his confidant, "I hope they all drown. What do you think of that?"

Awakened, the parrot protested. "Davy Jones," it squawked, and stretched its wings, wanting to fly. "Wock, Davy Jones, Davy..."

"My sentiments exactly," said Captain Lord and he poured himself another half tumblerful. It would be a long night, but somehow he would get through it....

"Here's to you, Lady Pomeroy, my love," he said, and kissed the glass as he drank.

FOR CAPTAIN RING of *Samson*, a Norwegian sailing vessel, the sight of *Titanic* through his binoculars caused fear. "We'll have to run for it now, Henrik," he said to his chief officer. "We've been seen."

"Aye, aye, sir," said Henrik Naess. He was not afraid. He knew he could slip any patrol boat in these waters, turbine engined or sail. No helmsman ever made by God or circumstance could beat Henrik Naess when it came to these waters off Newfoundland. This was his home ground, where he'd cut his teeth becoming the sailor he was...the renegade he was.

The hold of their barque was full to glory of illegal

sealskins taken from forbidden breeding grounds. To go to the aid of that poor damned ship would mean taking on survivors, seamen who knew what was allowed in these waters and what was not. It would mean attention, publicity—*Titanic* was a famous ship. There would be inspection, *exposure* to the authorities....

It would mean the end of his career; his license to work might be permanently revoked. At the very least he'd lose his reputation. And it would mean no money for his family all winter, his family and theirs, the rest of *Samson*'s crew. As things looked now, this winter would be fat for the Naess brood, and Henrik needed a fat winter: he was building his own boat. The *Nessie* would be smaller than *Samson* to be sure, but it would be a good boat. He would teach his sons to be sailors in that boat, teach them how to tuck in and out among the ice floes and escape the merchant marine. He would teach them how to isolate a seal pup and beat it to death with a bat, so as not to mar the pelt....

Oh, God, yes, he knew as well as Captain Ring that *Titanic* was doomed and sinking fast. You had only to look, and there she tipped, like an empress necklaced in glittering jewels—grand, even on the way down.... Captain Ring knew *Titanic* wasn't a patrol boat. But he had to say something, didn't he, to justify what they had to do? The captain was praying, of course, as he was; hoping, of course, as he was, that a respectable boat was close by, that a legal tender was even now steaming to the rescue, as *Samson* prepared to flee.

Naess moved the speed gear up a notch and

steered north where the ice glowed…where no boat that was not outlaw ever ran on ice-packed nights.

He gave *Titanic* one last look, one salute. She was hard down by the bow now. She'd be gone within the hour. Well, she had lifeboats, that one; the passengers were in for an adventure…and a little discomfort, perhaps, before they got picked up.

Still, it was a shame, wasn't it? She was the most beautiful liner he ever hoped to see.

Captain Ring stood beside him. "Take 'er up another notch, Naess, if you're able. I want to put distance between us and her. Long distance."

"Done, sir," said Naess. "Ava's gonna look real good in her new coat.…"

"And my Marlene, too," said his partner in crime.

DOVE WOULD NOT be hurried. She meant to look her best, to *devastate* Eleanor when the press pictures of their rescue showed her beside E.J. with his arm around her shoulder and her beautiful head lying possessively upon his medaled chest.

"Mother, do hurry. Don't go to pieces on me, now, please."

"I'm doing nothing of the sort, Nicola. I've told you to run along, I don't know why you're hanging back like this. Lord knows—" it was a pun and she knew it, a sly reference to that Captain Lord Nicola had confessed to bedding, and Dove would have her puns; it was part of her charm, being clever "—it's not like you. We'll be in different boats, anyway. I'm sure E.J. will wait until the very last one, and I'm staying with him, but don't you. So run along and don't scold, there's an angel." And Dove tried against light gray cashmere a triple-strand necklace of diamonds and sapphires.

Nicola was dressed as though for a grouse shoot, in trousers, boots to the knee, and two sweaters. For fashion's sake she had her life belt on under her sable.

Why am I waiting? she asked herself. It wasn't as though she'd never see her mother again....

Nicola turned on her heel and left.

It was the loss of Rolf that made her *unusual* these days, she thought, *unsure* where she used to be certain. Rolf...and now Rolls....

Amusing Rolls, whom she had taken to her bed after he had let himself be abused by Burty. She'd liked that; it had been an act of heroism on Rolls's part. She had liked his bedroom manner, too. He was experienced, expert; she hadn't minded that a bit. She didn't mind that he was not a gentleman, either. She was too secure to fret about that. If Theodore Royce was not a gentleman today, he would be the moment she *married* him, for society would have it so, and so it would be. No, what Nicola minded was that she cared at all, that she liked him, responded to him. She minded *needing* someone. She liked to be self-sufficient and free, wanted to be what Rolf had always said of her: Nicola, goddess of the hunt with conqueror's eyes. And if she allowed herself to be wooed by Teddy Royce, was she not, then, being *conquered* instead?

A deck was crowded with passengers, confused and milling. Jack Astor and Madeline stood like anxious parents, he holding their Airedale pup in his arms, she holding its leash, twisting it in lace-gloved fingers. Nicola stood for a moment beside Harry

Widener, and he said, "I asked the barman for more ice, but this is ridiculous, don't you think?" having a little joke. Another man she did not know said, "I've never been so put out. Do they call this a first-class trip?" But most of the assembled were silent, just standing around and looking odd, wrapped in coats and blankets over hastily thrown on clothes.

They were lowering the lifeboats now. Boat number seven, starboard, boat number four, port side. But the officers trying to get the women to line up to step aboard were having trouble; the women shrank back and looked for their husbands who, like a stag line, were lining up against the inside walls. It's like the first dance at a ball, thought Nicola, no one wants to go first.

Even in her sable she was cold. Her breath was visible, and the roar from *Titanic*'s funnels of released pent-up steam was like breath, too. Benjamin Guggenheim saw her and came over. He was bundled into two sweaters and trousers as she was. "I've been told it's no use," he said quietly. "The watertight compartments are flooding, the ship is going down."

Nicola disguised her shock. She kissed his cheek. "Thank you for telling me," she said.

"Get into the first boat you can, Lady Pomeroy, don't hold back. There are not enough seats for us all."

"Not enough seats—"

"Don't say I told you," he said. "I'm going back to my cabin now to dress appropriately to meet my maker."

"Mr. Guggenheim," said Nicola, "stay with me. We'll get into a boat together. We'll be all right."

He shook his head. "No, fair lady, it's women and children first, you see, and I am an old man. I've had my day.... Victor."

His valet was at his side.

"Are you ready, Victor? Have you seen enough?"

"Yes, sir."

"Goodbye, then—" Benjamin Guggenheim bowed over Nicola's hand "—and good luck."

"Good luck to you, sir," she said, her face white as she understood, at last, what was happening.

Mr. Guggenheim turned toward the staircase down to B deck. "We'll wear our evening tails, Victor—yes, you, too. And diamond studs. We want to look like gentlemen, don't we? Go down properly as gentlemen should?"

"Yes, sir, very good, sir," said Victor. "And overcoats, sir...can we wear our overcoats...?"

Not enough boats.

Not enough seats.

Not enough room.

I must save my entitlements, my bankbooks, and some remembrances of Rolf.... Nicola moved, as fast as she politely could, toward the servants' staircase down. It was closest. Out of a corner of her eye she saw Audrey and Bay and the twins in a group before a lifeboat. So they are all right, she thought, and batted down the stairs.... On B deck the water was already ankle-deep and as dark as old blood.

Her stateroom was far forward port side, but she saw no one in her long walk down the corridor. It was lighted as always, blue silk wallpaper and mahogany panels as always, but it was filling with water and so sharply slanted that she had to step along one foot at a time and hold the wall to keep her balance.

Some of the doors to the rooms were open and swaying to the pulse of the water that was invading. Lights were on in the rooms, beautiful rooms looking pitiful now with the furniture askew and the beds unmade, the covers thrown back and the impress of heads still flattening the pillows.

The door to B-16 stood open, too.

Was Dove still in there, her foolish, vain, *stupid* mother?

Angry, Nicola sloshed through the open doorway.

Teddy Royce was there. A leather satchel sat on the bureau, its mouth yawned wide, and Teddy was pawing through the dresser drawers, flinging her lingerie behind him in his hunt for...

Nicola's money and jewels, of course. He found her golden chest with a curved lid, the key was in the lock. He opened it for a peep inside. That chest held more than a million dollars' worth of gems. That chest held the turquoise-and-enamel necklace and five perfect strands of South Sea pearls and...

Nicola watched him toss the chest into the satchel, and go on rooting.

He uncovered her leather money envelope; there was more than thirty thousand dollars in it. He lifted the flap and fanned the bills. As he did, *Titanic* shuddered down a little lower. The room swayed, the chandelier above swung on its chain, and Teddy Royce glanced up and saw her in the mirror. She was standing in the doorway, her hands gripping either side of the frame.

"Is my mother here?" she said, and waded through water up to her shins toward a bedside table. There was a derringer in that table, fully loaded, and she was going to get to it before he did.

"Nicola," he said. "I'm saving what I can for you. Tell me what else is valuable, let's hurry."

Oh, yes, so smooth, the gambling man. He went back to his hunt with barely a pause to mark his surprise. He was very good, was Teddy Royce....

She was at the table. She had the drawer open and her fingers around the mother-of-pearl butt. She cocked its dainty silver hammer. "Is my mother still here?" she asked again.

"No," he said, and straightened up from the bottom drawer. "No—" He turned to face her, his hands spread along the bureau's face. "It's only you and I in here, my darling."

She raised the pistol, pointed it at his heart. The gun was only as big as her hand, but she knew how to shoot it straight.

"Put all my things on this bed and get out," she said. "Or you're a dead man, Teddy Royce."

He saw her eyes, her steady arm. He sighed and did as he was told.

"You're a rat," she said. "You're handsome and you're charming, and you're a rat."

"That I am," he agreed. "I've had to be to lead the life I want."

"If I shoot you now, no one would prosecute me," she said.

"That is also, unfortunately, true," he said. "No one would cry for me, and you would be applauded as a woman who acted heroically in her own defense."

"Put that box and that envelope into the suitcase under my bed," she said. "And the picture of Rolf, there, on the bureau. Add that."

He got down on his knees in the water, pulled out

an ostrich-skin case. He set it on the bed between them, opened the lid sideways so she could see his hands as he worked, and laid the chest and the envelope and her late husband's portrait on top of the bankbooks and the securities. Then he asked, his hands upon the lid, "What else can I do for you, Nick?"

She was thinking. "The satin box there, that goes in, too."

"Ah yes," he said. "I was hoping you'd forget that."

She smiled. He was a rat, but he was amusing. Even under fire—maybe only under fire—Teddy Royce was at his best.

"All right now. Close the bag and get out. If you hesitate I will shoot to kill."

"You're beautiful when you're angry.... Did I ever tell you that?"

And then he bowed, straightened his cravat and made his way through rising water to the door. "Don't stay down here too long, Nick. You'll drown."

"I can take care of myself and what's mine," she said.

"I wish I was yours," he said. "Then you could take care of me, and I wouldn't have to act the way I do, would I?"

"There is not enough room in the boats for all of us," she said. "Even if you'd stolen everything from everyone it might not have done you any good. It's women and children first, up there, so your chances, gambling man, aren't good."

"And just yesterday," he said, "Archie Butt was telling me how, with women wanting the vote and all, chivalry would soon be dead.... Seems no one gets to have his cake and eat it, too, eh, pet? But if I could, I'd ask for your hand, dear Nicky. And if you could, maybe you'd say yes.''

''Get out,'' she said.

And he did.

She listened to him sloshing down the hall until the sounds of him faded into the slaps of water against the walls, and then she tucked the derringer into her bosom. She checked; Dove had left her cloud-white jewelry bags behind. Nicola added those to the ostrich-skin suitcase, then buckled it closed, slung its strap over her shoulder, and high-kicked her way through the water, yellow green under the flame-shaped lights of the chandelier.

Rolls Royce doesn't deserve to live, she thought. He's a thief and a rogue. Better men, like Mr. Guggenheim, should get a place. But I'll miss him, dog that he is. I like him. He dares me, tries to get the better of me. He is a worthy foe, is Teddy Royce, and well made, too. The sharks will have a treat, feasting on him.

A steward, at the end of the hall, called to her. ''Hurry, madam, hurry. Is there anyone else you know of still on this deck? Everyone must be topside now, madam—topside, right away!''

21

In the wireless room John Phillips and Harold Bride worked on, sending to Cape Race, sending to *Mount Temple*, sending to *Frankfurt*.

"Try the new signal now, why don't you, John?" said Bride. "Try SOS."

"Yes, all right." Phillips was shaking with cold, but neither man noticed it. "MGY *Titanic* to MKS *Olympic*: SOS, we are in collision with berg. Sinking head down, 41°46'N, 50°14'W. Come soon as possible."

Incredibly—or so it seemed to the two operators; they had been working nonstop for almost two hours and had found no one to come to their aid—incredibly, *Olympic* wired back: "We are coming.... Our position 170 miles north...."

Phillips tapped furiously: "We are putting passengers off in small boats. Engine room flooding. Come with all speed—"

And then someone else was breaking in. Phillips switched to receive. "I say, *Titanic*," came through from *Carpathia*, "do you know there is a batch of messages for you from Cape Cod? Why won't you answer them? You're impeding our traffic."

Angry, Phillips tapped, "This is MGY, *Titanic*. Come at once. We have struck an iceberg. It's CQD...it's SOS. Position..."

"You require assistance?" *Carpathia* hummed back faint, fading away.

"Yes, come quick," Phillips tapped into the receiver. "CQD, SOS, come quick."

Harold Bride was looking up *Carpathia*'s position. According to the charts she was about sixty miles away. "She's nearer than most," he said quietly. "I hope she responds."

Phillips tried to get through again, but got no answer. "Hope is about all that's left, Harold," he said. "We've not much time now."

"I'll do the hoping and the praying, Mr. Phillips. You keep on sending, eh?"

"CQD...SOS, is anybody out there?" John Phillips labored on. "This is MGY, *Titanic*. We have struck a berg and are sinking fast. Please come, please come and help immediately. Position..."

"That's the way," Harold Bride mumbled to himself, proud of his superior. And then, because Phillips could not spare the time, Bride fit his life jacket on for him while Phillips broadcast on.

IN WEBSTER, MASSACHUSETTS, Bobby Powers, eleven years old last week, was playing with his birthday present, a new portable wireless receiver. It was a fine, clear night, and he was picking up marine messages as far away as Cape Cod. It was very exciting. He should have been in bed—his parents thought he was in bed—but he was sitting at his desk, listening hard, translating the code. He was getting good, he thought....

He heard again what he had been hearing for some minutes, clear as clear, almost no static around it; he heard the new international distress signal, SOS. And then the interference again, from the *Titanic*. Always it was the same. Someone calling for help, someone sinking, and then an identification: "MGY, *Titanic*...." And then the ship in distress would cut through again. "We are sinking fast. Require assistance, please come at once."

Suddenly Bobby's eyes lighted up. He had it! It wasn't the *Titanic interrupting*, it was the *Titanic* itself in trouble! It was the *Titanic* that was sinking.

Bobby leaned closer to be sure he had it right.

A few minutes later he sat back. He'd best tell his dad. His dad would know what he should do.

He ran down the stairs to the kitchen where his mother and father were drinking with friends, the Wilsons from next door.

"Dad, could you come?" said Bobby. "Come quick. I've got the *Titanic* on my wireless and they're sending SOS, SOS. They say they're sinking fast."

Bobby's mother was not amused. She gave an exasperated sigh and said to Corinne Wilson, "Really, I don't know what I'm going to do. He gets worse every day. Rob gave him that thing to stop all this showing off, but—" She swung to her husband.

"I'm not showing off, Mom," said Bobby. "Please, Dad, come."

"What are we going to do with him, Rob? Wash his mouth out with soap?"

"Dad," said Bobby, feeling his kidneys send out the urge the way they did whenever his mother spoke about him like that. "Come up and check—it's true. *Please come.*"

His father was eyeing Corinne Wilson's cleavage. "Not right now, Bobby," he said. "You listen, I'm busy."

"That *Titanic*'s unsinkable, Bobby," said Guy Wilson. "So it can't be the *Titanic* you're hearing." Guy Wilson was lazy and long legged, and Bobby wanted to be like Guy Wilson when he grew up because his mother liked Guy Wilson; her eyes went soft whenever she even mentioned his name.

"It is, too!" said Bobby, wanting to cry. He forced the feeling to go away and, defeated, turned back toward the stairs.

"He's supposed to have been in bed asleep two hours ago," said his mother to Guy Wilson, "but he's a bad boy, you see."

"What if the *Titanic*'s sinking," said Bobby's father. "What can we do?"

Grown-ups, thought Bobby. He'd never understand them if he lived to be a hundred.

In his room again, he hunched over the receiver. Yes, there it still was, coming in clearer now. "SOS," the wireless crackled through only a little static. "SOS, *Titanic* here.... Require assistance. Please come at once. We won't last the hour."

Bobby Powers sighed and, knowing his mother wouldn't like it, defiantly peed in his pants.

AUDREY HELD TIGHT to Bay's hand. Whatever happened, she wouldn't let it go. Whatever happened...

An officer who identified himself as Charles Lightoller was helping Madeline Astor into the boat. Audrey was close, next in line to board behind the

Strauses. Jack Astor was about to step in beside his bride, but the officer stopped him. Audrey tightened her hold on Bay's hand. She heard Lightoller say, "Women and children first, please," but there were not so many in their group; there was room for the men. Another boat had put down ahead of them, and men had been in that....

"I would like to sit beside my wife," said Jack Astor. "She is in delicate condition, and I need to be with her."

"I'm sorry, sir. We'll put you in after the ladies—how's that?" And Lightoller pointed out a section of deck where Jack Astor should stand.

Audrey's heart clutched and unclutched. The funnels had finished blowing off their steam, and the ship was death quiet. There were no more rockets to explode. There was no more milling of passengers; everyone stood quietly, dumbly. She could not even hear the water rising...it was all so still.... There was only Lightoller's voice of command and the creak of the ropes of the lifeboat as it swung, two feet off the rail of the top deck, from steel davits hung high from a hook.

John Astor kissed his wife and stepped back. He still held his Airedale pup. "Come, Kitty," he said, and rubbed the dog's head as he went and stood with several other men, over where the deck chairs were lined up out of the way to make room.

Dear God in heaven, thought Audrey. There was a full bottle of brandy in her coat pocket. She had put it in as they were leaving their stateroom, thinking they might want to warm themselves out in the cold in an open boat; thinking they might try to make a little party of it out there in the night—keep spirits up—while the engineers repaired *Titanic* if they could, or another ship came to take them on.

The thought came—she could no longer hold it back—that some of them, these dear, decent people, might die tonight. Not only Bay, but Jack Astor and Colonel Gracie over there beside him, and... With her free hand she gripped the neck of the brandy bottle in her pocket. It was hard and round: solid. It gave her a sense of strength.

The Strauses were next, and again it was the same. Lightoller took Mrs. Straus's hand and elbow to assist her in, but shook his head to Mr. Straus. "Sorry, sir, you'll have to wait over there," said Lightoller, and gestured back to where Jack Astor stood with others.

But he's an elderly man, thought Audrey. Surely they won't deny him a place—

"That's all right, then," said Mrs. Straus, and she removed her arm from Lightoller's grip. "I'll stand over there, too, for I'll not be separated from my husband."

"Now, Ida," said Mr. Straus. "I'll be along. You get into this boat and I'll find a later one. Don't worry about me."

Mrs. Straus snorted. "Isador Straus, I'll do no such thing. I've been with you all my life, and as we have lived so we will die—together."

"Oh, please let him in," said Audrey, unable not to plead for him. "He is elderly, can't you see? You *must* let him into the boat!"

Lightoller wavered, was about to say yes, Audrey could see that. But Mr. Straus was shaking his head. "Oh, no, no," he said. "I'll have no distinction not granted to others," and he stepped away toward the deck chairs.

Mrs. Straus followed him. "Please wait for me, Isador," she said. He waited, holding out his arms. She went to him, her arm around his waist thickened by his greatcoat. Tenderly, he wrapped an arm around her shoulders. He led her to the chairs and they sat down, side by side. They watched the filling of the boat proceed.

Oh, this is wrong, thought Audrey. They haven't thought it out properly. No one expected this. And now they are doing it wrong—

It was Audrey's turn.

Lightoller extended his hand to help her from the deck into the boat, two feet out in space. "Nor will I take my place without my husband," Audrey said, and squeezed Bay's hand; afraid he, too, would pull away.

Lightoller's eyes looked behind Audrey to Bay. Then he nodded. "All right, Mrs. Lockholm, he's coming. Lift your foot high now—" He was gripping her elbow, tugging, and she heard Bay, behind her, say, "I'm right here, darling, come now, let's not hold up the others." His hand slipped free of hers but he was lifting her, around the waist, and then she was skipping into space. There was a momentary frigid breath of ice up her legs as she stretched, and then she was in the boat, seated on a green board and tucking her skirts around her knees to make room for Bay.

But now another woman was being handed over, and *where was Bay?* She saw him, helping Smoke in, lifting her from behind. Audrey held the edge of her seat and tried to will Bay into the lifeboat with her eyes. There was a tightness around her throat, and a muffling, as of drums, roared in her chest. Do not leave me, she prayed.

Smoke was in, subdued and silent, different since she'd chopped her hair, *sadder*.... But Audrey could not think, could not worry, about Smoke now. She must *get Bay back beside her*.... "Don't sit just here," she said to her daughter as Smoke started to sink down to her right. "Leave a space for your father, please."

Smoke said nothing. She did as she was told, hugging her coat around her and looking away at the silent water, with no expression on her face.

Swan was next.

No, there was an older woman they were letting through, a tall woman in black right up to hat and veil....

Audrey gasped. For a moment the woman, who was strange to her, looked like the gypsy, looked *just like* in the way she held herself, furtively, *closed*, as though she had secrets to hide.... But no, it was just a woman, perhaps from second class, for they had allowed the second-class passengers up when they couldn't get the promenade windows open on B deck.

Bay was still in Audrey's sight, at least. He was helping Lightoller assist the woman in. He would send Swan aboard before himself, Audrey was reconciled to that. But then he would come aboard— and Jack Astor and the Strauses and Colonel Gracie, too—he wouldn't lie to her about that. They had never lied to each other.

Though I, she thought, was prepared to lie, wasn't

I, when I thought that to do so would save Bay's life....

Bay....

It was a silent prayer, a scream in a locked throat. Bay, don't leave me....

The woman in black was in now, settling herself on a far seat, as far from Audrey as she could get, ocean side of the lifeboat. Audrey sought the woman's eyes to reassure her, but the woman looked only at her lap. The cloak she wore was too small for her; it pulled over wide shoulders and reached barely to her knees, which were in men's trousers, men's boots....

Audrey looked away...and up, for Bay.

Swan was coming now, reluctantly, it seemed. That boy, the violinist, was hanging over the rail, separated from the crowd, watching, and Swan was gesturing to him. He waved to her. Being heroic, Audrey thought. He's smiling, pretending all this is nothing much.... Perhaps he is not a bad boy, and perhaps he does love her, or thinks he does....

A flash of silver caught the corner of Audrey's eye. She looked...*and saw a crescent moon, askew, pearl surrounded, upon the strange woman's throat....*

The woman was lifting her hair, freeing it behind from the collar of the cloak. Her picture hat was tilting; the veil was slipping. The woman's lifted hands strained the seams of her cloak. Too small, the cloak popped its buttons, the first and second, the ones at her bodice....

Audrey gave a little cry, a cry of recognition, for there, upon that alien woman's throat rode five strands of pearls clasped by a crescent moon. Audrey looked in horror at the woman's *red, red hair*.... Audrey leaned upon her knees, staring.

The woman saw. She stopped what she was doing, her arms stiffened, immobile in the air. And there, against a background of blue-black night dusted with millions of silver-sequin stars, Audrey saw Madame Romany's prophecy fulfilled.

There, visible to all, was the necklace Bay had given her in bon voyage, constrictively tight against a too-thick throat *just shaved*. And there, sliding now, slipping, was *red, red hair*, one of Nicola's false falls, wound around the head of a man, with hair dark and wavy...handsome hair just beginning to gray....

In a heartbeat the hat and the veil fell away, taking the handmade auburn switch with it, impaled by hat pins, off the side. All landed with a little slap on the surface of the sea. All floated, rocked only by water wrinkles.... Teddy Royce knew himself exposed, and smiled, charmingly, his top lip different with the mustache freshly gone....

Audrey stood, all thought gone, hate only in her heart. Lifting her skirts she sprang across the boat; people were yelling at her. The boat, held above by long ropes, swayed as Audrey upset the balance. She clutched at the side to keep herself upright, reached Teddy Royce and slapped his smiling face. That was *her* cloak he was wearing; those were *her* pearls he had stolen. That was *Bay's place* he had seized—

The boat was careening wildly now. Audrey fell against the detestable enemy. The davits whined, straining in their screws. She heard a high screaming and Bay's voice, from somewhere high, calling her name. She squirmed to *see*.... All was rocking, and *there* high above, in a billow of silk ruffles, as white as the moon in the night, *there, her daughter was falling from the side of Titanic....*

The lifeboat, bucking on its chains, struck Swan as she fell, bumped, *plunged* down the cliff of *Titanic*'s black side.

Swan clawed at the gunwale of the lifeboat, trying to stop her fall. She held for a moment...but the boat seesawed and bucked her against *Titanic*'s wall. She cried out; her fingers gave.... And in a flutter of petticoats and skirts, Swan dropped, sideways and flat down into the black pool of the sea....

Audrey, thrown to the boat floor, crouched to shocked to move, too stunned to speak....

What had she done to her daughter...?

They were lowering the boat away. By jerks, first one side then the other, the boat was descending. Audrey looked up, seeking Bay. Her eyes swept Smoke's eyes and shrank from the contempt that fired there.

She sought Bay...but saw only Danny Bowen leaping from *Titanic*'s top deck in all his clothes, save his coat. In shoes and sweater and flaring wide-cuffed trousers, she saw him sail out, arms spread, knees buckling; so she knew he was not a good swimmer. He is only brave, she thought, and in love....

Danny hit with a mammoth splash.

And still Audrey looked up, hunting her husband. But Bay was no longer to be seen.

Only then did she peer down for her daughter. And there Swan was, clearly visible in *Titanic*'s lights, thrashing, dog-paddling. Oh, get her quickly, Danny,

Audrey thought. She'll freeze if you don't get her quickly....

He had her.

Above on the decks and in the little lifeboat, people clapped for him and cheered. He had her; she was quiet against his chest. He was waiting, floating there, for the boat to set down and pick them up.

The boat bumped, rocked a little, and then they were afloat, the ropes thrown off; they were free....

"Row away," someone called down, and Teddy Royce took an oar and Smoke took an oar, and they pulled out from the shadowy hulk of *Titanic*'s sheer side. They pulled for Danny, waiting for them in the water, clutching Swan like a bouquet of flowers.

22

Dove, resplendent in soft white wool and silver fox, stood on bridge deck beside Captain Smith watching the passengers being put off into the boats. He was in his commodore's uniform and a heavy navy watch coat, its gold-eagle buttons undone. Desolate, stoic, he watched his last captaincy sinking into ruin. She, composed, with faraway eyes, merely waited.

"A captain, you know, my love," he said, "must stay with his ship. Go down with her if need be."

"I know, E.J.," she said, feeling the drama of it, feeling the *thrill*. She was going to win from Eleanor, after all: he, the last combat, her last conquest.... Dove found it fitting.

I could go on and on, older and grayer, remembering former triumphs, she thought. I much prefer it to end like this. He will be legend, and so will I, as his consort. Better, much better, this, than dying of boredom with Nicola, subservient to Nicola, while she—whom I have never liked—would be insultingly sweeter and kinder the more drab I became. Such an end is not for me, who once claimed all

Newport as my dominion…. This, at least, is a worthy ending….

She said, "Will it come to that?"

He did not want to dismay her. He was careful in what he said. "There are not enough boats, dear Dove, and the nearest liner is sixty miles away. She will be all night coming to our rescue, even if she races. And *Titanic* will be done, all done, by then. It will be all over now in half an hour." He stood straight, as a captain should. Warm tears stung on his ice-numbed cheeks. "The cold," he said, apologetically, "it tears at my eyes."

"And my heart," she said, admiring him. "I will not leave you."

"Oh, but you must."

"I wanted you to stay with me forever," she said, "and now I have my wish—you shall."

There was such a tenderness in his heart for her. This is what love feels like, he thought…. It was a caring beyond passion, beyond longing. It was…a contentment, a devotion….

"There is still hope," he said. Only a fool's hope, he thought. "I must release the men from their duty. Let me escort you down, dearest. I will personally hand you in to a boat."

She shook her head. "I'll wait here for my captain," she said. "My brave captain."

"I wanted to leave you," he said. "I was going back to Eleanor and little Helen."

"You would have left your heart," she said.

"I won't be long," he said.

"No," she said. "Hurry back. As you say, we don't have much time."

He left her then, not far. He stepped over to the

wireless room where Phillips and Bride were still, water pooling around their ankles, trying to connect with someone, anyone, who could save their souls.

"Leave off now," the captain said. "You've done your duty and more. It's every man for himself now, and good luck to you." And then, before they could reply, he was gone, to tell each officer individually that he was released from his captain's command and owed allegiance only to himself.

Oh, I like him, thought Dove, comfortable in the cold in her fur and happy with her decision. I like him exceedingly....

DURTY HADN'T BEEN by the pillar on A deck. She couldn't find Burty anywhere. She went from side to side of *Titanic*, where they were loading into the life-boats, went from port to starboard...and still there was no Burty.

Could he have gone into a boat ahead...? She'd looked over the railings, down into that black-green water lighted from *Titanic* as though by spotlights. But if Burty was out there, on the edge of the lights, rowing away, she could not distinguish him.

Tory hoped he was in a boat, safe.... For all the lifeboats had been filled and dropped. There were four collapsible rafts called Engleharts the crew was trying to get ready, but one was stuck and one wouldn't open, so there were really only *two* chances left...and Burty was not in line for either one....

The band was playing. The musicians had put on their red-and-gold coats and were standing in front of the grand staircase as though grouped to play for a ball, and they were playing the most rousing airs. Marches, mostly, and fast, happy tunes. And someone was blowing his bagpipe, someone out in the water there, beyond the circles of light. The bagpipe's melodies were sad; they threaded under the gay music like shivers, barely heard but felt—little aches around the heart....

Oh, where was Burtykins?

"Madam?" an officer called to her. "You must away, madam, right now. You and your child."

"Yes," Tory said. She stepped up to where the man was signaling to her. "I can't find my husband," she said.

"He's aboard another, I'm sure," said the crewman. "Now step aboard quickly, please."

She stepped over and in. It was a large canvas boat, flat bottomed. It was not much filled. There was the scandalous Lady Lucile and her husband Sir Cosmo Duff-Gordon, whom nobody liked. And Mrs. Twigg.

"Mrs. Twigg, have you seen my husband?" Tory asked.

Mrs. Twigg was frightened. Her eyes were wide with shock. She looked at the baby in Tory's arms, looked at Tory, and shook her head. She did not make room, so Tory sat on a board by herself. Nicola was being handed in now. So I will be with one friend at least, Tory thought.... Oh, where was Burty that he hadn't come to her?

Bruce Ismay came aboard as Nicola sat down beside Tory. They embraced each other, and Nicola lifted the baby. "Oh, Tory, I didn't know.... So this is what you were doing inside your room—I wondered."

Tory watched Nicola's expression as she unwrapped, just barely, the blanket around the infant's face. There was only joy in it as Nicola said, "Darling, it's *gorgeous*. What a face. I hope it's a girl."

"Yes," said Tory. "Nick...did you know...?"

"You mean the little skeleton in your closet, Tor?"

Tory nodded.

Nicola shrugged. "Not until I was told, and then I didn't give a damn. So don't you."

"It shows in her," said Tory. "I was afraid it would."

"Poop," said Nicola. "She's beautiful. You're rich. Who cares...? What will you name her?"

"I don't know," said Tory, and looked, again, for Burty, but the space on the deck where she had recently stood was bare.

"Mr. Ismay," she asked, "have you seen my husband? I don't know where he is."

Ismay had a ball of ice in his hand. He had picked it up as snow from the foredeck sometime before; he didn't know how long he'd held it, squeezing. It was ice now, packed tight. The heat of his hand had not melted it. He held the ice in his hand and nodded in reply to her question, though he did not look at her. "I saw him a while ago, Mrs. VanVoorst. He was talking with Bayard Lockholm and Jack Astor. I'm sure he's all right— don't you worry. Got aboard when he could, you know...." And Ismay turned the ball of ice in his hands, over and over.

"Yes," Tory said. "I see, yes, thank you." And she took Wisdoms back from Nicola and held her very close.

Titanic was slanting steeply now, and the collapsible boat was tilting with her, still held to her by davit ropes.

"Send us down," called out Sir Duff-Gordon, "or you'll take us with you, you dogs."

"But we're not nearly full," Tory said. "And there're people still up there, so many...."

No one answered her. The boat began to descend.

And then she saw him, saw Burty, there at the rail!

She almost stood, but Nicola pulled her down. "No, you can't," Nicola said. "You'll upset us."

Tory waved. "Burty! Burty, I'm here!" she cried.

He saw her. He was with Bay Lockholm. They both smiled and waved.

"Oh, there are seats here," cried Tory. "Why are we leaving them? We can't leave them!"

"We'll pick them up later," said Sir Cosmo. He was shivering though wrapped in pelts of beaver.

Tory counted only a dozen in a boat that could hold forty—fifty, if need be....

Burty was still waving to her, blowing kisses. He doesn't have his hat, Tory thought. He'll catch his death of cold.... He looked so little, far above, so vulnerable....

He's going to die here tonight, she thought. I've lost him, after all....

At her breast, snug upon chinchilla, their baby sighed, and slept.

Titanic was foundering, even as Tory watched her husband blow last kisses.

Water now topped the highest deck and rippled through all things. As though touched by a mighty finger at the bow, the ship's stern began to rise. Quietly at first, the fat bottom ascended as the nose dipped lower and lower toward its grave.

Fifteen hundred souls were still upon her, left boatless, *unsaved*.... Some, impatient, jumped from *Titanic*'s top deck the few feet down to the sea. Others waited. Archibald Butt, adviser to America's president, played a last hand of cards in the smoking room with his gentleman-friend Arthur Ryerson.

"My fortune against your fortune," Mr. Butt said, and dealt out the cards.

"That's not fair, mine is worth far more than yours," said Mr. Ryerson.

"Not anymore it isn't," said Mr. Butt.

As the great ship shifted in the sea, things began to break and tumble within her. Beds and chests slid and bumped against walls and each other. Chandeliers swung on slanted ceilings. Clocks fell and pictures dropped from their places. Washbasins tore free of their screws and bolts; tubs, overflowing, floated. All over, up and down nine massive decks, *Titanic* was disemboweled. Walls were crumbling, pillars were smashing down, great vents and pipes fell in disjointed pieces.... All *Titanic*'s gracious and handsome parts began to slide forward toward the bow, following gravity down, down, tumbling upon each other, crushing each other: it was a thundering sound.

And still *Titanic* lifted higher and higher in the stern. And still Mr. Wallace Hartley kept his band to a measure.... They played the most popular English song of that spring, "Songe d'Automne," to end their set, and, last, they stood as straight as they could while the floor beneath them tipped precariously and the ocean rose to their waists, and, last, they played the hymn that had ended the prayer sing of Sunday night. They played "Nearer my God to Thee" in the uproar and for as long as they could.

Danny Bowen was hanging now by life-belt straps to the side of Audrey's boat. He was unable to lift Swan up and into it. She was unable to help. "I cannot feel my legs, Danny, and my hips must be crushed, the bones are scraping."

He was afraid to get beneath and toss her, afraid of hurting her more. So he hung on the edge of the boat, next to Smoke, and held Swan in his arms.

"I'll pull her up," said Audrey. "I'm strong."

"Yes," said Danny, "but we will have to wait, Mrs. Lockholm, until the ship goes down. We could all be pulled down by her suction. I will hold her until it's safe, and then we will try to get her up."

"Don't disturb yourself, Mother," said Swan, almost too low to be heard. "It doesn't matter. I'm going to die."

Smoke, safe in the lifeboat, next to her sister, said, "I won't let you die, Swanny. We'll make it, you'll see. You've just got to hang on...."

"Pull away, pull away! She's sinking, heave to!" One of the stokers was at an oar and hauling. "She'll take us with her if you don't. Heave to!"

Teddy Royce renewed his efforts on the other oar, and together the men began to row. Swan laid her head atop Danny's shoulder and closed her eyes....

And Audrey looked for Bay.

She scanned the rows of people—hundreds of people—crowded upon *Titanic*'s stern. But if he was there, she could not see him. She strained to see in the dark where the other boats, rowed out beyond the circle of doom, floated idly, like dark ice sculptures themselves among shoals of it, blocks of it, shelf upon shelf of ice, fringed prettily with icicle crystals.

And *Titanic*'s bottom rose and rose. *Titanic*'s bowels thundered and broke. *Titanic*'s bow pointed deeper and straighter, until the whole majestic bulk of her, each window of her glowing an electric gold, stood outlined against the quiet black sky like the long and mighty finger of God.

There she held, for a moment, a minute, perhaps three. There she held.... And to the sounds of her innards tearing and the strains of the band still playing, there was added the cries of the drowning and dying. It all echoed for miles over the ice, come as quiet as ghosts, come peaked like tombstones....

And then, while distant stars shone, the ones adrift in boats were passengers no more, became *survivors* only. For the mighty liner shuddered, once, in her bones and *split* amidships like the crack of judgment.... And *Titanic*, beautiful *Titanic*, splendid *Titanic*, goddess of the sea, sweetly, slowly, electric eyes all gleaming, and with almost no tearing of the silken sea, *Titanic* slipped under the Atlantic and began her long swim down.

E.J. and Dove stood together on bridge deck in the captain's place. As *Titanic* tilted beyond standing, they leaped, hands locked, off the bow. As Dove smacked into the water, there came a celestial singing into her head. The awful cold took her breath, and then was warm. E.J.'s hand slipped away, but she could see him, hanging in the water, bright green in *Titanic*'s lights. He *dazzled*, luminous. As gentle water rocked over Dove's immaculate head, she smiled triumphantly. *She had held him to the end, and she did so love to win the prize....*

In a haze of bubbles, E.J.'s body was lost to her. She thought she saw, through water yellow green, the face of her late husband, Percy. He was calling to her—*she could hear him*—and he was smiling, as of old, and beckoning to her, *forgiveness* in his fishfine eyes. She let her fur fall away, and she swam for Percy. She opened her mouth to tell him *everything*, and all was a glorious light.

As Captain Smith leaped, he held Dove's precious body in his mind, but it was Eleanor's face he saw. She was at home in Southampton, watching out the kitchen window, waiting, patient as always, for him to come home to her....

And Audrey, pulled away under the stars, sought Bay. There were so many bodies in the water, it was like a school of frightened fish. There was such wailing, so eerie, shivering across the stands of ice, and arms and heads and bodies everywhere struggling, though some, already, were still. And all was shining *underwater* by *Titanic*'s generators, still pouring out the light.

Then, suddenly, invisibly, the great candle was snuffed. And the light was gone, *Titanic* was gone, and there was only a flat round circle widening on the cloak-dark sea.

A collective moan went up as darkness wrapped the scene. And Audrey could not stand it, *would not stand it*.

"I'm going now," she said quietly to Smoke. "Look after your sister. I'm going after your father."

Smoke said nothing. She was holding her sister's head on Danny's shoulder, and she was chalk white with shock. She only nodded and leaned away to give her mother room.

Before anyone could stop her, Audrey lurched out of her place and over to the rim of the boat. The man who had put himself in charge shouted at her, but she was over and in the water.

It was numbing cold.

But Audrey knew about cold water. From the time she was a child she had braved, early in the season, the cold whitecaps of Narragansett Bay. Her coat puffed up around her; as soon as it was waterlogged she would have to let it go. But she would keep it as long as she could. There was a bottle of brandy in it for him, and if she could find him and *get him to an ice floe*, she could cover him with the mink and her own body, and keep him warm enough. *Just barely warm enough, dear God....*

She began her hunt.

Now it was dark and the stars were distant, very

high, and small and hard. She swam clumsily, with cries and moaning like a fog around. She had to swim close to see faces.... The first was a dead man's. She shrank away and felt a rivulet of wintry ice at her knees; a current even colder than the top one flowing just under: it was a killing cold.

I will die now, too, she thought, and she swam through the destruction with long slow strokes to save her strength.

Two bodies, two little bodies, floated toward her. Two children. The girl, older, had long dark hair spread on the black sea's face like seaweed. The boy, small and fair, floated faceup. *The Miller children,* whom Audrey had met in third. *The Miller children, who had had no mother....* Their wrists were lashed together with a shoelace. Turning first one way and then the next, the little bodies spun by. *Keely*; Catherine had been the girl's name....

A woman whom Audrey had noticed from time to time, dancing, sank before her eyes. She was a young woman, pretty; Audrey had never said a word to her....

She swam on. She could see none of the boats, they had all pulled away. She was in the middle of a black and floating graveyard. All around there was nothing but bodies and debris. A man over there held on to a piece of wood, but it was not buoyant enough, it would not hold him up. And there was one of the collapsible lifeboats, overturned: at least thirty bodies were heaped upon its back. It hunched in the water like a turtle, almost submerged from the weight. They cannot last the night, she thought. One wave will finish them....

Finally there was no pity left and no anger. There

was only a little will. She swam because not to swim
would be to sink and so to give up. She rescued the
brandy from her coat, stashed it in her bodice, and
let the coat drown. Her feet were heavy, and her
fingers were too numb to loosen the strings and so
let the boots go.

And then a body floated by and it was Burty.

Audrey recognized him with horror. She touched
him. *"Burty...?"* And then she screamed, not so
loud, but long and wild. She screamed as she swam
away from his corpse, and then she heard—*what*—

"Audrey, Audrey! Over here!"

Like a bear, something humped on a slab of ice.
Like a bear... There he was! Still alive, coatless—
and there he was, his hair falling over his forehead
like a boy's.

Bay. Dearest Bay, darling Bay....

She swam, kicking past bodies. A cook, from his
whites.... An old man.... Another man in his prime.
Two stewards, still in their uniforms, the buttons lying on their chests like shells.

The ice floe had a jagged edge. She clung, though
it cut her fingers. "Bay," she said. "I can't lift up."
She didn't really care: she had found him, *found
him*....

His whole body, coatless, was shaking, but his
eyes were calm. The hands he reached out to her
were stiff, frostbitten already, almost frozen. "I'll lift
you," he said.

Yes, do....

He lay down on the ice and inched forward until
his arms extended over the edge beyond the elbows.
"Lie on my arms," he said.

She swam in a circle, trying to gather force. Then

she kicked for his arms and heaved herself up.... "There," he said, for she was upon one arm and the other was pulling, pulling....

She rolled onto the ice with him.

"Oh, but you're heavy," he said. And then they laughed, just a little, but they laughed on this night of nights, their hearts not broken after all, though their souls were.

"Put your hands in my blouse," she said. "There's brandy."

They huddled on the ice together, and waited for they knew not what.

SWAN WOULD NOT let Danny and Smoke haul her into the lifeboat.

"Please, no, I'm all broken," she said. "And the water is not so cold, and there's no pain."

So they stayed as they were, while Teddy Royce and the crewman pulled on the oars and sent their boat toward the horizon.

"You get into the boat, Danny," Swan said after a while. "Don't stay here with me."

"I'll stay with you," he said, numb now, too, not minding so much. The life belt tied around the seat inside where Smoke sat and then around him reduced the effort of holding her. Danny was content. He was glad now they had coupled on boat deck, glad he was not to die not knowing how it was, being with a woman. He said, trying to please her, "After all, we're engaged. I'm responsible for you."

"Oh no," Swan said, and tried to struggle.

"Don't," he said. "What's the matter?"

And Smoke, sitting above, holding Swan's head, said, "Mother will not find Father. They're both

gone. So when you marry, Swan, I will be alone."
She tried to joke. "Except for Twiggs, of course. I'll
have to keep Twiggs, just for her company."

"No," said Swan. "Smoke, can you hear me?"

Smoke sighed. "Yes." It was quiet now. The
sounds of people suffering had stopped, and the water was so still she couldn't hear it lapping at the
sides of the boat. The ticktock as the oars dipped into
the water and rolled in their sockets was the only
sound, that, and the tick, tick, tick as the oars lifted
out. And then ticktock as the oars swung the reach
of Teddy Royce's arm, and tick into the water....

"Yes, I can hear you, Swanny."

The dark glowed ever darker, *pulsed* inkier and
glossier. The stars seemed to recede. And the oars
ticktock ticked....

"Smoke," said Swan. "I'm fading, you see.
Please listen."

Smoke lowered herself to the floor of the boat so
as to be closer to her twin. She bent her head right
over Swan's and kissed her forehead. It was kissing
an ice cube, slick and wet and oh so cold.... "Do
you see, Swan, I'm close enough to kiss you."

"You must marry Danny," Swan said. "Say you
will, for my sake."

"What do you mean?" said Smoke. Beside Swan,
Danny jerked in the water, but said nothing. Smoke
could not see his face; he was looking away, toward
the black horizon. She was thankful he could not see
hers.

"If I die, it won't matter."

"What do you mean?"

"If I live," Swan said, "I'll be a cripple, I can't
marry, and I don't want to be alone. *Marry him.*

Danny, say you'll marry her so I'll have you both with me...." Swan twisted in the water, trying to see Danny's face, to see up into Smoke's. "Please, please, promise," she said. "I don't want to live alone in a bed or a chair without friends—"

"Of course you can marry," Smoke snorted, her heart hurting. "I'm going to be a sea captain. You must marry him yourself. *You* love him, I don't."

Danny's head was against Swan's. "It's you I want to marry, Swan," he said. "You're the one I love...."

"I'm all smashed inside, I know it," said Swan. "I'll never have children. You must have children, Smoke. The Lockholm line must go on—oh, promise me." Swan was twisting in the water and crying. Danny thought he would lose his hold....

"She's hysterical," he said. "I tell you what," he said, trying to warm Swan's face with his breath. "Let's say yes, Smoke. Yes, Swan, if that's what you want, yes. But if we get out of this, and you come out all right, then we rewrite all promises. How's that?"

"Yes." Swan was quieter. "Swear, Smokey. Swear on our parents' graves."

"Oh, Swan."

"Swear, or I'll die right this minute."

"Swear what, then? What must I?"

"Swear you'll marry Danny, give him children, and stay with me, the both of you, the rest of my life."

"I don't love Danny," said Smoke, though she did.

"I don't want you to love him," Swan said with

a sigh. "I love him. I want you to marry him, do the *physical side* for us Lockholms, since I can't."

"I could have children and not be married," said Smoke. "How would that be?" She thought: I will not marry him. It would kill me to marry him knowing he loves her. I must stay free....

Swan did not answer. Her head rolled back. For a long time she was still, and her pale, pale hair, which at first had floated, sank into the wet like weed.

Danny did not shake her. He seemed to have slipped from consciousness too.

Smoke shivered on the floor of the boat, with no energy to move away. The men stopped rowing, the boat swayed gently, like a cradle. Smoke could see none of the other boats.... They were alone—she—was alone in all the world, with only strangers who gave no comfort, and dark and ice.

She must have slept, for the sky was lighter now. It was not dawn, but the sky was grayer. She could begin to see again the ragged outlines of the ice....

"Swan!" She shook her sister's shoulders, rubbed her cheeks.

Danny murmured, and turned, just a little, from side to side in his life belt.

"Wake up—please wake up. I'm afraid," said Smoke.

Swan's mouth was open. There was frost on her lips.

"Swan!"

Her twin's eyes snapped open. "Smoke," Swan said. She tried to raise an arm, but could not. "Smoke."

"Yes, yes ."

"Promise. Please."

"All right, yes. Whatever you say, only *live*, Swan. *Live!*"

"I'll try...." Swan's head fell back, her mouth opened, her eyes closed. "I'll try, Smokey...."

Danny said, with cracked voice, "What do you see, Smoke?" So she knew he had heard.

"There is nothing to see," she said. And then, to be kind, she said, "Just hang on, Danny, and hang on to her. Someone must have heard.... Someone must be coming.... They won't be long now...."

Above, the sky lightened to the color of the stars, the color of ice. And there was nothing at all but them and the gray and the cold.

"THERE ARE ONLY a dozen of us," said Tory. "We must row back and pick up whom we can. Please, my husband was still on board. Please, let's try to find him!" And she held her baby closer. Even next to her heart under the fur and wrapped in a blanket, Wisdoms's tiny face was ice against her breast, and so quiet. Not a cry, not a whimper from her, and they had been—how long—out there in the dark?

A man named Symons, who said he had been part of the lookout crew, was in charge of their boat, had put himself in charge of these "rich landlubbers who didn't know a tiller from a cocktail." He heard what the woman said, but he was unsure what to do. On the one hand he was afraid of going back—who knew what might happen if *Titanic* exploded, or if a whirlpool suction started? He did not know, and he was not used to being in command. And he was worried about his job, his pay: he had a family, too, and who would pay him now? On the other hand, to turn back and rescue someone of importance might be the making of him. He could be a hero.

"Oh, we can't go back," said Sir Cosmo Duff-Gordon, with the authority of his class. "It would be the death of us. Row on, chaps. Keep us safely away."

His wife, Lady Lucile, had tried to comfort her maid, who sat beside her, on the loss of her nightgown, a lovely thing, as pretty as one of Lady Lucile's own. But her maid had not responded properly. She sat with her head bowed and hiccuped into a handkerchief. And the woman across from her, the Lockholm governess, with whom Lady Lucile had once condescended to converse, sat as though she were in heart attack. She had been stone since sitting down.

"Give the man a fiver, Cosmo," said Lady Lucile. "He'll feel better for it...." She knew how to buy instant obedience of servants when one could not purchase long-lived allegiance.

Sir Cosmo saw Symons's face brighten at the prospect. "All right, I will," he said, and held the lookout man with his eye. "Just keep rowing us safe, that's what we're all after." And he reached with lambskin-warmed hands for his wallet. He took his time, and saw that the man obeyed.

The man bribed, feeling safe now, Lady Lucile addressed Tory. "How sweet of you to hold your maid's child, my dear."

Tory had been in reverie, emotionally and physically spent. She had been through so much, she had only just given birth; and now strange thoughts, vivid images, filled her mind and made her dizzy.

I feel like a bird, she was thinking, *a bird long*

hooded who, finally freed, at first shrinks from the light, but then begins to shudder with an awful, awesome freedom....

And she shivered and shuddered and dreamed and *wished* she could fly, fly away....

The dreadful woman beside her had said something. Tory lifted her head. The dreadful woman had asked about her maid.... "My maid is not along this trip," said Tory, and she looked at the dark mirror sheen of the sea. "We must go back, there's so much room...." But the wails of the dying had ceased—hadn't they?—a long time ago now....

"Then whose poor baby can you be?" said Lady Lucile, and she reached out and tickled where the baby's middle ought to be.

Oh, Tory thought. *I see. She wants to know about Wis....* "She's not a poor baby," said Tory. "Her father is Burton Kingsley VanVoorst. He is worth more than a hundred million, and she's an only child."

Only child, her dazed mind echoed.

Only child, only child....

Abruptly, Mrs. Twigg spoke. "It's Mrs. Van-Voorst's child, you old fool."

Lady Lucile gasped in high indignation.

"Let's have none of that," said Sir Cosmo, glowering at his wife's inferior. "None of that in this boat."

"And will you give me a fiver to shut me up?" said Mrs. Twigg. And the bosom of which she was so proud heaved threateningly.

Tory could not understand what was happening. She knew she had some reason to be grateful to Mrs.

Twigg. She thought Twiggs would do very well for Wis...once they got back home....

"She gets her colored blood from me," said Tory.

And unaccountably, Mrs. Twigg barked again, "So put that where the sun don't shine."

"Well!" sniffed Lady Lucile. To be treated like this by riffraff; she would never travel White Star Line again. She would write such a letter... "Cosmo," she said.

Her husband patted her knees. "Just row on," he said to Symons. And Symons rowed.

Tory didn't hear the rest. She leaned against Nicola's shoulder, and the baby slid down upon her stomach. She's trying to get back in, thought Tory, where it's warm and quiet and safe.... Her coat opened, and infant Wisdoms lay on her mother's lap, pinned into a blanket but exposed, for all to see.

And in the polar-cold Atlantic, lightening now in prelude to the dawn, the bartender Wisdoms swam on, unwilling, yet, to let all end. He swam far out, trying to reach that almost-empty boat. If he could get there, it would be all right; they would pull him in. But the harder he swam the farther the boat seemed to recede and fade into the gray.... He pressed on, and gained. He was closing! He could see the occupants now, *so few!* He was very tired. His toes and fingers tingled. He saw a baby on a woman's lap, its cool quiet face turned up to heaven.

That must be my namesake, he thought. That must be Wisdoms VanVoorst, and inwardly he chuckled, and passages from the Bible filled his mind with comfort. He almost caught up; he called... But they must not have heard him, because the two at the oars, who had been resting, began to pull hard again…and Wisdoms knew he would not catch it.

Well, he was almost ready now.

Mine eyes have seen the glory and I seen my namesake, and she is fair…. His mind hummed. *Comin' for to carry me home….*

He relaxed then. And under a wash of water the diamond chip winked, indistinguishable from reflected stars.

In the lifeboat, Mrs. Twigg took the infant off Tory's lap and zipped it into Tory's jewelry satchel to keep it warm, and wrapped her arms around it.

And still there was only the ocean, flat and wrinkling, and the tombstones of ice, and the grayness…and each other….

The shelf of ice upon which Bay and Audrey huddled was breaking up. They were warm now. The cold was doing that, Audrey thought, slowly freezing them, taking away sensation. Audrey held her husband, he held her, quiet together. In the pervading grayness, Audrey saw, through ice-fringed eyes, *black* floating. Bodies…. Coffins…. She knew they were bodies…. But they all seemed to be the same, seemed to be the spread black skirts of Madame Romany, *circling, circling, coming back to…kill them….*

Audrey tried to close her eyes, but could not. She tried to shut away Esmeralda and this crystal ball into which they had been flung, this great ice-crystal ball where the future was not told but ended….

And still the bodies floated around the disappearing ice floe, floated in the gray crystal ball of sea and sky. Audrey saw, with eyes that would not close, *the iceberg come again….*

There, not far; in the grayness she could see it, high and sleek and pointed like a knife. It cut through the lesser ice packs, all black ice, so black the gray seemed pink behind it. It *steamed* for them, it *aimed* for them.... With arms that were all ice, too, she clung to Bay.

He murmured in her arms. "Audrey, do you see it?"

"Yes," she said.

"It was the brandy saved us," he said.

Saved us? she thought. They were not saved. Madame Romany had them surrounded....

"The iceberg has come back," she said.

"That's not a berg," said Bay, and he stirred. "That's a ship."

A ship? She looked. *A ship...?*

"Don't cry now," he said, tender. "But your hair, your beautiful golden hair, has gone all white...." He kissed her forehead and warmed her frozen lashes with his breath.

"No, dear Bay," she said, "it's only mist and ice, and fog from the crystal ball."

He knew better. "Can you stand, my love?" he said. "Look smart? We're going to be rescued."

She wanted to laugh, but she couldn't: Bay had gone mad. All right, she had gone mad, too. She looked for the body of the gypsy, but now there was only ocean spreading blue.... And the sky was glowing, yellow and peach and rose. And the pillars of ice were ivory and silver and fine-veined beige marble glistening in the dawn of a brand-new world....

She was in an ice palace of the most beautiful rooms.... "Have we died and gone to heaven?" she said.

She could not stand straight. She stood on the edges of her feet, her back bent. He could not use one leg; limp, it hung from his hip. He made it hold by bracing it against a stump of ice.

"Can you see it now?" he said.

She was afraid to rub at the ice around her eyes, afraid she would go blind. She looked, not knowing what he wanted.

And there it was, incredibly, *there it was*.

Steam blew from its funnels, people lined its decks. Its bow rode the water straight and high, it was unbroken by the sea.... There it was, speeding toward them.

Carpathia was its name.

"Oh," she said, and could not stop the tears. "Oh, Bay...."

"It's a magnificent dawn," he said. "Like the beginning of creation." He took her hands and pressed his cold cheek against her cold one. "And we're going home, darling, we've survived. Our children are safe, we're going to be fine."

Audrey shivered, feeling the cold again, remembering Burty turning in the water, remembering Swan crushed between—

Bay scraped flakes of ice from the floe, formed the ice into a ball. "Here's to tomorrow," he said, and he flung the ice skyward. Seeing that, the people on *Carpathia* cheered and steamed their way.

Audrey watched the ice ball split into fragments in the warm of dawn, and melt to nothingness....

"Welcome aboard," she heard the boatman say.

WHEN NICOLA LADY POMEROY BOARDED the *Carpathia*, Teddy Royce, already saved, was waiting for her.

"Ah, the bad penny," she said, letting him help her.

"Marry me," he said, "and I'll not need to steal."

"You're a gambling man," she said. "We'll cut the cards for it."

"I just happen to have a deck," he said.

"Not yours," she said. "Steward, do you have a fresh deck of cards?"

Captain Rostron, hearing, was prepared for eccentric behavior from the survivors. Shock, he knew, did strange things to people. He nodded to the steward, and an uncut deck of cards was brought.

"Do you know how to shuffle?" said Nicola.

"Yes, ma'am," the steward said. He shuffled and left the deck on a table.

"Ladies first," said Teddy Royce, his eyes aglint with the game.

Nicola turned up the jack of diamonds. "That's hard to beat," she said, and wet her lips, excited.

Unruffled, Rolls turned his card.

"I don't believe it," breathed Nicola. The queen of diamonds lay, triumphant, upon the knave.

"You're going to have your hands full with me," said Teddy Royce, enfolding her.

"And vice versa," said Nicola, lifting her chin to let him kiss her, and wondering how it was going to be.

And in that brilliant, roseate, ice-stabbed dawn, Captain Rostron turned *Carpathia* westerly...into the future.

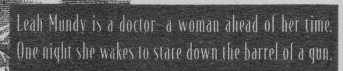

Leah Mundy is a doctor – a woman ahead of her time.
One night she wakes to stare down the barrel of a gun.

The Drifter

She is abducted at gunpoint by
Jackson Underhill, an outlaw
and drifter on the run…and
clearly in trouble. But soon none
of that matters, because he
needs her. More than that he
accepts her—as a doctor and as
a woman. Even knowing that he
will soon be gone, Leah can't
help herself from falling for the
man who has abducted her—
this man who has come to mean
so much to her.

SUSAN WIGGS

The rugged Pacific Northwest coastline sets
the scene for Wiggs's fast-paced romantic
tale of passion and impossible love.

MIRA®

Available in
May 1998 wherever
books are sold.

MSW459

Available in May!

National bestselling authors

JENNIFER BLAKE
EMILIE RICHARDS

Welcome to the Old South—a place where the finest women are ladies and the best men are gentlemen. And where men from the wrong side of town have more honor than all the blue bloods combined! This is a place where everyone has their place and no one dares to cross the line. But some rules are meant to be broken....

Southern GENTLEMEN

Sweeping romance and sizzling passion... and you will soon discover that
NOT ALL MEN ARE CREATED EQUAL.

Available in May 1998 at your favorite retail outlet.

MIRA

Look us up on-line at: http://www.romance.net

MANTHSG

Looking For More Romance?

Visit Romance.net

Look us up on-line at: http://www.romance.net

Check in daily for these and other exciting features:

Hot off the press

View all current titles, and purchase them on-line.

What do the stars have in store for you?

Horoscope

Hot deals

Exclusive offers available only at Romance.net

Plus, don't miss our interactive quizzes, contests and bonus gifts.

PWEB

One bold act—one sin—committed in an otherwise blameless life begins a family's descent into darkness. And this time there is no absolution...

Confession

THE TRUTH HAS THE POWER— TO DESTROY EVERYTHING.

When Rebecca has an affair with her daughter's boyfriend, all those close to her are forced to deal with the fallout and forces everyone to reexamine their own lives. CONFESSION is a poignant tale chronicling the destructive path of a wife and mother's confessed affair with a younger lover.

The newest blockbuster novel from the *New York Times* bestselling author of *A Glimpse of Stocking*

ELIZABETH GAGE

Available as a trade-size paperback in May 1998— where books are sold.

MIRA

MEG465

Catch all the passion, intrigue and romance you've come to expect from

JAYNE ANN KRENTZ

in a new movie!

THE WAITING GAME
premieres August 8, only on

Pick up your copy of *The Waiting Game* at your favorite retail outlet! Available in July 1998.

If you're not currently a subscriber to The Movie Channel, simply call your local cable or satellite provider for more details. Call today, and don't miss out on the romance!

The Movie Channel is a trademark of Showtime Networks, Inc., a Viacom Company. An Alliance Television Production.

MJAKTMC